A Poetic Love Story

Jacqueline Wrencher

Lisa Nicole Publishing
Orlando, FL 32824
www.lisanicolealexander.com

ISBN: 979-8-9878940-4-0
Printed in the United States of America

Acknowledgment

I dedicate this story to my son, Michael Simmons. I love you with all my heart. I could not have undertaken such a journey without your generosity. Your tower of confidence and unwavering support is what motivated me to finish my story. You called and encouraged me countless times to complete my book. I'm so thankful you were always there to mediate this journey.

To my granddaughter Skylar Katherine Simmons, who fills my life with joy every day. GG loves you beyond the stars.

In memory of my awesome parents, James Wrencher and Willie Mae, who continue to inspire me every day.

Many thanks to my sisters, Ella Mae Wrencher and Gloria Jean Wrencher, who were the first to read part one of my story. From your reaction, I knew I was onto something. Thank you so much for believing in me and encouraging me to move forward. I love you both immensely.

Special thanks to my astoundingly supportive sister, Shelly Jean Wrancher, who taught me the love of stories. I'm sorry you are not here to witness this moment. To my oldest sister Katherine, who was a beacon of hope, and my sweet niece, Leslie Muldrow, who left us too soon, but will never be forgotten. I know these phenomenal women are leading the cheers from heaven.

To my sister-in-law, Gia Bankhead, you were always in my ear, cheering me to write even when the words wouldn't come. You are my most profound inspiration and my forever ride or die. I love you so much.

Many thanks to my supportive nieces- Marteen Wrencher and Monica Wrencher, whose personalities inspired the creation of a few characters. You were my best audience. I love you dearly.

Thank you to my high school besties Debbie Bolden, Yvette Simpson, Anthony Wright, and Winola Brown who listened to my poems and stories. Our laughter was often heard throughout the halls of Westinghouse.

To my childhood buddy Yunace Bass aka Pumkin, my friend for life. You know all the secrets. Thank you for your love and support.

Thank you to my Paderewski classmate Charles Myart Jr., who also shared useful input. It was nice to have a male's point of view.

Thank you to my friend Thomas Byrd who always kept me accountable with my writing.

To my loyal friend Kim Harris, our weekly coffee dates were the perfect distractions.

To my wonderful friend Kim Nagle, who was my faithful sounding board. I will never forget those hilarious discussions we shared at Brooks Brothers. If those walls could talk!

To my beautiful friend Linda White, who made flyers and postcards, I will always remember your kindness.

My cousin Diane Fleming-Coker's suggestions were greatly appreciated and extremely useful. Thank you so much.

To my editor, Lisa Nicole, thank you for your insightful comments and constructive feedback. You make me look good on paper. Much respect to you and what you do so well.

I want to thank everyone who listened to me go on and on about my story, especially those who heard me sing the lyrics out loud. God bless you guys.

Finally, to myself for finishing what I started.

Broken Rules

A Poetic Love Story

A beautiful love story written with a poetic tone
Chicago, Illinois 2005

Karen is a successful business owner who just happens to be the wife of a famous singer and writer. While sitting in her beautiful office, overlooking the magnificent mile, she picks up a photo. It immediately takes her back to her much younger self, back to when she first laid eyes on her soul mate. The year was 1992. The year she started working for Bajem's department store. Karen had armed herself with four sets of rules, just mere tools she used to push herself forward and to guide her through.

Along her journey, she met a few interesting people. Carl St. John a handsome, smart playboy who captured her heart and caused her to break a few rules. Randy, a sassy salesman who keeps her real and makes her laugh out loud. Constance, a gentle soul and a seasoned sales professional. Coco, (whose real name is Dana) a beautiful young lady who has her hooks in Carl. And lastly, James aka Jumbug, Carl's best friend who is the smoothest brother in town.

"He Had Her Hooked"

Karen sat motionless, lost in thought.

Way deep in the corner of her mind,

She was reminiscing about Carl's intoxicating ways.

Like the time she saw him walk in the gangster-like trot,

Oh boy, he had one sexy walk!

The way his eyes sparkled when he laughed,

Oh, what an incredible smile he has.

The sexy way he twisted his lips,

When he thought no one was looking.

Yes, those sweet lips

And the perfect set of teeth that hide beneath them.

She knew she was breaking her rules,

Every last one of them.

This man had her attention.

She was clearly distracted by this dude.

Hot damn!

What's a sista to do?

After that first look,

He had her hooked.

CHAPTER 1

Beep! Beep! "Hey baby, where are you running to looking all foxy and fine? You got time for a brother to holla at ya?" Karen was rushing across Michigan Avenue to an interview at Bajem's Department Store. She didn't have time to talk small with no stud leaning out of a raggedy-ass car. She could not afford to be late! Karen shouted back, "Thanks, but I don't have time today," as she rushed inside Bajem's revolving door.

She passed the fragrance counter and walked over to the elevators. The doors opened, and she quickly stepped inside, "Five, please," said Karen to a well-dressed gentleman who stood near the controls. Karen felt nervous as the elevator door opened to the 5th floor. She stepped out and walked toward the double glass doors marked Personnel. She walked into the room and introduced herself to the receptionist.

Karen was told someone would be with her shortly. She eased onto a chair, careful not to crease her Emanuel Ungaro suit, and quickly surveyed the room. There were fashion magazines mixed with the store's catalog on the table, and the walls had plaques of employees of the month listed in chronological order.

Suddenly, a tall Caucasian woman with round-rimmed glasses and long auburn hair introduced herself as Mrs. Crane. "Ms. Karen Bosse, I presume," said Mrs. Crane as she extended her perfectly manicured hand. They shook hands, admiring each other's style. At that moment, Karen knew she had the job.

Karen smiled as she sat in her training class that contained five other new associates. Mrs. Crane was the training instructor, and Bajem's training program was very thorough. She had worked in retail before, but she had never experienced such an in-depth training regimen. Bajem was a well-respected, high-end department store known for only hiring the best of the best. Tomorrow will be Karen's first day on the sales floor.

* * *

From the first day Karen laid eyes on Carl, she was smitten. 'Oh, my goodness, if I never see another handsome specimen again, I can surely say I've seen one on this day,' thought Karen as she was introduced to her co-workers. Joseph Bobbs, the manager, was giving her a tour of her work area. She shook hands with Randy Walden, a tall, balding white guy, and then she turned and extended her hand to Carl St. John, the man who had her hooked. She wondered if he was as smart as he was fine!

"Ms. Bosse, what do you think of the department so far?" asks Carl, disrupting her thoughts. "Oh, just call me Karen, and uh, I don't know Carl, you tell me, how are the newbies broken in around here?" Randy chuckles under his breath, and Carl grins and stutters, "Uh, I try to uh," but before he finishes his sentence, Karen interrupts and says, "Never mind, I guess I'll find out the hard way." But little did she know, his way was much better.

Karen's philosophy of life consists of 4 rules.

1) No distractions. Remain focused.

2) Fall in love with yourself before falling for someone else.

3) Trust your inner self, listen!

4) No regrets!

Rule number one was broken into pieces because Karen was clearly distracted.

* * *

Karen moved into her new sales role with ease and precision. She was not afraid to seek help if needed. Karen had a client in the fitting area who needed assistance, so she asked for Randy's expertise. "Hey Randy, exactly what size length would a regular be in our men's dress trousers?" Randy, sounding pompous and arrogant, replies, "Well, first of all, there are three types of lengths in trousers, which are listed in the sales manual:

1) Short length, which is 30 inches,

2) Regular length, which is 32 inches,

3) Long length, which is 34-36 inches,

So, with this in mind, don't hesitate to call one of our tailors to lengthen or shorten your client's trousers."

Karen replied, "Okay, thank you, Randy." She turned to her customer, who, by the way, heard everything and said, "Sir, a regular length is equivalent to 32 inches."

Wow, thought Karen. Randy needs to take it down a notch because all that was unnecessary. She made a mental note to memorize the men's sales manual from beginning to end.

So far, so good. Working for Bajem's was smooth and educational. This was her first experience selling men's clothing. It was exciting to learn something new. As Karen turned and scanned the department, she noticed Carl staring at her from across the sales floor. Her lips slowly formed a smile as she realized she wasn't the only one drooling.

"Ms. Bosse, you look familiar. For some reason, I think we've met before," said Carl, walking over and standing next to Karen. "Oh, I doubt it, but I really wish you would call me Karen." Carl hunched his shoulders and replied, "Yeah, I guess, but you still look familiar. Anyway, where did you say you worked?" Karen swiftly answers, "I didn't say," and walks away. Her rudeness was not intentional, but Carl made her nervous like a teenager. Later, Karen had to check herself for being a smartass.

* * *

The next few months at work seemed bearable. Karen started getting the hang of things and had the entire sales manual locked inside of her brain. She even met a new friend named Constance Stonewall. Constance was a seasoned sales specialist in the women's shoe salon. She was aggressive and sassy as all get out.

She was also a no-nonsense person who knew what she wanted and wasn't afraid to go after it. And oddly enough, those were the same character traits Karen lived by. Except, Karen knew what she wanted. She just didn't know how to go about conquering Mr. Carl St. John!

"Huron and Michigan," shouts the driver. Karen is so immersed in her thoughts that she almost misses her stop. She quickly exited the bus and crossed the street. She turned up the collar of her drizzle trench to block the wind off the lake. Chicago was notorious for its wind gusts.

Today was Thursday, payday. Karen had been working at Bajem's for about eight months, and so far, things were going as planned. She got along with her coworkers with the exception of a few minor misunderstandings she sometimes experienced with Carl. Neither knew why they bumped heads over the silliest things.

For instance, on the sales floor yesterday, Karen approached a young couple. She introduced herself and told them to let her know if she could be of any assistance. As soon as she turns around, Carl comes out of nowhere and reapproaches them with the same speech. The code of ethics regarding the selling culture at Bajem's is that if you approach a customer and establish contact, that customer is yours to pursue and hands off. Well, maybe one could say his innocence was his excuse for the misunderstanding, but last Saturday was a different matter.

Saturday morning meetings were always encouraging. Joseph, the manager, ordered continental breakfast and sometimes lunch for his staff. His motto was if you didn't eat any other day, he had you covered on Saturdays.

Karen was lucky to have greeted the first customer and had him in the fitting room trying on Guess jeans and Missoni sweaters. Randy was in the back of the department sizing trousers, and Carl was conversing with Joseph. A problematic customer walked in with an alteration ticket for a pair of slacks he needed to pick up. Karen takes the ticket, which has Carl listed as the sales associate. She refers the gentleman to Carl since he was the original salesperson and still had her client in the fitting room.

Carl is visibly irritated. The rest of the day was filled with tension, as Karen was trending top sales, and Carl had the worst Saturday ever. In the midst of the feud, Randy seemed to enjoy the drama. As far as Karen was concerned, the day couldn't end fast enough.

* * *

The following day, Karen entered her department, feeling refreshed and confident. She was determined to have a good day, regardless of her failed attempt to have a decent conversation with Carl. Today was Randy's scheduled day off. So, fortunately, her department would have a substitute to cover his hours. Bajem called this individual a contingent.

As Karen walked into her department, Carl was just opening the register when he looked up and smiled at her, revealing all of his pearly whites. She was just about to return the smile when she turned and saw who he was really smiling at. What a beauty, thought Karen. This young woman looked radiant with her coal-black eyes, high cheekbones, and long shiny black hair.

Carl hurried over and immediately started conversing with this mysterious woman. They talked animatedly for a few minutes before they realized they had company.

"Oh, Karen, have you met Coco?"

"No, I haven't."

"Well, Coco, this is Karen Bosse, our newest sales specialist, and Karen, this is Dana Brown, but we call her Coco. She's our contingent for today."

After they made their introductions, Karen couldn't help but wonder about Carl and Coco's relationship. Coco was no ordinary lady. She was extremely attractive and stood at about 5'10, a decent height for a model. And there was no question about her being one. So, the only question in Karen's mind was, what in the world was she doing working at Bajem's?

After a little small talk, Karen soon discovered that Coco was only working part-time while she pursued her modeling and acting career, and Carl was an aspiring singer and songwriter. Once Carl finally went to lunch, Coco and Karen continued to talk shop. Karen discovers Coco and Carl's plans to have drinks after work, and she is surprisingly jealous. She worked beside Carl for over eight months, and he never suggested that she join him for drinks of any kind. Carl was a mystery she couldn't solve to save her life. The dude was just as complicated as she was!

Later that day, Coco surprised Karen with an invite. "Hey Karen, why don't you join us for drinks after work? A few of us are getting together. I'm sure you'll have a nice time. Before Karen accepted Coco's invitation, she caught a glimpse of Carl's reaction. His face was twisted, and then he quickly replaced his frown with a phony smile. "Yes, you should drop by and have a drink with us!"

"Maybe I will. Do you guys care if I invite Constance?"

"Constance?" said Carl with another twisted frown. "Oh yeah, the one who works in the shoe salon, right?

"Yes, is it okay to bring her along?"

"Sure, it's cool," says Carl with an unsure expression on his handsome face. Karen sensed his uneasiness, and somehow, it made her grin. She had him feeling uneasy and considered that a form of payback for never asking her out!

* * *

Karen and Constance stepped outside to flag a cab. They were leaving work and meeting Carl and the rest of the gang for drinks at a club called Charlie's. It was a beautiful night to go out. The wind was low, and you could hear the laughter of love as couples passed by laughing and holding hands. As they stood at the curbside, waiting for a taxi, Karen took notice of her attire. She was wearing a blue silk dress that fell over her knee.

She was annoyed that she wasn't wearing a sexy outfit. Nevertheless, her small hips had taken the slack as her dress clung to them perfectly. On the other hand, Constance was wearing a black knit dress that clung to her beer belly, which interrupted her otherwise small petite figure. Suddenly, a taxi drove up, and the girls quickly stepped inside.

Constance immediately took control using that rehearsed voice she sometimes used, "Charlie's Place, please. Oh, and do you need directions because we do not need a tour of Chicago!"

The cab driver shook his head and peered through his mirror. "No, ma'am, I know the location."

Constance could appear a bit direct with that voice that sometimes got on Karen's last nerve.

Charlie's Place was jumping and full to the max. Everyone was laughing and dancing up a storm. Karen was beginning to think she and Constance were a bit overdressed. Almost every woman in the place had on micro minis. Interrupting Karen's thoughts, Constance pulled on her sleeves and motioned her to the right. They didn't recognize anyone, so they took an available table and sat down. It was a smart decision because the club was getting crowded rather quickly.

Just then, Constance starts talking using her annoying voice. "Karen, do you think it was a good idea to sit down? We could easily get lost in this crowd. I hope they arrive soon because this crowd is making me uncomfortable. We should have met at that new club down the street called Nujack. Look at the clothes these freaks are wearing! Talk about potential victims. This place is full of them. Look at them showing all their assets. Karen, did you hear a word I said?"

"Oh yeah, I was thinking the same thing." Karen had just spotted Carl sitting at the bar talking to a young lady. Carl was a vision of fineness. She felt a wave of heat enter her body as she quickly recovered and turned her attention to Constance.

"Hey, Con's, I think I just spotted Carl sitting at the bar. I bet everyone else is here. Yes, I see him, with his fine ass! Girl, he can have all my money!"

They laughed out loud as Constance stood up and made a complete spectacle of herself. She waved frantically and shouted Carl's name across the room. Carl turned around, trying to find the fool who was screaming out his name. His head turns to their table, and just for a second, his eyes meet Karens, and a sly smile appears on his face. Then, it slowly disappeared as he noticed Constance. She was still waving frantically.

Carl lowers his head, whispers something to the bimbo, and starts toward their table. He thinks that Karen is so incredibly beautiful and hopes that he can swoop in and win her over tonight. Carl approaches the ladies and says, "So I see y'all made it. I'm sorry things got mixed up and we couldn't arrive together. Everyone's downstairs.

"Oh really?" says Constance. "I had no idea we were meeting downstairs.

"So, uh, did you order any drinks?"

"No." They replied

"Okay then, let's go downstairs where the real party is jumping."

As they approached the stairs, Karen stumbled over her footing, and Carl quickly grabbed her around her waist and said, "Are you okay, baby?"

"I'm fine"

Karen is light-headed and loves the way he calls her baby. Constance grabs Karen's attention and whispers, "I bet you did that on purpose! I understand because I would fake a fall, too, as long as I end up in his fine-ass arms. Get him girl!" They giggled as they took their seats.

Coco sashays over and asks what was so funny. She looked stunning in her black dress, which had a split up to her crotch. The back was low, and it almost met on the opposite side of where the split ended. What a dress! Carl was getting an eye full. "Oh, Hey Coco, we were just being silly. Have you met my friend Constance?"

The girls quickly become acquainted. Everyone at the table seemed to be smashed, so Karen and Constance decided to catch up and order drinks. Karen got the waiter's attention and ordered a glass of Chardonnay. Constance ordered her usual Bloody Mary, and Coco ordered a Dirty Martini. Typical, thought Karen.

They were seated at a small round table right off the winding staircase. Charlies was known for having a great sound system with the best DJs and a large dance floor. Karen and Constance were sitting next to each other, and Carl was seated between Coco and Constance. The rest of the group were sitting at surrounding tables. Sally Watson, John Baker, and Mike Bryant from men's suits were sitting together. They were also co-workers at Bajem's and mutual friends of Carl and Coco's,

As the evening progressed everyone seemed to be getting higher and higher. Karen was on her third Chardonnay, and Constance was on her second Bloody Mary. The Bajem's group had great chemistry. Coco and John were on the dance floor, working up a sweat. Constance had just accepted a dance from an older gentleman who watched their table most of the night.

The music was loud with Tone Loe. The Wild Thing had everyone on the dance floor going wild and crazy—all except Karen and Carl, who were the only two sitting down. Finally, the song ended, and Constance and Coco dashed off to the ladies' room to freshen up. There they were, Karen and Carl, sitting alone once again.

Keith Sweat started singing in the background, and that's when Karen put her pride aside and asked Carl for a dance. Carl looked stunned at first, but he smiled and took her hand. They slowly stepped onto the dance floor. Karen looked into his eyes as he took her into his arms, and at that very moment, she knew she couldn't hold back.

As they slowly swayed their hips to the music and held each other tighter and tighter, Karen wrapped her arms around Carl's neck, and slowly but with confidence, she tenderly kissed his neck. If it wasn't the middle of May, Karen would have sworn it was the fourth of July because the sparks that flew from that kiss must have created an uproar. Karen had made her bed, and now it was time to lay down.

Carl became the aggressor as he held Karen's face in his hands, looked into her eyes, and whispered, "I've been wanting to do this since the first time I saw you." The feeling was mutual as his lips touched hers. Karen tried to restrain herself from fainting in his arms.

At that very moment, it seemed the world stood still, and suddenly, they were alone in the room. Neither could hear the music or the voices around them. The only sound was their hearts beating to the same music, the music of love. Everything happened so fast. There was no time to think. She didn't even notice the strange looks on Coco's and Contance's faces when Carl announced that he was taking her home.

Although Karen was tipsy, she was well aware of the decision she made. She accepted Carl's invitation to his place, along with his kisses and touches that went on nonstop the second after she kissed his neck. The ride to Carl's apartment was nice and quiet. He drove a blue Mustang with a soft gray drop-top. Karen noticed how neat and clean his car looked inside, which led her to wonder if his apartment was the same.

Karen soon found Carl's living quarters just as tidy as his car. So many thoughts were running through her mind. Was she making the right decision? What type of underwear she wore? Did she have her diaphragm? Hopefully, she could take a quick shower. It seemed Carl was reading most of her thoughts. He told her to relax and have a seat while he selected a tape to play. Kenny G played softly in the background, and Karen was able to relax her nerves.

Suddenly, Carl comes over, lifts her off the sofa, and places her on his lap. He lifts her chin and gives her the sweetest kiss. Between kisses, he asks her if she is sure she wants him as much as he wants her. Not sure if she could speak coherently, she opted to nod yes. With some courage, she asked if it would be okay if she showered first. Carl smiled and said, "Of course, I'll get you a towel."

After her shower, Karen wrapped the towel around her as best she could. When she walked out of the bathroom, Carl was there waiting. At that moment, either they couldn't stand the suspense any longer or they went mad with passion because Carl picked Karen up and carried her into the bedroom. Carl gently laid her on the bed and stood up to ease out of his clothing.

He took more than an eyeful as he let his eyes travel down every inch of her body, and with his mind, he took a picture so that the moment could be revisited. Karen lay there mesmerized by Carl and his surgeon's hands as they skillfully roamed her entire body. She was beside herself because if the anticipation didn't kill her, the size of his manhood surely would.

Needless to say, she was more than ready to become his victim. Carl began to kiss her earlobes, then ventured down her neck, where he planted small kisses. He took her breast and sucked her nipples with extreme expertise as they swelled between his lips. After he was satisfied with her breasts, he took his long, happy tongue down to her navel and played and played and played. His next step took Karen to a place she had never been before.

His lips pressed the mound between her legs and traveled around and around. Then he ventured inside, where he sucked the juices that came from deep inside her. Karen screamed out as she frantically grabbed the sheets and held on for her life!!! That was only the beginning.

* * *

Karen's long cab ride home gave her a lot of time to reflect on the events that happened that evening. A few hours ago, she was sure she had died and gone into heaven. What she had just experienced was definitely something to write home about. Of course, she could never tell a soul because it would become one of the most talked about affairs at Bajem's. Karen couldn't have her name associated with cheap gossip. She was not the type of woman who slept around, but her behavior last night suggested otherwise. Despite the good time they shared, she just couldn't let it happen again. So, first thing Monday morning, she'd put in for a transfer.

CHAPTER 2

Carl was hanging out with his best friend, Jumbug. He was singing out loud as he rolled a joint. "Man, I hit the jackpot last night!" "What the hell are you singing over there?" asks Jumbug, Carl's old high school buddy. "You sound like a cat got a hold of your tongue and tore that mutha up," laughs Jumbug. Carl couldn't help but smile. "Nah, man, but on the real tip, I think I may have found the one. I got a sweet tooth for this shorty at work. We finally hooked up last night, and it was all good."

"Oh no! Don't tell me it's someone at work. Man, you know what happened the last time you messed around with someone on the job." said Jumbug in his big brother voice. "I hate to say I told you so, but I don't think it's a good idea to go down that road again." Carl knew his friend was right in his assessment, but somehow, he felt that Karen was different.

Bertha was the problem Jumbug was talking about. She was the sweetest thing Carl had met in a long time. And just like the old saying, Bertha had a big ole butt and big pretty legs to match. One would say that's what caught Carl's attention. Bertha started working at Bajem's as seasonal help. Carl spotted her in the employee's cafeteria, eating her lunch alone. As usual, he was the first to introduce himself, and that's how it all started.

Bertha was a beautiful woman. But she had one problem that pushed Carl away from her. The woman was as crazy as Richard

Speck. Even after she stopped working at Bagem's and her relationship with Carl was long over, she continued to call him every day at work. She was the type of person that did not respond well to rejection.

To make a very long story short, Carl had to get a restraining order against Bertha because she smashed out the windows of his Mustang. Even after a year passed, Carl continued to look over his shoulders because he didn't know when the nut could pop up. He definitely didn't need any more trouble at work. But Karen was special, and he thought they could go places.

Carl and Jumbug stayed up most of the night, tripping about the old days and listening to Kenny G. After Jumbug finally left, Carl walked into his bedroom and sat on the bed. Staring in silence, He couldn't get the image of Karen lying there next to him out of his head. Boy, was he hooked!

There are a lot of things that happen in one's life that are somewhat unexplainable. However, this wasn't the case for Karen. Being of sound mind, and not to mention a grown woman, a person of Karen's intellect just couldn't allow a work-related affair to continue. As much as she would have liked to have a relationship with Carl, she knew working together in the same department just wouldn't work.

Karen had to do the right thing and end the affair before it became one. After all, Carl didn't seem the type to commit to a monogamous relationship. Karen knew that a young talented black woman had enough to deal with in today's society, then to knowingly compromise her life with lust and irresponsibility. Karen had a goal in life, and her number one rule was no distractions, period!

Carl had cracked his knuckles so many times his hands were bright red. He was so nervous, and he had never been so messed up and confused over a woman. He just couldn't get the image of Karen out of his head. As beautiful as Coco was, she couldn't hold a candle to Karen. Carl was standing at his workstation contemplating what to say to her once she arrived. He hoped he would somehow find the right words.

Karen arrived at work just in the nick of time. As she approached her workstation, Carl was standing in the back, folding sweaters. Karen's heart was racing as she took a deep breath and started toward Carl. It seemed every step forward took her further and further away. Suddenly, Carl looked up, and the most glorious smile appeared on his face.

"Hey, sweetie, how are you feeling this morning?"

"Oh, I'm fine, and you?" replied Karen.

"Oh, I feel great now that you're here. I was hoping to talk to you before anyone arrived."

Karen felt hypnotized as she stared at Carl's sweet lips moving and those perfect sets of white teeth that hid beneath. She really wanted to taste his lips. Karen snapped out of her daze and quickly walked past him. She busied herself by opening the register. "Well, what do you want to talk about? I hope it's' not about the other night because I really don't know what possessed me, but I can assure you it won't happen again."

Carl walked behind Karen and wrapped his strong arms around her waist so that she could feel his hardness against her. He whispered in her ear, "Baby, can you feel that? I can't stop it from growing whenever you're near me. The other night was something special, and it will happen again and again and again because our chemistry is magnetic. We are drawn to each other; baby, please don't fight this."

Carl turns Karen around to face him and lowers his head to kiss her gently on the lips. Finally, Karen got what she prayed for. She deepens the kiss, holding him tighter and tighter. Footsteps in the distance forced them to break away just in time as Randy walked into the department. "Well, here we go, baby, it's show time!" announced Carl as he smiled and winked at her.

The day was running smoothly for Karen and Carl. They were able to keep the passion on low and remain discreet. It was two o'clock, and Karen was meeting Constance for lunch. They had not spoken since the other night. As Karen enters the cafeteria, Constance sneaks over and whispers, "Ooh, you little hussy, you! I can't believe you did not call me back last night. Girl, I know that stuff was good and plenty. Come clean and tell me everything."

Karen tried to appear shocked and confused, but all she could do was grin. "Con's, I don't know what you are talking about, but the man just dropped me off at home. End of story." Constance bucked her big eyes and said, "Honey child, I know my mother didn't raise no fool. Because the way Carl was burning rubber out of that club, you best believe something happened that night, and probably all night long. Girl, you got laid! You might as well admit it!"

"See, look at you. You can't even keep a straight face!" Karen busted out laughing as Constance continued to ball her out. "Mmmhmm, I knew it. I knew it when you walked in here like God sent you! Girl, you were blessed with the best! Look at you. You know you wanna tell me."

Yes, thought Karen, if only she could shout it to the rooftop! She was busting to tell someone about her exhilarating experience with Carl. Because just like Constance stated, she was blessed with the best!!! Lord help her. He had her hooked!

Karen and Constance finished their lunch and were walking down the escalator. Constance got off on the third floor, and Karen continued down to the second floor. The store didn't have much traffic today. She browsed through the Women's Designer Sportswear department. Karen enjoyed looking at all the latest trends. It made her adhere to all the whoop la in the world of fashion. Second to Carl, this was Karen's biggest turn-on.

As she approached her word station, she saw Coco from the corner of her eye, "Oh shit," thought Karen, she was not prepared to speak to Coco. Suddenly Coco spotted her and was on the move with her tail wagging behind her. "Hey, girlfriend, I was hoping I'd run into you. I wanted to make sure you two made it home safely. Ya'll left out so fast we didn't get a chance to say good night."

"Oh yeah, we made it home safe. Thanks for the concern! Catch you later, okay? Gotta punch in."

Before Coco could respond, Karen turned and continued to her department. Leaving Coco's response unheard and unwelcomed. Karen was well aware of Coco's intuitive nature and her concern for her and her soon-to-be man. Well, that was a boatload of bullshit!

* * *

Karen began to learn the true meaning of making good love.

Lesson one: Never quit until both parties are satisfied.

Lesson two: Don't speak until you have listened.

Lesson three: Be open and be adventurous.

Lesson four: Do unto others as you would like done unto you.

If one could interpret anything from Karen's learning experience, let it be a must-see, must-feel exchange because experience is indeed the best teacher.

Karen and Carl's wanderlust affair continued to flourish beyond the scope of their imagination. The attraction between them was so strong that silly rules were destined to be broken. The last rule on her list was the one she was clear on. No regrets! The night she boldly kissed Carl on his neck was the best decision she had made in a long time. Just thinking about all the moments they shared after that kiss made her smile as wide as the ocean- and she had no regrets!

Karen woke up one Sunday morning and fixed herself a strong cup of coffee. She was sitting on her black leather sofa with her head held back and her eyes closed. Karen's condo was intimate and quite contemporary. She didn't have much in her place, but what she had cost her a hefty penny.

That morning, Karen's body sank into her gigantic sofa, enjoying its comfort. Her sofa was custom-made using the finest Italian leather, and her dining room table was round and made of rich mahogany wood. She was still in the decorating phase, but for now, she was satisfied with the decor.

Karen was sitting there thinking about life. She had been fighting with her sins all night long. As she took a long sip of her coffee, she tried to remember the last time she went to church. She was a believer in Christ, but Karen knew belief alone wasn't enough. She needed fellowship and spiritual guidance.

Karen turned on her television and switched to a gospel program. A black minister was preaching about a temptation. He went on to preach about the times when he frequented lounges and drank alcohol with his buddies. After he became saved, he would come home from work on a Friday night, drink a can of Pepsi, and have the Chicken Shack deliver him a large order of wings with a side of coleslaw. That was the extent of his Friday night.

He admitted he was lonely at times and missed his rowdy buddies, but he remained strong. The minister later recalled another incident when a beautiful woman would call him up boldly seeking dates. He was baffled because women had never called before. He proceeded to tell this woman in particular that he couldn't go out with her.

He was a new founder of faith when she asked why, and he shyly responded, "I don't have a car." But that didn't stop her. She was persistent and told him that she would come over to pick him up. He prayed for guidance and strength because he was only a man. Somehow, his lips began to move, and unbeknown to him, from deep within his soul, he spilled the words he couldn't say before.

He told her he couldn't see her because he was saved and had been blessed with the Holy Spirit, and unless she was down with it, he couldn't be bothered. As Karen continued to listen to the pastor's sermon, she began to feel a stirring inside her. She, too, wanted to experience the Holy Spirit. But as the program ended, an announcement was made, and an address was given for donations to be sent in exchange for a holy cloth. Well, the divine moment passed through Karen's condo and out the door.

Karen switched the channel and continued to drink her coffee which was now cold. Life had an interesting twist, though, as she smiled at her television. Donald Duck was choking Bugs Bunny. Karen's laughter filled her four walls as she continued to watch the Looney Tunes. All else was forgotten, and the brief moment of savior had somehow passed.

* * *

Karen had some choice words with her doorman. She asked him to hold the elevator for her as she gathered her groceries into the building. The fact that she needed to ask was a whole other conversation. Tony, the doorman, only catered to a certain group of people. Karen was not a member.

He was a man filled with anger. At any rate, it wasn't her fault that she could see over the top of his head. Tony was only five feet tall. He most likely had a penis the size of a Vienna sausage. Heck, Tony would probably give anything to add a few inches to both of his woes.

'Mmmmm,' thought Karen as she put away the groceries. All of a sudden, she was craving Carl. So, she picked up the phone and dialed his number. Another rule is broken, but so what, thought Karen. She was horny. On the other side of town, Carl was hanging up his phone. He rushed into his bedroom, where he quickly threw on a pair of Levi's. Carl grabbed his car keys, and on his way out the door, he bumped his lower leg into his coffee table.

"Damn!" swore Carl as he went out the door. He got dressed so fast that he forgot to put on his jacket. But that's what happens when a man receives a booty call. They cannot afford to waste any precious time because women are forever changing their minds. Carl needed to get to Karen's place before she had a change of heart.

Life is a trip, sometimes, thought Karen as she lay in bed thinking about her relationship with Carl. They had just made passionate love that filled her heart with extreme happiness. But look at her now; the happiness is replaced with loneliness. Karen wondered why, as soon as the deed was done, the only thing men grabbed was the nearest exit. Why are they so quick to leave? Seriously, someone should please teach them that it will be in their best interest to stick around and fan the flames! All these thoughts ran through her mind as she stared into space.

Karen sat up in bed and flung her legs aside. She simply had to snap out of the sour mood she was in. She had to attend Joseph's little get-together, which he was hosting at his home tonight. Karen's boss had just received an award for Department Manager of the Year and wanted to celebrate with his staff. Carl and Randy would all be there that evening, and she had to make an appearance. She just didn't want to face Carl.

Karen started toward her bathroom to wash Carl's scent from her body. She stood in front of her floor-length mirror and wrapped her arms around her. As she stared at her reflection, she suddenly felt weak and ashamed. Too many rules were broken. Tears filled her eyes and slowly rolled down her cheeks. She did not attempt to stop them. Karen didn't have the strength to wipe them away. She stood in front of her mirror and watched herself cry. Sometimes, a girl has to cry to shed her pain and regain her strength. And frankly, this girl had to pull herself together.

As Karen finally got a grip on her emotions, she started searching through her closet for something to wear to Joseph's party tonight. She decided to go casual but sexy. She needed to give Carl an eye full so he could have something to think about. What appeared from Karen's bedroom an hour later was definitely a sight for cocked eyes.

Karen had just gone from a sad, weak soul to a confident Vogue candidate. She had never worn clothes as daring as she had on tonight. She wore a Donna Karen bodysuit and her black riding pants that fit like a glove, tucked inside her black lizard boots.

She pulled her hair back in a ponytail to compliment her big sterling silver hoops. Oh, she was looking good. Karen gave her reflection a wink as she threw on her leather jacket and sashayed her hips out the door.

* * *

Carl was standing next to Joseph's homemade bar, trying desperately not to appear as though he was choking. A small piece of ice was lodged in his throat as he caught a glimpse of Karen arriving at the party. 'Gott Damn!!' thought Carl when he finally recovered from choking.

Karen's confidence was slowly fading. She was starting to feel ridiculous wearing such tight pants. She decided to have one drink and then get the hell out there with a quickness. As Karen was plotting an exit strategy, Randy tapped her on the shoulder from behind.

"Hi Karen, did you just get here?"

"Yes, I just walked in."

"Oh, okay, what can I get you to drink? You need a glass of something in your hands."

"Okay, I'll have wine, preferably chardonnay."

"Coming right up," says Randy as they walk towards the bar.

Carl was checking out the entire scene from across the room. He was waiting for the right moment to approach Karen. Their relationship was still a secret, so he had to be cool with his approach. The small get-together was just that. A few friends gathering around to talk about a bunch of nothing.

"So, Karen, you are looking especially nice this evening," says Randy as he stares at her over his glass of brandy.

"Thanks. You don't think it's too much, do you?'

"Girl, please, did you see Carl choking over there when he saw you walk in?" replied Randy with a sheepish grin.

"Oh, did he now?" laughs Karen.

Suddenly, Carl walked up and asked what was so funny.

"Oh, nothing, just Randy telling one of his corny jokes, you know, the kind you can't help but laugh?"

Carl smiles and asks if he can speak to her alone.

"Okay, sure, Randy, I'll be right back."

Karen follows Carl toward a dark corner. They don't get far because Joseph runs over to hug Karen and ensure they are enjoying themselves. When Carl finally gets her alone, he can't help but drool openly.

"Damn baby, you look good enough to eat! I'm starting to imagine all types of stuff to do to you tonight."

"Oh, I don't think so. I've had enough of that for one day. So, you dragged me over here just to talk nasty or what?"

"Whoa, chill out, sweetie. I just wanted to tell you how much I enjoyed our afternoon together."

"Well, you left so quickly I didn't know what to think."

"O baby, that's why you are acting so cold tonight. You know we had to get ready for this so-called party. Had I known you wanted me to stay, I would've stayed. Please don't be mad at me." pleaded Carl.

"I promise to stay all night tonight. Just let me know when you are ready to make that exit, okay sweetie?"

"Uh, I don't think so. I'll probably leave early; I really need to be alone tonight. Is that okay?"

"Yeah, sure, I guess we better mingle, so I'll talk to you later.

Carl, feeling deflated, walks away puzzled and drowns his glass of gin. Karen was staring at Carl's back when Randy appeared with a full glass of wine. "Oh, thanks friend," Karen says as she accepts the full glass from Randy.

"Boy, you always know what a girl needs."

"Yep, now tell daddy what's troubling you."

Karen jerked her head up at Randy.

"Oh okay, you are talking kinda fly there. Maybe you better make that your last cocktail."

"Hey, we are in the same club. Because I think I feel the way you look. Sad and confused."

"Mmm Hmm yeah, well I got an idea, why don't we go to my place, pop open a bottle of champagne, and down our troubles!

Just as Randy and Karen's taxi drives off. Coco arrives at Joseph's party fashionably late.

Minutes later, they enter Karen's condo. Leaving Carl at the party wasn't easy, but she needed some space. Besides, Randy looked like he could use her ears tonight.

"Hey girlfriend, are we having champagne or what?" as he broke into Karen's thoughts.

"I'll be right there. I'm debating on whether to serve you the good stuff."

Randy laughs, "Girl, you better serve me the stuff that's fit for a Queen."

"Okay," replied Karen as she sauntered into the living room with a bottle of Veuve and two champagne glasses.

"Now that's what I'm talking about," smiled Randy as he accepted a full glass of champagne from Karen.

As bubbles dance down his throat, he takes notice of his relaxed surroundings. "Oh, l just love your place, girl! It looks like you put a lot of time and money into your decor. And this leather sofa is going on! Where did you get that black and white photo of Denzel Washington?"

"Oh, Carl hates that picture, oops, that slipped! Well, I'm sure you guessed Carl and I are sort of dating."

Randy grinned," Yes, I knew you two had the hots for each other. Hell, a person would have to be blind not to notice the chemistry between you two."

"Well, anyway, I just clipped that picture from a magazine and took it over to Photo King and had them copy it in black and white. You really like it?"

"Yes, I do," replied Randy. "It looks personal. I thought he was family or a close friend."

"Wow, thanks! Okay, enough chit-chat. Randy, tell me what's troubling you," Karen said as she took a long sip of her champagne.

"Girl, I don't know where to begin," said Randy in a voice different from his own.

"Whoa! This sounds serious, I better get comfortable."

She grabbed two decorative pillows from her sofa and made herself a seat on the carpet.

Randy remained silent as he sat there with his eyes closed. When he finally opened them, Karen noticed a sadness hidden behind them. "You know Karen, I must say that you have this sweet way about you that makes my being gay seem natural. I find that I can really be myself around you. Now, don't get me wrong, I don't hide who I am, but I can put my guard down when I am with you. I just hope Carl knows what a gem you are."

"Oh, Randy, that's so sweet of you to say, but the fact that you are gay doesn't change the way I view you as a person or a friend."

"I know, but most people are closed-minded and would waste time judging me rather than getting to know me. I can remember my first encounter with a male. Girl, are you sure you're okay with hearing this?"

"Listen," said Karen, "I told you I'm all ears tonight. So, let's fill up our glasses, and you can get whatever you need to off your chest, ok?"

"Okay, here it goes," Randy replied.

As Randy stroked the back of his head, words started to flow as if the champagne was laced with a truth serum. "When I was about nine years old, my mother would go to work and leave me and my brother with this babysitter. My brother was ten, and our babysitter was about sixteen. One summer day, the three of us were playing in this tree house, and our babysitter started touching us in a weird way. My brother would always struggle free and run, but not me. I'd stay because I was curious, and I enjoyed the touching. I don't know. I was too young to realize what was happening to me! As a child, I always felt different from other boys my age. My mother would catch me playing with her makeup and wigs. As I became older, I realized my behavior wasn't cool, so I quickly closed it up and put it in the nearest closet. At night, I would pray to God to change my ways. But change never came, and here I am, as gay as a jaybird! It is what it is, right?"

"In my heart, I know these feelings are not the classic way of life, but I was dealt this hand, and I am playing my hand, you know? Well, anyway, I just wanted to get that out. Every once in a while, I feel I need to justify my lifestyle. Or at least say it out loud. You know? Because talking about it is like my own form of therapy."

"Well, you never need to justify your life to me, but I hear you loud and clear. And I hope you know that I am always here for you. Heck, I just saved your butt two hundred dollars an hour," laughed Karen

"True that! Thanks, girlfriend. On that note, I think I'll end my session. I've said enough for one night. Do you mind if I doze off some of this alcohol before I head out?"

"Of course not. You can crash on my sofa any day. Here, let me get you a blanket and some bed pillows."

After Karen tucked Randy in, she went to bed, but not before she said a little prayer for her friend.

* * *

Karen woke up feeling blessed and highly favored. She had a brief but deep conversation with Randy about his sexuality. The reality of Randy's situation was major in comparison to her and Carl's minor spliff with some miscommunication. She was actually stressed for no reason at all. All things considered, Karen thought she could use some of Carl's expertise. So, she decided to pay him a surprise visit.

Karen got ready to see her man, and minutes later, she jumped out of a cab and made her way to Carl's apartment complex. She was just about to ring the doorbell when a delicious thought entered her brain. She was in the mood for some good champagne. Karen started walking back down the street to the liquor store.

Carl's Mustang was parked in front of his building, so he was definitely home. Ten minutes later, Karen sang Sweet Charlie Baby in her head as she stood across from Carl's place with a brown paper bag tucked in her arm. She was so into her song she almost didn't notice Carl and Coco leaving his apartment. Well, I'll be a monkey's ass, thought Karen as her heart hit the pavement.

She was about to storm off when suddenly Carl looked up and made contact. Coco was so busy talking a mile a minute that she missed the whole episode. Before their worlds collided, Karen swiftly turned and walked away. She dropped the bottle of champagne in a nearby garbage can and jerked her head up so high she almost popped her neck out of the socket. She stopped briefly to put on her sunglasses so no one would notice her tear-stricken face.

Maybe she should have listened to Illinois Bell's commercial and phoned ahead, thought Karen as she desperately flagged a cab. And to think she was buck naked under her trench coat.

Oh shit, thought Carl. "Uh, Coco, why don't I just drop you off at home, and we do a movie another day?"

"Oh, ok, no problem, but why the sudden change? After all, this was your idea."

"I know, baby but uh, I just remembered something I need to take care of right now."

As Coco and Carl approached his car, he was so nervous that he fumbled through his pockets, searching for his car keys. He noticed Coco's expression, but the only expression he was concerned about was Karen's facial expression. He had to find a phone and call her. He just couldn't believe his luck.

Carl didn't know how he was going to explain this mess he had gotten himself into. But he wasn't about to destroy his future with the woman he was falling in love with. When he finally found his keys, he quickly drove off, speeding to get Coco home so he could talk to Karen. He knew he couldn't show up unprepared. He needed a game plan and a damn good one.

* * *

Karen was furious as she walked into her place with steam coming out of her ears. She should have held onto her champagne because she could really use a drink. She couldn't believe that bastard just stood there looking stupid and did nothing. He should have run after her. She just couldn't believe the shit that happened, and why on

God's earth did she throw a perfectly good bottle of champagne in the garbage? Like, who the fuck does that? She thought as she continued to rant and rave.

Karen walked over to her answering machine and saw that she had nine messages, all from Carl, no doubt. Suddenly, the phone rang. Karen, still feeling the rage, her quick reaction caused her to throw the phone across the room and storm off to her bedroom. She threw herself on the bed, staring at the ceiling. That was one lesson she didn't need to learn. Karen rolled over on her side, closed her eyes, and prayed for sleep, deep coma-like sleep.

Karen rolled out of bed with a throbbing headache. For a minute, she couldn't remember where she was. Then, last night's event flashed down on her, and she whispered, "Oh, hell, Carl and Coco." Karen dragged herself over to her phone and prayed it was in working order. Her temper flared up because it's not every day a girl catches her man with another woman outside his damn house! But thankfully, a dial tone immediately fills her ears as she attempts to retrieve her messages.

The first few messages were all from Carl, "Karen, pick up. Baby, please talk to me." The last one was from her sister, Marteen, wanting to know if she was ready for her visit in a few weeks. Karen felt guilty after listening to her sister's voice. Once her affair with Carl bloomed, she rarely had time for her only sister. So, she picked up the receiver to confirm the itinerary.

Karen slowly laid the phone in its cradle. Her weak attempt to call her sister failed. She wasn't ready to talk to anyone. Maybe a large cup of black coffee would get the vocal cords in order. Karen proceeded to her kitchen to prepare a much-needed cup of coffee. She realized the incident at Carl's yesterday was the only reason she didn't want to talk to anyone.

As Karen waited for her coffee to brew, her conscience spoke. Maybe she had overreacted. She left before Carl could even acknowledge her or explain. Uh, oh, wait a minute. She was actually questioning her very own intelligence. Yep, not to mention about to break yet another rule. Not only was Carl seen with a beautiful woman, but the same women he had drooled over openly in the past.

Karen could answer yes to all of the above and still refuse to believe the obvious. Yep, it's true, love is blind. Across the street from Karen's apartment building, Carl was sitting in his car, having a serious conversation with his better half, himself! He remembered his mother's advice.

Never put yourself in a position where someone would think you are doing something you are not because it's just as bad as doing it. Lord knows he didn't even get the panties. Coco talked about her modeling career. The only reason he called her was to take his mind off Karen and give her some space. Big mistake. Huh?

Carl sighed and took another deep breath. He decided to bite the bullet and go up to Karen's place. He didn't have a plan, but he was confident enough that when the time came, he'd think of something. Now, if he could just dodge her little nosy doorman and get to her doorbell.

CHAPTER 3

Karen was drinking her second cup of coffee when her doorbell rang. Her first reaction was to ignore it, but what did it matter? She knew it was Carl because he was the only one who could sneak past her doorman. Karen opened the door and stepped aside to allow Carl to enter.

Carl swaggered into her place with an air of royalty and confidence. She was not prepared for this. "So, I see you are alive and well because I was concerned when you didn't return my calls. And what's up with you leaving so quickly yesterday? You never gave me a chance to holler at you. So seriously, baby, what's up? I mean, I know you are not tripping on Coco and me just hanging out together." Carl pauses, waiting for a response, unsure of what else to say.

Karen gave Carl an 'oh no you didn't' look right before she went at him! "Uh, I have one question for you, and after you answer, you may politely leave my house. Now, was that bullshit you just told me your own material, or was it plagiarized?" But before Carl could respond, Karen quickly opened her door, gesturing him to leave. She said in a calmer voice, "You know what, never mind, don't answer that. I'd much rather you leave now!!!"

Just then, Carl took a few steps toward Karen in an attempt to hug her, but Karen quickly thrusts her hands forward to stop him. As they stared into each other's eyes, Carl was the first to speak." Baby, you might as well close that damn door, because I'm not going anywhere until we straighten this out. You know I love you, and there's no one in this world I'd rather be with than you.

Karen smiled and said, "Yeah, well, three is a crowd, so tell that mess to Coco. Karen looked down at her feet for a few seconds, then raised her head and said, "Babe, I love you too. But evidently, something did happen yesterday. Right now, I really don't want to hear any oki doke, bullshit, so please. I just want to be left alone. There isn't anything you could say or do to make me feel differently."

Carl ponders Karen's words for a brief moment, and then he says, "Okay, but before I go, I need to know that we are cool. And maybe a small hug would be nice. But before Karen could blink, he leaned over, gently kissed her on the lips, and whispered, "I love you more than anything in this universe. So, whatever you decide, remember that." He walks out, and the door closes.

* * *

Carl stood at the elevator in total dismay. He just couldn't wrap his brain around the situation he had somehow stumbled into. He knew he would be lost without Karen in his life, and as far as he was concerned, he would have her back in his arms, come hook or crook! As he stood in Karen's hallway, his thoughts traveled back in time to when Karen asked him to dance. That was their beginning. That night was magical!

He remembers the feverish look in her eyes, the sounds of her heart beating faster and faster, the sweet taste of her lips, and the way she whispered his name as they became one! That wonderful moment when time stood still. The moment he fell in love! Carl turned around and made his way back to Karen's apartment. She was worth begging for!

* * *

Karen is left stunned by Carl's sudden departure. She couldn't believe the mess she was in. A woman knows when her guy is feeling another woman. And Carl is definitely into Coco, thought Karen. She began to wonder if she could walk away from Carl. Besides, a girl couldn't lose what she had never had, right? 'Yes,' thought Karen, as she had finally made a decision. She would simply ease out of her so-called affair with Carl.

As far as she was concerned, he could have Coco and let the whole world in on it! No more undercover, secret agent bullshit. Oh, hell! What was she thinking? She can't let him go, not without some form of drama! After all, he did confess his love for her, and God knows she loved him, too!!! This is crazy, thought Karen.

And who the hell is buzzing my bell like that? Someone was leaning on her bell. Karen pushed her intercom button. "Who is it?" she shouted. "Hey baby, it's me, Carl. I need to ask you something." Well, ease off the bell so I can buzz you in, answered Karen. 'Now what,' thought Karen, preparing to open the door for Carl.

Seconds later, Carl arrives, apologizing for ringing her bell like a madman. When he settles in, he asks Karen for a glass of water. While Karen is gone, Carl quickly tries to think of something to say. Of course, he didn't have anything to ask her; he just wanted to look into those big brown eyes again.

"Okay, now what's so important that it can't wait until work tomorrow? " Says Karen. "I just want us to be cool. That's all, babe. Please tell me we're okay. Because I am so messed up, l can't even drive home. I've been sitting in my car thinking about how I can make things right. I swear I didn't do anything that would compromise our relationship. You know... you can jump in any time," says Carl with that pleading look in his eyes.

The same eyes that Karen fell in love with many months ago. Karen's mood suddenly swings in his favor. She realizes that something is amiss but cheers to breaking yet another rule because she is a sucker for Carl's sad eyes and pleading manner. It was safe to say he was in, like Fin!!!!

Karen knew she was going against her rules. But her heart was cheering for Carl, and she just wasn't strong enough to fuss and fight! She just wanted her man! Before Karen could speak, Carl snuck up and planted a big, juicy kiss on her lips. She responded by wrapping her arms tightly around his waist and opening her mouth to a more fulfilling and powerful kiss. It is safe to say that everything was cool. "I need you," growled Carl as their kiss intensified.

Karen's heart skipped a beat as her blood boiled from Carl's heated touch. She didn't just want him. She needed him inside of her. She needed his lips smeared all over her body, and that was one wish Carl was more than willing to grant.

Karen and Carl had just finished the greatest makeup sex of all time. And now, with Carl finally at peace, his manhood softened along with all of his worries. As Karen walked to the bathroom, Carl's eyes followed her rump until it disappeared. His wicked thoughts were interrupted by a trench coat that was hastily thrown over Karen's closet door.

When Karen returns, Carl asks her why she hasn't hung up her beautiful coat. He knew it was expensive because his baby only wore designer labels. Karen just smiled at Carl's question and replied, "Oh, that was the outfit I wore to your house the other day, the day I saw you with Coco. Carl looked puzzled and replied," What do you mean, outfit? That's just a trench coat." "Exactly," answered Karen with a grin. Carl was confused for a moment, and suddenly it registered. Carl nodded his head and whispered, "Damn!"

CHAPTER 4

Karen was locked inside a hellish nightmare over Carl. She was still conflicted over the drama between him and Coco. Although it was supposedly water under the bridge, she was still stuck in her feelings. Raw emotions stirred in her dream as she continued to toss and turn in her sleep. She finally woke up in the middle of the night and decided to write in her journal, something she hadn't done in a month of Sundays.

Karen got out of bed and slid on her slippers. She walked across her bedroom and sat at her small desk. She switched on her desk lamp and retrieved the journal that she had kept in the drawer. She closed her eyes and immediately revisited that scene of Carl and Coco leaving his apartment. She remembered the smile on his face. The same smile that captured her heart. He was saying something to Coco that made her laugh out loud. The type of laugh that made Karen cringe with jealousy.

What was so damn funny, and why was she laughing in her man's face? Karen's heart was heavy, and she felt that deep feeling of betrayal in the pit of her stomach. She opened her damp eyes and wrote.

WHEN THEY LOVE YOU

Where does the heart go once it leaves your chest,

And it's retrieved...all broken up

Who's guilty of the mess,

Do you move on as if it was never done?

And when the going gets tough,

Just how far will you run?

If true love is caught with another...

What does one do?

Do you forgive them and make them choose?

What is a broken heart supposed to do...

When they love you...

Karen closed her journal and got back into bed. She decided to give Carl some space and rip up the rules she had made up many moons ago. It was time to live in the moment because, frankly, she was done worrying about him and Coco. Tomorrow was a new day for Karen.

* * *

Carl is sitting with his best friend, Jumbug. He had just left the stage after playing a few numbers, and of course, Jumbug was talking smack to him. "Man, you know you are my boy, right? So, I feel I can tell you when you're falling off your square. Now, that last song you sang, man, that was some love-sick shit! You were begging worse than Keith Sweat! What's going on with you and this chick? What's her name, Katie or something like that?

Feeling irritated, Carl frowns and says, "No, man. Her name is Karen! And she's a good woman, alright?" Jumbug raises his brow and responds, "Alright player, calm down. You swole up like I just insulted her. Wow, man, are you that much into this woman?" He shakes his head and gulps down his beer before saying," Man, I didn't see this one coming."

Carl quickly responds, "It's all good. I'm just tripping because she has this wall built up, and it's blocking me. Sometimes, I feel like she's the dude and I'm the shorty. She calls when she wants to see me. When I reach out, she puts her wall up and acts like she needs space. Man, she has me looking crazy as hell!

Jumbug thinks for a minute and says, "No, she's in your heart, now! You just whipped, player! Old mighty Thor just found his Achilles heel. That woman is your weakness, and that my brother is love. Yep, you done messed around and fell your weak ass in love! Damn! You want me to call sister Sally and have her put your whole birth name on the prayer list?" A burst of laughter fills the room, and now everyone is staring.

When Carl fully regains his composure, he says, "Man, you ain't never lied, but I am tired of this roller coaster ride. I have to give her some space, so I'm just going to chill a minute and try and think this shit out." Jumbug glares at Carl.
"Man, stop looking at me like that! I'm not whipped!"
"Hey, I'm just listening to my brother. Come on, let's get out of here! I need a joint to calm these nerves. I just found out my best bud is in

love and all that mess. Man, you did swell up on me. Thought I was gonna have to restrain your punk ass." They both laugh.

They pat each other on the back as they exit the bar, smiling. Carl parted ways with his friend so he could smoke his weed, and he decided to go to the one place where he could clear his mind: his studio. Minutes later, Carl enters his loft studio on the north side of town. He settles in and sits down at his piano, allowing his fingers to take him off to the land of soul. Almost instantly, he is wrapped in a song and begins to sing.

"I just want, I just want, I just want to love you baby.

Girl, I want to give you your space

Baby, take time to plan your day

Cause you're my Queen

For you, I will do anything

I just want, I just want, I just want to love you baby.

He continues to sing with pure emotion. Releasing a mountain of frustration.

Girl, you can call me, and you know I will come,

Cause what I'm craving, girl you are the one.

I've been patient, and it's driving me insane.

Are you for real or playing games?

Don't you know you are the one?

You know what I'm craving.

Come on and give me some.

I just want. I just want to love you.

Carl pauses in the middle of the song. He closes down the keys and grabs his jacket. He can't delay the obvious. He is whipped, and he knows he needs to talk to Karen sooner than later.

CHAPTER 5

Karen woke up in a panic! 'Oh, my lord!' she whispered out loud. In their haste to make love, she and Carl didn't think to use any protection. She reached over to shake Carl, "Babe, babe, wake up. Wake your butt up!" But Carl was clearly snoring up a storm. Karen jumps out of bed and runs around in circles. Panicking and swearing, "Shit, shit, shit!!!"

She walks toward the bathroom. Carl stirs in his sleep. He slowly wakes up and immediately reaches over to Karen's side of the bed. He sits up, wiping sleep from his eyes. Karen walks out of the bathroom and when she notices Carl is awake, she shakes her head at him and holds out her diaphragm! Carl appears puzzled and asks, "What is it, baby? What's up?"

"My diaphragm, I forgot to put it in, and you didn't use any rubbers! What the hell were we thinking last night!"

"Oh wow!" He's silent for a few minutes and says, "Well, don't stress baby, come here. We can't do anything about that right now. Come back to bed. I always wanted a Carl Jr.!"

Karen squeals and throws her diaphragm at Carl, barely missing his big head, and walks toward the kitchen. She is mumbling to herself as she starts up the coffee maker. Carl walks over to her with a sheepish grin and wraps his arms around her waist. He plants a kiss on her forehead and whispers," I'm sorry, sweetie. I just don't want you stressing over this. Let's just wait and see, okay? Let's wait and see. After some clever maneuvering, Carl convinces Karen to join him later for dinner.

* * *

Karen just could not believe her reckless behavior. She was making rookie mistakes and acting like a lovesick teenager! Carl tried his best to reassure her, but she was still stressed. These thoughts invaded her mind as she began to dress for work. Once Karen arrived at Bajem's, she prayed her day would end as quickly as it began.

Karen wanted to go back home and relax with a glass of wine and listen to Sade's greatest hits. If only, thought Karen. She walked onto the sales floor, ready to jump into work! She welcomed any and all distractions because it was going to be a long day.

Karen was working the late shift with Randy tonight. She busied herself with paperwork while observing Carl flip a customer into a client, ultimately selling him a head-to-toe wardrobe. Carl was good at his job, but Karen was better. Well, usually, but not today. Girlfriend had other matters to tend to.

By midday, Carl had managed to somehow talk Karen into joining him for dinner. As usual, she could never resist his charms! As Karen is closing down her department, she looks up and notices Randy eyeing her suspiciously, "Girl, what's going on with you today? I see the sadness in your eyes. You know you can't fool me! Did Carl do something?"

Karen smiles and says, "I'm just tired today, that's all. Carl is treating me real good! You know, I would tell you if he wasn't. As a matter of fact, he is waiting downstairs to take me to dinner.

"Yeah, okay, that's nice," Randy replies, looking skeptical. "Anyway, I guess you will tell me when you are ready because I know something's up! You know I'm here if you need me, right?"

"Of course I do. But right now, I need your butt to get over here and help me close out. I just wanna get the hell out of here!!" Karen replied, laughing.

"I know that's right. This was one long ass day! Carl was lucky to have an early shift."

Minutes later, Karen and Randy complete the closing process and say their goodbyes. Randy leaves out the side entrance, and Karen proceeds to the parking garage, where she is meeting Carl. As Karen turns the corner, she walks into Carl and Coco, who are having a friendly chat! Here we go.

Carl immediately looks over, smiles at Karen, and says, "Hey, so are you ready to go eat a monster steak?" Coco grins at Karen and says, "Hey lady, what's up?" Karen temporarily ignores Coco. She walks over to Carl and plants a big ole kiss on his lips, making sure there's no room for misinterpretation! She then turns to Coco and says, "Hey girl, thanks for keeping Carl company for me. Now enjoy your evening, okay?"

Carl opens the passenger door and Karen slides in with a whirl of confidence! As they pull off, Karen looks at Coco in the rearview mirror. Coco is still standing there, looking crazy as hell. Carl puts his hand on Karen's thigh and says, "Are you okay babe?" Karen sits back, fastens her seat belt, and says, "I am now!" They ride in silence.

CHAPTER 6

Karen finally made it home from her date night with Carl. She was bone tired and decided to soak her whole body in a tub full of strawberry-scented bubbles. Dinner was delicious, and Carl was so attentive that she almost felt sorry for him. He was overcompensating for that leftover drama with Coco. Karen was so over Coco. She had other pressing matters to stress about!

Karen's brain was still reeling over the probability of her being pregnant! Because God knows, she was not ready for parenting, and as far as she knew, neither was Carl. As Karen dried off, she was reminded of a poem she wrote during her teenage years called 'Teenage Pain.'

"Teenage Pain"

Hopelessly wondering if he'd call
That teenage pain will have you climbing the walls.
Crying yourself to sleep over a freckle-faced boy.
Wiping your tears with your teddy bear toy.
One day, you will laugh at your teenage pain.
It will be years before you'd entertain.
The depth of a grown woman's pain.

Oh yeah, thought Karen. She had grown folk's trouble because she was not ready for motherhood. But just as Carl stated, she had to wait and see, which was easier said than done. Karen climbed into bed, smiling and pondering on something else Carl said, "She needed to call sister Sally and ask to be put on the prayers list." Prayers definitely change circumstances. She said her prayers and finally drifted off to sleep.

The talented Mr. Carl. 'I just want, I just want, I just want to love you, baby!' Carl was singing to Karen as she listened with fresh tears in her eyes. Oh, how she loves her some Carl! They finally made it up to Carl's loft studio/mancave, where he was playing his new music for her listening pleasure.

As the song comes to an end, Carl reaches over to wipe Karen's tears away and says, "I guess you like it, huh?"
"Oh baby, I loved it. Oh, my goodness, it's beautiful. Now play it one more time!"
"Babe, come on, now, not again. You know I have other music, right?"
Karen pleads. "Oh please, just once again. It's not every day a girl has a song written just for her. This is like Christmas for me!!! I'm loving all this! She waves her hands in the air. Now sing my song, baby, please!'

Carl shakes his head and says, "Alright, sweetie, but this time, you need to dance. I want you to start stripping for me. You see that pole over there? He points to the huge bedpost attached to his king-size bed. Karen rolls her eyes and responds, "Boy, stop playing. I stripped enough for your butt this morning. Now sing my song. I think you may have a hit on your hands. Seriously. Especially when you sing that part, uh 'come on and give me some' Man oh man, that's sexy as hell!!! Now sing my song, please."

As Carl sang, Karen looked into his eyes and forgot all about her stress-related issues. She was no longer threatened by the Coco's of the world. And if by chance she was pregnant, well, so be it! She was not alone. She had strength in her heart, and she was thankful for loving a good man. A God-fearing, good man!

Carl went on singing for Karen until the wee hours of the night. They finally ordered some Chinese takeout and made a picnic in front of his grand piano. They were wrapped in the fabric of love and enjoying the conformity of its splendor! It was a great day. Definitely, one to remember.

CHAPTER 7

Enough time had passed, and it was time for Karen to have a real pregnancy test. Karen's world was spinning in a swirl of love and happiness. The two people who share her heart will meet tonight. Marteen was flying in for a quick visit. Karen couldn't help but wonder how her sister would respond to Carl. She sounded so skeptical over the phone. Marteen was always protective of Karen and would move mountains for her baby sister.

Karen made the mistake of sharing her concerns about Carl's relationship with Coco and the fact that she had unprotected sex with him. She wished she would have never shared her drama with her sister. Because although the drama was over and things with Carl were great, as far as Marteen was concerned, it was fresh and salty! This is going to be both fun and interesting, thought Karen as she prepared herself for Marteen's arrival. Fingers and toes crossed, and maybe eyes, too.

On the other side of town, Carl was so excited at the thought of being in the company of two beautiful women, and it showed all over his face. Karen and her sister would sit front and center as he performs tonight. He made it to the club early. Carl wanted to practice his set before the staff arrived. He was performing the new song called 'I Just Want to Love You Baby." Karen's sister, Marteen, was also joining them for dinner and drinks, so he had to be at his best tonight!

Carl sat down at the piano, closed his eyes, and began playing the song that made his woman cry. He was going to rip the roof off tonight! Oh yeah, thought Carl as he sang, 'Come on and give me some.' Karen's favorite verse. Carl got in a few more songs before the club began buzzing with people. He was nervous, but the energy in the club was pumping up his head. It was almost showtime as Carl checked his watch and dashed off to his dressing room, or as Jumbug would say, the closet room.

* * *

Marteen's plane was taxiing in. She was always happy to come home to sweet home Chicago! She smiled openly as she exited the aircraft. Everyone was staring at her in awe. Marteen was quite striking. She had a walk that demanded attention and was a combination of sexy and fierce, all woven into one sophisticated lady. Girlfriend could stop traffic on her worst day!

Oblivious of the commotion, she followed the signs to baggage claim. She had to retrieve her luggage and pick up her rental car. Marteen couldn't wait to see her baby sister. She wanted to slap some sense into her because, apparently, this Carl dude had her doing dumb stuff. Dumb, like having unprotected sex, so now, she could be pregnant. Oh yeah, thought Marteen, she had to do some damage control. Lord help my little sister, prayed Marteen as she made her way over to baggage claim.

Across town, Karen was so excited to see her big sister! She had just spoken to her, and she was finally on her way to the house. Their plans were slowly unfolding. Once Marteen freshened up and they did some catching up, they headed to Carls's club to hear his performance. Karen hoped and prayed that the two would hit it off without incident.

As Karen sat anxiously waiting for her sister's arrival, she took a trip down memory lane. She went way back to when they were little girls in pigtails, foolishly competing for their daddy's attention. Karen remembered that time Marteen had found her diary and had read every page. She even had the nerve to share a few details with their mom and dad.

Karen became so angry she went ballistic and whooped Marteen's butt. That was the first fight she ever won against her sister. They tore the house up, fighting like total strangers. Afterward, their dad had a heartfelt talk with them, and they were so ashamed. From that day forward, they formed a bond that would bend over the years but never, ever break! They were more than sisters; they were best friends.

As sisters, they shared everything, from clothes to makeup, secrets, and once, boyfriends. When they were teenagers, they dated twin brothers. Marteen pleaded with her to switch twins because she wasn't feeling her twin. Of course, Karen argued that the boys were identical and, therefore, exactly the same. But Marteen swore they were different. So, to keep the peace, Karen persuaded her twin to go out with her sister. Karen laughed openly at those childhood memories.

The sound of the doorbell brought her back to the present. She quickly jumped up to buzz her sister in and opened her door.

Marteen was barely inside before Karen was hugging and squeezing her so tight! And just like old times, they picked up right where they had left off.

Karen immediately starts talking a mile a minute. 'Ooh, look at you. You're still a Diva! I love that camel blazer you're wearing. Who's the designer, Ralph? Oh, yes, I must have it, and give me those boots, too, girl, you look like a million dollars!"

"Well, Damn! Can I at least put my bags down before you start stripping my ass!"

"Ok, dang, give me your bags. Ooh, you packed heavy, huh? How long are you planning on staying, sis?'

"Oh, it's your fault. Those bags are heavy because I knew you would want this jacket, so I bought you one, and I got you a pair of black boots. Also, look inside my garment bag and take that Donna Karen white bodysuit! But just wait until I leave town before you wear anything. Because we haven't played that twin role in years!"

Karen squeals as she ruffles through Marteen's bag. "Oh, my goodness! I love you so much! This is awesome. You are the best! And how did you know I wanted this body shirt? I was just looking at it inside my Vogue magazine. Whew! Girl, this feels like Christmas." Marteen smiles and shakes her head as she flops down onto the sofa. "I'm glad you like it, sis. I just hope your butt isn't pregnant so you can wear it this winter."

"Well, I am not claiming anything. Besides it's too soon to know anything. And I am stressed enough, so please don't start in on me. I know it was dumb and irresponsible! Trust me! I know!!!!

Marteen puts her hands up and says "Okay. But you know I have to give you some grief. So, tell me about this slick-ass Carl that has your brain turned upside down! And I hope he can sing because you know I cannot fake a compliment." She grabs her carry-on bag and walks toward the guest room.

Karen rolls her eyes and whispers, "Here we go." Marteen, sensing her sister's reaction quickly says, "Stop rolling your eyes. You know I am speaking the truth, but you can fill me in later because I am going to take a quick shower."

"Okay, I put fresh towels on the bed, and everything else is as you left it. I am going to call Carl and give him a heads-up, ok?"

"Yeah, okay, tell him I cannot wait to meet his slick ass! Oops, sorry. Let me leave your boo alone. But seriously, I won't be long. Just tell him we should be there in an hour or so."

Marteen and Karen walked into the club minutes before Carl hit the stage. The place was packed, and Karen was thankful for their reserved seats. Carl looked so dreamy as his earthy voice filled the room! Marteen leaned in and whispered, "Oh yeah, his slick ass can sing!" They gave each other a high five.

They bobbed their heads as Carl sang one of his older songs. The crowd went wild! Tonight was going to be epic, thought Karen, as she swayed her head to the music! Karen leaned over and shouted into her sister's ear, "I told you he was good."

"Oh yeah, he can sing, and he is easy on the eyes. But I need to see where his head is at. You know I got to interview him, so calm your ass down! He ain't all that," laughed Marteen as she gave her sister a playful slap on her arm!

"Well, he's all that to me. Just wait until you hear the song he wrote for me. Girl, it's so damn sweet. I fell in love with him instantly!" Ooh, look at my baby singing! You see him! Seriously, do you see him?" more laughter.

"Yes, I see his slick ass, and you see those groupies over there?" Marteen motions to Karen's left to a group of women licking their lips and throwing air kisses in Carl's direction. "Now, can you handle that? I mean, they are coming at him hard! Just remember, he's an entertainer, so you know what it all entails little sis. That's all I'm saying."

"I see them, and all that is good for business! Just as long as they look and don't touch! Carl can handle it. I mean, he's used to it!" Karen says as she stands up and throws Carl a big ole kiss! Carl gives Karen a sexy wink as he closes the song. The crowd is on their feet as Carl receives a beautiful standing ovation!

When the crowd simmers down, Carl announces his next song and gives Karen and Marteen a big shout-out! "This next number was written for a special lady, my baby, Karen Bosse, who's sitting up front with her lovely sister, Marteen! I call this one, 'I just want to love you baby.'" As Carl starts to sing, the crowd goes wild.

Karen is on her feet, staring at her man with tears in her eyes. Marteen is taking it all in as she watches and listens with her ears and intuition! 'That Carl was something else,' thought Marteen, as she stared in silence. Before Carl finishes the song, a tall slick thuggish brother swaggers his butt over to their table and introduces himself as James (aka Jumbug), Carl's best friend. Marteen smiles and whispers in Karen's ear. "You see little sis, wolves always travel in pairs.

CHAPTER 8

Watching the rain fall was so therapeutic to Marteen. She was lost in the wet, foggy morning as her thoughts danced around inside her head. She was sitting by the bedroom window, listening to the raindrops on the windowsill. Marteen was just steps away from the most important person in her life. Her baby sister, Karen Denise Bosse.

As her sister slept across the hall, she thought about how much she enjoyed the other night. Although that night was epic, hanging out with her sister's friends, she remained conflicted because she knew her sister was no more ready to be a mother than she was ready to be an aunt. Carl was a great guy and all, he just wasn't father material, at least not in her eyes. Marteen knew their parents would never forgive her if she didn't take better care of her little sister.

Marteen was the closest thing to a parent for Karen. Their parents died young, and they were left with each other. She had to have her sister's back when it came to her life choices. Now, his friend, Jumbug, was quite the character with his ghetto-acting self. Marteen shook her head as she remembered his last words before they retired for the evening.

He was like, "Sweet lady, don't you dare leave town without me. Now, I have two ways to make you sleep like a newborn baby, and that's either with this joint in my left pocket or this big thing in my front pocket. But since you are a lady, you can hit this joint in my left pocket."

Ugh, so gross, thought Marteen. Oh yeah, that dude, called Jumbug, was something else with his dirty jokes. Hopefully, that was the last time she'd be in his company.

As Marteen's thoughts circle back to the present, she glances over the guestroom and notices a picture hanging over the queen-sized bed. She smiles because her sister had pictures of Denzel Washington posted all over her house. In that particular picture, he was sitting in a chair, reading a book. Karen didn't know Denzel from the man on the moon! She literally had more photos of him than those of her own flesh and blood.

With that amusing thought, Marteen shakes her head once more as she walks into the bathroom to shower and dress. They had an appointment with Karen's OB-GYN. Today was the day! Yep, the big pregnancy test because her sister refused to take an over-the-counter test. She wanted the real deal, one without false positives. Oh boy, thought Marteen, somebody call Sally!

* * *

Karen lay in bed, wide awake. She couldn't sleep because her stomach was full of butterflies. Just thinking about Carl singing his heart out on stage and the way the words flowed from his sweet lips. Man, oh man, Karen was so wrapped up in reliving that night she almost forgot about her appointment with her OBGYN today. "Oh heck," squealed Karen as she jumped out of the bed!

She got down on her knees to pray. "Lord have mercy. I hope and pray that I am not pregnant. Please, God, I pray that you will fix this for me. I promise to never put myself in this position, and please don't let my sister roll her big eyes at me today, for haven't I suffered enough, Lord? In Jesus' name, I pray, Amen."

Karen remains on the floor with her back against the foot of her bed. She pulled her knees up and wrapped her arms around them. For the first time in a long time, she was afraid. If she was double-jointed, she'd kick herself in the butt. She definitely needed a butt-whooping. This was plain stupid and careless of her. But like Carl stated, what's done is done. She had to get up and pull herself together because this was just a short chapter of her life.

Karen stood up and walked out of her bedroom, shaking off the sadness as she shouted for her sister to wake up and fix breakfast. It was her turn to cook. After all, she wasn't staying in a hotel! "Marteen, it's your turn to fix breakfast!!!" screamed Karen as she went to search for her sister.

* * *

Carl was pacing back and forth in his living room as he waited to hear from Karen. He didn't know if he should be mad because he was told to stay away or relieved because he didn't have to see Karen's sister browbeat him to death with that accusing look of hers. Man, oh man, he just couldn't figure out what her problem was.

He was in love with her sister, and if that's a crime, then lock him up for life. Because he had that mad, crazy-ass love for his baby, and if she was pregnant, then bring it on. So be it because he was running to Jewelers Row to buy the biggest damn diamond he could afford. Oops! Thought Carl, I think I found the love of my life. Ooh shit, wow!

Carl quickly took the nearest seat because suddenly his legs were standing on shaky ground. Carl was so caught up in his own thoughts that he forgot his buddy, Jumbug, was sitting on his sofa. Jumbug was being way too silent, and Carl was so thankful for his silence. But this wasn't like his friend. He was acting very strange ever since they left the club the other night. As a matter of fact, he was starting to behave like a love-sick puppy! Mmmm, thought Carl. This ain't right. Nah, this joker must be into something slick or, maybe, someone.

Carl stared at Jumbug until his phone rang! He and Jumbug jumped at the same time. Was this the call he was waiting for? Could this be the beginning of the next chapter of his life? Carl quickly picks up the receiver and says, "Hello?"

CHAPTER 9

Jumbug had somehow made it over to Carl's place. He was in a daze ever since he laid eyes on Karen's sister, Marteen. He had never seen such beauty in all the days of his life. He had to find a way to win her heart because she had him inside the palm of her hand. Jumbug no longer craved weed...not anymore.

Marteen was his new drug, and he was high as a kite. On nothing but pure, sensual love. The kind of love that keeps you full and thirsty. He was talking about that love that has you calling your Mom for advice over the silliest thing and dreaming during the day. He was everything he had laughed about, joked about, and swore would never happen to him. He was hopelessly in love.

Jumbug was sitting on Carl's sofa, watching him walk holes in his carpet. For the first time, he knew what his friend was going through. At least he finally understood. He was just praying he didn't blow things with Marteen when he told her those awful jokes. Suddenly, he jumps up and back into reality. Carl's phone was ringing.

* * *

Karen and Marteen had just arrived at the doctor's office. They were late because Karen couldn't find her house keys, so they had to wait for the next available time slot. Karen decided to call Carl and invite him for lunch. Her sister wasn't happy about this, but Karen couldn't give a rat's behind about her sister's feelings because she wanted her man by her side. Carl answered on the first ring.

"Hello?"

"Hey babe, listen, uh, we are still at the doctor's office, and the next available appointment isn't until 3:15 pm, so I was wondering if you wanted to meet us for a quick lunch at Carmine's."

"Oh, okay, is everything okay sweetie? I thought your appointment was at 11:30 am."

"Yeah, we missed the appointment, and now they can't see me until later. It was my fault. I misplaced my keys. You will not guess where I finally found them."

"Where? Inside that big purse of yours?"

"Nope, they were on the desk, in that tray where I always put them. My head is all screwed up. I am such a scatterbrain."

"Wow, and neither one of y'all thought to look there, huh? Yeah, you gotta calm down. But listen, I will head on over. Is it okay to bring Jumbug? He's hanging out with me."

"Of course. Marteen and I will meet you guys at the bar area, okay? See you soon, baby. Love you!"

"Okay, sweetheart, I love you more."

As Karen ends the call, Marteen is giving her the evil eye look and turning beet red. 'Here we go,' thought Karen.

Marteen was livid. She couldn't believe how hot her sister was for that slick-ass Carl! She couldn't help but hear her gushing on the phone. And no, she didn't just agree to have his ghetto friend join them. Oh hell, no!!! Marteen glances over at her sister and says, "I can't believe you just invited them to lunch. I did not travel all the way to Chicago to hang out with your man and his ghetto-ass friend."

"Oh my gosh, what is with this guy? Did he drug you? I mean, seriously, you can't be without him for a few hours? Damn! You're lucky I love you because I would take my butt straight to a hotel. This is crazy! Why are you smiling? You know this shit ain't right. That doggone Jumbug is a hot mess.

They begin walking to the restaurant. "Girl, come on and do this for me. It's just lunch, dang! You don't have to talk to Jumbug. Just take one for the team, please, please, please, with sugar on top! If the tables were turned, I wouldn't hesitate to do this for you. Do you remember those twins we dated in high school? I switched my guy for your guy. Now, that was some freaky mess, but I did it with no complaints. Yep, so technically, you owe me one."

"Mmm, I still think that damn Carl put some voodoo on your ass. But ok, I will sit through lunch, but I will be damned if I have dinner with y'all." Karen quickly gives her sister a big hug. Stop hugging me, you know this shit ain't right, stop it, I can't stand your butt."

"Awwww, you know you love me. Thanks sis. This means a lot. Karen and Marteen enter the restaurant and proceed to the bar area.

* * *

Carl placed the phone in the receiver and turned to his friend. "Hey man, are you cool? Because I just told Karen that we would meet them for lunch at Carmine's. Trying not to appear too excited,

"Yeah, that's cool, but can we swing by my place so I can change clothes? I need to up my game with that Marteen. She got my nose wide open, for real! Man, I am really digging this chick!"

"Awww hell no! I knew it! I knew something was up with your no talking ass. You've been quiet since you walked in. Man, that woman is too stuck up for you. I mean, she is foxy as hell, but her attitude is wack," Carl says, pacing back and forth. He throws his hands in the air and continues ranting. "But hey, knock yourself out, player! I will say a prayer for you. Because I thought I heard you offer her a joint the other night!'

"Man, I know I was acting like a complete idiot. Wow, I just hope I can redeem myself. But check this out. Let's take my ride so I can show her what I'm working with. You know, she probably thinks I am some knucklehead ass fool from the hood. She hasn't met my other half because I am about to blow her beautiful mind!'

"Okay, well, let's roll so I can have a front-row seat to this freak show starring your crazy ass."

"Yeah, okay, just pay attention. You might learn something today."

Jumbug's thoughts were racing through his mind as fast as a slave running for his freedom... woo! He just hoped this was the last time he would ever fall in love. His heart was too fragile for this mess! Man, oh man. Jumbug was never that guy who chased women. He didn't have to. Women were always chasing after him and threw everything but the kitchen sink at his azz.

There was this one chick named Amy who followed him all the way to Europe and back! She had mad detective skills. To this day, he never figured out how she retrieved his itinerary or discovered his mother's unlisted phone number. She definitely gave Columbo a run for his money! But his last girlfriend, Tanya, was super jealous and bipolar. Of course, she never showed this part until he called things off! Oh boy, he thought he was gonna have to put a hit out on her crazy azz. Yeah, that Karma is a son of a gun! Because he was straight chasing this Marteen and God help her when and if he actually catches her.

As they pull up to the valet, Jumbug pops a tic-tac in his mouth and strokes his goatee before handing over his black Mercedes Benz. Carl and Jumbug walk into Carmine's like they own the joint! Two kings looking for two Queens.

* * *

Karen and Marteen ordered an appetizer while waiting for Carl and Jumbug. The restaurant was starting to pick up as the lunch crowd flowed in. Karen loved their steaks and roasted chicken. She never had a bad meal at Carmine's. The atmosphere had a sexy, romantic flair. The combination was fabulous, with candlelight and small vases stuffed with fresh-cut roses all cleverly placed throughout. It is so elegant, thought Karen as she surveyed the room.

Karen turned her attention back to Marteen, who was talking about her house plants. Suddenly, Carl and Jumbug entered the bar area. Karen had to take a double look at Jumbug because he looked like he had just stepped out of GQ. He was looking quite dapper. He had a certain air about him that Karen hadn't noticed before.

Marteen stops talking mid-sentence as Jumbug and Carl suddenly enter the room. Karen says, "Hey babe!" and gives Carl a quick kiss before hugging Jumbug and re-introducing him to her sister. They have an awkward moment as Carl steps in to give Marteen a brief hug and hello. As if on cue, the host walks over and asks if they will be eating at the bar or dining area.

As they wait for their table, Carl and Karen are having a private conversation, and Jumbug swoops in and smoothly compliments Marteen. "Wow, I didn't think you could be more beautiful, but here you are, looking gorgeous as ever. So, tell me, what's your secret to fineness? Oh wait, don't tell me. I think I got it. You are what the elders called 'highly favored.' Yeah, that's you! Because baby, God gave you everything!"

Marteen laughingly says, "That's one compliment I never saw coming, at least not from the same man who offered me a joint, and what was that other option you gave me? Mmmm."

"Oh, wow, I was hoping you wouldn't remember that foolishness. I must apologize for that. I am so sorry. Let's start over. James extends his hand and says, "Hello, my name is James, and my friends call me Jumbug. It is a pleasure to meet such an elegant and stunningly beautiful young lady."

"Okay, I will play along." She shakes hands with James and says, "Hello, James, nice to meet you. Now, are we good?"

"Uh, nope, not until you allow me to take you out to dinner, a movie, or both, before you leave town. After that, we are cool in the gang! So, what do you think about that?"

Marteen smiles and responds, "Let's get through lunch. Okay?"

"Mmm, okay, fair enough, my lady." But not willing to give up he continues and says, "So uh, what's your favorite cuisine?" If you like Italian, I know this quaint restaurant over in Little Italy called Sol" Marteen is laughing at him.

"Maybe we can go there or, uh, what? What's so funny?"

"You know what, I can see how spoiled you are. You just command your way, huh? We are having lunch, and that's it. Stop making plans for dinner."

"Okay, I see how you are. You wanna make a brother wait. That's cool. I have been waiting all my life for you, so I can wait until tomorrow." They share a laugh.

"Boy, whatever, and stop giving me that puppy dog look. I am not falling for it." They continue conversing, and suddenly, the iceberg is broken, and the big elephant has left the room.

CHAPTER 10

Marteen was blown away by the new and improved version of Jumbug. He was very cultured and quite handsome. He was all over her at Carmine's, and surprisingly, she enjoyed the attention. But she was not having dinner with him. She didn't want any distractions, so she had to decline all of his offers. She was easily annoyed by men who boldly pursued her, but James. And yes, she prefers James because Jumbug didn't fit the man she met today.

James' relentless behavior had her laughing and smiling through all his clever attempts. He was a charmer, and his eyes were dangerously sexy. Marteen was having a tough time looking into them. She wouldn't admit it, but this man was stirring up something deep inside of her body, and that was...well, she didn't know what it was. She had to ignore it and keep her distance because he was danger with a capital D!!!

As lunch was ending, Jumbug insisted on driving them back to the doctor's office. As they exit Carmines, Marteen has an 'ah-ha moment.' First, Karen and Carl swing through the revolving door. As Marteen steps in, James gently places his hand on the small of her back to help guide her inside the revolving door. Immediately, her back feels the heat from his touch! Her back is burning like fire, and the pit of her stomach is filled with the sensation of fluttering butterflies! What the hell is happening!!

Marteen is having a hard time wrapping her mind around the obvious. She's thinking, this can't be, not now, and certainly not with this man. Please, God, don't allow it. I beg of you!!! Inside her mind, she is screaming. NOOOO!!!!! She couldn't, she just couldn't. Oh, hell no, she was actually feeling this dude!!! Dang!

* * *

Lunch was delicious, and now it was time for Karen's truth. She had stressed and prayed as much as any sane person would in her predicament. Karen was finally back for her exam, and Carl and Marteen were with her. Jumbug is parked out front, waiting to take Carl to his car.

Carl insisted on walking her inside the doctor's office. He was trying to stick around, but Karen wanted him to leave her to face the news alone. She wanted some space and some time to sort through her thoughts and concerns. Just as Carl is about to leave, her OBGYN appears from the back office and immediately greets Karen, explaining that he will be with her shortly.

Carl looks confused as he whispers to Karen. "Uh, is that dude your doctor?"

"Yes, he has been my primary physician for years. Why?" Karen replied, "For years that Denzel-looking joker has been all up in my candy jar. Oh wow! Man, that's not cool. What's wrong with a female doctor? I don't like this dude checking you out, nope. Carl notices Karen looking annoyed and says, "Baby, don't give me that look! You would feel the same if my doctor looked like Halle Berry. Let's be real baby. Let's be real!!"

Feeling impatient, Karen responds, "Baby, I know this looks weird to you, but he is a professional, and I am comfortable with him. He is the best in his field. There is absolutely nothing to worry about. I am not thinking about him like that, and I definitely do not have time to babysit your feelings right now, okay? They just called my name, so let me take this test, and I will call you later. Please, you know Jumbug is outside waiting."

"No, I'll wait right here, and Jumbug is cool. I am not leaving. As a matter of fact, I wanna meet the doctor. I need to check his credentials. Yeah, I will be right here when you're done. No way I'm leaving now."

Karen shakes her head as she walks away. Marteen was sitting in the background, taking in the entire scene. She chuckled to herself because she was glad to have something to take her mind off of James. They were hilarious. Two lovebirds fighting. She just wished she had a bag of popcorn and a box of goobers.

Carl is pacing back and forth like a tiger, watching his prey. Marteen is sheepishly watching from the corner of her eye. She is about to offer him the seat next to her when he walks over and says, "Uh, Marteen, I am going to run out and talk to Jumbug for a minute. Would you please let Karen know that I am right outside? Thanks." Before Marteen can respond, Carl swiftly walks out of the doctor's office.

As soon as Carl jumps inside the car, he is talking a mile a minute. "Damn man, what took you so long, and slow down?"

"Man, I am tripping right now. I decided to stay and wait for Karen, she just went in."

"Ok, so where is Marteen? Is she inside waiting by herself?"

Annoyed, Carl snaps, "Man, what do you think? Who else would be in there with her? Hell yeah, she is by herself. You see me sitting in here with you."

"Ok, bro, what happened in those 5 minutes that got your panties in a bunch? And take a breather before you get jacked!!!

Carl exhaled and said, "Man, I'm sorry, but listen to this. Karen's doctor is a black dude who just happens to resemble Denzel Washington! Now, would that have your panties in a bunch?"

"Well, first of all, I don't wear panties, so..."

"Man, be serious. This dude is in there right now, examining my woman's stuff. That realization has me all messed up!!"

"Mmm. Ok, I see. Yeah, that's a lot to digest, but he's a physician and just doing his job. That brother can't help it if he looks like Denzel. He is just trying to get paid, man, so don't trip about it. You should be concerned about these other cats on the street."

Carl says, "She also has a huge crush on Denzel. Her entire house is full of pictures of him. And now her doctor could be his twin! I'm having a hard time getting over this one."

"I see how that can make your blood boil. But as long as she continues to prove her love to you, then that's all you can ask for. Whatever you do, don't let your insecurities bring drama into your relationship. Trust me on this, alright?"

"Yeah, I know, but I wish I would've never walked my ass inside that building. So, tell me, if you and Marteen were a couple and she had a handsome doctor examining her privates, would you be cool and take the advice you gave me?"

"First and foremost, let's just let the idea of Marteen being my woman soak in. Man, oh man, having her as my woman would be the greatest feeling of all. And I wouldn't want a male doctor examining her. I don't care if he looked like a gorilla's ass. But that's something I would keep to myself, especially if she had him before I came on the scene. Besides, he already had his hand in the cookie jar, so why trip?

"Okay, I get that. He's seen it all, but I am having a hard time with him looking like Denzel because that's her favorite movie star. Man, I know I'm probably tripping over nothing, but I can't shake it off."

"I feel you, but uh, not to change the subject, now, tell me the truth. Do you think Marteen likes me? I mean, you heard her laughing and stuff during lunch. I wanna say yes, but what do you think?"

"Man, I need you to focus on my dilemma right now because my woman is in that damn building getting touched, and God only knows what else is happening. Awww, this is killing me, man, it's killing me!!!!

"Ok, I just told you to let that shit go. Karen ain't going nowhere, man. That woman loves the shit out of your punk ass. Now pull yourself together and act like you got some sense. That dude has seen more cats than the two of us will ever see in our lifetime. So that shit he's doing with Karen is just business as usual."

They are silent for a few minutes. Carl is rubbing his hands through his hair with a distant stare. Jumbug has his head back on the headrest with his eyes closed.

Jumbug is the first to speak. "Alright player, let's find a spot to park and take a walk. You need to cool off.

Carl replies, "Okay. Yeah, okay, let's do that.'

* * *

Carl has his emotions in check. The walk with his best friend did the job. They were parked and waiting in the lot for Karen and Marteen. Karen's test results will be ready in a day or so, and she was happy to know that all the drama will soon be laid to rest.

Marteen grabbed her purse and the book she was reading, and they exited the building. As they walk to the car, Marteen hugs her sister and whispers, "I hope you know that I am always going to be here for you and support you, no matter what. She squeezes Karen tighter and says, "You hear me, sis? I love your butt, ok?"

"Aww, thanks sis. I know you love me. I just can't wait to find out, and I hope Carl has calmed down. Did you hear what he said to me?"

"Yes, I heard everything. But that's his own insecurity, and if I know James, he has already talked him down from that cliff. Carl was just tripping because that man really loves you. I saw it in his eyes today! He reacted with his heart and not his head. You know how it is when you really love somebody. That's all it was."

"I hope so because I've never seen him so angry. He has to know that I love him, and my doctor is no threat to him, none whatsoever. Uh, wait a second, did I just hear you say James? Girl, when did you start using Jumbug's birthname? Oh wee. I bet you're going to dinner tonight. Yep, you like him."

Marteen is blushing. "OMG, look at you, I have never seen you blush like that! Lord, this just made my day!' Karen is as giddy as a teenager as she claps her hands with excitement. Marteen, trying her best to remain poised, says, "I am not feeling him like that. He just told me his full name. Now stop laughing; they are staring at us. Stop it!"

As they approach the car, Carl gets out and immediately gives Karen a big hug. Jumbug exits the car and walks around to greet Marteen. And far, far away, on this bright sunny day, you could hear the chatter and laughter of these four extraordinary souls. The calm after the storm.

* * *

Marteen was stoked about having dinner alone with James. She was both frightened and excited to hang out with the best friend of her sister's boyfriend. Just hours ago, she didn't want to have lunch with him, let alone dinner. It's funny how a few heartbeats will change the mind, like two snaps of your fingers! Bam, just like magic!

Karen was out with Carl, so she was alone in her sister's apartment, thinking about things. Marteen was standing in front of the mirror, holding outfit after outfit up to her chin. She was looking for something to wear to dinner. Too many choices thought Marteen.

She held the last dress up, tilted her head, and smiled at her reflection. She whispered out loud, "Yes, this will do."

Hours later, Marteen opens the door, and in steps James, with that Denzel walk. The Training Day walk he took when he crossed the street to his car that bounced up and down in anticipation of his arrival-his swag was off the chain!!! Oh yeah, James aka Jumbug, had it down packed!

James gives Marteen the look a boy has when he receives his first bicycle, and he wants to ride it. James plants a kiss on Marteen's cheek and then swings her around and back into his arms. It was an old steppers move. He says, "Wow, look at you, you look stunning, baby! You got me feeling like the luckiest man alive! Thank you for accepting my dinner invitation. You are so beautiful."

"You're welcome. Thank you for all the compliments. And might I add, you are looking handsome tonight in your blazer and white dress shirt. Now, can I have my hands to grab my stuff so we can make our dinner reservations?"

"Absolutely, just as long as I can hold them again. I hope you don't mind if I hold your hand tonight. Because I know I am about to turn every man in this universe green with envy!"

Without a second thought, James lifts her hands and delivers a light kiss on each one. As he raises his head, he stares into her big brown eyes and leans in to brush a loose strand of hair from her beautiful face. They just stood staring into each other's eyes with such intensity that one could cut the air with a knife. The silence was loud.

The night was young as the locals and visitors strolled down Michigan Avenue, a famous street located in the heart of Chicago. Laughter danced in the air. It was a storybook night for lovers. As the starlight twinkled from above, someone was laughing out loud, and that someone was Marteen!

"James, would you please stop talking just long enough for me to catch my breath? You are making my mascara run with these wicked jokes of yours! Oh, my goodness," laughs Marteen. James, showing no mercy, continues with his jokes. "No, seriously, I didn't see his lips move. Was he even talking to me?"
"You know as well as I do that man was talking to you. Now stop! Just stop!'

After dinner, Marteen and James decide to leave the car with the valet and walk off the wonderful meal they had just devoured! The night was so beautiful, so they decided to enjoy it with a brief walk around the Avenue. Suddenly, a horse carriage appears, and they hop in. James didn't waste a second as he quickly pulled Marteen into his arms and whispered, "You know Cinderella had a ride just like this."
"Uh, yes, she did, but you know, at the stroke of midnight, it all went downhill, right?" she laughs in reply.

They shared another laugh, and James snuck a quick peck on her cheek and another one on her forehead. He didn't dare kiss her anywhere else because he knew his heart couldn't take the explosion that kiss would ultimately bring down on him. The night was going so well, and he didn't want to mess up. He was on his best behavior. No way was he showing her his other half, at least not again. No way, she was his future. This beautiful moment was their beginning, their first.

After the carriage ride, James wanted to prolong the evening, so he took Marteen to his favorite restaurant on the other side of town. He wanted the night to last forever. They drove further north to a family-owned spot called Shelly Jean's. The owner was a sassy old broad who greeted her loyal clientele with a warm hug.

Whenever James was missing his mom, he'd stop by Shelly Jean's for cocktails and some old-fashioned motherly love. It was a quaint little place, and the menu looked like an old map of the city. The main entrees were named after different streets in Chicago, and meat eaters loved her Lake Street pulled pork sandwich or her Dr. King Italian beef sandwich with steak fries. Every meal was a trip down memory lane.

They were seated in a cozy booth sipping coffee with a splash of Bailey's, sharing stories from their childhood days. What a discovery for James! He was thrilled to learn that this beautiful, elegant lady was a tomboy in heels. She ran marathons, climbed mountains, and drove race cars as a hobby. Most importantly, she designed software for the United States government.

She was the stranger in his dreams. He always wanted a GI Jane. He wasn't into those damsel-in-distress chicks. He was attracted to a woman's strength and strong character as well as her beauty. She was rare

When Marteen and James finally left Shelly Jean's, the night was over, and the sun was making its way inside for a new day. James wasn't ready to leave, but he had to get some rest. So, they made their way back to Karen's place. Marteen walked to the door, and when she turned to say goodnight, James had cleverly placed his whole body dangerously close to her. They stood toe to toe.

James lifts Marteen's chin up and plants a sweet kiss upon her lips, her nose, and back to her lips. Before she can respond, he pulls away and takes a few steps back. He stares at her for the longest time, and then, in a weak voice, he says, "Thank you for tonight. You have my undivided attention. I will call you later. Sleep well, my Queen." Before she can respond, he quickly exits the hall, and she is left listening to his footsteps as he leaves the building.

CHAPTER 11

Marteen walks into her sister's place in a daze. Wow, what a night, thought Marteen as she slipped off her heels and flopped down in a chair. She closed her eyes and shuddered at the thought of James kissing her lips. He was such a little tease. And it was so cute how he stole glances at her throughout the evening. He was sweet and incredibly funny.

She was smiling as she recalled their waiter who had those thin lips. James had her laughing so hard because he said the man was a rare ventriloquist because he didn't have to worry about his lips moving. James was hysterical. The carriage ride was so welcoming because she was able to give her calves and her feet a much-needed rest. And, of course, the quaint little bar called Shelly Jean's was a gem. It was so warm and inviting, just like being at home. James was an interesting man. She couldn't wait to see what was around the corner because he also had her attention.

Marteen slowly got up and tiptoed toward the guest room with her shoes in her hand. But she doesn't get far because Karen walks out of her bedroom with her hands on her hips and says, "Well, good morning to you, and where have you been all night? Just because you are grown doesn't mean you can't call or something." Marteen continues to her room with Karen on her heels, fussing like an old lady.

"Girl, I called Carl and woke his ass up, and he told me, Jumbug probably sold you to some high-paying trafficker. Girl, I was like, boy, stop playing with me! I was not in the mood for his sick jokes."

"Well, I am sorry you were worried about me, but as you can see, I am home and in one piece, so if you don't mind, I need my beauty sleep. Before you ask, yes, I had a wonderful time with James; he was the perfect gentleman, and yes, I am still a virgin! They both fall to the floor, laughing like teenagers.

Marteen says in between laughing, "Girl, go back to bed so I can get some beauty rest. I'll tell you all about my day in the morning Karen."

"Okay, crazy lady, wake me up if you get up before I do."

"Okay, sis, see you in a few hours."

Karen retreats back to her room, and Marteen walks into the bathroom and draws herself a bubble bath,

* * *

James walks into his place after dropping off Marteen with a big ass smile on his face. In his head, he is singing Keith Sweat's 'Make It Last Forever.' He was a man on a mission, and if he played his cards right, he was certain he'd be married by this time next year! From his heart to God's ears! He had to have Marteen, and he was not going to mess up. But for now, he needed a cold shower, though, because she had his stuff hard as a brick!!

Across town, Marteen was soaking in a tub full of bubbles. She had her head held back with her eyes closed, thinking about the kiss

James teased her with. She wanted to respond with full force, but she was treading in deep waters, and she didn't want to mislead him. She just wanted to get laid and move on. She sensed that James wanted more, and she wasn't ready for a relationship. She wanted friendship with benefits! No more, no less.

Marteen woke up a few hours before Karen and decided to let her sleep. She needed a few minutes to collect her thoughts. She was heading home in a few days, and she wanted to make sure her sister was straight with her baby issues. God willing, she would be blessed no matter what her test results revealed. Life would go on.

She was also thinking about James and his kissable lips. She wasn't sure if hanging out with him was in his best interest, but it was definitely good for her. When it came to dating, Marteen was always undermatched in the bedroom. She had a wild appetite and was hard to please, but James made her tingle, and that was something many men could never accomplish. But he seemed too emotionally attached, and she needed his head in the physical arena, not that emotional one. She had her work cut out because she had to at least test the waters.

Now, what Marteen really needed was a partner who could toss her around, throw her in the air, then catch her with one hand, all while never missing a stroke! Oh, yes!!! She was betting on James to get the job done. She had a lot to think about. But first thing first, she had to start breakfast and wake her nosy ass sister up so she could call in her pregnancy test! Today was the day, thought Marteen, as she set the coffee maker and then screamed for her sister to wake up! She almost forgot it was her turn to make breakfast.

Marteen and Karen were just sitting down for breakfast when Carl and James stopped by to join them. Karen wanted everyone together when she received the test results. Breakfast was delicious and entertaining. James imitated the waiter from the other night, and Marteen joined him in her assessment of the story. Marteen noticed her sister's weak laugh, so she suggested that maybe it was time for Karen to call in for her test results.

Karen slowly walked over to the phone and picked up the receiver. All eyes were on her, and Carl quickly stood next to her, just in case she needed him. Karen spoke into the phone for a few minutes and then hung up! She turns to Carl, smiles up into his eyes, and says, "Do you mind pouring us a glass of mimosas? Cause I think it's okay for me to have one!"

Carl looks confused for a moment, and then he picks her up and spins her around as Karen shouts, "It's negative. I'm not pregnant!!!!" Marteen is thrilled, and James is as well. Ole James was just happy to be there. Any time he could be in Marteen's company was always good news to him!!

* * *

"Just be thankful that you are not pregnant and can learn from the experience. I'm sure you will be extra careful from now on because you and I both know that a baby is not something you need in your life!" They both reach over to give high fives. Marteen says,

"So, did you ever talk to Carl about his reaction to that fine azz doctor of yours?"

"Oh, nope. We were so focused on the pregnancy test that I guess it slipped our mind, but I am definitely going to tell him about himself. You saw how jealous he was acting, girl that was so out of character for him!"

"Yeah, he came out of nowhere with that behavior, but like I said, he spoke from his heart and not his brain. Don't stress about it. He's entitled to at least one meltdown."

"Yea, that's true, you called it, sis. A meltdown is exactly what he had. His eyes were wide open, and his hands were moving a mile a minute!"

They laughed. "I know, right? And all I was missing was some popcorn and a jumbo box of goobers because that was some good entertainment!!"

"Mmm, ok, now. Enough about my drama. What's up with you and Jumbug? Oh, oops, I'm sorry, you and James. Are you going to continue seeing him?"

Marteen leans back, stares at the ceiling, and reveals, "I honestly don't know. I want to, but girl, I don't want anything heavy right now. It's just complicated. Karen gets up, walks over, places her hand on her sister's forehead, and says, "What the hell is so complicated about dating? Are you running a damn fever? Sis, would you please stop overanalyzing your life and just live!!"

Marteen laughs and says, "Look who's giving advice on drama! You have a lot of nerve. I'm not like you. I don't lead with my heart. I use my head, so yes, it's complicated. Because for once in my life, I'm going to think before I jump in the sheets with, oh, wait, let's find the right word, oh, with a damn practical stranger!

Karen puts her hand over her mouth and whispers "Oh my, I was just talking about dating; you done moved up to the bedroom! Well slap me because I must be sleeping! Damn sis, you must really like him. We can have a double wedding next year and save money, like a two-for-one! Right?? Come on, let's plan it."

Marteen shakes her head as she grabs a pillow from the sofa and hits Karen with it! Now it's war. Karen jumps up and screams, "Oh, it's on now!!!" She grabs another pillow and hits her sister in the face! And just like when they were teenagers, a pillow fight was brewing, and they were giggling and squealing as feathers danced in the air!!

Oh yeah!! It's about to be champagne popping, pillow flying, music blaring, great time!! And within those four walls, if one was really listening. They would hear the expression of sisterly love and the bond that carried them along their journey—no more, no less.

Unbreakable Bond
A Poetic Love Story
Part 2

CHAPTER 12

Carl had just finished a set and was breaking down his instruments when Jumbug walked into the club. The club was small in size but known for having great entertainment. They had a small stage with a few surrounding tables and a long L- shaped bar! Carl loved the smaller clubs because being up close and personal allowed him to capitalize on the vibes of his audience. Carl waved to his friend Jumbug, aka James.

"What's up, player? How does it feel to have that load off your chest?"

"Hey, man! I'm feeling good. You missed my set. We were jamming a new jazz number. What are you doing on this side of town?"

"Aww, man, damn! I was just sitting around the crib, and it hit me that you were playing tonight. Sorry, I missed that jazz number. But check this out. Let's call the girls and see if they want to come out tonight."

"Mmm, I don't know about that, my man. Karen said they were having a slumber party or something like that, and she was in for the night."

Looking disappointed, he replied, "Oh okay, well, I guess I can look upside your ugly mug for a few minutes, huh?"

"Man, you the one looking like a love-sick bulldog in the face. I don't know why you are so hung up on that Marteen. You need to snap out of it because you ain't hitting that! Trust me when I tell you, she ain't going, my brother."

"Yeah, okay. Just watch and learn because this time next year, you will be getting fitted for one of those penguin suits. I'm telling you, she can have all of my riches!"

"Mmmm, well, grab that table in the back while I finish breaking down my equipment. Oh, and order me a gin gimlet on the rocks!"

"Ok, cool." He orders a drink and a beer. Carl finally settled down to drink his gin gimlet and shoot the breeze with his friend, Jumbug.

They are talking trash as usual until Carl brings up Doctor Denzel, his girlfriend's obygn. "So, is your friend Gia still working at that new artist gallery up north?"

"Uh, last I heard, she was. Why? You need some artwork for your studio?"

"Nah, I was going to buy Karen a few pieces to replace those pictures of Denzel that's hanging in her bedroom! I can't look at that joker the same anymore. Definitely not in the bedroom! I'm just going to put my foot down because that's kinda disrespectful, wouldn't you agree?"

Jumbug takes a chug from his beer and slowly responds, "Uh, well, let's see, you are going to walk into your girl's apartment, where she pays the bills, and remove her portraits from her wall. Now stay with me...I said her walls and hang up something you think she should have on *her walls*. Man, get out of here with that foolishness!! You sound crazy! Leave that woman's stuff alone and get over that doctor before you make a mountain out of a little hill!"

Carl attempts to say something, but James interrupts. "No, no, let's just rewind what you just said. Better yet, why don't I record what you just said and replay it for you because you need to hear the shit that you are planning on doing. Man, please don't ask that woman to remove her shit off of her wall for your insecure self. Uh-huh, don't do it!!"

Carl laughed, "Man, I know this sounds crazy, but she must know that now that I know her doctor favors Denzel, well, she should. At least take the mess off of the bedroom wall! Seriously, what's wrong with me, replacing it with some beautiful art? No, I'm serious. Stop looking like that! You mean to tell me you can't see where I'm coming from."

"I see your point, but you can't take it upon yourself to remove her pictures. You have to talk that shit out which I wish you would just let go! I mean, Karen loves you, man! You need to bury that, enjoy your relationship, and live happily ever after before you mess up something for real! "

"Alright, I'll try to, but I don't know. I'm just having a hard time getting past this. You know, it's killing me inside, and I'm not even the jealous type. Well, forget I said anything. Why don't you tell me how you're going to win over Marteen so I can have a good old-fashioned laugh."

Jumbug smiled "Yeah well at least I'm not going crazy and talking like a damn fool. Unlike you, I'm not going to jump into anything. I'm going to treat her like a Queen, so she'll be so hooked that she'll be begging me to touch her!"

"Yeah, in your dreams!"

"Yep, first my dreams, but later in real life! I know it's gonna happen. All I gotta do is take it slow and keep praying every night!

Carl laughed, "Okay, we will see. Now let's get out of here. I need to see my baby tonight. I'm going to crash her little slumber party!"

"Alright, player, let's bounce." They settle the check and exit the club.

* * *

James had just left Carl and was unlocking the door to his crib. He was happy that his best bud wasn't going into fatherhood. 'That joker dodged a bullet,' thought James as he entered his living room. He walked over to his pioneer stereo to turn on some sounds. Just like his best bud, he was a music lover.

When it came to music, he didn't discriminate. James loved every form of music. He could bathe his soul into the depths of each chord. The more instrumental, the better. From the beat of the drum, the range of the horn, and every pound of each key. Music told the story that seasoned the soul. James often referred to music as a tenderizer. A good soundtrack could soften up a tough day, lighten up any mood, and put a smile on an old bulldog's face!

James grabbed a beer from the fridge and sat down on the sofa. With Kenny G. playing in the background, he sipped his beer, and his thoughts immediately took him to Marteen. She was like the forbidden fruit. He knew it would be bad for him to taste her, but he just had to have her. Nothing could stop him, and as long as he played his hand to the end, we would win the cat-and-mouse game!

Come hook or crook, James was determined to have Marteen in every position known to mankind! James smiled as he continued to bob his head to the music and drink his cold beer. If one was ear hustling in on his thoughts, they would hear his heart beating fast. He had a picture of Marteen in his head, and she was smiling with her eyes. They are wrapped in a tight embrace, and the passion was burning a small hole into his soul because he was falling in love!

Fall in Love

What's that fullness you feel?

Why are you smiling from ear to ear?

Suddenly, the burdens and all the pain,

Poof into the void

The world has changed.

What once was urgent,

Can simply wait,

Time to smell the flowers

Time to escape

Love.

Love is the medication prescribed today.

Be silly, make love, eat lots of cake!

No crystal ball,

No gimmicks at all,

Listen to your heart,

Relax and fall in love.

CHAPTER 13

Carl's drive from the club to Karen's place was therapeutic and eye-opening. Maybe his best friend was smarter than he thought he was. He had to let the doctor business go and find a way to get those pictures off the wall by Karen's own doing. Yep, he had to be smart about the way he handled it. Before you know it, he'll have her doing everything he wanted. Yes, yes, thought Carl as he turned down Karen's street. He pulled right into a parking spot in front of her building.

Inside Karen's place, she and Marteen had retired to their own rooms after straightening up the living room. They made a big mess of things from that silly pillow fight. It ended with them on the floor laughing and reminiscing about the time they snuck out to see 'Prince and the Revolution' but had the dates mixed up. As a result, they were put on punishment for a month and ended up missing the real concert. They were blaming each other for getting the dates wrong! To this day, they cannot figure out how they screwed up.

Karen was posing in her floor-length mirror, trying to imagine herself pregnant, when her doorbell chimed. Karen quickly pulls her T-shirt down and walks out of the room to answer the door. As she waits for Carl, she glances across the room. She notices her sister making a face as she returns to the guest room and closes the door. She made it obvious that she had no intentions of making small talk with Karen's boyfriend!

Carl walks into Karen's place and greets her with a hug and a kiss. Karen says, "Hey babe, what brings you here tonight? Oh, and how did your show go?" She takes his hand and walks him into her bedroom. Carl replied, "It went well. Jumbug stopped by, and we had a few drinks, you know. But how was your little slumber party with your sister? I'm surprised I didn't see her when I walked in. I thought I was crashing y'all lil sister's bonding party.

"Oh, so you were hoping to crash our party, huh? Karen reaches over to poke him in his chest and says. Well, it just so happens that we had a lot of fun and a pillow fight!" She raises her arm, flexing her muscles, "And you know who won, right? I was like, take this and take that! Man, oh man, we were acting like little girls up in here!

I know that's right. My baby can take care of herself! Look at you. Come here and show me some of your moves. Boy, uh un umm. Ain't nobody trying to tussle with you. I was just going to bed, I'm bone tired! Carl reaches out, and Karen quickly crosses over to the other side of the bed, puts her hands on her hips, and gives Carl that sexy smile, the one that stole his heart.

"Nope, you know you owe me an apology for acting so jealous of my doctor. I was embarrassed because people were staring at us, and you know my sister heard it all!" Karen said.
"Awww, come on, babe, can we discuss this in the morning? I don't want to talk tonight. Come here. I know I was tripping, but let's not talk about that right now! Please, baby, I just want to hold you tonight."

"We just found out that you are not pregnant, and I'm feeling sad and happy at the same time, you know! Part of me was looking forward to being a dad, and the other half was, well, you know, just nervous about being one! I mean, I know I acted crazy about that dude being your doctor. I'm sorry if I embarrassed you, okay? I'm sorry baby!"

Karen walks over, holds hands with Carl, stares into his eyes, and says, "Babe, I'm so in love with you. There isn't a man alive that can ever and hear me, okay, I mean ever, take me away from you! Won't happen! So..." She kisses his hand, takes it to her heart, and says, "This heart, right here, belongs to you, so don't question my love by being that insecure, okay? It hurts me to see you so angry like that!"

Carl suddenly becomes his father's son and his mother's child. He is feeling real, unapologetic, pure love as he fights within to hold back a tear. To love someone so much and have that same love reciprocated, wow!!! He's too emotional to speak. But somehow, he manages and mumbles, "I know, I know." That night, Carl and Karen made passionate love, and a bond was born. One that, over time, would prove to be unbreakable.

* * *

Marteen is lying in bed wrestling with her feelings about James. She's tempted to call him, but she's conflicted. Should she cross the line and discover what James has to offer, or should she just pack her bags and go back home because it's obvious that she is no longer needed. As quiet as it's kept, her sister is in good hands with Carl.

Of course, she would like to have seen Karen with a more stable person, but that's not her decision to make.

Marteen was bored and horney, so what the heck, thought Marteen. She opens the door to her room, sneaks out into the hall, and brings the phone into her room. She is careful not to make any noises as she pulls the cord along the floor. Once inside the room, Marteen turns her purse upside down, searching for James' phone number, and she finally has it.

Marteen dials his home, and James picks up on the first ring! "Hello?" James answers. "Hello, James, this is Marteen. I hope I didn't catch you at a bad time." James' heart is beating a mile a minute. "Uh, no, I wasn't doing anything. Is everything okay?" Marteen replies. "Well, I was laying here bored out of mind, and I was wondering if you were up to some company tonight?" "Oooh, hell yes! I mean, sure, you uh want me to pick you up? I can be there in 20 minutes. Are you at your sister's house?" James replied "Yes, but I have my rental. Sooo, uh, were you dressed for bed? What are you wearing right now?" James, caught off guard, says, "Oh uh, just some Levi's and a white t-shirt. Umm, I can change if you want me to. What's up, baby?" Marteen laughs, "I'm just playing with you boy. Give me your address and I'll be over within an hour! James laughed, "Oh, ok. You got them jokes, huh? Alright. I feel you." James gives Marteen his address.

I Want You

It takes a certain person to run toward danger,

So, I am running with no fear.

I must have you. Right now, right here!

I can't explain.

Lost for words.

My butterflies are swarming.

I am guessing you heard.

Counting the seconds, baby, I am going to explode.

Feeling like a teenager.

Laughing because, finally, I know!

Checking my hair and fixing my clothes,

Hoping you can feel it too,

Because damn,

I really want you!!!

* * *

Karen awakens to the sound of her front door opening and closing. She reaches over to wake up Carl, but he's dead to the world. So, she eases up, grabs her robe, and walks out to explore. She looks around and knocks on Marteen's door before going inside. Her sister is nowhere to be found.

She checks her front door and notices the deadbolt is unlocked, just leaving only the automatic lock, locked. Mmm, I know this heffa didn't leave and not tell anyone! Now, where did she run off to? Karen's mind continued to wander. She uses the bathroom and then climbs back into bed, and slowly drifts back into dreamland. Knowing her sister was probably just going for a drive and smart enough to take care of herself.

Across town, James is pacing back and forth, looking from window to window for Marteen to arrive. He quickly showered and changed into a different pair of Levi's and a white shirt. He put a bottle of champagne on ice and played some soft jazz music. He was not sure what the night would bring. But he didn't give a damn. His soulmate was coming over, and he and his heart were grateful for that!

"Man, oh man," thought James. "God is good! Ooh, He's so good!!" Just then, his thoughts are interrupted as the doorbell chimes. James throws a big kiss up to heaven as he opens his door, and Marteen fills his doorframe with her beautiful presence. Marteen tilts her head to the side and licks her lips. Her eyes were on his, and she slowly unwrapped the belt of her wrapped dress, revealing her birthday suit!

Firefighters are most likely on their way because James' ass just caught fire as he stares at the most beautiful creature God has ever made! From the perky round breasts, small waist, long shapely legs, and that diamond in the middle!! Sweet Jesus. James reaches out for Marteen and pulls her into his arms. From behind, she kicks his door shut with her 5-inch stilettos. Marteen wraps her arms and legs around James as he lifts her by her bare ass, as their lips lock up in fire and passion.

James carries her towards the bedroom, and Marteen breaks the kiss. She repeatedly kisses him on his nose, cheeks, and forehead.

James buries his head between her breasts, trying to get a mouthful of sweetness. Finally, they are at the doorframe of his bedroom. Marteen opens her eyes, looks up at this object hanging above the door, and says to James, "Omg, is that what I think it is, hanging over your door?" James is too involved to hear anything, so Marteen wiggles around until he glances up, and she says. "Boy, is that a bone over your bedroom door?"

James, a bit disoriented, puts her down, glances up, and smiles. "Oh, yeah, that's some shit from my mack days. Between laughter, he finally says, "So, uh, let me welcome you to the bone room! They laugh so hard, and James says, "Now, baby, uh, you know what happens inside the bone room, right?"

Marteen can't stop laughing. James lifts her back up, carries her across the threshold, and lays her on his bed. They both continue to chuckle over that big ass bone over his doorway. There's one thing for sure: there is never be a dull moment with ole Jumbug. He was a fool, for sure.

So, with the passion on hold, James wraps Marteen in his arms. They hold each other, laughing ever so slightly at their inside joke. That night, the ice was broken. After the tears of laughter were finally over, James skillfully examined every inch of Marteen's body. Dutifully satisfying her to the twenty-first power!!!

It was safe to say that all was good on that side of town. Marteen finally falls into a deep coma-like sleep. Next to her, James was sleeping like a newborn baby, with a big ole smile on his face!

And we all know he'd be thanking the good Lord come Sunday morning.

In the middle of the night, Marteen opens her eyes to James, staring up at his ceiling. She stares at him for a moment, taking in his handsome features and remembering his smooth moves and sweet lips before she says, "Mmm, do you have another bone up there or what?"

"Oh, hey you," says James as he turns and smiles. "Nah, no more bones around here. How are you feeling, babe? Do you need anything?"

"Nope, I'm good. I think you gave me enough last night.

Smiling, she says, "What we're just thinking about?

"Mmmm, you. Thinking about you and wondering how I got so lucky. Well, blessed is more like it. Just reliving last night. Is that alright? "Yes," says Marteen as she props up on her elbow, holding her chin in her hand. She looks into James' eyes and says, "Have you ever thought about doing stand-up comedy?"

James smiles and says, "Nope, you are the only one who laughs at my corny jokes. "No way, I know that can't be true. I mean, right in the middle of you know what, and I almost passed out from laughing so hard! You keep me laughing!" Marteen replied.

"Good, I'm going to work on keeping that smile on your face. And if you let me, I'll also keep those toes curled up and keep you screaming like you were a few hours ago. But that's on you. I mean, I wanna be a gentleman and, uh do what I'm told." James reaches over and kisses

Marteen with such intensity that she responds with a moan, her body longing for his touch again!!!

James lets go of her just long enough to flip her on top of him. He smiles into her eyes and says, "Do your thing, mama. I can feel your fire burning. Just do what you wanna do to me." And just like he said, Marteen puts on a rodeo show that will make all the horses in the barn steam with envy! James whispers, "Oh yeah, oh yeah!! It's yours, baby, claim it, claim it!!" As Marteen continues to ride him all the way to glory!!

Marteen wakes up for the second time. James is freshly shaven, fully dressed, and grinning like a Chinese cat at an all-mouse party! Marteen stretches and rises and says, "Boy, where are you going this early in the morning?" James, still grinning, "Uh, apparently to your search party. Carl called about an hour ago."

"He's talking about you being missing since last night and your sister losing her mind trying to organize a search party!" Marteen squeals, "Omg! What? Boy, why didn't you wake me up?
James shakes his head, hunches his shoulders, and says, "I don't know, babe, selfish reasons, I guess. I mean, you were sleeping so peacefully, and I didn't wanna interfere with your rest! You know, you needed that rest!"

Marteen looks at him like he has lost his mind and attempts to throw a pillow upside his head, "Boy, what time is it?"
"Oh, uh, about 1:30 in the afternoon?" he replied.
"Oh my god! What did you say to Carl when he called? Can I use your shower? I gotta get out of here, damn!" Marteen said.

"Yes, I got everything in the bathroom waiting for you. And uh, I told them I was on my way to help look for you," he says with too much humor in his voice.

"Ooh, you make me sick! Call over there and tell them I'm okay! James follows her into the bathroom and says, "Uh, how you want me to spin this? Maybe you should call. I mean, I don't know what to say, babe!

Marteen takes a deep breath, pulls her hair up, and twists it around before stepping into the shower. She shouts, "Never mind, I'll call myself." James walks back into the bedroom, grinning from ear to ear. Anxious to see the look on his friend's face when he walks in with Marteen on his arm! Oh yeah, thought James, that joker is going to have a massive stroke!

* * *

Marteen walks out of the bathroom with a towel wrapped around her and starts barking off orders. She gives James her car keys and directs him to grab her workout bag from the trunk of her car. She orders him to please fix her a cup of coffee, black with one sugar. Finally, she wants to use his phone to call her sister.

James is standing in the middle of the room trying to figure out what to do first when Marteen says, "Uh, I need my bag please so I can get dressed."

"Oh, okay, I'll be right back, uh where did you park yesterday?" James asks.

Marteen stares at him and says, "Out front. The red convertible. Where's the phone, please?"

Feeling like a little boy, James gestures to his right and walks out to Marteen's car. Mumbling to himself. Marteen reluctantly picks up the phone and dials her sister's line. She immediately gets a busy signal! James walks in with her bag and hands it to her. He then turns around and mumbles that he is going to make some coffee if she needs anything.

Marteen pulls out a pair of leggings, a T-shirt, and tennis shoes. While getting dressed, she makes another attempt at calling her sister again, but the line is busy. James enters his bedroom holding a hot cup of coffee. Marteen hops up, kisses James on the lips, and says thanks before taking a sip of her coffee!

"You're welcome. Did you square things up with your sister? "Not yet, couldn't get through. The line was busy, so I guess we should go. Oh, and why don't you follow me? Can we just pretend we bumped into each other or something like that? Is that cool? James, a bit confused, says, "Uh, so, you want to keep our lil thing a secret?

"Well, until everything calms down, yeah. I'm pretty low-key when it comes to my personal life. I hope you are cool with it. No need to complicate things. I enjoyed you, and you enjoyed me, right?" "Yeah, right! No need to complicate anything, so why don't you go on and get a head start, and I will come in a few minutes behind you, alright?" James replied as he walked into the kitchen, trying to keep himself busy.

Marteen grabs her bag and purse and walks into the kitchen. She puts her empty cup in the sink and squeezes James's butt before saying, "Bye, lover!" She quickly walks out to her car! James is left in his kitchen with a surprised look on his face. "Well, I'll be a monkey's uncle. I think she just pulled one of my old moves on me.

Man, oh man, thought James as he grabbed his keys and walked out to his ride. James laughs out loud and shivers, realizing the rules of the game have changed! James was now on the receiving end because the bitch, called Karma, finally showed up!

* * *

Marteen had to park a block away from her sister's apartment because every space was taken. Marteen grabs her purse and starts walking back to her sister's place, mentally preparing herself for Karen's hysterics. Karen's apartment is packed with her friends and a few of Carl's. They had called every hospital in the area, and her friend Randy was on the phone with the city morgue.

Karen was wide-eyed, scared out of her mind, and sick to her stomach, wondering what was happening to her only sister. The police had informed her that they couldn't do anything because her sister was an adult, and she had been missing for less than 24/48 hours. But Karen wasn't waiting around. She knew every minute her sister was out there was viable, and she called everyone she knew to help her. Her sister was a level-headed person and would never leave like that and not tell her or write a note! Nope, not the Marteen she grew up with!

Suddenly, the doorbell chimes. Carl buzzes the bell without pushing the intercom and opens the door to someone he assumes is

James or another friend who is stopping by to help out. Surprisingly, it's Marteen!! Everyone is clapping and thanking Jesus as Karen runs to her sister, almost knocking her down with a monster bear hug! They are rocking back and forth. Randy is wiping his eyes as he hangs up the phone because he knows someone, somewhere, would be crying today. He was told that an unidentified African American female was found last night.

CHAPTER 14

Twenty-four hours after Marteen walked into Karen's place, safe and unharmed, across town, a young woman's body was being identified at the county morgue. A dark cloud is looming over Karen and Carl's relationship. The strength of their love and trust will be put to another vigorous test.

Karen is over at Carl's place cooking dinner for the two of them. She made steak and gravy with scallop potatoes and a mixed green salad! Carl's favorite meal! While Karen prepares dinner, Carl relaxes on his sofa and enjoys a basketball game. The Chicago Bulls are playing the Detroit Pistons, and Scottie Pippen is on fire!

"Oh yeah! That's my boy," yells Carl from the living room. Karen runs into the living room, screaming, "What did I miss?" "Scottie just hit a three-pointer; look, baby, watch the replay! Whoosh, all net baby!!" All net!! Karen yells, "Yes!! Alright, Pippen!" And gives Carl a high five before returning to the kitchen.

Carl asks how long before dinner's ready, and Karen says, "Almost babe, maybe another 15 minutes, okay! You want another beer?"

"Nope, I'm a good baby," he replied. Like clockwork, dinner is served, and Carl is one happy dude.

"Wow, this looks amazing baby! How blessed am I to have a woman who's beautiful and a great cook!"

"Why thank you, my King," laughs Karen.

Between bites, Carl asks about her sister Marteen. "So, what's up with your sister? Is she still fuming over her rescue party?" Carl laughs. Karen chuckles, "Nah, she's okay, but that's what she gets for not telling us anything. She knows I'm a lil crazy, and you better not agree with that."

"Nope, I'm not getting between two sisters. My lips are sealed, he replied. "Smart man, but anyway she's back in DC doing her thing! She'll be back this weekend, though."

"Mmm, okay. I know James will be sniffing around like an ole hound" They laugh more as they continue to enjoy their meal.

Just when they were really chowing down, the phone rang. Carl gets up and walks into his living room and picks up the receiver. A minute or two pass by and Karen hears a sound from Carl that gets her up and out of her chair. She walks into the living area, and Carl is sitting down with his head in his hands. Feeling Karen's presence, he raises his head with a look of dismay on his face. His eyes are tearing up, and at that moment, Karen is afraid to ask him what's going on. But she walks slowly over and says "What happened baby? Omg what!?!"

Carl shakes his head, and in a shaky voice, he mumbles. "She's dead. Coco is gone, baby. They found her by the lake." Karen takes a step back and says, OMG, that's terrible. I'm sorry, who was that person who called? Ignoring Karen's question, Carl walks into his bedroom and grabs his jacket and keys. Karen is right on his heels.

Carl turns to Karen and says, "I'm sorry, sweetie, but I need to pay my respects to Coco's Mom. Would you mind putting my food away? So, you, I mean, let's go and I'll drop you off at home. I'm just in shock right now! Man, this is crazy," Carl sighs.

He sits down on the edge of his bed, and for the longest time, Karen sits with him while he stares off into space and quietly mourns another woman. Not sure how to make sense of the situation, Karen is feeling some kind of way. She's struggling with how not to respond to Carl's reaction to Coco's death. After all, she was a friend of his, right? Right? Mmmmm. A question she can't answer with accuracy.

* * *

Carl was still in disbelief mode. He had just seen Coco days before her death, and she was smiling and talking about her contract with Essence magazine. She was nervous about an upcoming interview because she didn't want her past to resurface. Coco was on her way to stardom! A young black girl from Arkansas was making her mama proud.

Carl was in his studio, and he knew he was behaving strangely. Karen was trying so hard to support him, but there was only so much she would endure before asking questions that he wasn't prepared to answer. He closed his eyes and started playing a song he would sing at Coco's service, tomorrow. Her mom asked him to say something, and he said he would sing, instead. Carl rehearsed a song he wrote for his friend, Coco.

Going Home

Hey there, lady with the mask on,

Show the world where you come from.

Share your dreams,

I know you have some.

Don't be shy,

Put your crown on.

Leaving soon,

You ain't got long.

The Lord is coming,

To take you back home.

Hey there, lady with the mask on.

Show the world where you come from,

Oh, your haters,

Yeah, you got some.

Don't be shy,

Put your crown on.

Reveal your eyes.

You are not alone.

I see you smiling,

Cause you are so strong.

Fix your crown.

All your worries are gone,

I'll miss you.

Girl, strap your wings on,

You going home.

He couldn't finish. Carl broke down and cried because, in all honesty, Coco was more than a friend. Time passes, and later when feeling better, Carl pulls out some old photos from his past! He remembers the first time he saw Coco. It was about 12 years ago. He was shooting hoops with some friends, and she flew past him on her bicycle, and he was like, who is that!!?

Carl didn't see her again until his junior year. They hooked up and had the best time. There was no sex, just great conversation. She was fine as hell, but she was like one of the boys. Her conversation was so laid back that you wanted to hear more of whatever she had to say. She inspired him to write music, and soon, a friendship developed.

Her mom was his biggest fan. But life happened, and they grew apart. Then, one day, out of the blue, she shows up to work at Bajem's Department Store, and they instantly reconnect! Coco aka Dana was a complicated lady. The industry she was in brought a lot of pain, and she hid behind a mask of secrets. One she regretfully shared with Carl.

One night, after smoking some weed, she told Carl that her dad was a rapist. He raped her mom when she was a teenager, and she was born as a result of his crime! And unfortunately, she looked just like her dad. A constant reminder of how she was created. Growing up, Coco had to find love in all the wrong places. Her mom loved her, but not the way she loved her baby sister. She tried so desperately to earn her mother's love, but the older she got, the more she resembled her dad.

Coco often said she died the day she was conceived, and so, she was living on borrowed time. Upon hearing the news of her death, echoes of her saying those words filled his mind, and he lost it right in front of Karen. He wished he could've held back his reaction that day. Carl closed the book of memories and grabbed his belongings. He turned off the lights and left for home! The service for Coco - aka Dana Brown was tomorrow, and he had to do her right because she deserved it!

Coco's homegoing was tomorrow afternoon, and Carl hadn't even talked to her about how and when they were going to the service. Karen was sitting at Barbara Jean's Cafe on Elm Street, heavily in deep thought as she sipped on a glass of Chardonnay. Randy was meeting her for a few minutes because he had a previous commitment to get to.

Karen was thankful for his friendship. She could always count on him to show up and, if needed, to show out! Karen was seated in a booth for privacy. Besides, she loves the cushy orange leather loveseats and the hexagon-shaped espresso wooden table, which is just fabulous by all standards. Karen was looking for any distractions.

So many thoughts were dancing inside her brain. Just how well did Carl really know Coco? Were they ever lovers? Who called him that night, with the news of her passing? At some point, she needed some answers. As far as she knew that girl could have been his damn ex-wife! Okay, maybe not that, but her mind was starting to play all types of tricks on her.

Randy walks into Barbara Jean's carrying a large shopping bag from Bajem's! "Hey, my precious, how are you doing, boo?"

"Oh, you don't have time for me to begin with all the mess my brain is dealing with. What's in that big ole bag?" she asked him.

"Oh, girl, that's just a wedding gift I had to pick up for this reception, I'm going to do it in a few hours, that's all. Nothing special.

Randy makes eye contact with the waiter and gestures for him to come over, "Girl, what are you drinking?"

"Wine. Chardonnay, it's not bad. I think I'll have another one. Order whatever you want. My treat today, Ok?"

"Well, alright, big shot! I'll just have what you're having and maybe, mmm, let's see, oh, hello!" says Randy to the server who just walked up to the table.

"Afternoon sir, will you be ordering lunch today?" the server asked.

"Yes, but first I would like what she's drinking, but in a larger glass. And bring her another one as well. Also, I'd like to try the small seafood salad, please. Thank you!"

The server looks at Karen and asks, "Anything else for you, madam?" "Oh no, just another one of these, thanks," says Karen as she finishes off her wine.

"So, how are you holding up? I am still in shock over Coco. I mean, that girl was about to really be someone! There was a small article on her in Ebony last month. Word on the street is that she was doing a movie with Pam Grier and Richard Roundtree next summer. Just sad," Randy said, shaking his head.

"Oh wow! I didn't know all that. We barely spoke. After that incident with her and Carl, well, I just kept my distance, but do you know what really happened to her?

"No, I haven't heard anything except what's in the paper. You know she made the news the other day? I'm just waiting for someone to interview me because we all worked with her. But hold up, you don't know anything? I thought Carl had all the information. Weren't they going out, a few years ago? He should know something. Have y'all talked about her?"

"Not really, he's been to himself lately. He's taking it really hard, so I'm just waiting for him to open up and talk about it. I didn't know they used to date, though. Well anyway, I'm just in an awkward position, you know? I wanna know, but part of me is afraid of what he may confess to me. I'm just waiting for a bomb to blow!"

"Well, I'm sure it's not anything to worry about. Carl is mourning her like we all are. Maybe just a little more, that's all. She was a coworker who died mysteriously, and we are all shocked over her death! I know I am. I just saw that girl the other day, and we were talking about that new restaurant on Erie. Wow, can't believe she's gone!"

Just then, Randy noticed the sadness in Karen's eyes. "Girl don't be sitting around stressing over stuff you can't change. Carl is crazy over you, girl. So, get that look off your face and let's talk about something else. Oh, I know what I wanted to ask now. What happened again when Carl walked into that clinic office and saw your fine-ass doctor? Girl, you had me hollering. You are lucky he didn't start flipping furniture upside down in that place. Girl, you a bad bitch, though, because I would have run home immediately, taking all those pictures of Denzel down and throwing all of them in the garbage. Come on and give me some skin," laughs Randy as he reaches over to hit Karen's hand!

Karen, giggling "I know, right?! I need to at least change the ones in my bedroom. But we had a talk, and he should be cool with it. Now that you mentioned it, I'm going to move some stuff around but, I'm keeping my black and white portrait, though, that's my favorite."

Randy replies, "Mmm ok, like I said, you a bad one, cause..." Randy's words were interrupted by the server as he delivered their drinks and bread with Randy's seafood salad.

After lunch, Randy suddenly had to rush off to get ready for his friend's reception. Karen decided to stay and have one more glass of wine. She didn't want to say anything to Randy, but from the grave, Coco was making her feel jealous, again! Carl was so not himself. He also failed to share the song he was writing about Coco, because he always shared his new music with her.

That just made her feel so left out. The truth of the matter was Carl was really hurting her feelings. The hardest part was she was forced to watch him mourn the woman he almost cheated on her with. She was looking for answers she may or may not handle well, once the genie was out of the bottle. Karen was starting to feel a little tipsy, so she paid the bill and grabbed a cab to take her drunk butt home.

Karen makes it back to her place, and all of a sudden blood rushes straight to her head as she stumbles into her apartment. She tries to walk straight to her bedroom, but the doorbell chimes. Realizing she's expecting her sister for the weekend, she opens the door. She continues to her bedroom, leaving her front door wide open. She finally makes it to her bed and falls on top with all of her outside clothes on, shoes, and all.

Carl walks into the bedroom, looks down at her, and says "Uh, hey you, what's going on around here? Why did you leave the door open like that? Karen tried to raise her head, but the effort was too much for her, so she lay back down and said, "Oh hey handsome, I thought you were Marteen. She's on her way from the airport. I'm sorry baby, but my head hurts. I had a liquid lunch with Randy, and I think I'm drunk," she giggles.

Carl climbs into bed beside her and starts taking off her jacket. Karen, thinking he's being fresh, tries to kiss him. But Carl says, "Nope, not tonight. You need to sleep this off, okay? Here, raise up so I can get you out of these street clothes." Karen smiles and immediately closes her eyes and says, "Thank you for not taking advantage, but I'm ok if you do, okay?"

Carl replies, "Yeah, I know, why did you drink so much on an empty stomach? That wasn't smart, now was it, baby?
Karen smiles and says, "Nope!
Carl finishes undressing her and asks if she still wants to go to the service tomorrow. Karen mumbles, "Nope, and tells him to go on and enjoy the party."

Carl looks confused and kisses her on the forehead before saying "Hey babe, if you change your mind, just call me, and I'll pick you up around 10 am, okay? Do you need anything before I go? I need to revise my song, but I bought a copy of the rough draft so you can look it over. Okay? Hey babe, you okay?

Karen had fallen into a deep sleep. Carl shakes his head and pulls the covers over her before tiptoeing out. He leaves a copy of his music on top of her dresser. As Carl was preparing to leave, the bell chimed again, and he buzzed Marteen in. Marteen walks in, and as soon as she sets down her luggage, she gives Carl a sisterly hug and offers her condolences for Coco.

Carl thanks her and tells her that Karen was sleep drunk and that he had left a song on her dresser for her to look over if she wakes up anytime soon. They talk a bit about the service, and Carl tells her about Karen not wanting to attend. Then he leaves to go take care of some loose ends.

Marteen shrugs her shoulders and turns her lips up because she thought for sure that her sister wanted to attend that service. But, oh well, thought Marteen, she must have changed her mind. She stops to look in on her sister, musing that her sister was always a lightweight and never could hold her liquor. Marteen smiles as she closes the door and continues on into the guest room to shower and wash the flight smell off of her body.

Karen wakes up the next morning with a throbbing headache and the smell of fresh coffee brewing. She brushes her teeth and gargles that nasty taste out of her mouth. She walks into the kitchen and sees Marteen sitting down at her kitchen island. Karen asks her, "Hey girl, what time did you get in last night?"

"Well, good morning, sunshine. How are you feeling? Carl told me about that liquid lunch you had yesterday!" Marteen replies.

"Carl was here?"

"Oh yeah, you were out of it. Carl opened the door for me. He said y'all talked. Don't you remember?"

Karen squinted her eyes before saying, "Uh, yeah, vaguely. I think he undressed me. I can't think straight. What time is it?"

Marteen replies, "About 11:15 I think." Karen grabs a cup of coffee and stops in mid-air. "Oh, my goodness! Did Carl call because I need to be at that service today! Damn! Did anyone call me?"

Marteen replies, "Not that I know of. I just woke up myself. I took two sleeping pills last night. But wait, I thought you had changed your mind about going. At least that's what Carl said yesterday before he left." "Omg," screams Karen as she races to take the quickest shower in world history. She screams for her sister to get dressed because she needs her to go for moral support!

CHAPTER 15

Karen and Marteen made it to Coco's Service just in time for Carl's solo. They were in the Medina Temple, a well-known Chicago landmark with standing rooms only! Dana Brown, aka Coco from Arkansas, was having an extraordinary send-off! The Temple was filled with yellow and white roses, apparently her favorite. As the piano started playing, you could hear a pin drop!

Carl sang from his soul this song:

Going Home

Hey there, lady with the mask on,

Show the world where you come from.

Share your dreams,

Know you have some.

Don't be shy, put your crown on,

Leaving soon

You ain't got long.

The lord is coming.

To take you back home.

Hey there lady with the mask on.

Show the world where you come from.

Oh, your haters.

Yeah, you got some.

Don't be shy.

Put your crown on.

Reveal your eyes, you are not alone.

I see you smiling

Cause you are so strong.

Fix your crown.

You ain't got long,

I'll miss you, girl

Strap your wings on.

No more stressing cause you're awesome,

You know you're awesome, girl you awesome.

Hey there lady, with the mask on,

Show the world where you come from.

Fix your crown,

You ain't got long.

You know I'll miss ya,

Ya, so strong.

Sorry girl, I wasn't there long,

When ya called, I didn't pick up my phone.

I can't undo what I have done,

I'll miss you girl,

You were the first one.

Yeah, you were the first one.

Hey there lady with the mask on,

Show the world where you come from.

Your haters hating, cause ya so strong

No second guessing.

Girl, you got some backbone.

Yeah, you got some backbone.

Girl, you so strong.

You know you so strong.

I'll miss ya,

Strap your wings on.

You know I loved ya,

Put your crown on.

Your mom, your sista, they remain strong

Hey there lady with your mask on.

Show the world where you come from.

No more stressing.

Put your crown on

You'll soon be resting

Strap your wings on

You going home yeah

You going home.

Carl received a minute-long standing ovation. Karen finally cried. Not entirely for Coco but because she was sad for Carl, and she now understands why he mourned so. Coco was obviously his first love. Feeling blindsided, she quickly wipes away her tears and tries her hardest to make it through the day.

Karen turns to her sister and says, "Wow, that was beautiful, wasn't it?" Marteen replies, "Uh, yeah, he sang that!" Are you okay, though? We can sneak out before anyone sees ya." "Mmm no, I'm ok, I am here for Carl. If you want, you can go back home.

I'll get a ride with Carl, ok?" Karen replied. Are you sure you're ok? Marteen asks.

"Yes, I'm good. Go on, I'll be fine."

"Well, ok. I'll see you later," Marteen says.

As soon as Marteen leaves, Karen is bombarded with coworkers from Bajem's as they share stories of Coco. Everyone is whispering about how wonderful the service was and raving over Carl's song! Wow, Coco was really a beautiful lady. There were pictures of her floating everywhere, and her obituary was magazine size and full of photos of her, some of which were taken with Carl from his younger days.

Karen is furious that Carl never said anything about them being high school sweethearts. She had to find him. Karen loses sight of Carl and is forced to move with the crowd as everyone is lining up to exit the building. Thankfully, she spots Carl hugging an older lady, who could be Coco's Mom. Karen squeezes her way over to Carl. He is surprised to see her and quickly introduces her to Coco's mom as his friend and not his girlfriend.

Karen is trying her best not to show how hurt and ashamed she is feeling. She's suddenly feeling sick and whispers in Carl's ear that she will see him later because she isn't feeling well. Carl grabs her arm and says, "Ok, just give me a minute, and I'll take you home." Karen replied, "No, you stay. I'll get a ride with Marteen, she's waiting for me, okay?" Before Carl can respond, Karen disappears into the crowd.

Knowing she didn't have a ride and sorry she had asked Marteen to leave, she walks towards the lake to get some fresh air. She can't believe how Carl is behaving, and she's had enough! She's tired of being a supportive friend! Well, he can just crawl his ass in the casket with his first love because she was done kissing his ass! The hell with him! Karen finally hailed a cab and went back to Barbara Jeans. But this time, she would avoid all things alcohol and have a cup of coffee because she never had her morning coffee.

* * *

Karen was glad to be home. Marteen is asleep on the sofa. Karen walks past Marteen and into her bedroom to change into some loungewear. While searching for her slipper, she finds Carl's song sheet under her dresser. Karen sits on the bench at the foot of her bed and reads his song. She reads it over and over until her eyes are red. She folds it over and drops it in the waste basket in the corner.

Karen climbs in bed, pulls the covers overhead, and prays for sleep, which she does when she's mad at Carl. She knows she'll feel better tomorrow. But her wish wasn't granted because her bell chimes, and guess who it is? Carl. Karen buzzes in Carl and Marteen is still sleeping soundly.

Carl walks in with flowers. "Hi, are those for me?" Karen asks. Carl replies, "Of course, how are you feeling?"
"Oh, much better. So how was the repast, assuming she had one?" she replied. Karen walks into the kitchen to put her flowers in a vase, and Carl walks into the bedroom, ignoring her question. Karen shrugs

her shoulders and finishes arranging her flowers before placing them on the entry hall table.

Karen walks back to her bedroom, where Carl is lying down, snoring and calling the cows home. She's tempted to wake his ass up, but she walks back out and sits at her kitchen table, staring into space. Minutes pass, and she walks over and wakes Marteen up, so she can get into bed. Marteen stumbles into the guest bedroom and instantly falls back asleep.

Karen sits in her living room in the dark, and she notices the flowers in her vase are yellow roses, not flowers. Most likely they are from Coco's service. Now she's really anxious to have it out with Carl and he has the nerve to be sleeping like an angel. How ironic, muses Karen as sleep finally consumes her.

Right before dawn, Karen wakes up, and Carl is standing over her. She sits up and says, "Mmm, did you get enough rest?"
"Not at all. I woke up, and you weren't beside me. Why are you sleeping on the couch?
"I didn't want to disturb you, and you were snoring so loud!"
"I don't snore. That was that alcohol. I needed to sleep it off."
"Hey, I missed you today. He grabs her hand, and they walk into the bedroom. I'm sorry I wasn't myself this week, but I really appreciate you being there for me. I know this was hard on you. I'm so sorry sweetie," he kisses Karen.

"I'm glad you said that because I felt so blindsided today. My feelings were hurt. I cannot believe you never once said anything about you and Coco being high school sweethearts. I mean, you didn't think not once that I needed to know that? You let me walk into that place in total darkness. I'm supposed to be your girl!"

"Well, everyone knew Dana, and I went way back. I mean, I thought you knew all that. Wow, I'm sorry sweetie."

He tries to kiss her again, but Karen steps back and says, "What? No, I didn't know anything, and I'm kinda pissed right now. Can we stop with the kissing? Because I'm not in the mood, ok?"

"Ok, so you're mad because you didn't know I had a past? Babe, I did not know you were clueless about this. I'm sorry, ok?"

"No, it's not okay. You don't get it. I felt like an outsider, and you had the nerve to introduce me as your friend. What the heck was that? Last I checked, I'm your woman, your boo thang, your girlfriend, definitely not a freaking friend!

Laughing, Carl replies, "Ok wait, I'm sorry, babe."

"What's so damn funny?"

"No, no, it's just the way you try to curse; it's cute. You say freaking instead of, you know, like... well anyway. I'm not laughing at what you said, baby. I'm laughing at how you said it! I'm so sorry. Now, can I please be forgiven so we can do what grown folks do?" Carl replied

As she looks at Carl, tears start falling. She is trying to talk in between sobs but, realizing she can't speak, she runs into the bathroom and locks herself inside.

Carl is standing in the middle of the bedroom, wondering what the heck just happened. Using one of Karen's curse words,

Carl knocks on the bathroom door and says, "Hey, are you okay? I get it. I'm the biggest idiot for not listening to you. Please come out so I can apologize to you."

Karen opens the door and steps out. Her nose and eyes are red, and she is still visibly shaking. Carl attempts to hold her, but she stops him and says, "I don't know why I'm so upset, but the fact is, I am. I think it will be best for us to have some time apart just so I can put myself back together again. Is that okay with you?"

"Uh, I don't know what that means. Why can't we just talk this out, baby? I'm sorry."

"Well, uh, I just need a little space. I'm not talking about forever. Just a vacation, without you, to clear my head and try to understand why I'm so emotional about you and Coco.

Carl raises his voice, "Baby there is no me and Coco. She's gone. Literally, I stopped seeing her the minute I fell for you. I broke her heart because I chose you. Never for one second have I regretted that decision! I'm sorry, I didn't do things right, and I put you in a bad situation, but it was never intentional. Please forgive me. I don't want you to leave me right now! Please, baby, I'll go home, and you can rest, and maybe tomorrow we can have dinner and..."

Karen cuts him off. "That sounds great, but maybe when I come back. I am going to DC to have some alone time. That's all. I'm not leaving you or anything like that, ok?"

Carl slams his fist into his hand and walks away. He stops and runs his fingers through his hair and sits on the bench at the foot of her bed. Minutes pass as the silence becomes louder than their heartbeat.

Carl finally says, "So you are still jealous of Coco, baby she's no longer a factor. Why in God's name are we still discussing this, and why do you need so much damn space! Or better yet why are you leaving me at a time in my life when I need you? I don't know if I can take another loss." Karen sits down next to Carl and says, "Mmm, another loss, huh? Well, I'm not leaving you, okay? The best way I can explain it is this. You know how a flight attendant instructs passengers who are traveling with children to first put their masks on before helping their child with theirs? Well babe I need to heal my heart before I can help heal yours. I'm just putting my mask on! That's all. Baby, you lost your first love, the same woman I thought you were cheating with. So, imagine how it makes me feel to have to comfort you and be in the middle of people treating you like a widower. Baby, I am a strong woman, but not that strong."

"Well, do what you gotta do, and I'll do the same," Carl says as he grabs his jacket. He walks into the living room and out the front door leaving Karen standing there as the door closes behind him. Karen stares into the darkness, wondering how a dead girl could cause such a rift in her life. As her friend Randy would say, 'Damn! That's a bad Bitch!"

* * *

Minutes ago, Karen and Carl were talking, and now she's standing alone and confused in the middle of her living room. She turns to walk back to her bedroom, and the vase full of yellow roses catches her eye. Suddenly her heart races, and she's filled with rage as she storms across the room, crashes the vase to the floor, and then collapses. Water from the vase soaks her pajamas. Broken glass and roses are scattered everywhere. Hearing the crash, Marteen runs in and sees her sister on the floor crying. "My God, what happened, are you hurt?" Marteen asks.

"Yes, he bought me her roses, he, he," and she sobs in her sister's arms.

"Ok, ok, come on. Can you stand up? We need to get you cleaned up, okay? It's ok, it's ok, don't cry, I got you, I got you.

Marteen runs a warm bath for her sister and fixes her a hot cup of tea with a shot of bourbon, to relax her nerves. After helping her sister pull herself together, and cleaning up the mess left in the hall, she sits her down and asks her what the hell is going on.

Karen takes another sip of her tea and says, "What did you put in this tea because I'm starting to feel pretty damn good?"

"I know right? That's my secret potion. Now tell me, what's going on with you?

Karen takes a deep breath and tells Marteen everything.

"Wow! And He just walked out like that? Mmm."

"Yes, and I'm like, is he just walking out the door or walking out of my life? So strange, you know? Like what's the big deal? I can't go on a vacation without him?"

"Mmm, you really wanna know what I think?"

"Yes, I do, I wanna know. Just go ahead and tell me how I brought this, all on myself."

"Girl, listen. Now, let me start by saying this. A while back when you called me and told me that you had seen Carl with another chick, and the next day, y'all made up? Like all was well and good. I was like how she not at least punish him, for a few days, longer, but you took him right back, and that, little sister, was your first mistake. In America, you do the crime, you do some time. Carl got off with no punishment. Therefore, he never learned anything. So now he's confused because now you want to punish him, and he's not used to being held accountable for taking your love for granted. You have to teach a mf, that you will not stand for their bullshit! And another thing, he should have never told you about breaking Coco's heart and shit because now, you gotta carry that drama along with all this other crap he's throwing in your face!"

"Yeah, I didn't need to know all of that."

"Exactly but let me finish what I was saying. Now, you know you don't just fall in love like normal people. When you fall in love you love deeply, and you give so much of yourself. You have to remember to put yourself first."

"I know, that's why I'm taking my vacation and going on a spiritual journey with me, myself, and I. If he cannot understand that, then we are in more trouble than we thought."

"Oh, he will come to his senses and realize that you epitomized the phrase, in sickness and in health. You were there for him in more ways than any woman would've ever been. Because it couldn't have been me holding him while he cried over another woman. So, trust me, once he wakes the fuck up, he'll come running to you! So don't you dare second guess yourself. And stop worrying about his feelings and concentrate on healing yours. Oh, and if I ever catch you on the floor like that again, I'm going to slap the shit out of you, and then kill that mf! Does he even know I have a conceal-and-carry permit?"

Karen laughs and says, "I think I might have mentioned it to him."

"Good. Now let's get out of here and go to Barbara Jean's restaurant you keep raving about."

"Uhh, can we go somewhere else? I'm tired of that place!"

"What? After all that talk about that place, uh, we're going to Barbara Jeans, baby! Don't even try it!"

"Well, okay, dang! Can I at least see if my friend Randy can join us?"

"Sure, call him. He's a lot of fun."

* * *

Barbara Jean's Restaurant was so pristine and unique in its design just as Karen had explained, and then some! Marteen was in awe of the orange leather loveseats and the citrine candle holders with shiny pennies sprinkled on the base of the holder, so clever! Oh, and the food was so darn good, thought Marteen as she cleaned her plate.

Marteen was very impressed with Barbara Jean's and Randy's charm, which was the icing on the cake! They were laughing and crying over something Randy's wicked tongue had said. Karen was finally enjoying herself until Marteen announced that she had a date with James and must leave to get ready.

"Aw, but we are having fun. Do you really have to?"

"Uh, yes. I need to unwind after dealing with all of your drama. I am leaving you in good hands. Besides, we'll talk tomorrow. And we have DC to look forward to, okay?"

Karen, still pouting, says, "Mmm, okay, sis, thanks for hanging with me. I love you so much."

After hugging, Marteen said "I love you more. Start packing tonight because you know how long it takes you to pack. We are leaving in a couple of days!" Karen replied, "Okay."

As soon as Marteen leaves, Randy starts quizzing Karen about her and Carl's situation. "Well, let's order a cocktail because I am going to need something strong in order for me to tell this story again. Karen tells Randy everything from the moment Carl found out about Coco, until the present day. Randy was silent for a few minutes. He takes a sip of his Long Island iced tea and says, "Please don't take this the wrong way, but I think you should have given Carl some."

Confused, Karen replied, "Uh, what do you mean, gave him some? Gave him what exactly?"

"Girl, stop acting slow. You should have had sex with him. And then told him you were leaving because then he would've been more relaxed."

"Excuse me? Relaxed? I don't believe you, why are you defending him?"

Randy replied, "I'm not defending him. He was wrong for the part he played in this, but I am looking at this from a man's perspective." Karen twists her lips and raises her eyebrows. Noticing the look she's giving him, Randy quickly adds.

"Uh, don't give me that look! Just because I'm gay, doesn't mean I can't give a man's point of view. It was clear that Carl was looking to get laid, and you basically said no. So of course he walked out mad, the man couldn't hear you, because he was horny! Now he's walking around here with a heavy heart and a heavy pee wee! Case closed! You should've taken care of your business, boo boo. Don't worry about it now. He probably took care of it, but I bet my last dollar that the outcome would've been different had y'all had sex first!"

"No, I disagree. Sex is what he used to get me to forgive him that last time. So, he's on his own. I'm not on board with your opinion! That's crazy talk! And I'm surprised that you would even tell me that mess!" Karen argued back.

"Fair enough, but keep in mind that he's hurting. A life was lost, and Dana Brown is never coming back. Just don't be too hard on him, ok?

"Yeah, I know."

CHAPTER 16

Karen had a few loose ends to tie up before her vacation. She had to ensure that her high-maintenance client, Mr. Mark Conway's merchandise, was altered and delivered on time. She walked into the employee entrance of Bajem's and ran into her old friend, Constance. Constance worked in the women's shoe salon and was one of Bajem's finest. She was known as Lady Bird because she had bigger balls than most men and could sell raids to a roach! She was highly respected.

Constance said, "Well, hello Ms. Bosse. Where do you think you're going showing those pretty legs?" Karen replied, "Oh, hello, Cons. How are you doing this morning?"

"Girl, I don't have time to tell you, and I know you don't want to listen. Now come over here so I can look at that outfit you're wearing." They laugh and share a brief hug.

Constance asks, "What are you doing here? I heard you were on vacation.

"Wow, that was fast. I just started my vacation. Oh, that's right, I forgot you and Randy held the rally this morning. But uh, I'm just in for a hot second to finish up some customer orders, and then I need to start packing!

"Oh, okay. Well, have fun and give Carl a kiss for me. I know he's torn up over Dana. It's just a shame, isn't it?"

"Yes, it is. I'll be sure to give him a hug and kiss, ok? Well, take care, I need to get upstairs before the store opens, see ya later."

"Okay, Sweetie, see you later and call me when you get back in town."

Karen continues on her way to the service elevators to hopefully avoid anyone else who may have a message for Carl. As far as she is concerned, she can't get out of the building fast enough. Half an hour later, Karen is all done and on her way home, and who does she run into at the employee's entrance? Mr. Carl! And if looks could kill, she'd be dead! Carl looks across the hall and eyes her up and down with a mean look on his face.

Karen's first thought was, oh he looks so handsome, until she noticed the look he was giving her. Now, she's like, what now? Dang. Carl says hello as he opens the door for her, and they walk outside. "Hey, are you working today?" Karen asked him.

"No. I just filled out some paperwork. I'm taking some time off. What are you doing down here in that short-ass skirt? I thought you were on your way to DC?'

"Uh, first of all, my vacation just started, and my skirt is not that short. Is that why you were mean eyeing me in there?"

"Yeah, it is very short. I've never seen this outfit. Why did you wear that down here?" he replied as he raised his voice and people were staring.

"Uh, you don't have to scream at me. I am not your child. So don't talk to me like I'm about to get a whooping or something."

"Yeah, okay. I should spank that ass! But that wouldn't be a punishment. Anyway, I'm parked by the meter. I'll take you wherever you go. Because I'd be damned if you are walking around half-naked on public transportation."

"Excuse me," as she looks down at her skirt and says, "My skirt is perfectly fine. You just wanna pick a fight with me."

"Why would I want to do that? I'm just saying the skirt is too short for any woman of mine to have on unless I'm with her."

"Mmm. Well, I am going back home, so let's go."

They start walking down Huron Street.

"Ok, I'm just parked a block away. So, uh, is this a new look? I notice you're wearing your hair down. I always liked it down."

Carl says, "What's up?" to someone passing, and he grabs Karen's hand.

"Oh no, I just had it trimmed, so I left it down today. So, you like it?"

"Yep!" Carl replies. Carl asks another guy if he needs help. They make it to the car, and Carl stops, looks down into Karen's face, and says, "I'm sorry about the other day. I was too angry to be around you, so I had to leave, ok?"

"Okay," Karen answers back.

Carl opens the passenger-side door for Karen and then walks around to the driver's side. He hops inside and looks over at Karen. He stares at her, looks down at her legs, and smiles. "You know, you got a man, right?"

Karen replies, "Uh what are you talking about?"

"No, I just want to clarify things because you're dressed like a woman who doesn't have a man. That outfit is sexy as hell, and your hair like that! Man, oh man, I thought I was going to catch a case today. You didn't notice all those dudes checking you out, huh? If I wasn't with you, they would have been on you, like white on rice!

"Oh, yeah, I probably shouldn't have put this on. Maybe it is too short."

Carl says, "So you agree with me, huh?"

"What? I can admit when I'm wrong. Oh, and can we stop on the way? I'm hungry, and I'm craving a grilled chicken salad.

Carl laughs.

"What's up?" Karen asks him.

"Bae, who craves a chicken salad? I mean, that's not even a real meal." "Yes, it is!"

They stop for Karen's chicken salad and drive back to Karen's place.

"So, when are you leaving for DC?" Carl asked.

"Tomorrow evening," Karen replied.

"Can I at least have a copy of your itinerary?"

"Of course, I had planned on giving you a copy."

"When? Because I haven't seen or heard from you since we had those words. Were you mad at me?"

"Yes, I was more confused than anything because you told me to just do whatever, and you were going to do the same. I didn't know if you were breaking up with me or what!

"No, I was not breaking up with you. That ain't never happening, baby! I'm not going anywhere, okay?

"Okay babe, do you want me to get you a beer or something?"

"No, I'm good. Have you noticed that I've been the perfect gentleman today? I haven't tried to be fresh with you. I'm keeping my hands and my lips to myself. I'm trying very, very hard to respect your wishes, but you gotta change out of that short-ass skirt and maybe pull your hair back up or something. Please, a brother like me can only take so much.

"Oh, is that what ya doing? I'll change, but I was hoping we could clear some things up about that argument we had. Let me just say that I'm not running away from you. I'm just taking a vacation. I'll be hanging out with my sister and getting to know me again. I've been so caught up in you that I'm losing myself. That's the only reason I'm leaving. If you ever really needed me, I would drop everything and be there for you! I'm hurt because I was somehow lost in your world, and you were so consumed with grieving that you never noticed, and I get that now! I know you love me. I just need you to realize that I am your plus one. You have to let those who don't know, well you should, let it be known. Don't ever introduce me as a friend. I'm so much more than that. And from now on, please keep me informed of what's going on, and let's not assume anything about anything. And if you're angry, let's try to talk it through and not leave with the unknown hanging in the air. Because together, we are one. I'm your half, and you are my half. Okay? Now let me change it to something more appropriate."

"Wait, you don't have to change. And for what seems like the 100th time, I'm so sorry. I'm so blessed to have you. From this day forward, I'm going to work on being a better man for you, baby. I understand why you need this time. You have been my rock, and you handled this crisis like a champ! Baby, you are that strong, and I will never take you for granted! Okay? Now, do you want me to help you pack? Because I uh, don't want you packing stuff like you have on, okay? So, I need to inspect that suitcase."

Karen giggles, "Ok, I deserve that. Come on, let's pack me all up! Oh, maybe I'll come back a few days early so we can have some time alone.

"Yes, I would love that! Oh, and uh, you think you could maybe hook me up before you leave?"

"Boy, you know, I'm going to take care of you before I go."

Karen turns the radio on, and Keith Sweat is singing 'Make It Last Forever.' Karen slowly takes her skirt off, and before she can pull her top off, Carl picks her up. They are wrapped around each other, and just like the song, they will try their hardest to make it last forever.

* * *

Karen is lying in bed, wrapped in Carl's arms. They are both feeling blissful and thinking about the future. Karen is starting to have second thoughts about going to DC and leaving Carl. She is having what some would describe as separation anxiety. She unconsciously holds him a little tighter.

Carl is having a similar anxiety. He doesn't want Karen to leave just now. He is starting to miss her already. He looks down, lifts her chin, and kisses her with so much passion that she is feeling lightheaded, and her body is responding with a burning desire. They make love again, much slower this time. Like newborns, they are exploring each other as if it's the first time. God only knows how electrifying it feels to love someone so fiercely and have it mirrored right back at ya. As Karen moved her hips, matching every thrust of her man, she felt victorious. Once again, their bond was so strong, and though it did bend some, it remains unbroken!

After making love for what seems like forever, Carl shares a shower with Karen. Of course, he manages to hit it one more time! They are laughing like toddlers as Carl is trying to get dressed, and Karen is being silly, imitating him by saying, "Hey man, you need some help?" and "Oh, hey, stop looking at my woman," "What's your problem?" She is cracking up at her own jokes. Carl says, "Okay, we will see what's funny once I remove this garbage you got hanging on your walls!"

Carl walks into Karen's kitchen, grabs a trash bag, and proceeds to remove her portraits of Denzel from her bedroom walls. Karen has her hand over her mouth with a look of astonishment. After Carl puts the two pictures in the large trash bag, he goes into her living room. Karen is on his heels, screaming, "Don't you touch my black and white picture. That's my favorite!"

Carl takes it down, anyway, and says, "Oh, you stopped laughing, huh? You know, you should've been pulled these suckers down. I'm sorry, baby but I gotta put my foot down. You can put them anywhere you want, except these walls, ok? Stop giving me that look because I'm not hanging this mess back up, and you better not."

"Well, I can put one in the guest room. You won't see it, ok?" said Karen. "Mmm, baby I really don't want this joker hanging anywhere but go ahead. You know you're wrong for having them up in the first place. That was straight-up disrespectful!

"Well, I didn't know they were causing a problem. It is just a picture. I don't know Denzel from The Man on the Moon, and my doctor doesn't even look that much like him!" Carl, looking at her with skepticism, says," Let's not talk about that, ok? And I'll take you to this art gallery and buy you some real art, okay? Would you like that?" Karen smiles, "Ooh, yes, that's so nice of you, babe! I would love that, thank you." To show her appreciation, she gives Carl a big ole kiss!

CHAPTER 17

So, with the girls in DC, the fellas, Carl and James, are having a light snack at a coffee shop in High Park. James walks into the coffee shop and sees Carl sitting on a stool near the window. James greets him, "What's up, player? How you doing, man?" They hug and slap each other on the back. "I'm good. You want some coffee or something? I didn't think you were coming," Carl replies.

"Sorry, traffic. But uh, no, nothing for me. I'm good. I just had a steak burger. Man, I'm stuffed like a turkey on Thanksgiving. So, how's superwoman doing?" Carl questions

"Who?"

"You heard me, superwomen. Your girl?"

"My girl? Man, what are you talking about?" Carl replies as he stirs some cream in his coffee.

"Karen, you know she's a superwoman, right?"

Carl laughed, "Man, you tripping."

"Nah, Marteen told me how she stayed by your side after what happened with Dana. That was alright. You know most women would have looked the other way."

"Yeah, she's something special, for sure."

"I know that's why I call her superwoman. That girl is the real deal. You better not be taking her for granted, 'cause I'm kicking some sense into you! You feel me?"

Carl answered, "Man, whatever. I know how to treat my lady. We're good!"

"Yeah, okay, you had her over there blowing your nose for you. and shit. I bet she was like blow baby, blow, it's okay. Yeah, now, remember that shit the next time temptation comes knocking on the door!"

"Man, stop with that shit! I know how to treat my girl. I don't feel like hearing that! Listen up, I just found out how Dana died, and that shit was messed up!"

"Oh wow, what happened?"

"Man, she fought like hell. They said she had some major defense wounds. One of her fingers was broken and two of her nails. They have a lot of DNA, so the perp who did it will not get off. My girl fought with everything she had! Man, I'm just torn up. She was a good person and didn't deserve to go like that! She was on her way to being a superstar. She told me she was going to make her mama love her by being a movie star! Just sad. But anyway, I'm just blowing off. What was it you wanted to talk to me about?"

"Oh man, it can wait. Again, I'm sorry for your loss. I know Dana meant a lot to you. Don't pay me any mind. I was kidding before. You wanna shoot some hoops at the gym or something?"

"Nah, I'm about to run over to Coco's mom's crib. She said she wanted to see me about something. Let's hook up tomorrow or the weekend, ok?"

"Ok, cool, you're leaving now?"

"Oh yeah, I'm sorry. I need to run over there and see what's going on."

"Ok, hit me up if you need to talk, alright? You know I'm here if you need me."

"Oh yeah, for sure!"

Carl leaves some cash on the table. They slap each other on the back and take off in separate directions.

* * *

Carl arrived at Mama Jo's house, Dana's Mom. He pulled up to an old, ranch-style house, cut his engine, and just sat there. He was thinking about the last time he was over here with Dana. It was a few years ago. They had stopped at Rib Lady and bought her mom an order of rib tips and hot links.

They sat in the kitchen and played spades for hours, good times. He could hear Dana laughing because they were winning almost every hand. He could hear her telling someone, "Hey, you better not be cutting hearts. If you don't have one, then you better pull yours out of your chest!! You got a heart, sucker!!!"

Carl was smiling and shaking his head. Yeah, that girl was something else! She could step her butt off! Man, oh man, the way she would swing her hips around the dance floor. She was a master at just about everything she set her mind to. Carl came back to the present because someone was knocking on his car window.

Carl got out of his car and walked around to give Mama Jo a hug. "Hey baby, I thought that was you. What are you doing sitting out here? Come on inside. They got my baby's murderer in custody! Hallelujah, and praise Jesus! You know, she loved you, didn't matter what was going on. She would say, y'all were going to get married one day. I told her she should let you go, but she wouldn't hear of it!" "Yeah, I know. We always talked about how we would live in Hollywood and build you and my mother a big house right next to us. But you know, we were just kids back then. Eventually, I met someone, and she went on to pursue her dreams. So, you were saying they caught the guy? Wow, that's great. Do you know who?"

Mama Jo replied, "Yes! It was that ole cross-eyed agent of hers. The detective said he confessed." They were walking inside the house when a little girl ran up to Carl and hugged his leg. She was the sweetest little thing. Carl stoops down and says, "Hey, cutie, what's your name?" She laughs and runs away.

"Oh, I see you have company. Did you want me to stop by another time?

"Oh no, that's my granddaughter, and you know I have people stopping by every day, so today is as good a day as any. Besides, it's just me and Mona here right now. Come in here. I want to show you some papers Dana's sorority sister found and see if you can help me figure out what it is.

"Oh, sure. I didn't know you were a grandmother. Lil Mona has a baby?" Mona was Dana's baby sister. Just then, they heard a big thump and a wailing scream! Carl and Mama Jo took off down the hall. The little girl had fallen down the back staircase. Coco's little sister, Mona, was trying to comfort her, but it wasn't working. The little girl was screaming at the top of her lungs!

Mama Jo asks, "OMG, what happened, Mona?"
"Mama, she fell before I could get to her. Oh, hi, Carl."
Mama Jo tries to soothe the little girl. "It's ok, baby." She instructs her daughter to pull the car around so they can take Carly to the emergency room.
"Uh, is there anything I can do? My car is out front."
"No, that's ok baby, we can take her. I guess I'll have to call you later in the week so we can talk. Ok? And thanks for coming."
Mama Jo had the little girl in her arms and was moving fast for an old woman. Carl helped them in the car and watched them race away. He climbed back into his car, praying for the little girl and wondering why Dana never mentioned she had a niece.

* * *

Karen and Marteen finally made it to DC. Marteen unlocks the door to her condo, and Karen's mouth hits the floor. The espresso-colored wooden floors are so shiny you can almost see your own reflection, and the long white leather sofa with tan colored pillows is to die for!! "Wow, sis, this is bigger than the last one. Look at that view, staring at us. Girl, this condo makes mine look like a doll house."

Karen walks out onto the terrace just off the living room, and Marteen joins her. "Girl, I am so proud of you. This is beautiful, and I haven't even seen the bedrooms. "Thanks sis. Oh, and the master suite also has a terrace and a spa bathtub. Come on, let's put our bags away. I'm ready to wash that flight off me."

"Oh, okay. What does that mean? Wash the flight off because you always say that?"

"Girl, being locked in the air with strangers, you are bound to have all types of germs on you and your clothes. You know how I am!"

"Oh yeah, ok. Makes sense now."

After the girls unwind, they sit in the living room, drinking wine and laughing out loud! "So, what did James say about Carl and Coco's relationship?"

"Uh, he said they dated in his senior year and some in college. Apparently, she was a virgin when they met, and he was her first. Oh, and he said she was good at gymnastics and could have gone to the Olympics."

"Oh, okay. Do you think she was doing flips in the bedroom and stuff? Because he was really infatuated with her. But hey, I was a cheerleader. I wonder if I can still do a cartwheel."

"Girl, that mess doesn't make you an expert in the bedroom. Carl must be happy with your butt because he apparently left her for you, remember?

"Mmm yeah, but he's still thinking about her, and sometimes I catch him staring off into space. He never used to do that. I think he's thinking about his past and wondering what if."

"Girl, why are you stuck on this woman? She is in heaven right now, probably cheering for you and Carl. At the end of it all, she really loved him."

"I know, I'm just tripping. Let's move this table back so that I can do a cartwheel." Karen stands up and starts stretching her legs.

Marteen rolls her eyes, "Sis, really? Uh, girl, sit down. You are not flipping around in my living room. Save that mess for the gym or someplace else."

Karen flopped back down and took a sip of wine. "Yeah, ok. But I bet I can still do it. Ooh, I'm going to search for my old cheerleader uniform and wear it for Carl one night! You know, just to keep things popping."

"Mmm, ok, now that's better than trying to do a damn cartwheel in my living room. Now you are talking like my sister!" She leans over and gives Karen a little shove.

"Girl, I'm all over the place when it comes to my man. Sometimes I wish I could just shrink his ass and carry him in my purse. Ooh, I love that man!!! Do you hear me?" Karen says while laughing.

"Well damn! Girl, that's some fatal attraction stuff! But I get it. You are in the beginner stages, that new love feeling, but once it gets old, you will be begging him to hang out with the fellas."

"Mmm, I don't know, sis, I think I'm going to be loving him like this forever. He's my soulmate! Karen leans back against the sofa and closes her eyes.

"Okay. I guess you wanna call him then, huh?"

Karen squeals, "Yes!"

Marteen replies, "Well, go ahead. I'm going to bed. So, you are on your own tomorrow because I have meetings all day. I booked a massage for you at 2 pm, and all the information is in the bureau. But we can have dinner together, ok?"

"Ok, cool. Thanks! Goodnight sis!"

"Goodnight, knucklehead!

* * *

Karen dials Carl's number. Carl answers on the first ring

Karen says, "Hey babe, you miss me?"

"Hey, you! You know it. How was your flight?"

"It was good. We had a direct flight, so it was smooth all the way. What did you do today?"

"Mmm, not much. I never got to the gym. I saw Jumbug for a minute, and you know he was talking smack. Oh, and I went by Mama Jo's house for a second."

"Who is Mama Jo?"

"Oh, sorry, she's Coco's mom. She wanted me to help her with some paperwork, but things got crazy, and she said she'll get back to me later. I'm not sure why she's asking for my help, but anyway, tell me something sweet so I can sleep good tonight."

"Mmm, well, first, keep me posted on what this, uh, Mama Jo lady has to say. And do you know what's going on with James and my sister? Because she's not saying anything, and I think they are creeping around?"

"Babe, that's their business. We ain't got nothing to do with that. Now, what are you wearing? You in your pajamas?"

"Boy, you know I'm nosy, but anyway, I'm just sitting around here, naked," Karen laughed

"Girl, don't start no shit! You better stop playing before I book a flight tonight. Real talk!"

Karen replied, "Boy, I'm wearing a T-shirt, actually one of yours. Now tell me what you got on?"

"Some shorts and a T-shirt. So, uh, what are y'all doing tomorrow?"

"Oh, I'll probably relax and chill tomorrow. Marteen scheduled a massage for me, and we are having dinner later. She's working a lot, so I'm on my own time, which is cool with me."

"Yeah, that sounds nice. I got a message on my machine about some producer from LA who wants to meet with me. I guess he heard me singing at the funeral. So, I'll call him back first thing tomorrow."

"Ooh, that's great, babe. You never know because you sang the heck out of that song! You had me crying and everything. I'll send a prayer up for you, okay? Now tell me again how much you love me."

"Mmm, ok. Now, if you take all the numbers in the world and multiply them by all the numbers in the world baby, I'll still love you more than that!"

"Ooh, I love it when you say that. Well, pucker up because I just threw you a big ole kiss! I love you so much. Call me tomorrow because I'll be here most of the day. This number is in the itinerary I left you."

"Ok, yep, got it. Sleep tight sweetie!"

"Ok, good night."

Karen hung up with Carl and immediately thought, now, what the heck did this Mama Jo want with my man? Dang, why can't she leave him alone? He's not her son-in-law. Damn, thought Karen.

CHAPTER 18

"Never trust a man, never trust a man,

never trust a man with a prize in his draws.

Learn from me. Ya hear me?

If he ever calls, turn your phone off, turn your phone off.

Learn from me, ya hear me.

Never trust a man, never trust a man, with a tongue in his mouth.

Y'all hear me. Ya, hear me?

Cause when he takes it out, when he takes it out.

Girl you'll be climbing up the walls.

Learn from me. Ya hear me?

I say never trust a man, never trust a man.

Listen little one.

I'm all for having fun.

ain't trying to block, no one.

If the prize is in his draws, a long tongue in his mouth.

he ain't the one.

Girl, you better run, you better run.

Learn from me, ya hear me?

Never trust a man, never.

Beep! Beep! Finally, traffic was moving again. Gia was singing one of her latest songs while riding bumper-to-bumper on Lake Shore Drive. Gia had that southern flair, being born in New Orleans and raised by the strong hands of her mama and nana. Her father left them the day after she called him, dada! She was 11 months old. Growing up, folks would ask her if she ever missed her daddy, but Gia shook her head full of curls and told them, 'Nope, you can't miss what ya never had!'

Gia eventually moved to Chicago, where she met her BFF, Dana Brown. They were college roommates and sorority sisters! Gia was on her way to the hospital to see her goddaughter, little Carly! Mama Jo called and said she had fallen down some stairs. Gia was thinking, "Lawd, if it ain't one thing, it's another. First Dana, and now lil Carly! Give me strength as she continued singing her song. Never trust a man, ya hear me!

* * *

Gia walks into Carly's room with determination. She says hello to Mama Jo and Mona and walks over to Carly's bed. She kisses her on her forehead, and Carly tries to reach out to her, but the tubes are in the way. Gia holds her little hand and talks to her, "Hey sweetie, I'm here, I'm here. Ooh, I know, I wanna hold you. But you have to stay still, okay?" She brushes her hair, and tears swell up in her eyes because a 2-year-old doesn't understand hospital rules.

Gia finally calms Carly down, and she asks Mama Jo what happened. "Well, I was talking to Carl when I heard her scream. Mona was watching her. "Carl? You mean Dana's ex?

"Uh, yes, he stopped by to see how I was doing?"

"Mmm, well, did he see Carly?"

"Yeah, he saw her. And I was watching her, but she ran so fast, and I tried to catch her," Mona explains, crying.

"Don't cry. I know it was just an accident. Babies are so curious and…"

Mama Jo, interrupting "Well, we were keeping a good eye on her, but she just took off running like she always does. It ain't nobody's fault."

"I know. What did her doctor say?"

"Oh, she has a little bump, and they are keeping her overnight, just for observation. She can come home tomorrow."

"Oh, well I'm staying the night. She can't stay here alone. Y'all can go on back home, and I'll call if anything changes, ok?"

"Well, okay, let me kiss my sugar goodbye. And don't worry, I won't say anything to Carl. He just showed up out of the blue."

Mona raises her eyebrow as she glances at her Mama. "Oh, okay. Well, you know we have to honor Dana's wishes. She never asked you for anything except what she told all of us. And Mama Jo, you gave your word on the King James Bible, and I expect you to honor your daughter's wishes. I'm surprised Carl would show up like that without calling or anything."

"Please let us know if anything changes. Thanks, Gia. I really am sorry," Mona says.

"I know. Come here and give me a hug, girl."

Mona smiles and hugs Gia.

"Well, okay. Goodnight then. We'll come back early in the morning to check on her." They kiss Carly before leaving the room.

As they are walking to the elevator, Mona asks her mom, "Uh, mama what are you up to? Because you know you called Carl and told him to come over."

"Child, hush your mouth. That girl is not running anything but her damn mouth, and I don't care what Dana said. That boy needs to know that he has a daughter. Now, I won't tell him. But if he's smart enough, he'll figure it out all on his own." Mama Jo and Mona step into the elevator. When the door closes, Mona stares at her mother with astonishment.

Back in Carly's hospital room, Gia is singing to Carly. It's a grown-up song, but it's one that she and Dana had fun writing together.

'Never trust a man with a finger and a hand. He will hold you in his arms. And then leave you alone. Learn from me. Ya hear me? Never trust a man Never trust a man. If he's driving a mus-tang He will break your heart, tear it apart. Learn from me. Ya hear me? Oh Carly, that man is your daddy. Gia sings to Carly as she drifts off to sleep.'

Gia's crying openly. She misses her friend more than anyone will ever know. She knew Mama Jo couldn't be trusted. Dana told her that the day she went missing. Gia tiptoed out of the room to find a nurse so that she could have a cot brought inside the room. She really needed to lay down.

* * *

Gia was drowning in her own blood; she couldn't breathe! Mama Jo was standing over her with a blood-soaked bone in her hand. She was grinning like she had won the jackpot. Carly was calling for her, but she was fading in and out. "Oh God, please help me!" Gia gasped, and her eyes opened to darkness and the sound of Carly's voice. "Mommy, Mommy!!

Gia sat up and adjusted her eyes, realizing she was still in the hospital and had just experienced a nightmare. Gia got up and went to Carly to soothe her back to sleep. Still shaken by the dream, she went into the bathroom to splash water on her face. Gia dried her face with Kleenex paper and stared at her reflection in the mirror.

Her heart was beating rapidly, and her eyes were blinking away some tears. For the first time since Dana's death, she was afraid. Not of Mama Jo but the reality of the situation she was in. Carly was her daughter now, and she had to protect her from everyone and everything! Maybe it was time for her to move back home with the people who love her and Carly.

She knew that dream was a warning because somehow or another, Mama Jo always got what she wanted. And the only way she would have Carly was over her dead body! Gia was planning on living a long, prosperous life. She wiped her tears, looked straight into her own eyes, and said, 'The devil is a lie!'

Gia walked over to the phone beside Carly's bed and asked the operator to connect her to a phone number in Louisiana. The phone rang somewhere in Louisiana.

"Hello?"

"Mama"

"Yes, Soja, is that you?"

"It's me mama. I'm coming home with Carly, okay?"

"Ok, is everything okay? Have you been crying baby?"

"Not anymore, mama. I just needed to hear your voice. I'm sorry I woke you. But I'm bringing Carly home in a few days, and I need you and Nana to watch her for me while I pack things up. Because, Mama, I'm coming home for good, ok?"

"Ok, baby, we'll take care of Carly. You don't have to worry. You already know that. Stop worrying because you are a child of God and a child of mine, so you are covered! You hear me, Gia Soja Dubai! No more crying. I'll get ready for the baby. See you soon, okay?"

Gia, wiping tears, responds, "Okay, mama, we'll see you in a few days. Love you!"

"Love you more. Now let me get back to dreaming about your soon-to-be stepdaddy," her mama giggles.

"Oh, my goodness, mama, you're a mess! Good night!"

"Good night baby, kiss my little pumpkin pie for me!"

Gia hangs up from her mom with a clearer mind and a lighter heart! She knew exactly what she needed to do.

CHAPTER 19

Mama Jo and Mona arrived at the hospital a few minutes after Gia checked Carly out! Mama Jo was furious, but she remained calm with the doctors and the nurses. She had everybody eating out of her hand! The minute Mama Jo made it to her car, she let out a howling scream! People passed by looking at her as if she was indeed insane or in grave pain!

Mama Jo ignored the stares and climbed into her car. Mona knew from experience to keep her mouth shut! Mama Jo took a deep breath and started up the car. As she pulled out of the hospital parking lot, she spoke out loud, "I know my Dana is missing her best friend, don't you agree?" She looks over at Mona and asks. Mona nods her head.

Mama Jo, "Open your mouth and answer me! Don't you think your sister should have her best friend with her? She's all alone and should have some company!" Mona, fighting back her tears, answers Mama Jo, "Yes, mama, I think so, too!"
Mama Jo says, "Mmm mmm, yes! That bitch will soon be a pain out of my ass! It's about time she met her maker. Someone should have told her that I am not the one to be fucked with!"

Mama Jo smiled in the rearview mirror. She seemed much calmer now. She sang Amazing Grace as they rode home. Mama Jo had a beautiful voice. Mona remained silent, but inside Mona's mind, she prayed repeatedly for someone to save her!

Mama Jo made it back from the hospital with fire in her blood. She was still boiling from the hospital visit. She tried calling folks but didn't get an answer at Carl's place or Gia's condo. She was beside herself! Mama Jo stormed down to her basement and entered a back room. Dana and Mona called it her lair because neither one of them had dared to go back there.

Mama Jo walked into a dark room filled with what she called trinkets. Every trophy, ribbon, and paper reward that Dana ever received was displayed in the room. Mama Jo always went back looking for every reward she threw in the garbage! She loved Dana in a way only she could understand! It was love mixed with hate and a sprinkle of rage! Dana's death tore her up, but the words Dana said to her the day before she was murdered hurt her to the core of her being. Dana died, knowing her truth.

Mama Jo sat down in an old leather recliner and removed her eyeglasses. She reached for an urn filled with Dana's ashes. What Mama Jo did next would wake up the dead! She spreads Dana's ashes all over her face and neck as if she were putting on some Jergen's lotion. She leaned back in her recliner and smiled as she stared at her daughter's shiny trophies and satin ribbons, with ashes all over her face. Mama Jo was proud of her baby. She would tell anyone who would listen, anyone except Dana.

Mama Jo stayed in her lair for hours thinking about the time Dana did a triple-double and landed on her feet with her arms in the air. She was number one! Yes, lawd thought Mama Jo, her baby girl was number one! Mama Jo got up and walked over to a cabinet. She took another urn and placed it next to Dana's. It was empty! Mama Jo hummed Amazing Grace as she busied herself, polishing the empty urn as ashes fell down inside her blouse. She didn't seem bothered. She was lost in her own world.

Mama Jo locked up her lair and went upstairs to clean up. She knew exactly what she needed to do and the person to do it. Mama Jo still looked good, and her body was still tight! She took off her old mammy clothes and admired her figure in the mirror. Mama Jo took a hot bath and changed into what she called her work clothes.

She put on her red mini dress and black high-heeled pumps and splashed on her Coco Chanel perfume. It was Bugger's favorite. Bugger, aka Bobby Ford, was a friend Mama Jo grew up with in Arkansas. He left his wife and kids for Mama Jo. He was smitten with Jolie Mae (Mama Jo) and would do just about anything for her!

Mama Jo could always count on Bugger. He took care of all her needs. When Dana decided she wanted to be a model, it was Bugger who gave Mama Jo the money to pay for all of her clothes and lessons. It was safe to say that ole Bugger was always her ace in the hole! Mama Jo arrived at Bugger's place just in time to watch the Jeffersons, her favorite T.V. show.

Bugger was thrilled to see Mama Jo, and he wasn't interested in no T.V. show. "Hey baby, look at you with your sexy self. Come here and give me my sugar!" Mama Jo put her hands out to stop Bugger in his tracks.

"You know you gotta feed me and make me my drink before you can get some suga! I am still mourning my baby, and I need more than your lil pecker tonight! You understand me? Now did you order my hot links from Rib Lady?"

Bugger replied, "Now baby, you know I got your food. Don't I always take care of you? Sit on down, and I'll fix ya plate and ya drink! As long as you take care of me, I'll always take care of my sweet, sexy lady. Ooh, you look good, baby!! Damn!"

"Mmm mmm, just fix my plate. I haven't had anything to eat all day."

After Mama Jo was good and full, she took care of Bugger. Mama Jo laid Bugger down on his back and sat on top of him. She kissed him from the top of his nose down to his baby toes. And finally, when he thought he had enough, she rode Bugger until he was dizzy and calling out for Jesus. But Mama Jo told him to stop calling Jesus's name because he wasn't doing nothing for him. So, Bugger went on screaming out, 'Oh Jolie Maeeee! Oh, sweet Jolie Maeee!!!' Until the wee hours of the night.

When Bugger was good and satisfied, Mama Jo told him her plans to get her granddaughter back! Bugger leaned back against his headboard and said. "Baby, for you, I would break a bitch in half." And he slid on top of Jolie Mae and made love to her, just the way she was used to.

CHAPTER 20

Coco was her nickname. She never knew who gave her the name, but over the years, she heard why. Her skin was as smooth as butter and the color of coco with a splash of cream. Her mother told her she was just like her rapist father, and for years Dana tried to hide her features. She wore big, baggy clothes and oversized hats that covered her beautiful face. Her mother told her that her beauty was a curse and ugly was in her blood.

After years and years of hiding, Dana's high school drama teacher told her she was gifted and could be anything she wanted. So she stopped doing gymnastics and started modeling and acting in every school play. Dana rushed home and told Mama Jo that she was going to be a model or an actress one day. Mama Jo laughed at her every time she mentioned her dreams. Until one day, Dana won a contest and got a monetary gift! Mama Jo stopped laughing and started begging for every dime Dana had.

Dana was lost inside her own world until she met Carl. He showed her what love was supposed to feel like, and for some reason, her mother adored him. Carl could do no wrong in her eyes. They became inseparable. And one night, she became a woman, as Carl showed her that her hip movements were for more than just dancing.

Dana Brown mastered the art of making Carl scream for Jesus and shake like a drug addict! Dana was good at just about everything she set her mind to, except gaining her Mama's love! Mama Jo was two-faced. Dana was convinced! She showed the world one side, and Dana was privy to her other side.

Dana excelled at gymnastics. When she won trophies and first-place ribbons, Mama Jo would beam in front of everyone and brag about her to anyone who would listen. But as soon as they were alone, Mama Jo would rip Dana apart with words and throw her trophies in the nearest garbage can! She told Dana her trinkets didn't make her the best. Dana didn't understand why her mother was so upset.

One day, Dana said something to Mama Jo after winning her division with a perfect record. "Mama, I beat everyone with the highest score." Mama Jo replied, "And? Do you think that means something to me? You ain't gonna make no money winning trinkets by flipping your ass in the air! And you will never be the best of anything!"

With tears in her eyes, Dana said, "But Mama, you can't be any better than number one! I'm number one, Mama!" Mama Jo slapped Dana so hard that she fell to the ground. "Bitch! Don't you ever talk back to me. And get your lil ass up before someone sees ya down there! Now wipe your face and get in this motherf'ing car before I half kill you!"

Dana never spoke up again. Because no matter what Mama Jo did, she still loved her mother. Yet, more than anything, she wanted that love reciprocated!

* * *

Carl is on his way to California with all expenses paid. He had a meeting scheduled with one of Teddy Riley's assistants, and he was riding high! "Yes! Yes!" screamed Carl as he hung up the phone. Teddy Riley was one of the best producers on the scene. He produced hits for Keith Sweat and the king himself, Michael Jackson. Carl's heart was so full, it could bust any moment. "I gotta call my girl, oh, my god! This is exactly why I hump all day and all night," thought Carl.

Carl grabs the itinerary from his dresser and makes another long-distance call to Karen. Karen picks up. Carl says, "Hey baby, I have some good news!" Karen replies, "Ooh, what is it, baby?!" Carl talks to Karen for a few minutes and hangs up with an even bigger smile on his face. Man on man. The celebration his baby was planning had him floating above the clouds.

He had to run by Jumbug's and then hit the studio to brush up on his skills. He would call his mom from James's crib! Carl was riding so high that nothing could bring him down. Well, except Mama Jo.

* * *

Carl And Jumbug were at his studio, sitting around his grand piano, talking smack and smoking weed. Just like the good ole days Carl said, "Man, do you remember Dana's best friend Soja?" Jumbug replied, "Uh, yeah, but I never met her. She came on the scene around the time I was playing ball overseas. Do you remember?"

Carl replied, "Mmm, oh yeah, that's right. Well, anyway, I thought I saw her at Speedway, buying baby clothes, but she was moving so fast, I didn't get a chance to holler at her! Anyway, she was at Dana's service, and she was talking about coming down here and maybe doing a duet with me. What ya think?"

Jumbug asks, "Uh, well, can she sing?" Carl answered, "Nigga, that girl can shatter glass. Hell yeah, she can blow. But we'll see because I'm about to work on getting that contract first!" Carl leans over and claps hands with Jumbug.

Jumbug said, "Man, you are about to get paid my brotha. I'm amazed that Riley was even in the city, let alone at Dana's service. I mean, did he actually hear you sing, or what?"

"Uh, I guess so! But his assistant said he was impressed with me and needed me in his studio, pronto! So I'm like, done. I'm there!!" Carl takes a pull and passes the joint over to Jumbug. Jumbug replied, "Wow! I know moms was happy for you. What did she say when you told her?

"Uh, you were in the room. I called her from your crib, man, your old ass, getting amnesia, quick!"

"Oh, yeah, I forgot. I'm just happy for you, my brother. I remember when you used to sing on State Street and pass out those flyers! Man, you came a long way, and I couldn't be happier for ya. Real talk!!"

Carl laughs, "Yeah, all that hustling is about to pay off. But check this out, I'm working on this new number, but I can't get the beat to flow like I want it to. Listen to this."

Carl walks around to his piano, selects some music, and then plays this song: 'Got me thinking'

Hey baby, with that smile on ya face,

Stop whatever you're doing, pack a suitcase.

I've been thinking, hope it's not too late.

Come on baby, let's try to escape.

Got me thinking, oh oh.

I've been thinking.

You see we've been dating for a long, long time,

and you ain't complaining.

But it crossed my mind.

About the time that I changed my life.

Been thinking of making you my wife.

Oh, oh, oh, Girl I've been thinking.

Oh, oh, I've been thinking.

Carl stops singing and says "You see what I mean? That beat didn't land like I needed it to. I can't get that verse to flow."

"Mmm, yeah, I like it, maybe go with... 'Hey baby, I've been thanking.' Instead of thinking, you know, put a lil slang in it. Maybe rap to her, instead of talking to her. Try that!

"Oh, okay," Carl says,

You see, I've loved ya, for a long, long time,

You ain't complaining, but it crossed my mind.

Oh baby, I've been thanking.

Yeah, I've been thanking.

"Mmmm, still not right!"

Carl and Jumbug continue with the song until Carl has it set in play. They laugh and talk stuff about the past and the up-and-coming future. Just two soul brothers with real love for one another, smoking weed and reminiscing.

* * *

Karen was so excited about Carl's news that she decided to cut her trip short and fly back home to celebrate with her man. Carl arrived at O'Hare Airport to pick up Karen. They put the luggage in the trunk of his Mustang and are on their way to Karen's place. Karen settles into the car. "Hey baby! So are you still riding high about your record deal?"

"Oh yeah, you know I am. But let's not assume anything I really don't want to celebrate until the ink is dry, okay?"

"Uhh, really? I wanted to have a Lil get-together with all of our friends. Are you sure, babe?"

"Well, after thinking about it, yes, I'm sure. Oh, and I want to get you a flight out to LA tomorrow for Wednesday because I want you there with me, alright?"

"Oh, absolutely. I'll call around as soon as we get home. I'm just so happy for you baby. You are going to be walking the red carpet with the likes of Keith Sweat and my boy, Prince! Ooh, I'm so excited right now!!"

"Yeah, I see. You gotta calm down, babe. Let's just get there and see what Mr. Riley's talking about, ok?"

"Awww, ok, you do have a point. I'll try to relax, but you know, I'm hard-headed, right?

"Oh yeah, you are definitely my hard-headed baby, and I'm glad you flew back. Those were the longest two days without you sweetie. Carl reaches over and rubs Karen's thigh.

"Yes, it was. I can't wait to get home and show you how much I missed you!" Karen rubs Carl's hand with hers as they ride down the expressway.

Sweet silence as they continue the drive to Karen's place. Carl is thinking about holding Karen in his arms, and Karen is wondering what's in her closet that she can take with her to L.A. They remain silent as the radio is playing 'Angel' by Aretha. A nice ride home with two souls in love, entering into a new chapter of their life.

* * *

Karen and Carl finally made it to Karen's condo. Karen is reading her mail when Carl sneaks up behind her, wraps his arms around her, and whispers, "Thought you missed me?"
Karen leans back into his arms and says, "Mmm...you know I missed you, babe." She drops the mail she's holding, turns around, and wraps her arms around Carl.

They hug for the longest time. Carl finally releases her, grabs her hand, and walks her over to the sofa. Carl sits down, and Karen sits beside him. She says, looking up at him, "Babe, tell me again how much? Carl smiles and says, "Mmm uh, how much of what babe?"
"Boy, stop playing. You know what I mean!"

"Oh yeah, I remember. Let me see." He takes a deep breath and says, "Uh, you take all of the numbers in the world and multiply them by all the numbers in the world, and baby, I will still love you more than that."

"Mmm, thank you. I love it when you break it down to me," she gives him a little kiss on the lips.

"Glad you approved. You know what I was thinking about as I was waiting for your flight to land?"

"No, what?"

"I was thinking we should take that next step and move in together. What do you think? I mean nothing much would change. I feel like I'm here every day anyway."

"Mmm, well, I don't know. It's definitely a big step, but if you think you could deal with me on a daily basis. You know how I am in the morning."

Carl sits up and says, "Well, it was just a thought. We don't have to make any decisions today. Why don't you think about it, ok?"

"Mmm, baby, it's not that I don't want to, it's just that I think I'd rather be married or at least engaged before we do the moving-in stuff."

"Well, I mean we are getting married one day, right? I just think my going back and forth across town is meaningless! I'm always here. But I guess you want to hold on to your space, huh? I mean you are always talking about how you need room to breathe and everything."

"No, that's not completely true. I just don't wanna play house, babe. When you make up your mind that you want to marry me, then we can move into a damn shoe box. I wouldn't give a damn about my space because I'm with you in the Biblical sense. But until then, I think we should keep things the way they are, okay?"

"Mmm, okay, I guess you're trying to tell me something, huh?"

"Nope, I'm not. I love us the way we are, and when the time comes for us to take the big step, I'll still love us. No pressure, baby! I'm happy."

"Yeah, okay. Well, I'm tired so I'm gonna take a shower. You coming?"

"Yep! That sounds good." Karen and Carl get up and walk into Karen's bathroom, each lost in their own thoughts.

CHAPTER 21

Gia was home in Chicago with Carly. While Carly was napping, she started packing a few bags for their trip to Louisiana. She knew it was imperative that she take Carly back home to Louisiana as soon as possible. Mama Jo had been calling her all night, and each message she left was laced with more and more sarcasm.

Gia had tried calling Mama Jo all day yesterday, but it went straight to voicemail. So Gia left a message that she would call her back today. But the heck with Mama Jo thought Gia because she was probably somewhere scheming on how to take Carly away from her. Dana had warned her about her evilness, so she made plans. They're flying out tonight on a red eye. Gia's intuition was telling her to move her ass and get Carly somewhere safe.

Gia wasn't a pushover, and her Mama raised her to always listen to that inner voice. Gia was handling her business accordingly. She didn't want to disrespect her elderly, but if Mama Jo came for Carly, she'd beat the devil out of her and pray for forgiveness later... and she put that on, everything! Trust and believe, Dana had left Carly in the best and most capable hands.

* * *

Days before Dana (Coco) died, she uncovered the truth about her and her mama's past. Dana made up her mind that she needed answers about her family. So, after doing some snooping around she drove to Clarksville, Arkansas where her mother was raised, and her grandma still resides.

She arrived during the Peach Festival. Dana's grandma lived on London Street, down the street from what folks claimed to be the best rib joint in town. Dana made a mental note to buy an order before leaving town. Dana didn't know what to expect, but from the way Mama Jo behaved when she told her she was coming, it couldn't be good!

Dana braced herself as she climbed the steps of her grandma's red brick house. Just as Dana was about to push the doorbell, a beautiful old woman opened the door.

"Oh, hello ma'am. I'm looking for my grandma, Hattie Jones."

The old woman gasped as she stared at Dana, and tears filled her eyes as she whispered, "I'm Hattie, baby. I'm your grandma."

"Oh my gosh! Hello grandma!" They hugged each other for the longest time.

"Oh, look at you. So pretty, just like your daddy!"

They walk into a room with plastic covering the carpet and the sofa. The room is filled with French provincial furniture and lots of framed pictures on the walls. Hattie takes Dana into the kitchen and offers her a cup of tea.

"No thank you, ma'am."

"Oh, baby, you can call me grandma. No one in these parts calls me Hattie."

"Yes ma'am. Oh, I mean, grandma."

"It's ok, practice makes perfect. So, I gather you want to know about your family and such?"

"Yes, like I said over the phone, I always heard stories about my dad, but my mom never talked about you or anybody else in the family. I'm being interviewed next week and I just wanna know where I come from, if that's okay with you?"

"Mmm, so Jolie Mae hasn't said anything about her family? Huh, well, that doesn't surprise me. I did the best I could for Jolie Mae, and Lawd knows I tried. But your mama was a handful. When she set her mind on something, she would lie, cheat, or steal to get it! Now what do you wanna know, baby?"

"I wanna know everything."

Hattie gets up and walks into the next room. A few minutes later, she returns with a few books. One was a family album full of old pictures. Hattie sat back down next to Dana, held her hand, and said, "I'm sorry I wasn't there to help you along the way. I tried to find you after your mama ran off with you, in the middle of the night.

Your daddy searched everywhere. We hired private detectives, but your mama hid you so deep that we just couldn't find you." She cried softly.

"It's okay, grandma. I'm just happy to finally see you. But I thought my dad was in jail for what he did to my mom.

Hattie, looking surprised, "Uh, what did that Jolie Mae tell ya about ya daddy?

"Mmm, well, that uh, well, you know, he raped her!"

Hattie gasped, put her hands on her chest, and shook her head. "No, no, no... Oh, sweet Jesus, your daddy was a good man. He never did anything to Jolie."

She reached for Dana's hand, "Your mama destroyed that man's reputation, and if anyone did any raping it was your mama! She seduced that man, lied and, well, it's too much for me to talk about. But your father did nothing wrong. You hear me? Nothing!!!"

Dana stood up and walked away. She was visibly upset and turned and ran outside. As soon as she reached the street, she threw up everything in her stomach. All the years of her life, she believed she was a child of a rapist. Her mother had lied to her, and she was beyond hurt.

Hattie finds her granddaughter crunching on her knees, and she lifts her up and walks her back into the living room. She held her granddaughter as she cried. When Dana is feeling better, she tells Dana everything about Jolie Mae and her amazing father, who was an athlete, scholar, and brilliant professor.

* * *

It was early in the morning when Gia arrived in Baton Rouge, Louisiana. She didn't know it, but she came close to getting her back broken and joining her BFF in heaven. Back in Chicago, Bugger arrived minutes after Gia left, and he was pissed! He had failed Mama Jo, and he knew she wasn't gonna give him any sugar for a month of Sundays! But ole Bugger wasn't giving up, he knew Gia had to return, sooner or later, because she left her car and a closet full of clothes.

Bugger continued to creep around Gia's place, searching for clues about her whereabouts.

He decided to keep an eye on her condo until she and Carly returned. Bugger left Gia's place with enough information to make Mama Jo very happy. He had a smile on his face as he drove to Jolie Mae's with his unused duct tape, shovel, hammer, and tranquilizer. He just might get his sugar.

Back in Louisiana, Gia was so thrilled to be home. And so was Carly because she took off running to her Nana's room as soon as they walked into the house. Carly woke up everyone in the house, as her lil feet were scrambling about.

Gia's mom started cooking breakfast, and just like she remembered, they, three generations of strong women, sat around the kitchen table cutting vegetables and catching up on all the neighborhood gossip and well, just enjoying the moment. "Oh, how I've missed this," said Gia, as she smiled at something her nana said. She threw back her head full of long curls, as she laughed out loud. And for now, all was good.

* * *

After getting Carly settled with her family, Gia made plans to go back to Chicago. The move wasn't as easy as she had thought. She needed to sell her condo and honor a few commitments. Gia suddenly realized that she would be commuting back and forth for a lot longer than she thought. She sat down to check her voicemail.

Gia decided to call her old friend, James. He left her a few messages, so she decided to catch up with him. Gia dials James Home.

James picks up on the first ring.

"Hello, may I speak to James?"

James replied, "Speaking?"

"Oh, hey stranger, this is Gia. How are you?"

"Oh, hey beautiful! I was wondering when you were going to call a brother. What's up with you?"

"Oh, wow, where do I start? I'm making it, you know, I just flew home for a minute. But anyway, I was returning your call. What's up with you?"

"Oh yeah, well, a buddy of mine wanted to get some art for his girl, and I was hoping you could help him. Are you still managing that Gallery out east?

"Yep, I'm on vacation right now, but I'm flying home tomorrow. I'll give you a call in a few days and we can schedule something, ok?

"That's cool. You okay? You don't sound bubbly like Gia, I remember."

"Boy, uh huh. You still think you a psychic, huh?" They both laugh.

"But, yeah, I just buried my sis a few weeks ago, so you know, it's been tough."

"Oh, I'm sorry baby, my condolences to you and your family. I thought you were the only child, though?"

"Oh yeah, I am. She wasn't blood, but she was still my sister. We were pretty tight. But anyway, I'm just trying to readjust my life.

Sometimes I pick up the phone and call, and be like, 'Oh, wow, my girl is gone.' Just hard to swallow, you know?"

"Yeah, I know, my buddy just lost someone, too, and he is pretty down about it. I'm sorry sweetie. Listen if you wanna hang out or grab something to eat, just call me, and I'll swoop you up, okay? Real talk."

"Okay, I would like that. Let me finish packing so I can get ready for my flight."

"What time are you flying back? I can pick you up. I'm home all day tomorrow with nothing going on."

"Are you sure? I don't wanna bother you."

"Baby, come on, now, you know I wouldn't offer if I didn't think I could."

"Well ok. I'm flying into O'Hare on American Airlines. Let me get the flight info."

Gia returns to the phone and gives James her itinerary.

"Okay, I'll see you tomorrow. I'll be the finest brother in a white T-shirt, alright?"

Laughing, Gia replies, "Boy, I see you haven't changed a bit. Thanks so much, and I guess I'll see your fine ass tomorrow."

They hung up, and James wondered what the hell he was doing. He was still into Marteen. But with the long distance and with her not wanting to complicate things, it had him walking around confused. James didn't want to give up on Marteen, but she had it clear that they were just enjoying each other, so maybe he should see other women.

Back in Louisiana, Gia hangs up with James, and she sings,

'Never trust a man, never trust a man... if he's wearing a white T-shirt... ya hear me...cause, girl, he's just a flirt...

Girl, he's just a flirt... learn from me... ya hear me?'

She smiles to herself as butterflies are swarming inside.

* * *

James arrived at the airport to pick up Gia. He hadn't seen her in a few years. They still talked over the phone now and again. But life happened, and they sort of moved on. James was always into Gia. She was the prettiest redbone sista and could sing her butt off. She was always humming a song, and her mama was just as sweet. James always felt like she was the one that got away.

Well, maybe he could try to make amends. Well, that's if, Marteen would stop playing and decide what she wanted. But if he still had feelings for Gia, then he was not about to mess up the second time. He was too old to play games. And besides, he wanted to settle down and maybe have a few kids.

Man, he already knew Gia would be a great mom. She took care of his grown ass enough. Like that time when he was sick or when he broke his foot while playing ball. Man oh, man, she never left his side. And she could cook her ass off! She was a package deal. But Marteen had him dangling from a string, so a brother was confused.

Suddenly, he spotted Gia, and good golly miss Molly! She was still as beautiful as the day she bounced her long, curly hair into his life some years ago! Oh yeah, he was still feeling her, thought James as Gia walked up to him.

"Hey! Damn girl, you uh, gotta man, or what?" They hug and kiss, as friends would do.

"Boy, I can't be with you. You are still as crazy as ever."

He carries her luggage over to the car.

"Ooh, look a here, babe. Is this your ride?"

James opens the trunk of his Mercedes Benz and says, "Oh nah, I just stole it. Now hurry up and get your fine ass in the car before the cops see us! They laugh.

"Boy stop playing. This is sweet. I'm feeling all special."

"That's right, you are special, baby. Real talk. And you look good to me! That's why you need to call that nigga and tell him it's over."

Gia laughs.

"I'm serious. That ain't no joke. Call ya man, and tell him your future baby daddy is back. He needs to kick rocks. Tell that chump it's over! You okay, baby?"

Gia is choking from laughing so hard.

"Baby, you okay over there?"

"No, I'm choking. You really want me to call him, huh?"

James looks over at Gia and says in a more serious tone, "Absolutely, call him today!!"

They pull off and drive down to Gia's place. All of sudden, it's quieter now, and James breaks the silence. He asks Gia if she's still in the same place, and she says no, and gives him her new address.

"So what are you doing besides working, are you still volunteering at the boys club?" Gia asks him.

"Oh yeah, you remember that, huh? Mmm, yep, whenever I can, I'm down there, trying to make a difference in someone's life. What are you doing? Are you still singing at weddings and stuff?"

"Yes, I am. As a matter of fact, I have a gig to perform at this weekend. That's one of the reasons why I had to come back today.

"That's nice. I'm glad to hear you are doing something with that beautiful voice of yours. So how is your mom doing? I miss her and your nana. She used to be crazy about me."

"She still asks about you and nana too. You could do no wrong in their eyes."

"So, what are you doing later today or tomorrow? I wanna spend some time with you if that's okay."

Gia tells him, "Now, James, don't start nothing you can't finish."

"Trust me, I know, baby. Because the minute I kiss you, we are going to be in a relationship. I already know. I'm not in a relationship, but I'm sorta talking to this woman. But after seeing you, I know exactly what I want. So you tell me how this story goes."

"How long have you been seeing her?"

"Few weeks"

"Okay, that makes me feel better. But James, I'm dealing with a lot right now. So I think I need a friend more than a boyfriend. I'm not saying no to a relationship with you because I still love you, but my life isn't the same. I need to know that you are ready to be the man I need."

"Okay, so you don't have a man, right?'

"No, I don't have anyone to call," Gia responds as they share another laugh.

"Good, because I didn't wanna have to beat the shit out of anyone."

Gia smiles and says, "We both know how you get down, so..."

"Oh yeah. You remember that dude that used to follow you? I had to choke his ass. Sorry you saw all that."

"Yeah, I was scared for him because you were trying to kill that man!"

"Yeah, it's called territorial. He got too close to you. And as your man, I had to let him know, that's all."

James continues, "So, are we going out tonight or tomorrow?"

"Mmm, how about tonight and tomorrow?" Gia replies.

"Now that's what I'm talking about. Damn, I missed you, baby! One thing about you, you always spoke your mind. Glad to see you are still the same."

* * *

James and Gia pull up to her condo, and James carries her bags to her door. "Well, okay, I guess I'll see you later, ok?" James says.

"Ok, thanks again. Do you want to come in? The least I can do is offer you something to drink."

James looks awkward and says, "No, I'm good babe. Just call me when you get settled. I better get out of here, you know how it is."

"Boy, get in here. I am not going to bite you. And if you get too fresh, I'll just do what I used to do!"

James holds his hands up, "Now see, you trying to start something. I gotta go, baby. Let me be a gentleman, ok? Call me."

James starts to walk backward and waves goodbye.

Gia yells, "Chicken!"

As soon as Gia walks into her place, a coldness touches her soul. She drops her bag and lets out a low cry. James runs back and asks her, what's going on. Gia turns to him with a frightening stare and says, "Evil has been inside my house."

James, familiar with Gia's sixth sense says, "Are you sure?"

"Yes, someone has been here. I cannot sleep here tonight."

"Okay. Let's make sure your stuff hasn't been damaged or anything."

"Okay, I'm coming with you because I'll know if anything was taken."

They enter her place, and Gia turns on the light. Although everything looks ok, Gia knows someone was there. They checked everything, and nothing was missing, except some of her bills and documents were out of place. Gia immediately thought of Mama Jo because she would be looking for some type of leverage to use against her.

Gia grabbed a few more items and asked James to take her to a hotel because her home wasn't safe anymore. James grabs her luggage, they lock up and walk out. Gia asks, "Uh, babe, could you follow me to a hotel? I'm going to drive my car."

"No, I don't think you should be driving. Look at you, baby, what's going on? You are shaking like a leaf."

"As soon as we are far enough away, I'll tell you everything."

"Okay, well we can come back and get your car tomorrow. You can stay with me. I have a guest room, okay?"

"Are you sure? Because I don't want to be a bother."

"That's the second time you have said that. Now, baby, you are staying with me and that's final. You know your mama would kill me if I let anything happen to her baby girl! Come on, let's get out of here because you got me looking at everybody with suspicion."

James and Gia arrive at his house, and he sets her up in the guest bedroom. While Gia is taking a shower, he throws on a few steaks and makes a salad for them. When Gia finally comes out of her room, dinner is served.

Gia says, "Mmm....look at you, cooking for me. I'm surprised you didn't ask me to fix you something."

"Uh, the kitchen is all yours after today, ok?"

"Oh, I knew it wouldn't last. But thanks babe. I love your place. It's so cozy!"

They eat dinner and play catch up on their life's work and interests. Gia finally tells James about Carly and Mama Jo. James still hasn't put two and two together about Dana, but he's intrigued about Carly.

"So, why are so quiet?" Gia asks James.

"Just trying to soak up all this new drama in your life and the fact that you are a mother of a two-year-old. Tell me more about her.

Gia gushes, "Oh, she's the cutest baby and so smart. She can count to ten already and she can tie her shoes. Now she still wets the bed at night but she is out of diapers and can run like the dickens! She is so fast. I think she will be athletic like her mom was. She calls me mommy. It just warms my heart. I miss her so much already, and it's only been a few hours.

"Wow, I can't wait to meet this little person."

"Well, I sense that you are really into this woman friend. I think you should ask her what she wants from you. Get a better understanding because she could want the same thing, you need to communicate with her."

"Here you go with that. What, you don't wanna give me another chance to do right by you?"

"I would if you didn't have someone else in the picture. I will always feel connected to you, but I gotta protect my heart, babe! You need to have closure with your friend before we can begin anything, ok? You know I'm right."

"Yeah. I love your honesty and strength. Carly is blessed to have you, baby! Well, I'll finish the dishes. Why don't you call home and let them know, you are with me. You know your mama will fly here in a minute, looking for ya."

"I know. I need to check on Carly. Anyway, thanks so much. I won't be here long. I don't want to block your romance."

"Stop with that. So, you really don't want to give us a chance?"

"I would but, it's never the right timing with us babe. It's either too soon or too late. I hate to admit it, but I'm too late. Somebody else has your heart. You know, I'm right."

Gia walks back into the guest room and closes the door. Later that night, Marteen calls James. "Hey, did I catch you at a bad time?" Marteen asked. "No, I'm up. What's going on with you?"

"Nothing much. Karen flew back to be with Carl, and I've been thinking about coming back this weekend. Are you free this weekend?"

"Uh, I don't know. I have a friend here from Louisiana, so I'll let you know, ok?"

"Oh, okay, well is everything okay? You don't sound happy to hear from me."

"No, I'm cool. Just trying not to make things too complicated. I mean those were your words, right?"

"Mmm, yes, they were. So, you wanna stop what we're doing?"

"Baby, I don't know what we're doing. You know how I feel about you, but you want me to stay in the background and wait until you say I can come out and play with you. I'm a grown man, and I can't keep this up. Now, I don't know about you, but I think things just got complicated, so. Now what? Tell me what ya want from me. Do you wanna be my woman or what?"

"So, the long-distance relationship wouldn't bother you?"

"Not if you wanna be my woman. We can work that out, but I need to know what you want from me."

"So, are we going to discuss this over the phone?"

"Yeah, I guess so. Tell me what you want, baby.

"Well, I want you, and we can try to do this relationship thing. Is that cool?"

"Yes, that's cool. So, no more secret agent shit, right?"

"Right no more, baby. I'll be back this weekend, so let me know if you are free, okay?

"I'll make time, but my friend from Louisiana is a lady friend. She's staying in the guest bedroom, okay?"

"Oh, okay, well, just let me know. I'm not worried about that. I think you know how to behave yourself, right?"

"Oh, absolutely, on my best behavior."

"Is she cute?"

"Yep."

"I'm flying back tonight."

"I thought you weren't worried...

"Well, you didn't tell me she was cute!

"Awww, you good babe. I can't wait to see you. Are you coming in early or late?"

"I don't know, I haven't booked anything yet. But I'll call you tomorrow evening, ok? I miss you so much!"

"Damn, miss you too, sweetie. I'm just glad you finally came around and decided to do the best thing for us, you know?"

"Well, I know, I've been neglectful, so I'll make it up to you when I get back there. Okay, baby? I'm sorry. See you soon and give me my kiss goodnight."

James throws a kiss, and they hang up. James smiles and says, out loud "Gia was right, just like always... damn!"

CHAPTER 22

Karen calls Marteen. "Hey sis, are you awake?"

"Yes, just got off the phone with James. What's wrong?"

"Ooh, so you and James are together, I knew it! With your secretive ass!

"Whatever, why are you calling me this late?"

"Oh, well, I couldn't sleep, and you don't have sense enough to call me. But anyway, I'm conflicted, sis. Carl wanted us to move in together. But I'm like, no, because then, he'll never marry me. You know how mom used to say that a man won't buy the cow if he's getting the milk for free."

Marteen laughing says, "Yeah, she always said that but your relationship with Carl is on a different level. He really cares for you. But if you don't want to move in, then don't. But make sure your reasoning is your own, and not about something mom said. Because if I was living in Chicago, I wouldn't hesitate to move in with James. I know he's the right man for me and that's all I'm saying. So, don't ask me questions about my relationship, okay? You know I'm private about my business."

"Mmm hmm. I know you are. And I understand, but back to Carl. I just don't want him to think that I'm giving him an ultimatum, you know? Because he sorta insinuated I was. I don't know. He was really quiet tonight.

"Well, he's a big boy, so stop trying to analyze him. Just take things as they come. Just relax and enjoy your relationship, okay? But I do have something I want to ask you about James. He said he had a friend staying with him from Louisiana, and it was a lady friend. Have you ever heard them talk about her or anything like that?"

"Mmm nope. But I know Carl told me one day that James used to have a girlfriend he never met. And she had James's nose wide open. I think she was Creole, so maybe she was from Louisiana, but I'm not sure."

"Mmm, well I trust him. I was just curious. I'm just trying to connect the dots. Anyway, I need to get up early. If you want to talk more, I'm flying back this weekend, okay?"

"Oh okay. I'll be in California with Carl, but you have the keys to my place so enjoy the solitude."

"Ok"

"Uh, I think I'm going to stay at James's place, but thanks."

"Well, alright then, I know that's right! I'll talk to you tomorrow night, okay?"

"Bye, sis."

"Good night knucklehead." Marteen hangs up and tries to go back to bed. When sleep finally comes, it's a restless one.

* * *

Bugger sat directly across Gia's condo. He was staking out Gia's place, wearing a workmen's uniform. Just in case someone said something, and he could pretend he was with maintenance. So far so good. The car was still parked, and no movement was going on through her 3rd-floor window.

Back at James's place, James woke up to the smell of bacon and all the fixings. He walked into his kitchen area, and Gia was setting the table while humming a song about men.

"Good morning, babe," James greets Gia.

"Hey, perfect timing. I hope it's okay. I cook when I'm feeling troubled."

"Oh, you good, babe, I'm happy to have this old-fashioned breakfast, wow! Is that the smothered potatoes over there? Got damn, I should have married yo ass years ago," James walks over and gives Gia a kiss on her cheek and says thank you.

"Oh, you're welcome, babe. Now eat before it gets cold."

"Mmmmm, this is everything, baby, just everything."

After breakfast, James decided to take a cab to pick up Gia's car.

"Oh, okay, and while you are gone, I'm going to contact my realtor and see if she can help set my place up for some showings. I'm praying it will sell quickly."

"What? Why are you selling your place?"

"Oh, I forgot to tell you, I'm moving back home to Louisiana. I can't raise Carly here without the support of my family, and I just don't trust her grandmother.

"Wow, I guess that's why you were so quick to push me away, huh?"

"No, I stopped us from both being hurt. So have you made things clear with your girl because you look happier this morning?"

"Yeah...you know, you are creeping me out with that psychic stuff! But yeah, we're finally on the same page. I'm sorry I was all confused with seeing you again because you were always supposed to be my wife. But you were dead on when you said the timing with us is always off. I'm sorry babe!"

"Hey, I'm happy you're happy, no worries. I really appreciate your thoughtfulness. So, if it's okay, I just need to stay one more night. Then I'm staying temporarily in the room in the back of the gallery. I just need to make it livable, ok?"

"Hey, stay as long as you want. My girl knows you are here, so she's cool with it."

"Uh, trust me, she's probably trying to fly back here today because no woman is okay with her man having another woman sleeping in his house, so I am out of your hair tomorrow, okay?"

"Oh, okay, so you think she's tripping on the low about you being here?"

"Oh, hell yes, she is definitely in her feelings. So be reassuring, but on the low, because she's probably trying to play it off."

"Mmm, well that serves her ass right, had me dangling from a string. But I'll make sure she is secure with me because I don't want her stressing over nothing."

"Good. So, here's my keys and stuff. Be careful because Mama Jo is crazy, OK?"

"No problem, I can take care of myself," James replied

"I know, but still stay alert. And please come straight here so I'm not worried."

"Ok, babe, so what are we having for lunch?"

Gia threw a sofa pillow at him, "Boy, get out of here, you ate enough to last all day. But I'll see." "Alright, I'll be back in a few."

* * *

Across town, James makes it to the condo and decides to thoroughly check out the locks and windows. As soon as he approached her floor, he noticed a maintenance guy walking away from the direction of Gia's apartment. "Hey, do you work here? "Oh uh, yes sir, excuse me."

James says: "Whoa wait, a friend of mine had an intruder in her apartment, so who should she contact about that?"

"Oh well, she can call the uh office, but I am off now, so sorry, gotta go."

"Well, I..."

The guy walks off quickly like he is scared or something. James shakes his head as he unlocks the front door and checks her locks for any tampering. He goes inside and inspects all of her windows. After finding nothing out of the norm, he locks back up and leaves the building. As James is climbing into Gia's car, he hears a noise, turns around, and sees the shadow of a person running in the opposite direction.

James steps around to survey his surroundings and check under the car and all the tires before climbing back into the car. He pulls out of the garage with an uneasy feeling. He makes a mental note to carry his gun from now on.

* * *

Gia and James are just leaving her Condo association office when they run into Mama Jo. Gia introduces James to Mama Jo and asks him to wait for her in the car.

"Are you sure?" James asks Gia.

"Yes, I'll only be a minute."

Mama Jo twists her lips but remains silent.

"So, were you coming to see me or coming to break into my house?"

Mama Jo says, "Lil girl, I have been real patient with you, but you are wearing my nerves. Now where is my grandbaby?"

"She's doing fine, thank you. And that fall she took while under your care, is loosening up her front tooth. But thankfully, she's a lil fighter like her mother."

"Mmm ok, you think you're smart. But you still haven't told me where you took my baby. I'm not going to ask you again." She steps closer to Gia and places her hands on her hips.

Gia stands her ground and says, "Carly is somewhere safe, with a real grandma who knows how to love and care for her."

"Hmmm, well, last I checked, she's not at my house. So, she must be over to Carl's mama's house because we are her blood grandparents. If I don't have my baby at my house tomorrow, I'm coming for ya ass. And I'm going to call Carl, and tell him he has a daughter, ok? You hear me? Because I only tell a grown person something once! Just once!!!"

Mama Jo starts to walk away when Gia says, "Well, since you're calling people, call Dana's dad because he's blood too, right? Tell him how you destroyed his daughter."

Mama Jo took her pistol out of her purse and pointed in Gia's face, "Keep talking, and I'll shoot you in yo mother fuckin face, you high yella, bitch!!"

Gia walks up so the gun is touching her nose and calmly says, "Go on and do it because, unlike you, I'm willing to die for mine. I know how to love, so pull that mother fkn trigger, 'cause that's the only way you'll ever see Carly. Pull!"

James comes out of nowhere and tackles Mama Jo and takes the gun. Mama Jo is screaming for him to let her go, and Gia screams, "Yeah, let her ass go because I am done running. Let her go!!" James lets go of Mama Jo and stands between the ladies. Suddenly, Mona runs over and grabs her mom, pleading with her to get back into the car. Police sirens are blasting.

Mama Jo walks back to her car and James unloads her gun and gives it back to her. Gia and James jog to their car and pull off before the cops get there. James says, "Are you out of your fuckin mind? Why in God's name would you walk into a gun, huh, what's...." Gia interrupts, "I'm just tired of this mess. You have no idea how stressful these last few weeks have been. I'm sorry," Gia starts to cry. James pulls the car over and holds Gia in his arms. Finally, she can release the last of her tears. She emptied those burdens that were weighing heavily on her shoulders.

* * *

James is still holding Gia in his arms as he tries to soothe her.

"It's okay, sweetie I'm sorry. I wish I could carry all of your burdens for you. I swear I do." He leans over and grabs some Kleenex from his glove compartment. He lifts Gia's chin and wipes the tears from her eyes. He puts one of the tissues up to her nose and tells her to blow. She laughs between crying and blows and gives him a big hug. She looks up into his eyes and says, "I'm sorry you had to see me like this. I just couldn't keep it inside anymore, you know?"

"I know, that's a crazy broad, and I think you need to go back home. Why don't you let me deal with the sale of your place, and just get out of here, like tonight? I'll give you whatever you need to get settled, okay? Because seeing that gun in your face, man oh man, I'm angry, now! This shit just got real! Look at me," James says. James holds her face between his hands and continues, "I love you, okay? And seeing your life in danger just made me wonder why am I letting you go. I don't know, babe, I just don't know, and he leans in and kisses Gia.

A slow kiss, not forceful, until Gia responds. Then, they are wrapped up into one another so tight that Gia comes up for air. James looks into her hazel eyes, and the past comes flashing back to him. He's remembering why he fell in love, and he's wondering why in the hell he ever let her go.
Gia was unique and spicy, like hot sauce. That natural beauty, light skin, big round hazel eyes, kissable lips not too small but just right. A gorgeous figure, like Halle Berry's but better. Her bowlegs were so damn sexy. But that smile, ooh, that smile, and her inner strength and

caring ways, those were the icing on the cake. She had the most generous heart. He should have married her! Damn!

Gia interrupts James's thoughts and says, "Well, I think the adrenaline of this drama has us, you know, just..." It's James's turn to interrupt by kissing her again, and this time, it's serious because James is unbuttoning her blouse, and Gia is helping him. Oh no!! Freeze!!! Should I stop them before it gets complicated, or should I let them continue on with you know what...now, I'm conflicted.

* * *

James suddenly pulls away from Gia. He quickly apologizes as he fumbles with her blouse. Gia takes his hand and says hey, it's okay. She buttons her blouse back up, straightens herself up, and puts her seat belt on. She glances over at James, and he is staring at the steering wheel. "Are you okay?" Gia asked James.

"Uh, I don't know what came over me. It's just, you know, I'm sorry." He looks over at Gia "Are you good?"

Gia replied, "I'm good, and I'm not sorry. This was bound to happen, baby, we have chemistry and history. So don't beat yourself up. We came to our senses, so don't feel bad; you are an amazing man and like I said, our timing is always off. I hope your girl knows how lucky she is to have you."

"Yeah, me too. I'm so sorry. I just, you know, I got feelings for you. I don't want to lose you. And you out here thinking you bulletproof and shit. So, I mean, you need to take care of yourself. You have a little girl that needs you. So, don't be walking in front of guns ok? Just keep yourself safe, and I am going to keep my hands to myself because I love my girl, and I don't want to hurt her. And I definitely don't want to hurt you, so, let's get you back to the gallery, ok?"

"Okay, and thanks again for saving me. I'm like that damsel; I'm always in distress, but I won't be anymore. I'm going to take your advice and stay alive because I love that little girl, so let's get the heck out of here."

James drives Gia to the Gallery and after he unloads all of her belongings, they say their goodbyes. James drives home with a clearer mindset. He is missing his girl, and although he will always love Gia, he is in love with Marteen.

James enters his place, takes a cold shower, and pours himself a shot of bourbon. Just when he is about to relax, his doorbell chimes. Wondering who it could be, he opens his door, and it's Marteen. Marteen smiles and says surprise! I couldn't wait until the weekend, baby!! James pulls her inside and kisses her, and in between kisses he tells her, I'm happy you couldn't wait.

CHAPTER 23

Mama Jo drops off Mona at the house and continues to Carl's place. She is done fooling around with Gia. Thanks to Bugger, she had Carl's address and Gia's mother's address in Louisiana. Her plans were to talk to Carl and then go on a road trip to get her granddaughter. She was done playing with that yella belly bitch! Mama Jo's motto was, you should only tell a grown person something once! After that, you gotta show them!!

Mama Jo arrived at Carl's place and found no one home. She was beside herself, so she waited out front for a few hours before going back home. Back at the house, Mona calls her father and asks him to please come and get her because her mother is losing her mind again. Her dad told her he was on his way and would put her up in a hotel until things were back to normal.

Mama Jo returns home and immediately instructs Mona to start packing a few of her things because they are going to Baton Rouge, LA, to get Carly. "Mama, where did you get that gun? I'm not going anywhere with you," Mona says

"Excuse me? Did you say what I think you said?"

"I'm sorry, Mama, but I can't let you do this. It's wrong, and Dana, well, she gave Carly to Gia, she told us, remember?

"I don't care about that. I want my granddaughter. She's mine. She belongs with family. Now get ya ass in there and start packing. I'm not going to tell you again."

Mona walks over to her mother with tears in her eyes, and she says, "Mama, I have watched you belittle and beat my sister every day of my life. She took everything you threw at her with grace and dignity. All she asked of you was to honor her wishes, so I am begging you, to please let this go."

Mama Jo reaches out to slap Mona, and Mona blocks her hand and says, "No more, mama...no more..."

Mama Jo, filled with rage, lunges for Mona, and they tumble to the floor.

* * *

The paramedics strap Jolie Mae (Mama Jo) in and lift her inside the ambulance. She is unconscious, and they are administering CPR, giving her oxygen. Bugger pulls up as Mona is climbing into the ambulance. Bugger sways, "Oh God, what happened Mona?"

"She fell down the stairs headfirst. It was an accident, and they are taking us to Cook Country." Bugger looks into Mona's eyes and notices a bit of strength that he has never seen in her before and he asks her if she is okay.

"I'm good, Dad, I'm good.

The door closes, and the ambulance rushes Jolie Mae to the hospital. Bugger stands in the street looking lost because something doesn't seem right. He's wondering why his daughter isn't distraught, and unlike her, she's not crying.

The next morning, Mama Jo's condition was critical. She has suffered major brain damage and is currently in a coma. The doctor just left the room. Bugger and Mona are at her side. Bugger is crying openly, and Mona is comforting him as she stares off into space.

She's not worried or sad, just different. Her heart is lighter, and her back is in an upright position. She's taller now. Her head is in a well-rounded state of mind. She's feeling free for the first time. She looks to the heavens because God still loves her, thought Mona. He finally heard her. She looks down at Mama Jo, and she forgives her because the Bible says thou shalt honor thy mother and thy father. Mona knows God will forgive her for throwing her Mama, down the stairs.

CHAPTER 24

Carl and Karen arrive in LA, California and a car is waiting to take them to their hotel. Carl is getting the royal treatment, and they are soaking it all in. "Ooh, I'm so happy I was able to get a seat on your flight because I would've missed all this!" Karen tells Carl.

"I know, babe. Now this is what's happening. Man, oh man, I wish ole Jumbug was here, that joker would be grinning from ear to ear.

"Oh, speaking of him, you know, he's been dating my sister. I think it's getting serious. So, you better keep an eye on his butt because I don't want him trying to be no player and all that mess."

"Oh, wow, that joker slid in there. Mmmh...well, you know that's none of our business baby so, I'm sure your sister can handle him. I know for a fact that he is crazy about her."

"Oh, yeah, how much do you know?"

"Baby, can we just enjoy this moment and not talk about them? Let's just have some fun."

Carl fills their glass with more champagne.

"Awww, look at you, are you nervous, because I know I would be? This is living baby, ooh look at those houses on top of that hill. We should try to do some sightseeing."

Karen sips on her champagne and leans back into Carl's arms. Carl tilts her chin up, kisses her, and then whispers, "Let's pretend we're on our honeymoon when we get to the suite, ok? You know, uh, get some practice in before that day comes. Cause you know, it's coming, right? Yep, it's coming baby."

Before Karen can speak, he kisses her again, but with more passion this time, and she wraps her arms around him, and they slide on down into the cushions of the limousine.

* * *

Carl is in a recording studio with Mr. Riley. They are discussing the music industry and how Carl's uniqueness will set him apart from many other artists in the game. Carl's smooth voice can carry him over into a new multi-age R & B category, not just the young listeners but the old as well. With his handsome face, he was solidified. The ladies will fall in love with him, and the fellas will respect him for his rapping abilities. The only thing left to do was start recording and, of course, find a name that's complimentary.

Riley wanted Carl to keep his plans of marrying Karen on the low until after his single release and maybe his first album. Carl had plans to propose to Karen while in LA, but now he wasn't sure. So, Carl agreed to keep his plans on hold till after the release of his first single, but he wasn't waiting for the album because he wanted Karen to be his wife as soon as possible.

Carl had his attorney look over his contract, and once he was given the ok, he signed the dotted line! Carl was on his way to stardom. He couldn't wait to call his mom and celebrate with his lady!!!

Back at the hotel Karen was out shopping. She picked Carl up a silk shirt because she had noticed all of the guys were wearing them, with jeans and a sports coat. She knew he would be hesitant, but she bought some magazines to support her case. Karen heads back to the hotel, carrying a load of shopping bags, just as Carl is exiting a limousine.

"Damn girl, let me make some money first, alright? What did you buy, the entire shop or what?"

"Nope, and don't worry, I got you a little something, something." Carl carries the bags, and once they are inside their suite, he tells her the good news.

"OMG! And you walk into that hotel like nothing happened. I can't believe you didn't tell me right away! OMG! What did they say? Do you have to move to LA? Are you going on the road? I mean, how does this work? Boy, you better call your mom. Right now! I'm so happy for you. This is everything you have ever wanted, right?"

"Yeah, it's a lot to process, but my mom can wait. Come here and check this out." He shows her a copy of his signing bonus, and Karen gasps and has to sit down because her legs are shaking. "Yeah, that's us, baby. We are buying a big ass house, and whatever else you want, you hear me? This is us. Our future is set! And speaking of our future..."

Carl gets down on one knee and takes the ring out of his pocket, and Karen is speechless. "I know I haven't been the best boyfriend lately, but you have always had my back and never left my side. You have seen me at my lowest, and now, I want you with me at my highest, so ride this roller coaster with me, baby. I don't want you to ever feel insecure or stressed about us, ok? You are the only woman for me. So, Karen Denise Bosse, will you marry me?"

With tears falling down her face, she shakes her head. "Uh, baby, I'm gonna need to hear you say yes, ok?"

Karen whispers, "Yes!" Carl stands up and puts the 3-carat solitaire diamond on her finger. Karen throws her arms around his neck, picks her up, and they kiss. Carl takes Karen by the hand, and they sit down on the bed.

Carl says, "Baby, I hope you are ok with us not saying anything about our engagement until after my first single is released. I sorta agreed not to announce anything to the public, you know, it's for my image and stuff. I'm sorry. I know this is a lot to ask, but..."

"No, it's fine. I don't care. I just need to look at my ring for a few minutes. Can you leave us alone please?"

Carl laughs, "Are you serious? You want me to leave the room, so..."

"Boy, I am just playing with you. And, of course, I'm ok with keeping things quiet, but can I at least tell my sister?"

"Yeah, but don't tell Randy or Constance shit because you know they can't hold water. I'm serious, baby. This has to stay between us, ok?

Karen twisted her lips. "Oh, ok, I won't say anything to anyone, but why didn't you just wait until after the single was released to propose?"

"Well, because I had already made plans to propose today, and when he hit me with the news about my single image, well, I just didn't want you to be feeling all insecure about us again. You know how crazy you are, and I don't wanna hear you talking about how you need some space and all that. I love you so much, and I just couldn't wait, baby. I had the ring, and I didn't want to wait, so... why? Are you upset?" Karen puts her finger on his lips and says, "No, I'm so happy, baby, and I'm glad you proposed today because you were getting on my nerves with this let's pretend we are on our honeymoon mess. I was like, he better hurry up and get my damn ring, so you made the best decision, baby! Now let's pretend I'm your wife..." she pulls him down on top of her.

"Yes ma'am. Whatever you say, Mrs. Carl St. John."

And they celebrate love, success, and happiness.

CHAPTER 25

James is lying in bed, watching Marteen sleep. He is restless because he is still worried about Gia. She is alone out there, and some crazy ass people are trying to hurt her. He knows he has heard that name, Mama Jo, before, but he can't remember where. James eases out of the bed and sits on the sofa with another shot of bourbon. He lays his head back and closes his eyes and tries to remember who was that crazy ass woman.

Suddenly, he remembered. Dana's mom was also named Mama Jo. Carl went to visit her last week, and he saw a little girl fitting Carly's description. James has finally connected the dots, and suddenly, he needed to talk to Gia. Because if what he was thinking was true, his friend could be the father of that little girl. Just then, Marteen walks into the room and asks him, "Hey baby, what's wrong?"

"Oh nothing, just didn't want to wake you up. I couldn't sleep, so I'm having a shot of bourbon. Come here and sit beside me."

Marteen sits down and lays her head on James's shoulders and says, "Are you sure you're ok? Should I be concerned?"

"No, no, I'm just relaxing baby. It's all good. Nothing to worry yourself over."

"Okay, then," she sits up and says, "I guess I'll join you. Pour me a shot of that bourbon, baby."

James pours Marteen a shot, and she laughs and says, "I'm surprised you are not in here smoking weed because I never took you as a bourbon man."

"Oh, yeah, I guess there's a lot more to me than you thought, huh! Now come sit on my lap and tell ole Santa what you want for Christmas...."

Marteen throws her head back, laughing, and sits down on her man's lap. They make love until they both fall into a deep coma-like sleep.

* * *

The minute James left for work, Marteen walked into his guest bedroom. She wasn't sure why, but she was curious. It was neat and clean. Nothing was out of place except a pink barrette on the floor. Mmm, thought Marteen definitely wasn't something a grown woman would wear, maybe she had a daughter. Marteen had so many questions, but she wasn't prepared to hear the answers. Who was this woman who had her man's attention and had him up late drinking bourbon? Who the hell is she... and what did she look like? For the first time in Marteen's life, she had competition, and she'd never admit it, but she was afraid of losing James's heart. And it was all her fault. Marteen had no one to blame except...her damn herself!

James was meeting Marteen for lunch today, but he had hoped that he could run by and talk to Gia during his lunchtime. But what can he do? Marteen was on his ass, and she was being overly attentive. He wondered what was up with her. Oh, wait, thought James... Could it be that Marteen was feeling insecure? James smiled and made a mental note to reassure her that he was all hers.

But James was thinking about Gia a lot, and he had to see her ASAP. So James called Marteen and told her he couldn't do lunch because something came up, but he would stop and bring home some dinner. Marteen sounded okay so he drove over to the gallery to hopefully see Gia.

James got to the gallery and found that Gia had quit and was on her way back home. She left him a note. James waited until he was back inside his car to open up the letter.

James,

Thank you so much for being my hero. I owe you big time!
I guess you know by now that I am on my way back to my little princess. I am taking your advice, and I am going to live my best life, starting, right now! So, you take care and enjoy the next chapter of your life. Thank you for that last kiss goodbye, it was magnificent!
Sorry I was late.
Love always, Gia.

James read that letter over and over. Then he looked over at the passenger side, and he remembered her, sitting over there, buttoning her blouse. The blouse he tried to rip off of her, he saw her lips still swollen from his kiss, and he heard her heart beating fast. He saw the look in her eyes when she lied and said that all was good. He knew they had started something. And suddenly, some words he had once said came to him.

One of the first things James said to Gia when they met was, "Girl, you know if I kiss you, that's it; you are going to be my woman." And she was his woman until he screwed up! James snapped back to reality, folded Gia's letter up, put it inside his wallet, and drove back to work.

* * *

Bugger was sitting in Jolie Mae's (Mama Jo), hospital room watching over her. Jolie Mae was his whole world. He didn't know how to get along without her. Bugger held Jolie's hand, and he smiled as he remembered the first time he laid eyes on her.

It was on Maine Street, right around the time of the County Peach Festival. He was walking with his wife and twin boys, Bobby and Robby. It was a scorching hot day in Clarksville Arkansas. The year was 1972. His wife Ann was talking about something, but Bugger couldn't remember what she said if his life depended on it.

He saw the most beautiful woman walking down the street and just like that model Beverly Johnson, Jolie was strutting her stuff down Main Street. She had on a bright yellow dress with a black patent leather belt covering her tiny waist. She held her head straight up and her hair was bouncing with each step. She didn't see him, but he saw her. Bugger stopped and turned all the way around, and his wife popped him upside his head for staring like that. But Bugger had already left her world. He was in Jolie Mae's world, and that was that.

Jolie Mae satisfied his thirst. She was his tall glass of lemonade on a hot sunny day. And he wanted that glass of lemonade. Sadly, he didn't give a rat's ass about his wife and kids. He had to swallow the whole glass of lemonade, he just had to. So, he stalked her.

One summer night, Jolie Mae left the house with her bags and lil Dana in her arms. Bugger pulled up in his Buick and Jolie Mae was crying and smelling like someone had poured gasoline on her. Bugger asked her if she needed a ride, and Jolie said yes! He took her to a motel outside of town and fed her and Dana. The next day, Bugger robbed the First National Bank, and they drove away and never looked back.

Bugger found out later why Jolie Mae smelled like gasoline. As the story was later told, the fire started in the basement, and Dana's father escaped, but his wife wasn't so lucky. She was found locked inside the attic. She died of smoke inhalation. No one knew she was up there. They were newlyweds, married only 24 hours.

Bugger knew he could never go back home to his wife and kids, so he erased them from his mind. He had his tall glass of lemonade and that was all he needed. When Bugger finally came back to the present, he knew he had to finish what he and Jolie Mae aka Mama Jo started, because it ain't over, thought Bugger as he kissed Jolie and left the hospital.

CHAPTER 26

When you're sitting around in the dark,

Mending the same ole heart

Trying to figure out

When did it all fall apart

Left alone with your thoughts

Not sure if you played the right part

Now he's gone and

You're sitting around in the dark

Mending the same ole heart.

Gia was restless and writing in her journal. Somewhere deep inside her soul, she knew she had to get as far away as possible. So, she typed up her letter of resignation and grabbed her belongings. She locked up the gallery, packed her car up, and drove home to Louisiana. What the hell. She'd sell her condo over the phone. Chicago wasn't big enough for her and James. She couldn't face him again. She loved him too much. That kiss in James's car, well, it raised feelings she never knew she had.

* * *

Marteen was restless and deep in her feelings, so she left a note for James and went for a drive. She had to clear her head and just relax because she wanted to shake the mess out of James. Because if he was out cheating with this woman, she was going to hurt him. He could have just left them the way they were!

As Marteen was walking to her rental car, she ran into a strange man, Bugger. "Oh, excuse me, I thought you were someone else.

"Oh, no worries, and she continued. As she was opening her car door, she felt like she was being watched. Marteen put her purse on the front seat. She had her gun with her. For the first time in a long time, she pulled it out and laid it in her lap because she knew that dude was on some bullshit!

Marteen pulled her car out, and as she passed the creep, she made sure he saw her gun because she wouldn't hesitate to empty every single bullet in his whole ass! And the way she was feeling, she would probably beat his ass and then shoot the shit out of him! Damn what is the world coming to, thought Marteen, as she drove off. Bugger was thinking, 'Oh, she was packing, wow! Well, that wasn't Gia, but she acted like she knew him.

Bugger hunched his shoulders and walked back to his ride. So where was that bitch? She wasn't at work, and she wasn't at her Condo. Bugger had followed James home the other night, so he figured Gia was held up in the apartment. But he had a feeling that Gia was probably going back to Louisiana.

Damn, he couldn't leave Jolie Mae alone, not with Mona acting strange. He would have to wait because she had to come home sooner or later. He made a mental note to stay out of sight of that pretty lady he just bumped into because she could be a cop or something like that. Bugger drove back to the hospital.

Marteen drove down Oak Street where she found a parking meter. She went into Barneys New York and did some shopping. She needed some retail therapy! She picked up James a little something and went next door for a quick lunch. She had two glasses of wine, and she was feeling a lot better when she finally made it back to James's place.

James was pacing back and forth when Marteen used the spare key and walked in. James notices the shopping bags and says, "Oh hey, you got your shopping on, huh?"

"Yes, I was just trying to kill some time waiting for you. How was your day baby?" Marteen asks as she kisses him.

"Not bad, I uh, stopped at Barbara Jean's and picked up your favorite. But it's cold so I guess you can warm it up, if you want, ok? I'm going to take a quick shower."

James walks off as if he's mad about something.

Marteen, still feeling tipsy, calls after him and says, "Sounds good, babe. I'll join you in a minute."

James is lathering his arms when Marteen opens up the shower door and climbs in.

James says, "See, I was supposed to be mad because you weren't here when I came home. I was starting to worry, but now, I can't even be mad anymore. Damn, baby you women always know what to do.",

Marteen smiles and says, "Aw what did I do? I just went shopping. What, I can't go shopping, you want..."

James silences her with a wet kiss, and they make up by making love to the sounds of water sprinkling down their bodies.

Later that evening, Marteen is lying on the sofa with James watching TV. She has her legs stretched across his lap. They are laughing and enjoying each other when the phone rings. James picks up, and it's Carl and Karen calling from LA. James gives Marteen the phone and Karen tells her about their engagement. They are squealing and jumping up and down like teenagers.

James is like, what the? And finally, Marteen hands him the phone and Carl tells him that he had to start planning his bachelor party because it was going down. The girls are both screaming no! Absolutely not! After they hang up the phone, James looks at Marteen and says, "Alright now, don't you get any ideas about taking my freedom away, ok?"

"Boy, your freedom is already gone, like poof! It's out of here. Look up, you see it? Wave goodbye, baby, it's gone."

Marteen pulls him in for a kiss, and between kisses, James says, "Yeah ok, just have your ass in this house when I come home. That's all I'm saying, you hear me?"

Marteen replies, "Mmm, yes papi!"

CHAPTER 27

James and Marteen are eating dinner at Carmine's. They are laughing and flirting like teenagers and not wanting the evening to end. They head over to hear some live music at Club Electra, one of James's favorite spots.

Marteen is wearing a beautiful Escada strapless fuchsia and red print dress with red Jimmy Choo stilettos. Her hair is up, and she's wearing her teardrop diamond earrings. She looks stunning, and James beams as he walks into the club, Marteen draped on his arm. Nothing could burst his bubble, well, let's just say, not until the next act hits the stage. James and Marteen are having the best night, ever.

Backstage, Gia is getting ready to perform a new number she just wrote. She is a little nervous and sleep-deprived. She flew in earlier today to honor her contract with Club Electra. After tonight, she was planning on sleeping like a baby. The show is about to start. The next act is being introduced as the club's favorite, the one and only...Ms. Gia Soja!!!

James whispers, "shit," and Marteen realizes that the singer is James's ex and lady friend. James says, "I'm sorry, I had no idea she was even in town. Let's just go, baby."

"Oh no, we are not going anywhere. I want to hear her sing, so let's just enjoy the rest of our date, ok?"

James reaches over to kiss Marteen, and he whispers in her ear that he loves her past the moon...'

Gia takes the stage and is wearing a long white beaded gown that fits her like a glove. While she's talking about her next number, she spots James and Marteen sitting up front. Her heart is on fire because Marteen is beautiful, and James just reaches over to kiss her. James wants to disappear, and Marteen thinks that Gia is not just pretty, she is gorgeous!

Gia sings the blues...

Sitting around in the dark mending the same ole broken heart

Left alone...with your thoughts...

Not sure if you played the right part...

Now he's gone ...and you're left sitting in the dark.

Wondering when did it all fall apart

Not sure of what you're supposed to do....

Oh, baby...hope you're missing us...

Hope you're missing us too...

Oh ohhhh

Lost without... you...

Oh baby...

Sitting around in the dark

Mending the same ole broken heart...

Wondering where did it all fall apart

Baby if you're tapping in on these thoughts...

I still love you...with the same ole broken heart...

Ohhh the same ole broken heart

Gia is staring straight into James' soul as she sings the last verse. She holds on to that last note, everyone is on their feet. James and Marteen slowly stand up and look at each other, like...what the f'k?

* * *

Gia exits the stage, and Marteen decides she has heard enough live music for one night. So, they drive across town to Shelly Jean's for a nightcap. But, before they leave for Shelly's, Marteen goes into the ladies' room to refresh herself. Gia is in the mirror fixing her hair. "Oh, hello, we haven't met, but I'm Marteen, James's girlfriend." Gia smiles and shakes Marteen's hand, "Oh yes, hi...nice to meet you. I hope y'all enjoyed the show."

"Oh yes! You have a lovely voice. You should be on Broadway with that little number."

Gia, not sure if it was a compliment, says: "Thank you, and it's so nice to finally meet you. Please thank James again for his warm hospitality." She smiles and continues fixing her hair. "I'll be sure to tell him," Marteen says as she smiles and re-applies her lipstick before saying good night.

"Oh, you're not staying for the rest of the show?" Gia asks.

"Oh no, sorry. We are not into the blues; it's just so sad. We like happy upbeat songs, you know? Sorta like we are, happy! But good luck tonight, or should I say, uh, break a leg!"

"Oh, just as well. Y'all would not like my next number. It's called "I had him first." Gia looks in the mirror and smiles at Marteen.

Smiling back, Marteen says, "Well, like I said, break a leg." and whispers 'bitch" under her breath.

Marteen walks back out, and she and James leave the club. Now At Shelly Jean's restaurant, they are seated in a cozy booth next to the window, drinking coffee with a shot of Baileys and Cream. James is holding Marteen's hand across the table, and he says, "Hey sexy lady, did I tell you that you look amazing tonight? I can't help but stare. Is this a new dress?"

"Yes, I just got it the other day. I'm glad you like it. Ooh, I forgot to give you your gift. I picked you up a little something. Also, remind me to give it to you, ok?"

"Oh, ok, so you were thinking about me, huh?"

"Of course, I'm always thinking about you. You know I'm crazy about you."

"Yeah, I know. Sorry about tonight at the club."

"Oh, no worries baby. I'm in a good place, and I told you I'm crazy about you. We are solid. I'm not thinking about that."

"Oh, is that right? So, you're crazy about my black ass, huh? So crazy that you wanna move to Chicago and live in sin with me?"

Marteen reaches over, kisses James, and says, "Yes baby, and I can't wait to do it!"

"Aw, thank you baby. I know it's a lot of me to ask, but trust me, I'd move anywhere for you. Now, can I ask you something serious?"

"Yes, of course."

"How many kids do you want? I mean, do you dream about one day settling down and raising a family? Getting married, you know? The whole nine yards?"

"Yep, I have been thinking about a lot of things lately, especially now that I can admit that I'm in love. This is exciting and new for me. So yes, I'm thinking about all that. What about you?"

"Oh, hell yes, I want a house full of kids!"

Marteen widens her eyes. "But since you looking at me all crazy, I'll be happy with 3 or 4. Because the way you spend money, shi'd two of our kids will have to be geniuses and get full scholarships because I could only afford to send two of them to college. All the rest of my money will be in your closet, right?"

Marteen's eyes are holding back tears. She laughs and says, "I won't spend that much baby. Not if we have all those kids!"

"Are those tears of happiness or sadness?"

"Happiness," Marteen answers.

"Okay, good. Now let's get out of here because I want to take my time and polish my beautiful, sweet diamond."

Marteen grins, crosses her legs, and says, "Boy, why are you talking dirty to me in this expensive dress?"

"I'll buy you a new dress."

"Mmm hmmm...lawd have mercy. Well, I'm driving us home because I drive faster than you."

"Okay, let's get out of here." He gives her his keys.

Stay tuned because happy doesn't last long.

CHAPTER 28

James is up again watching Marteen sleep. He's wondering if that song Gia sang was really about him. The last thing he needed was her trying to make Marteen jealous. Damn, he needed to talk to her, though, like ASAP, before Mama Jo gets in the way of his best friend's happiness. He is still staring at Marteen.

He was so happy and ready to commit to her. Like all in, because he loved Marteen with everything in his soul, and he knew she was feeling the same. But he was conflicted. He really needed to find out about this little girl because he knew his friend would want to know if he had a daughter.

Marteen was stirring in her sleep, and James reached over to pull her close into his arms. He kissed the back of her head. Damn, he was the luckiest man alive. He was going to love her for the rest of his life.

Marteen pushes back into him, and James holds her tighter as he drifts off to sleep. Marteen is awake, but her eyes are closed. She's wondering why her man can't sleep at night. She hopes he's not thinking about Gia because she didn't trust that woman as far as she could throw her. The way she smiled when she mentioned her new song, she really wanted to wipe that smile off her face.

James was hers, and if need be, she'd fight for him. But only if he was completely over Gia. In her heart, she felt that he was. She just wished she knew what was keeping him up at night.

* * *

Gia was walking into her hotel suite with one shoe on and one shoe off. She was bone tired and kinda pissed. First of all, she didn't like Marteen. She was low-hating, and James had the nerve to leave without talking to her. How rude and so unlike him.

She wasn't even trying to mix her sugar in their bowl, but that bitch brought it. So she was going after James with everything she had. Game on missy. So she said she didn't like sad songs? Well, she was going to be singing one when she finished with her ass!

Gia was never this chick. She always stayed away from drama, but Mama Jo changed her. Seeing James kissing Marteen had her deep in her feelings. Gia undressed and ran some bath water. She called the concierge for a wake-up call. While Gia soaked, she started humming a new tune to a new song, "Happy Doesn't Last Long."

* * *

Gia was back at her old place packing up some things. She wasn't worried about Mama Jo because Mona called and told her she was in the hospital. Gia still had the feeling that someone was watching her. She changed all the locks on her condo because she was sure Mama Jo was using Dana's old key to enter her place.

Gia had calmed down and she was no longer thinking about Marteen or James. As far as she was concerned, they could have each other and live a blessed life. Because her mother didn't raise her to be jealous, hearted, and vengeful. She wasn't perfect, so that inner bitch would come out if poked, and Marteen poked the hell out of her! But she was not going there, and besides, James kissed her!

She wasn't even hitting on him. She even made sure she was always fully clothed when she stayed with him those few days. As fine as James was, most women would have laid in his bed naked, but she kept it classy and friendly. Suddenly, Gia's thoughts were interrupted by some noise outside her front door. Gia went to her door and asked, "Hello, who is it?"

The noise stopped, and she heard footsteps running away. She opened her door just as a man's shadow turned the corner. Gia quickly locked her door, put the chain across, and thought, now who was that man, and why was he trying to open her door? Thinking about something James said, she really wished she had a man to call. She was feeling like a damsel in distress, again.

* * *

Marteen and James are enjoying breakfast at Annette's Kitchen, a family-owned business. Across the street from James's condominium. "So, did you enjoy your long weekend with me?" James asks Marteen.

"Yes, it was fun, even the Club was fun. And your friend Gia has a beautiful voice. Oh, we uh, introduced ourselves in the ladies' room last night. She told me to tell ya thanks for your warm hospitality."

"Oh yeah? Mmm, surprised you didn't mention this before."

"Oh, I didn't see the point. I'm sure she thanked ya enough."

"Mmm, what does that mean? Is that some encryption I need to figure out?"

"No"

"Good, because I don't like puzzles and shit. You know I want things to be smooth and as drama-free as possible. So, I'm going to say this again for the last time. I didn't sleep with her, and our past is in the past. I'm looking at my future, and that's with you, okay? Anything on your mind? You need to say it because I don't want you getting on the plane feeling insecure about anything, ok?"

"Mmm yeah, I understand, but it's just so typical, you know? It's almost always the man with leftover drama because I don't have any exes calling me or trying to get in. Because when I walk away from someone, I don't go back and forth! I close the door, and they can't get back in. So, if you keep the door to your past closed, women like Gia wouldn't even be a factor, and you could live your drama-free life." Marteen says as she sips her tea.

"Damn, you hot this morning, huh? Mmm, well, ok, you went there. Uh, Gia wasn't just a girlfriend. She was a real friend. Like family, and I don't close the door on family. She needed me, and I was there. Her door was and is the only door to my past relationships that remained open. But now that I have you, I'll close that door. No problem, baby! Consider it closed. But she's still like family so if she needs me, I don't know if I can just leave her hanging. But she's not staying in my crib. I am not putting her before you, not ever. Now, is there anything else you want to hit me with?"

"Mmm, well, I'm not comfortable with her calling on you for help. Doesn't she have another friend to call because that's not okay with me?"

"Baby, I'm not talking about lil stuff, I'm talking about family crisis and shit like that. I'm not trying to fix her pipes or put oil in her car. I'm talking about my mother dying or my leg falling off type of shit. So, don't worry about me being used, okay? I'm a grown-ass man. I know when a woman is coming on to me."

"Ok, just checking. But if anything falls off her ass, I'm coming with you, and we'll both put her ass back together again, ok?"

James laughed, "Yes ma'am. I'm not even playing with you. I'm scared of you."

"Mmmhmm, don't be scared. Just think with your brain instead of that monster between your legs."

"You like my monster?"

"I love your monster. That's why I don't wanna share him. So, are there any dark secrets I need to know? Like, uh, are you somebody's dad, or husband?

James smiles and says, "No, I have never been married, and as far as I know, I'm not a dad!"

"Ok, I guess I'm good."

"You sure?"

"For now, yes."

"Ok good. I'm starting to miss you already. I don't know how people can deal with long-distance relationships. This shit is for the birds, you feel me?"

"It's a big test, babe, and you better not fail, ok?"

"Oh no, I ain't failing shit. I'm graduating with honors. Now come on over here and sit with me...with you hot ass!"

"Getting all sassy with me, you might need a spanking."

Marteen laughs, "Oooh, probably. I think I need one before I leave!" Marteen sits next to her man, and they enjoy each other's company until it's time for her to fly back home.

* * *

James had just dropped Marteen off at the airport and was driving back to his place. He was seriously considering going by Gia's condo to see if she was still around. He really needed to talk to her about her little girl, Carly. James was thinking about Marteen's last words. 'Love you,' and he knew she would flip if she knew he was even thinking about visiting Gia.

But his buddy's happiness trumped her little feelings. Besides, he was gathering information to help her sister as well. James made a left turn and headed to Gia's condo. Back at Gia's place, Gia was just hanging up from her condo associate hotline when the doorbell chimed. Gia hesitated but spoke into the intercom system, and she was so happy to hear James's voice.

As soon as James walks inside, she hugs him and says, "Boy, you are psychic because I was wishing you were here. Some man just tried to open my door. It scared the mess out of me."

"What? When? Just now?"

"No, like 20 minutes ago."

James opened her door, checked her lock, and noticed some scratch markings.

"Yeah, I see some scratches here. Did you call building management?"

"Yeah, I left them a message."

"Good, so are you cool with sleeping here now?"

"Yes, I can't continue spending money on hotels. Especially now that I quit my job. So, I'm just going to stay here just another day or so, and then I'm going back home."

"Do you need any money to help you out?"

"No, I'm good. I'll just pinch my pennies until I find work, but thanks anyway."

"Okay. Have you heard from that crazy-ass lady, Mama Jo?

"Oh, I forgot to mention, her daughter called me and told me she was in the hospital. I guess she had a bad accident, and she's in a coma."

"Oh damn! When did that happen?"

"The same day she pulled that gun on me, ain't karma a mother fuck'r?"

"Yep! She is right where her crazy ass needs to be, in the hospital. She is one crazy broad!"

"I know, right? We should pray for her though..."

"Yeah ok. Uh, is that some greens cooking in that pot over there?"

"Yep, and my short ribs are almost done. Are you hungry?"

"Yes ma'am, I'm always ready for your cooking. What else you got over there?"

"Well, some sweet potatoes and cucumber salad, and I'm making your favorite cornbread pancakes."

"Oh lord, help me, I'm in heaven. Baby, fix me a plate as soon as it's ready, and I'll take two to go."

"Okay, I got you. So, your girl is gone back home?"

"Yeah, she left earlier today,"

"Oh, okay, she's very pretty."

"Thanks. Uh, I wanted to talk to you about something."

"Okay,"

"Well, I think my best friend used to date your friend, Coco. His name is Carl."

"Uh, your Carl is the same Carl that dated Dana? Omg I never put that together. Wow, that's crazy. Why didn't I know that? But I always refer to her as Dana, I forgot her nickname was Coco."

"Well, I was playing ball overseas when they were dating. And then I was down in Louisiana, so we were always missing each other, I guess. But the reason I'm here is because I was wondering if that little Carly is his daughter."

"Mmm, well, honestly, I'm not sure. Dana wasn't even 100% sure herself because she was messing around with this dude named Charles. But I assumed she was his because she named her Carly."

"Mmm, ok. Well, don't you think he should know about this?"

"Dana made me swear I wouldn't say anything, and she left Carly to me in her will. I'm her godmother, so I am not giving her to Carl. I don't care what he says."

James interrupts, "Baby, all I'm saying is he should know, and I think you need to be the one to tell him. He can get tested, and then y'all can sort all this shit out. Because if you don't tell him, I will. That's my boy, and he needs to know. Dana had no right to keep this from him."

"I know. So, I guess you can tell him because I can't break my promise, I just can't."

"Well, he just proposed to his girl. So, I'll wait until after they calm down because they are riding high, and I don't wanna rain on their little parade, alright?"

"Ok, just let me know. I'll bring Carly back to Chicago, or he can come down to Louisiana and do the test there. So, no one knows because she may not be his. Ok, is that cool?"

"Yep, now is the food done?"

"Boy, you act like nobody feeds you. Sit at the table, and I'll fix your plate. How is the boys club doing? I heard about the new center being built. I'm performing at the ribbon ceremony," Gia said

"Oh yeah? Wow, that's alright. I'll be there for sure. Yeah, that's my greatest accomplishment working with the youth. It's the best feeling, you know?

"That's why I volunteered to do it, and I didn't even hesitate," Gia replied.

"Mmm yeah, you are really something, you know? In case I forget to tell you, I miss your friendship, babe. No matter what was going on, we could always talk it out. I miss talking to your mom and nana. I love those women. They're good people and that's why I can't let nobody hurt you. Please be extra careful and make sure you talk to somebody in the building. Find out if there's been any break-ins and if that ain't talking right, just call the police and show them the scratches on your lock because someone was trying to pick that lock."

"Mmm, now I'm really scared. But Mama Jo is in the hospital so, I must have a stalker or something."

"Mmm, the more I think about this, the more I want you in a hotel because this shit is weird and unsettling."

"Mmm unsettling? Boy, your woman has you around here sounding like a professor."

"Oh yeah, well damn, I know how to speak intelligently. I just choose not to on a daily basis.

Laughing, Gia replies, "Ok, silly, are you ready to eat?"

"Hell, yes!!"

After dinner, Gia makes a big doggie bag for James, and she assures James that she is just fine staying in her place. "Well, lock up after I leave and sleep with the phone next to you. Oh, and put a knife under your pillow, okay?"

"Boy, the way I sleep, I'll probably kill my damn self," Gia laughs.

"Oh yeah, I forgot. Yeah, forget everything I just said. Just call me, if something happens, and I'll be here in a matter of minutes, okay?"

"Okay, but I'll be okay. I need to learn how to get along without your help because you are someone else's man. If you were my boyfriend, I would not want you to be anywhere near another woman, especially your ex! So, I'll be okay, but thanks so much! And let me know when to have Carly ready for the paternity test, ok?"

"Ok. Now are you sure you're okay? Because I can sleep on the couch! Oh damn, sorry, I cannot do that, but..."

"I know. Just get out of here and call your lady because she's probably looking for you."

Gia gives James a hug and kiss on his cheek and pushes him out the door. James checks to make sure she locks up. He walks to his car and drives home.

* * *

As soon as James enters his home, his phone rings, and it's Gia. "Hey, everything ok?"

"Yes, I just thought of something. I think we can have the test done sooner because they just need some DNA from them, and the test usually comes back in the mail. A friend of mine had one done last year."

"Oh, ok! Good to know. I'll talk to him when he gets back from LA. And thanks again for the food. I got enough to last a couple of days."

"Mmmhmmm... you know you are going to knock that out tomorrow! So, before I leave, I'll cook your favorite steaks and smothered potatoes, ok? Goodnight, babe."

"Ok, my mouth is watering. Thanks, and have a good night." James said and hung up.

He then calls Marteen. "Hello?"

"Hey you. Are you all unpacked and showered fresh? Because I know you are a clean freak."

"Yes, I'm on the sofa, watching the news. I called earlier."

"Oh yeah, I haven't been in long. Sorry, I missed your call. So, do you miss me yet?

"Yes, and I was looking at my work calendar. I am going to Maine for a briefing from Thursday to Sunday. So, I guess we'll have to see each other the weekend after. I'm so sorry. I forgot all about that."

"Aww man, well, it is what it is. I was hoping to take you to the ribbon ceremony for the new boys' center that's opening soon. I know Carl and Karen are coming because Carl is playing a jazz piece for me. Yeah, that's too bad, babe."

"Awwww, now I'm really bummed, this really sucks."

"Well, they say absence makes the heart grow fonder. So that just means we'll have fun catching up when we finally see each other. Don't worry, I won't dance with anyone."

"No, I want you to enjoy yourself. I know this is a big deal. Just celebrate, responsibly. It's your night!"

"Yeah ok. Just remember you said it was ok."

Marteen replies, "Mmm well, don't do anything you wouldn't want me to do, ok? Because you know I'm traveling with 4 men, and 1 female, ok?"

"Oh, now you tell me? You weren't going to say a damn thing about that. Yeah, you just work faster on getting that transfer in for Chicago because I don't trust those blue-collar boys. Them jokers are sneaky. They are just waiting for me to slip up. Then they'll be like, oh, do you wanna talk or see a movie? And the next thing you know, bam! They are slipping off the panties!!" James replied.

Marteen laughed, "No, no trust me. You don't have to worry about that. I'm loyal, baby, always have been. So tell me something sweet so I can have a restful night…"

"Well, just tell my diamond, I miss her too, and just remember what I promised her, and you'll sleep like a baby, ok? Goodnight, sweetie, I'll call you tomorrow."

"Oh my goodness, I can't wait to get back to Chicago! Love you, baby."

"Love you more. Night!" James says as he hangs up. He's smiling because he knows Marteen is probably trying to figure out how she can get back to him quicker than a fly eating shit!!

* * *

Marteen hangs up with James, and as a distraction, she calls her sister's hotel in LA. Carl picks up. Marteen says, "Hello brother-in-law, how are you guys doing?"

"Oh hey, sis, we are doing good, just getting back from a late dinner. You want to talk to Karen?"

"Yes, if she can climb off the clouds for a minute,"

Laughing, Carl replies, "Well, she's not climbing down any time soon, but here she is."

"Hey sis, I cannot believe you are calling. Did the cows come home or something?"

"Whatever, I just wanna hear your cheerful voice. When are y'all coming home?"

"Well, Carl has that fundraiser event on Saturday, so we are coming back in a few days. Then he'll be in Chicago for a few weeks, then back here again. We'll probably have a private engagement party. Just us and...Oh, have you heard from Chase? Because he's another one that doesn't have sense enough to call people."

"Mmm yes, he called me last week. He's on an assignment, but he said he had been trying to reach you all week. I told him you were out of town. Anyway, he is taking some time off as soon as he can. I'll tell him you asked about him."

"Ok, I know he's always under cover, so I don't wanna bother him too much. So, what's going on with you and James? Is he acting, right?

"Yes, he's doing good. As a matter of fact, I just got back from Chicago a few hours ago. I had fun hanging out with him."

"Awww, that's good. Carl told me he was crazy about you. Oh, hold on, let me go in the other room..."

Karen goes into the bedroom for privacy. "Ok, I'm back. So, did you find out more about James's ex? Because Carl won't say anything. He acts like they got some kind of a blood oath or something. He's so closed lip about everything."

"Oh, yeah. I finally met her. She's very pretty and could almost pass for a white girl. And that sister can sing her ass off! She definitely got some vocals."

"What? How you know that? You heard her sing?"

"Yes! She was performing at this jazz club. But it was only by coincidence because we just showed up out of the blue, and there she was."

"Mmm. How did James introduce y'all?"

"Girl, he didn't get a chance to because we left after the performance. But I ran into her in the powder room."

"Oh, okay. His ass dodged a bullet then. Well, was she bitchy or trying to act all social?"

"She was a little of both, but we were cordial. I don't know if she's the type to cause any problems. James and I have a mutual understanding, so it's cool."

"Mmm hmmm, well just don't sleep on her because they have history. So, she knows him better than you do, at this point, anyway. Okay, sis? Because James used to be something else back in the day!"

"Yes, I know. Well anyway, I was just calling your knuckle-headed self, because I kinda miss your butt."

"I know, I miss you too. I'll be home in a few days, and we can talk more. And oh, when are you coming back?"

"Well in a few weeks. James is coming out next. I guess we are going to be back and forth for a while. So, I'll see you soon. Tell Carl I said goodnight and I'll talk to you later."

"Ok, sis, love you."

"Love you more! Bye"

CHAPTER 29

Marteen woke up feeling a bit under the weather she was a little lightheaded and her throat was scratchy. Oh hell, all this traveling is taking its toll on me, she was thinking as she pulled into the parking lot. She made a mental note to pick up some Dayquil during her lunch. She wanted to get ahead of her cold symptoms. She dragged herself out of her car and into her workplace.

Later at work, Marteen was burning up and feverish. One of her associates, Donald Mack noticed. Now Donald was one of the software engineers who specialized in high-tech explosives, and he was as nerdy as anyone could get. He walked over to Marteen's immaculate desk, put his ashy hand on her shoulder, and asked her if she was feeling okay

Marteen looks down at his hand on her shoulder, and he quickly removes his hand. She says, "Uh, I'm fine, Donald. I'm probably coming down with a cold or something, that's all.
"Well, you don't look too good. Maybe you should get out of here early you know and get some rest."
"Yeah, maybe, thanks," Marteen replies but continues working. Donald shakes his head and walks back to his desk.

Marteen tries to finish her report, but she's feeling weak. As soon as she stands up, she falls hard to the floor. Donald and a few others rush to her side, and she is unconscious. Marteen is rushed to the hospital. Her heartbeat is irregular, and she has a fever of 104.

Donald, a close friend of Marteen's stepbrother Chase, calls his commander and leaves word about Marteen.

Marteen's next of kin is Karen, but they are unable to reach her. Thankfully Donald is friends with Marteen's stepbrother Chase. As soon as Chase's commander informed him about Marteen, he broke every speed limit to get to her. Marteen had a special place in his heart. He knew if she wasn't his stepsister, he would have married her. They were very fond of each other. But because of their parents and well, it was awkward to even consider such a thing. But they always wondered what if they were strangers and met at a mall, or grocery store. They would have instantly connected but they never really crossed that line. Well not exactly.

Chase made it to the hospital, and he tore ass to get to his lil sister. Chase was what women would say was easy on the eye. He was 6"4, solid build, nice tight end, with just enough muscles but not too much. He was dark like milk chocolate, he had big brown sexy eyes and very big hands. He walked with a purpose, and boy could he stop traffic. Well, if women were driving, of course.

He was handsome and didn't even know it. He was clueless and always felt awkward when women would flirt with him, so he usually dated very shy women. Because, like his name, he preferred to chase after his woman. And he'd been lowkey chasing Marteen for years.

* * *

Chase was outside Marteen's hospital room, being briefed on her condition. Doctors told him she had most likely contracted a virus, was severely hydrated and her fever was still high. They were administering fluids through an IV and keeping her overnight for observation. She was conscious and alert.

Chase breathed a sigh of relief, because seeing her hooked up to all the equipment almost gave him a heart attack. He hadn't seen Marteen in months. Even lying there ill, she was still the most beautiful woman he had ever seen.

Chase enters Marteen's room and sits down beside the bed, "Hey, if you wanted my attention, all you had to do was call instead of being all dramatic laying up in this hospital," Chase jokes.

"Hi! Well, I guess it worked, huh? How did you know I was here?"

"Uh, Donald got in contact with me."

"Oh, I forgot y'all were friends. How long have I been here?"

"Uh, some hours, I think. Did they tell you? You were admitted and staying the night."

"Mmm, I guess all that flying back and forth finally caught up with me."

"Yeah, it did. You need to stay put for a while and take better care of yourself. You scared me for a minute. Do you need me to call anyone?"

Marteen answers, "Oh no. And please don't tell our sister because she will just get on my nerves and I need my peace, right now."

Chase laughs and says "Well, I'm not going to have her mad at me, so you better call her tomorrow and just say something."

"Well, I'm probably going home tomorrow, I hope. And I thought I told you she was in LA!"

"Oh yeah, that's right. Well, you want me to call your lil boyfriend?"

"Well, first of all, he's not little. And no, don't call anyone, ok? I'm just glad you're here."

Marteen closes her eyes and doses off. Chase reaches over, holds her hand, and prays silently. Then he kisses her hand, sits back in his chair, and watches her sleep.

* * *

James was becoming anxious. Marteen wasn't answering her phone, and he hadn't spoken to her since yesterday. He left a message with her sister in L.A. He had a restless night.

Back in DC, Marteen was released from the hospital on 48 hours of bed rest and instructions on hydration. As soon as Marteen and Chase made it to her condo, she took a warm bath and went straight to bed. Still no call to James. Chase made plans to stay in the guest room while Marteen recuperated.

Marteen's phone rings and Chase picks up the phone. "Hello?"

"Uh hello, Marteen? May I speak to Marteen?" James asks, wondering who the hell is this dude.

Chase says, "Who's calling?"

"This is James. Her man. And who may I ask am I talking to?"

"Oh, hi. This is Chase. I'm Marteen's brother. She's sleeping right now, but I'll tell her you called."

"Oh, okay, well is uh she doing okay? I've been calling since yesterday. I kinda need to talk to her, if you don't mind."

Chase says, "Well, like I said she's sleeping, and I don't wanna wake her."

Marteen picks up the line in her bedroom. James replies, "Yeah, I heard that the first time you said it. But could you wake her up, please?"

"Listen, uh..."

Marteen jumps in, "Chase it's ok. I'm awake, you can hang up, please. Chase, hang up."

"Babe, what's going on? Are you okay?"

Marteen tells him, "Uh, I am okay."

"Why haven't I heard from you? Did you get my messages? Where have you been?"

"Well, I was sick. I was dehydrated and nauseous and anyway, I spent a day in the hospital. I just came home a few hours ago. I'm so sorry, I was so out of it. I was just about to call you."

"What!? You were in the hospital? You should have had someone call, baby, this ain't cool. What happened?"

"Uh, baby I was at work one minute and the next thing I knew, I was waking up in the hospital and my brother was staring down in my face. Apparently, I contracted a virus of some sort but I'm feeling better. I just need to rest for a few days."

"Wow, this is crazy. I was losing my mind. I didn't know what to think. So, Karen doesn't know anything? Why didn't your brother reach out to me?"

"No, I told you. I was in and out, so I haven't talked to anyone. I'm sorry."

"Mmm, oh okay. I understand sweetie. Well, as soon as I hang up with you, I'm going to call the airlines and try to get a flight to DC as soon as possible, ok?"

Marteen says, "No, it's ok, I'm fine. You have a lot going on. I'm ok."

"Now baby, I'm coming. I got the address in my book, so just get some rest, and uh, do you want me to try to get a hold of Karen for you because you know, she's going to freak out."

"No, I'll have Chase call her, ok? And trust me, I know how she is."

"Right, right. Mmm ok, does anything hurt? I mean are you in pain? Are you sure you're okay?"

"Mmm, no just tired. And I am fine, don't worry. My head hurt a little from my fall. I think I fell and hit my head. But I was cleared of any concussion, so please don't worry about me."

"So, you fainted? You already know I'm worried, so don't waste your breath on that one. Girl, I'm losing it, over here. I hate this long-distance crap. But get some rest and I'll be there as soon as I can. You know you're my big baby, right?"

Marteen sighs, "Yes, I know."

"Ok, good. Well, go on and rest. I'll get there as soon as I can sweetie. Love you baby."

"Ok, love you too."

Marteen hangs up and walks into her living room. Chase says, "Hey sleepyhead, how are you feeling?"

"Ok, I guess. I need you to try and call Karen for me. She's staying at the Wilshire Hotel in LA under the name Carl St. John. Get ready because you know the dramatics, are coming."

Chase laughs and says, "Yeah, I know. She is so emotional. She's been like that since the day I met her."

"Yeah, I know. Remind me to tell you about the time she organized a search party for me, and I was only across town with James."

"What, are you serious?"

"Yes, it was so embarrassing."

"Damn, I really don't want to get her started," Chase replied.

"I know just tell her I had a cold or something, cause I cannot deal with her worrying about me. But please leave her a message because if she finds out that we didn't call her, first she's going to raise hell. Trust me, I know my lil sister like a book."

"Alright, I'm on it, Are you sure you're ok? Because you don't look too good."

"Yeah, I'm going back to bed. I'll be okay. Thanks for staying with me."

"Of course. Is your guy coming out?"

"Yep, he's coming. And don't be giving him a hard time, cause I really like him, ok?"

"What do you mean?"

"You know I'm serious. I'm not playing with you."

Laughing, Chase replies, "I can't make any promises, you know I gotta check his ass out."

"No, you don't, and I know what you did to Jackson!"

"Oh, that dude was on some bullshit, and you know it."

"Whatever, just don't mess with James. He's not like Jackson, so don't play with him, okay?"

"Hey, if he passes the big brother test, then I will gladly welcome him into the family."

"Aw, I can't stand you. I'm going to sleep, and if he calls, you better wake me up!"

"Mmm, yeah ok," Chase mumbles.

"Just wake me, ok? Please?"

"Mmm, you really like this dude, huh?"

"Yes, I really do. So please don't play them games with him."

"Alright, get some rest."

Marteen lays back down and is asleep as soon as her head hits the pillow. Chase is left thinking about the new man in his sister's heart. He had a funny feeling about this one...

* * *

Back in LA, Karen and Carl are on a retreat with some producers and other new artists. They are living their best life. They were cut off from the outside world and clueless about what was happening in DC.

Back in Chicago James is taking the rest of the week off and packing his bags for his trip to DC. He is worried sick about Marteen, annoyed with her, for not calling him and he thought her brother was an asshole. But he was still trying his hardest to get to her house.

* * *

James parks his rental a block away and walks into Marteen's condo plaza with awe. The building is beautiful, and he expected nothing less from his baby. 'Damn,' thought James, he was in love with a true diva, for real.

Chase opens the door to James, and he is immediately impressed. James was about an inch taller than him and looked like he could hold his own. He still had to vet him out, thought Chase.

Chase greets James, "Hey, you must be James."

"Yeah, what's up? Nice to meet you."

Just then Marteen walks out of her bedroom and straight into James's arms. Chase walks away as they kiss and embrace. James steps back and looks at Marteen and says, "How are you feeling, baby?"

"Good, now that you're here," and she grabs his hand and leads him into her bedroom.

James looks around and says, "Damn, girl, this place is beautiful Wow! That bed is round, huh? What is it made of?"

James walks around the bed and inspects the curved headboard.

"It's marble. I designed it, you like?

"I love it! I can't wait to get in it with you. Come here, let me look at you. Are you sure you're okay?"

Marteen shakes her head, yes, and James kisses her again, but with more passion than before. He comes up for air and says,

"So, you sure you're okay? You look a little tired. I can see it in your eyes."

James sits on the chaise lounge, pulls Marteen onto his lap, cradles her in his arms, and feels her forehead. "Mmm, you are a little warm. Now tell me again what happened and start from the beginning."

Marteen tells him everything, including what her doctor told her.

"Wow, you need to stay put for a while. Let me do the traveling, ok?

Now, show me the rest of your little palace, and then I can let your brother try and punk me because I know he wants to. They both laugh.

"How did you guess? Because he does that to all of my friends."

"Well, if I had a fine ass sister, trust, I'd be scrutinizing all of the male friends. Come on, show me your palace, baby." James asks again.

"Ok, well, the master bathroom is right through here. I have a spa tub, so we are going to get in there tonight."

"Oh yeah, trust me, before I leave, we are going to baptize every corner in this place," James replies.

"Ooh, and you know diamond can't wait for you to take care of her."

"Oh yeah, that's on the top of my list. Now let's get this tour over so that I can take care of my baby.

Marteen shows James around her place, and now they are relaxing out on the terrace. Chase announces that he is going back to his office and he'll call her tomorrow. Chase briefly talked with James, and he felt that he was leaving Marteen in good hands.

As soon as Chase leaves, Marteen sits on James's lap and hugs him really tight. They sat out on the terrace for the longest time, just holding each other and enjoying the beautiful view.

Later that evening, James is undressing Marteen when he realizes he didn't pack any condoms. "Oh, shit, baby, I, uh, don't have any condoms. You're on the pill, right?"

"Uh, yes."

"Well, we don't need condoms anymore, do we?"

"Mmm...no, we don't."

"Ok, you sure? Because once we in, I'm not stopping."

"I know. I said it was ok."

"Then why are you staring at me like I said something wrong?"

"Because I'm pregnant!" Marteen says as she puts her hands over her face and cries into her hands.

* * *

James is quiet as Marteen continues to cry. He finally gets up and goes into the bathroom to bring some tissues for Marteen. He wipes her tears away. He looks into her eyes and says, "You know, you woke something up inside of me, baby. I loved you the minute I laid eyes on you. I was like, lord, please let me have this angel.

You know, I opened up my Bible, found some scriptures, prayed, and prayed for you. Yep, I had church in my living room and God answered my prayer because here we are. I don't know where you want this relationship to go, but I want my forever to be with you. I hope you are not crying because you don't want to have my baby. Please don't tell me that.

Marteen shakes her head and says between sniffles, "I'm sorry. I don't know what came over me. Of course, I want our baby. I love you. That's the sweetest, deepest thing anyone has ever said to me. I don't know why I'm crying, but it's not because I don't want our baby James. You know I want this baby. I just wish we were further along in the relationship. It's only been a few months, and I'm pregnant, already!" She starts crying again.

James smiles, "Oh, okay, well, I think the tears are just hormonal. But I'm glad we're having a baby. Doesn't matter if it's now or later. We talked about this last weekend, remember, and you were already growing our baby inside. Wow. How do you feel? Do you want me to go get you anything, like a pickle or something?" Marteen laughs. "See, I made you laugh," James says.

James kisses her tears and lips and nose and back to her lips and says, "So, uh, no condoms, right?" Marteen laughs, "Omg, you are a mess. We need to figure this out. Sex is what got us here!" "Baby, there's nothing to figure out. We are having a baby, and we love each other. Now come here. Let me take your mind off this, okay?"

Marteen answers, "Mmm, okay. But a pickle does sound good."

"Okay, I'll get you a pickle in about 3 or 4 hours," James replies.

"What?"

"Alright, 20 minutes, damn!"

Marteen laughs, "Boy, I love me some you. Lord knows I do."

"Thank goodness because I am the happiest man on earth. Now come here, baby. I need to make good on my promise.

Marteen squeals like a teenager.

CHAPTER 30

The retreat was awesome, and Karen was talking a mile a minute, and suddenly she stopped talking. She was listening to her messages from Chicago. Carl walks into the room and says "Hey, what's up?"

"I don't know, but it's Marteen. She needs me. Her job left me a message."

Back in DC, Karen calls her sister and finds out all about her stay in the hospital.

"Omg, are you sure you are okay? Is Chase still with you?"

"Yes! He went to the grocery store with James. Everything is ok."

"Well, we are booking a flight now. I'll be there tomorrow morning and don't even think about stopping me. I'm coming, ok?"

"Ok, I know you are, well I'll see you tomorrow."

"Wait, don't be trying to get me off this phone. What's up? Are you and James fighting?"

"No, we are good. He's been so helpful, and Chase too. Girl, they are acting like best friends! James wanna introduce him to one of his friends."

"What? Chase, ain't trying to run him off? Wow! He must really like James because it took him a minute to warm up to Carl.

"That's because Carl was impatient with him. James just listened to him and told him he would do the same if He was in his shoes. They hit it off, perfectly."

"Oh okay, that's nice, but you just don't sound like yourself."

"Well, I'm not going to have you trying to analyze me. I'm good."

"Ok, I'll know when I look at ya. You cannot hide anything from me you know I'm the best PI in town."

"What's a PI" Marteen asked Karen.

"Private investigator," Karen replied

They laugh. "Oh yeah, and nosy as hell. Don't forget about that one."

"Well, ok, I'll see you soon. Carl said hello and asked James to call him."

"Okay, bye, knucklehead."

"Bye, sis."

Marteen hangs up and unconsciously rubs her stomach. She knew her sister would see through her and guess she was pregnant. She just knew it.

* * *

James and Chase were driving and talking about Gia. James was trying to get Chase's take on her situation and fixing him up with her on the low. "So, you need to come back to the Windy City and put your investigative skills to use my brother because she really needs help."

"Mmm... well, I was planning on taking a long vacation anyway, and that uh, ribbon ceremony sounds interesting. I always had a soft spot for the boys club. Yeah, I'll stop through, and just give my portable phone number to your friend."

"Well, I'll introduce you as my friend and make sure she's comfortable. You might need to stake out her place and maybe sleep on her couch to be there to catch that mf!"

"Man, I don't know about all that. Is she that afraid?"

"Yep, and I'm worried about her safety because, you know, I have my hands full. Plus, your sister would kill me dead if she knew I was even thinking about helping her. But she's like family. Her mother and nana are the sweetest people on this earth, and they would want me to keep an eye on her. But trust me, she's a cutie pie and can cook her butt off. When she's nervous, she just cooks dishes of food, like all day.

"Damn, if she's so awesome, why did you let her go?"

"Man, young and dumb. I wasn't ready, and she got tired of waiting for me to get ready, so she was like, see ya!"

"Mmm she sounds like a good, level-headed woman. I can't wait to meet her. If she's half as cute, I'll take her out for dinner or something. I'm not involved with anybody. Now tell me more about this Mama Jo character because she could be a career breakout case!" They laugh.

James says, "Man, that's one crazy lady. Did I tell you I had to tackle her ass?"

"I know! You could've been shot! Usually, I have to report shit like this, so I'm going to pretend I'm not hearing this shit. But I wanna meet her. She probably got a few dead bodies in her backyard."

"I know, right? That's why I need you in Chicago, doing what you do best."

"Man, I'm on vacation, but I won't lie, I wanna see this superwoman named Gia. She sounds like a damn damsel in deep distress. This Mama Jo may have someone assisting her. That's what my experience is telling me so far."

Yep, that's exactly what she is. A damn damsel, but now let's just keep this between us."

Ok, and yeah, this all could be about that crazy ass lady."

Chase says, "Oh, no doubt."

They pull into the garage and start removing the groceries from the car. Help is coming for Gia. I just hope it's not too late.

* * *

Karen and Carl made it to DC. Karen hugged her sister so tight for the longest time. The guys are looking down at their shoes. No one is saying anything. Suddenly, Chase breaks them up and gives Karen a big hug and kiss. It's late, so after everyone is settled, the guys are drinking beer and playing spades. Marteen and Karen sit on the terrace and have one of their sisterly talks.

Carl asks the girls if they want to be partners against him and Chase, but they decline and continue with their conversation. They make plans to spend a spa day together. Just like always, they get everything in, except, Marteen never mentions anything about being pregnant.

Later that night, James and Marteen are getting ready for bed. James asks her, "So, did you say anything to Karen about the baby?"

"No, but we are hanging out tomorrow, so maybe then. I don't know; she's just so excited about the wedding, and I just don't want to interfere with her happiness."

"Well, I wanna tell Carl, but I guess I'll have to wait for you. I'll support whatever works best for you, ok?"

"Thanks baby. Did I tell you how much I love you today?

"Yep, you just told me, baby. Now why don't you get some rest because you know your sister is going to drain your ass tomorrow."

"Mmm no, she's not that bad. I'm excited to hang out with her."

"Ok, how are you feeling? Did you make your doctor's appointment?"

"Yes, he's checking me out next week."

"Oh okay. I'm sorry I won't be there with you. I need to get back to work now that I have another lil mouth to feed. So, you sure you're alright with me leaving Friday? I really need to be there for the ribbon ceremony.

"Yes, I told you to go. I'm fine, and Karen is staying until next week. I need to get back to work myself. So, it's time for us to get back into our daily routine.

"Oh, did I tell you your brother is going to the ribbon ceremony and he's donating $1,000.00 and some of his time? Bae, he's doing a safety course on Crime and Home Security."

"Oh wow, that's awesome. I'm glad you two are getting along."

"Yeah, so it's going to be just the three boys this weekend. You know, Carl is going to play a jazz number for me, and uh, Gia is also singing.

Marteen says, "What? She's performing? How long have you known about this?"

"Baby I just found out she's only doing one song."

"Well, I guess you are going to run into her somewhere so, I guess you can enjoy yourself without me breathing down your back, right?"

"That's not true. I would love to have you on my arms, and you know it, so don't go there, ok?"

"Mmm ok, well I'm going to sleep," Marteen says as she kisses him on the lips and turns her back to him.

"Good night sweetie."

He decided to leave her alone because he didn't want to argue, and he was tired of saying how sorry he was.

Marteen turns back around and faces James, "So, you don't care if I'm upset about this?"

"Yes, I care, I'm just not in the mood for drama. I cannot do anything about Gia being a performer, baby. And I don't wanna upset you, so let's just go to sleep, ok?"

"Awww, you make me sick with your cockiness, you know, just, oh, forget it! Goodnight," and she turns her back to him again.

"Good night baby. I love you," James says as he lays on his back and puts his hands behind his head. He stares at the ceiling until he can't take it anymore. He turns over, hugs Marteen, pulls her into his arms, and says the dreaded words, "I'm sorry."

He kisses the back of her head and whispers, "Stop acting mad."

"Okay, so you don't wanna talk hun?"

Marteen still says nothing. James pulled her closer to him and slowly drifted off to sleep. Marteen is furious, and she really doesn't want James to go without her, but she can't ask him to stay. It's too important to him. She just has to get over it. She finally falls asleep, mad as hell!

* * *

Marteen wakes up, and James is already dressed and cooking breakfast for everyone. Marteen takes her time getting dressed. She and Karen have an early spa appointment and then they are doing some shopping. James walks into the bedroom and announces that breakfast is ready.

"Ok, I'm not hungry, just some orange juice for me," Marteen says.

"Mmm, you don't wanna eat anything? You got another person to think about."

"No, I'll just get sick, I'm okay, thanks."

"Are you feeling okay?"

"Mmm hmm, I'm fine."

"Alright, stop this shit right now. Stop being short with me baby and acting mad at me."

"I'm not mad, well, not anymore. I'm just not hungry because of morning sickness baby, that's all. I'm ok, really, and she walks over and gives him a long, passionate kiss."

"Mmm ok, that's more like it. Now let's at least sit at the table with everyone, ok?"

"Ok, I'm right behind you. I just need to finish getting dressed."

"Ok," James answered.

Chase comes over just in time as they sit down and enjoy a table full of pancakes, bacon, eggs, and hash browns! No one really noticed that Marteen wasn't eating, well, except Karen, the famous private eye. Breakfast is over, and Karen and Marteen are on their way out when Karen stops and goes back to give Carl another goodbye kiss.

"Babe, what time are we going to the movies again? "I forgot," Carl asks.

Karen replies, "Uhm, the 8:00 show. I'll be back in plenty of time ok, baby? I promise. She gives Carl another kiss and straightens the collar of his shirt. Carl grabs her hand and kisses it.

James shakes his head and says to Karen, "Hey Karen, uh, did you leave a bottle in the fridge for Carl, just in case you're late getting back, and this nigga start crying and shit?"

"Man, go on with that bull shit, you play too damn much."

"Then get off the titi, nigga with yo whipped ass!"

"Man, I ain't thinking about you, fake ass Eddie Murphy wanna-be," Carl tells James.

"Yep, he always got something smart to say," says Karen as she rolls her eyes at James.

Chase and James give each other a high five and continue cracking up. Carl is looking at them and shakes his head, trying not to laugh himself. Marteen says, "Now, James, you know the only reason I didn't fix you a bottle is because I'm still breastfeeding you."

"That's right, shut his butt up, sis!" Karen laughs.

Marteen and Karen give each other a high five as they leave.

James says, "Yep, she ain't never lied. That's how I get down nigga. No shame in my game."

"Man, both of y'all asses are whipped. My sister's locking shit down around here. Now that's what's up!! I'm so proud of em.'"

Everyone starts laughing.

The three Amigos sit around watching basketball and talking smack. Later, Chase goes back home to pack, and James has the long-awaited talk with Carl. James sits down and tells Carl about Carly and the possibility of her being his daughter. Carl is pretty shaken by the news. He walks out onto the terrace and stays out there, deep in his head, until the girls return. James steps out onto the terrace and whispers to Carl, "You good man?"

"Yeah, just trying to process this. I'm not saying anything to Karen until I know for sure, ok?"

"Ok, cool. They are back, so get that sad look off your face."

"Oh ok, and thanks for looking out man. Love you."

"Love you too, my brother."

"Hey man, I saw her once, you know. She looked up into my eyes. She's beautiful. Damn."

"Wow, well come back inside man, and fix your face, ok?"

"Alright...ok," Carl replies

* * *

Karen burst into the house carrying shopping bags and laughing with her sister. She shouts to Carl, "Guess what babe? We got a little one joining the family soon!"

Carl looks sick.

"Boy, stop looking crazy. It's not me, silly. It's Marteen. She's pregnant with James's baby."

Carl relaxes, "Oh wow, congratulations!" He turns and looks at James and says, "Yo ass ain't said shit all day!"

"Man, I was dying to tell you, but I was waiting on Marteen to say something."

Marteen says, "Well, Miss Ace detective over here figured it out all by herself."

"Yep! First, you fainted at work, then you didn't drink any alcohol last night, and finally, you didn't eat any pancakes this morning. I was like, yep, she's pregnant!"

Carl walks over, gives Marteen a sisterly hug, and says, "Congratulations sis! I'm so happy for you guys."

Marteen replies, "Thank you."

"Yeah, I can't wait to be a dad myself," and smiles at Karen.

"Oh boy, baby, let's just plan our wedding first, ok?" Karen replies.

"Ok, oh before I forget, I bought everyone portable phones, so we can all stay connected. I'll set them up and program our numbers, ok?"

Marteen said, "Aww that's nice. Now I can have access to my baby's daddy 24/7.

"Aw shit, yeah, thanks a lot buddy," James says.

They all laugh.

Later that evening, Carl and Karen get ready to go to the movies, and Carl packs up his stuff in his suitcase. Karen says, "Baby, why were you so freaked out earlier?"

"What do you mean?"

"When you thought I was the one pregnant?"

"Oh no, I was just shocked, you know. I don't care about that. We've been down that road."

"I know. That's why I was confused about your reaction."

"Well, I don't know what to tell you. Now come here and help me pack so that we can get to the show on time." Karen helps him finish his packing, and they leave and make it on time for the show.

Across the hall, James and Marteen are sitting in bed discussing their flight schedule. James and Carl are going on a camping weekend trip in a few weeks, and Marteen is open to travel the same weekend.

James says, "Well, like I said, I'm not home those days, so if you come, baby, you'll be alone."

"Well, you can't, like pick another weekend to go with Carl?"

"No, because he'll be recording. This is the only time we can go and hang out, okay? It's not the end of the world.

"I know that. Why are you being so cocky with me?"

"Because I told you a hundred times that's the only weekend, and you're still trying to rearrange stuff."

"I'm just trying to spend time with you. Sorry if that's a problem."

James shakes his head and walks out into the living room, just so he doesn't lose his cool because Marteen is making him angry. James makes a cocktail and walks out onto the terrace to clear his head. Marteen comes over to him, hugs him from behind, and says

"You're right baby, I'm so sorry. I'm just being a bitch about everything. Just have fun on your trip, ok?"

James sips his drink and says, "Yeah ok. I'll be with you in a minute. I just need to stand here for a moment. Is that cool?"

Marteen, knowing she has somehow pissed him off, walks back into the bedroom and sits down on the bed and waits.

James is trying so hard not to snap on his woman, but she is pushing all of his buttons. She's choking him. He knows it's her hormones, but they have only dated a few months. He's wondering if this is just who she really is because if so, he should have been more specific when he prayed for her. James finishes off his drink and goes back in to talk to Marteen. He walks into the room, and she's folding his underwear and putting everything neatly in his suitcase.

Marteen says, "Oh hi, I hope it's okay. I washed all of your dirty clothes, so you don't have to worry about it. I really hope that's okay."

"Yeah, that's cool, thank you."

James walks over and sits down on the chase. He pulls Marteen over to him and says, "Hey sit here with me, I wanna talk to you about me, ok?"

"Ok," Marteen replies.

"I wanna spend time with you, ok? So, that's pretty clear, right?"

Marteen nods in agreement.

"I am an easygoing guy, no drama, low maintenance. It doesn't take much to make me happy. But what really makes me angry is when I feel like you are intentionally ignoring me. I told you several times that the weekend was filled. I even explained why, and yet, you ignored me, and tried to just make me change everything. Baby, if I tell you, no, I mean that shit, okay? Maybe you're not used to hearing no. I could be wrong, but I think you're spoiled. Now that you got a man, who's a no-nonsense man, you don't know how to deal with it."

Marteen replied, "Yeah I think you're right. I've never had anyone challenge me the way that you do, and so forceful. It's so sexy to me. I'm just so turned on by you. It's the best feeling in the world. I'm so sorry, baby. Will you forgive me?" Marteen is rubbing his thighs.

James says, "Mmm, ok. I'm going to forgive you, but you need to listen to me and stop trying to get ahead of whatever I tell you. I'm your man, ok, not your little toy. You feel me?"

Marteen kissed him, "Yes, I understand baby,"

James holds her hands and says, "So, you know what I need you to do for me?" He nods towards her closet.

"What, the uh wrap dress?"

James nods his head.

Marteen asks, "Now?"

"Yep."

Marteen runs into her big walk-in closet, searches for the dress, and puts it on with her high heels. Before she walks back out to James, she undoes her hair and fluffs it out just the way he likes it. She walks out and stands in the doorway. She tilts her head, licks her lips, and slowly unwraps her dress.

James walks over to her and says, "Damn. Now, see...I already forgot whatever the hell you did." James picks her up and carries her to her big round bed, and kisses every inch of her body. Marteen is beside herself and tries to force James inside of her. But he whispers in her ear, "What did I just tell you? Stop trying to get ahead of what I'm trying to do. Now, relax, and let me spend some time with my diamond, ok?"

Marteen sighs, "Oh God, baby, please!!"

James put her legs on his shoulders with her stilettos still on her feet. He takes Marteen on a mind-blowing trip, and when he finally brings her back home, she is whimpering like a little girl. Suddenly, she gets the monster inside of her, and she goes back around the world again. This time, she's riding the waves with her man, and they ride and ride, until finally they make it back to earth together, at the same got damn time. He holds her until she finally drifts off into a restful, uninterrupted deep sleep. She promised to never ever get ahead of her man, again.

CHAPTER 31

James and Marteen wake up and share a long shower. They are both behaving like newlyweds. Marteen is giddy and overly attentive. James is all over Marteen, rubbing her down with lotion and kissing her belly. They are pretty sickening. Carl and Karen are out on a morning walk.

James asks Marteen, "Hey, do you think you can eat something this morning?"

"Mmm no, just orange juice. This baby is so picky."

"Mmm ok, well just ask the doctor if he has any suggestions because breakfast is an important meal, ok?"

"Ok, I'll talk to him. But you better eat something too because that airplane food is really bad for you."

James kisses Marteen on the lips and says "Ok, I'll make something. Oh, I think I hear Karen and Carl. They must be back from their walk.

Marteen finishes getting dressed, and James makes a light breakfast for the three of them. Karen is washing the breakfast dishes, and James and Carl are sitting on the sofa talking when Marteen comes out wearing some daisy dukes. James happens to look up and immediately stands up, "Oh, hey baby, uh, uh, let me talk to you for a minute." They walk back into the bedroom

Carl looks over at Karen and says, "Now you see, wearing that shit ain't cool."

Karen replies, "Well, that's the style."

"Yeah if you are on the beach, but not walking around without a man at your side, that shit looks like you wearing panties. I better not ever see you in that shit!"

"Oh yeah, well, maybe I won't let you see me."

Carl said, "Baby, stop playing with me, seriously."

"What? We were going to wear them to the mall today!"

"Nah, you know better than that. I don't play that. Girl, don't let me find out..."

Karen laughs, "Just playing, but I did buy 'em, but just to wear around the house, for you."

"For real?"

Karen nods.

Carl said, "Let me see."

He grabs Karen's hand, and they run into the guest bedroom.

Back in the master bedroom, Marteen says to James, "What's wrong?"

"Uh, you wearing that outside?"

"Mmm maybe, why?"

"Baby you don't think those shorts are showing too much? I can see your ass cheeks and I don't think the citizens of DC need to see your ass."

"Baby, these are stylish, and it's hot. So, I don't see anything wrong with wearing them."

"Mmm ok. But, uh what if I ask you nicely not to?"

Marteen looks at him, walks away, throws her hands up, and says

"Alright, I'll change."

"Thank you baby, you are the best."

"Yeah, whatever. But you know you cannot be telling me what I can and cannot wear, ok? I'm a grown woman."

"Okay, I know, you are. I really appreciate it. Uh, can I help with that?"

Marteen is pulling her shorts off, and James walks over and pulls her panties all the way down to her ankles. Marteen steps out of them and James starts kissing her.

Marteen says, "You better stop. You are going to miss your flight!"

"Fuck that flight," James replied.

Long story short, James and Carl are running through the airport, barely making their flight because of those damn shorts. Chase is smiling at them when they board the aircraft and sit in their seats. Shaking his head, he says, "Mmm hmm...My lil sisters made y'all late, didn't they!"

Laughter erupts.

* * *

James and Carl were hanging out at James' crib. They dropped Chase off at Karen's place and were sitting in James' living room conversing. James says, "So, how do you feel about taking this paternity test?"

Carl replies, "I'm good, just wanna get to it, you know? A part of me really wants her to be my baby. I just pray that Karen is cool with being a stepmother."

"Yeah, I think she'll come around. It's not like you were cheating on her when she was born. She loves you; she'll be okay. Just give her time."

"Yeah, maybe we should just go to city hall and get married, so she'll be my wife, and then she'll be more inclined to stay with me."

James replied, "Man, try talking that girl out of having her dream wedding and she'll bite your head off. Just be cool. She'll still marry ya ass. That woman is insane over you. Don't you know that?"

"Yeah, I know but she's just been through so much with Dana and now she's going to have to be her daughter's stepmom. Man, she's going to blame this mess on me."

"Well, just let her get it all out, don't say shit. Let her have a tantrum, shit, she'd deserve one."

Carl asks James, "So, how are you coping with the idea of fatherhood?"

"Wow, I still can't believe it. I wanna house full of kids man, just didn't think it would happen so soon. But I'm ready, and I know Marteen will be an awesome mom. You know what I caught her doing yesterday?"

"What?" Carl replied.

"Man, she was folding my clothes all neatly and packing up my suitcase for me. She washed all of my dirty clothes and had them smelling all clean and fresh. I liked that shit man. I gotta marry her ass, like quick!"

"Damn, I had to ask Karen to help me pack. But she will wash my stuff for me, but she ain't packing for me, she'll tell me in a minute, she is not my mama!"

They laugh.

"Yeah, it just surprised me because she's so high maintenance. Yet, she's thoughtful and looks after me. Yep, she's going to be my wife. She don't know it, but she's going to be pregnant again because I wanna knock two out of the way so they can grow up together."

"Man, good luck. Marteen may have something to say about that. She might need a break."

"Nah, she'll be so busy taking care of the baby, she won't even know she's pregnant again until it happens. I'll help her with everything."

"I guess you wanna stay-at-home wife, huh?"

"Yeah, she'll find out that she doesn't have to do shit because she got a husband that got them papers," James says.

"Oh, she doesn't know your ass is wealthy?"

"Nope. As far as I know, she just loves my black ass, just for me."

"Good, but she has a nice career, and from the looks of her place, she got it going on, all by herself. Man, did you see that art hanging on her wall? And that big, long-ass white leather sofa? That girl has her own paper."

"Oh yeah, she's doing well. And she can continue with her career. It's just nice for her to know that she doesn't have to. I think I'm going to buy her a new car. Her ride is nice, but it's a two-seater and she's going to need a family-style ride. I'll take her shopping for another car."

"Yeah, makes sense," Carl agrees.

Changing the subject, James asks, "So, how was California?"

Carl replied, "Man... it's crazy. Parties all night and meetings all day. I recorded my song. We're putting it on the album. I was wondering if you could come out with me soon because I wanna record you in this one song. It's like a party song, and we got people in the background, but I want your crazy ass on it, too, you know? Might as well make it authentic."

"Oh, yeah. We can definitely do that. Just let me know when. Damn, you are about to blow up! Man, oh man, this shit is real!!" James says.

"Yep, and too bad you're about to be tied down because the women in LA are fine as hell and willing to do whatever!"

"Damn! Well, you know, we did that shit already. Time to pass the torch, my brother. I got my brick house, and she is everything I need and more. I ain't missing nothing! As a matter of fact, I already bought the ring. You wanna see?"

"What? Yeah, let me see."

James walks back into his bedroom and, a minute later returns with a Cartier box. Carl says, "Wow, that's beautiful man. She'll love it. Now when are you planning on proposing?"

"Mmm... haven't thought that far ahead. But I'll do it here in Chicago because that's where we met. Maybe at that restaurant she's always talking about."

"Yeah, or right here in the living room, that way you can celebrate immediately, you know what I'm saying?"

They do their handshake.

"Mmm yeah, sometimes you use that brain," James says.

"Man, whatever."

"I like that idea. I can have a chef come and make dinner for us, play some sounds, get down on my knee, and pray she says yes."

"What? You don't think she will?"

"I'm like, 99% sure, but you know, with her being pregnant, she could be having a moment and be like, I hate ya ass, or something."

Carl laughs and says, "Mmm, well just don't piss her off that day. She'll probably say yes. I think she loves you. I mean, she's washing your nasty ass clothes and folding up your clothes, having your big head baby, yeah, she's expecting a damn ring."

"I hope so because I wanna spend every minute with her, you know? Damn, I love her."

"Yeah, I feel you. I love my baby, too. Man, who would have ever predicted that we would be marrying sisters, like blood sisters." Carl says.

"Yeah, that's alright, huh?"

"Yep, now roll that joint up. I need to chill my nerves."

"Alright, I got you," James replied.

CHAPTER 32

James had just hung up the phone with Chase. He gave him Gia's address. Chase was headed over to check out her condo and maybe stop by her place to introduce himself. Gia was walking as fast as her legs would carry her. Someone was following her, and she was so scared because they were on her ass and moving fast.

Gia finally made it to the front of her condo building, and thankfully, one of her neighbors was walking in, so she quickly got on the elevator with her.

"Oh, hello Sharon? How are you?" Gia says.

"Can't complain. Were you just out jogging or something? Girl you sound out of breath."

"No, just power walking. Have a good day!"

Gia gets off on her floor and is digging in her purse for her keys. Her purse and most of its contents hit the floor.

Gia mumbles, "Oh lord, help me." A tall figure is walking her way

Gia stands up and screams, "Please leave me alone!!"

Chase steps back and says, "Hey, I'm sorry. My name is Chase and I'm a friend of James. He said the password was Soja and Carly.

Gia, with her hand on her heart, breathes a sigh of relief and says, "Oh Jesus, Joseph and Mary. I thought you were that man, who was following me. Did you see anyone?"

"Mmm no, some lady buzzed me in, which wasn't smart, but I didn't see anyone. Are you ok? Can I help you with that?"

Chase helps her put her items in her purse, and with her hands still shaking, he puts her key inside the lock and opens her door.

"Thank you so much. I'm sorry. I'm just a nervous wreck. Please have a seat. Can I get you anything to drink?" Gia asks Chase as she puts her things down.

"No, I'm good."

"So, James told me you were an FBI agent. Is that correct?

"Yes, I'm on vacation, but that's correct. And I understand you are a wonderful singer, right?"

"Yes, I'm actually performing this evening at a fundraiser event, but I guess you know that, huh?"

"Yes, I'm supposed to be your escort. Is that still okay?"

"Oh goodness, yes, I'm so glad you're here. I don't know who would want to harm me, well, except Mama Jo. Now, you know about her, right?"

"Yes, but why don't you tell me in your own words about your relationship with her," Chase says as he pulls out a pen and pad.

Gia starts from the beginning and tells Chase everything. While she's talking, Chase is wondering why she doesn't have a boyfriend or husband because she is drop-dead gorgeous! Man oh, man, he made a mental note to thank James because this lil woman was incredibly beautiful.

He couldn't stop staring at her eyes. Her lips were the perfect size and very kissable. Lawd have mercy, he hoped she was interested because as soon as he solves the case, he was asking her out, for damn, sure!

Gia finally finishes and walks into the kitchen. Chase notices her ass and her bowlegs. She calls out to Chase and asks if he wants to join her for a late lunch. She told him she had fried chicken, cucumber salad, grilled potatoes, and asparagus. Chase declined but said he would take a glass of water. "Are you sure? Because I don't want to eat alone. What about a salad? I can make you one."
Chase responds, "Ok if you insist. I'll just have whatever you are having.

Gia smiles and says ok. Gia is thinking, wow, he is so freaking handsome! She didn't notice a ring on his finger, so she made a mental note to ask James about him. Because she could just eat him up, he was so damn fine. They ate lunch, and Chase teased her about that scream of hers.

He told her she needed some mace or something because that scream wasn't enough to protect her. After lunch, he checked her apartment and gave her some safety tips. He got up to leave and thanked her for lunch. He told her he'd swing by and escort her to the event at 7 pm, and they made a date for brunch on Sunday. Well, it's more like a second interview. He wanted to go over any angry exes or anyone who may have a crush on her. He joked that he would need a larger notepad because he knew she had a lot of admirers. Gia was blushing like a teenager

As soon as Chase was inside his car, he called James. James answered, "Hello?"
"Man, you did not tell me that Gia was so damn fine. Nigga I'm sitting outside her house, like, I dare anyone to come near her. I'm locking

mf's up for just staring at her. Man, I wanna take her out! What does she like to do? She is super cute, and you were right. She served me some fried chicken, better than my mama's, man. I wanted to get a doggie bag, but I'm trying to be professional. Because she could put the ball and chain on my ass, for real!"

"Alright, alright...slow down partner. Just be real with her because she doesn't play games. I told you she has a two-year-old daughter to raise, so you will have a package deal, ok?"

"Man, I will be the best damn stepdad ever known. I like this woman, real talk."

"I know. She's really special."

"Absolutely, and remember when you said I should sleep on her couch? I can do all that!" Chase says as he laughs.

"Nah man, you said you didn't wanna do all that."

"Changed my mind. Just hint around to her, and I'll do the rest."

"Ok, I'll see y'all later."

Gia calls James.

"Hello?" James answers.

"Hey, I met my bodyguard a few minutes ago. Where did you find him? In the book of fineness?"

James laughs, "Damn, I guess y'all hit it off, huh?"

"What? Did he say something? He just left!"

"Yep, he called from his car. He definitely likes you."

"Really? Now tell me exactly what he said about me."

"Girl, look, I am not a matchmaker. Just get to know him, okay? And stop feeding that nigga, because he'll be too full to catch your stalker."

Gia giggles, "Oh, okay. Well, thanks for looking out. I'll see you later."

"Alright, see ya later. Oh, and Gia, you sure you're okay?"

"I am now. I finally got someone to call other than you."

They laugh.

"Yep! Thank goodness. Ok, see you soon,"

* * *

Marteen was restless and missing James, so she and Karen decided to go out for dinner at a restaurant and bar. They didn't wear those daisy dukes, but they had on their mini dresses. As soon as they stepped into the bar area, all eyes were on them.

Karen says, "Let's eat in the bar area."

"Ok, sure."

They sat down, and a handsome Hispanic waiter took their order. The atmosphere was dark and electric. They had an upscale clientele, and the girls fit right in. Marteen ordered steak, baked potatoes, and a glass of lemonade. Karen ordered the grilled chicken salad, her signature, and a glass of Chardonnay.

As soon as they were deep into their conversation, two handsome men in suits walked over, complimented them, and offered to buy them drinks. They declined and said they were waiting for someone. As soon as the two men walk away, the waiter comes over to tell them that another two men offer to send them any drink of their choice. Again, they decline.

Finally, they switch to a booth just so they can enjoy their food. Marteen says, "I forgot how this dating game was. Do you miss that life?"

"Mmm sometimes, but then I remember who I'm with. I don't trip over it. I'm happy with my life. You always think the grass is greener, but it never is. Do you think you and James will get married before the baby comes?

"Mmm, I don't know. He makes reference to us being married, but I don't know if he's seriously thinking about it. But who knows? I'm still trying to wrap my head around becoming a mother, you know? I can't believe someone is going to call me mom. It just freaks me out."

"Yeah, and someone is going to call me auntie."

"Funny how this all happened. I came to town because I thought you were pregnant, and I ended up being the one pregnant!"

"I know, right? They say everything happens for a reason, so we just gotta roll with it. But I think James is gonna ask you to marry him. I got a feeling."

"Mmm, oh, okay. I'm not thinking about it, one way or the other. I mean, I love him, but we need to figure out how we're going to do this. I'm in DC, and he's in Chicago. If I move to Chicago, it will be at lower pay, and my chances for a promotion become zero to none. So, I'm just trying to figure this out. I know James has his practice and the boys club, so his life is in Chicago. So, I was thinking about taking a leave of absence so I don't lose my seniority. I can move in with James and maybe rent out my condo. But I don't want strangers in my home, so I honestly don't know what to do. The only thing I'm sure of is I wanna be in the same place with James. I don't want to live apart," Marteen says.

"Well, I don't think you should give up your career just to move. You better wait and see if he marries you. Because if you don't get married, then you are going to be a single mom, and you will need your high-paying job. You told me you were next in line for a promotion, so just keep things as they are. Don't move to Chicago for a man, move for a husband, ok?"

"But I don't need a piece of paper to validate our love or our commitment. Yes, I want it, but I don't need it. Can you understand that?" Marteen asks Karen.

"I guess I just want you to be happy, and if you're happy, I'm happy. But if I were you, I wouldn't make any major changes until after the baby comes."

"The more I think about this, the more I think you're right. I need to stay in DC with my doctor and my comfort zone. Oh, look, he's taking pictures. Let's take one!"

"Where?" Karen asks, looking around.

"Over there, that guy with the Polaroid camera. Let's get a photo of us." Marteen points at a man in the back of the bar setting up a back screen to take Polaroid photos.

"Oh, ok."

They take their pictures and leave behind a few broken hearts as they exit the bar with their minis on and drive back home.

Gia could not decide what to wear to the fundraiser. She was torn between a short, beaded black dress with a long silk chiffon scarf draped down the back. It was a showstopper, for sure. The long, off-the-shoulder, navy beaded gown, with a high split up the middle, was also a crowd pleaser. She was wondering which one Chase would prefer.

Time was slipping away from her, so she decided on the short, beaded dress with the long scarf down the back. It was a warm night so short was better. Chase was on his way up, and she was all dressed. The zipper on her dress was stuck. She needed help, and she didn't want to ask Chase, but what could she do?

Chase walks in and is looking super fine in his tuxedo. Upon seeing Gia, Chase somehow lost all sense of time and space because Gia looked incredible, and for a minute, he couldn't breathe.

"Hi, you look so handsome tonight," Gia tells him.

"Mmm, thank you, and if you don't mind me saying, you look unbelievably beautiful. I'm at a loss. Just so incredibly beautiful."

"Oh, thank you. I'm not trying to be fresh with you, but I sorta need your help."

"Ok, whatever you need baby, oh, I mean Gia, sorry."

"Oh, it's ok," and she turns around, lifts up her beautiful hair, and asks if he could zip her up. Chase looks at her smooth skin, and he has to get control of himself because he wants this one.

He slowly zips up her dress, and without thinking, he smoothly runs his hands down her shoulders and gently turns her around to face him. Realizing she wasn't his woman, he steps back and says, "Ok, all zipped." He's staring into her eyes, and he says again, "Uh, all zipped." Gia was not sure what had just happened, but she was feeling lightheaded from his touch, and she was scared to walk because her legs were weak.

"Oh, ok, thank you. She takes a step and loses her footing. Chase quickly grabs her, and they are just too darn close. Gia grabs his arm, and she is thinking uh, oh what the hell is under his clothes because his arm is so hard! She snaps back and says jokingly, "Oh Chase, what are you going to do with me? Seems I'm always in need of your help!"

In a serious tone, Chase replies, "Trust me, it would be inappropriate for me to tell you what I really want to do to you."

Gia blushes, "Oh, mmm... well let me uh, do some retouching and we can go, ok?"

"Ok, hope I didn't offend you!"

"Oh no, I can appreciate a man who speaks his mind. I'll only be a minute," Gia says as she walks away.

Chase whispers, 'Hot damn,' and he's thinking that he should really treat James to a Bulls game or something! Praise the lord and his Kingdom!!

* * *

They arrived on time for Gia's introductions. Chase escorted her up the platform and then took his seat. He is seated at a round table covered with a silver tablecloth with Carl, James, the alderman for James's ward, his wife, and an alumnus of the boys club. The gala is packed, and the ceiling is full of gold, silver, and white balloons. Everyone is decked out and shining like new money! James is on ten, as he shares a joke with the alderman and his wife.

The lights are low, and the curtains open up. Gia has her back to the audience, and she is one badass! She performs 'Rock Steady' by Aretha Franklin. She turns around, swings her hips from left to right, and looks straight at Chase.
She sings...

Rock steady baby
That's what I feel now
Let's call this song, exactly what it is...
Rock steady...
Awww, rock steady baby
It's a funky and low-down feeling
Swing your hips from left to right, rock rock steady, baby

Gia licks her lips, swings her hips, and is singing Aretha's song!!! If you close your eyes, you would swear it was Aretha Franklin on that platform. Chase is mesmerized. He looks over at James and mouths, 'Thank You!' James nods in response, and he too, is mesmerized by Gia. He is thinking to himself, 'damn girl'.

She is swinging her hips, and her dress fits her like it was poured on. Her beautiful legs are on full display, and the entire room is nodding and moving in its seats. She raises her arms above her head and jams to the beat. She sings and throws her hands up in the air...

Rock...steady...
Rock steady.. baby...
It's a funky and low-down feeling awww,
Move your hips from left to right...
Rock steady

As soon as she is done she throws kisses to the crowd. People were standing, and one man shouted, "I love you, baby!" Gia waves and says, "I love you too, baby," as she exits the platform. Chase is on her ass. He meets up with her at the rear. She whispers in his ear that she is going to the ladies' room.

He grabs her hand and walks her to the lady's room. Gia freshens up and reapplies her lipstick. Chase is standing outside the door like a bodyguard waiting for her. Chase says, "Damn girl, you just gave the Queen of Soul a run for her money. Your voice is solid, and the way you move them hips had me feeling some kind of way!" "Well, thank you, and uh, what way were you feeling?" Gia asks. "Well..."

Before he can finish his sentence, James and Carl walk up. James hugs Gia, gives her a kiss on the cheek, swings her around, and compliments her on her performance. Carl hugs her, gives her his personal phone number, and asks her to call him so they can discuss Carly. He rushes off to get ready for his performance. Gia nods, ok.

Chase walks over and stands next to Gia because people are walking up to congratulate her and compliment her on her singing.

The night winds down, and Carl plays his number, a jazz hit by Peter White. He also has an outstanding performance.

Gia and Chase make a quick exit out the back for a nightcap. They end up at Shelly Jeans. They are sitting in the back in a cozy little booth sipping coffee with a shot of baileys and cream. "So, I'm curious: how is it that a beautiful lady like yourself is single?" Chase asks Gia.

"If you find the answer to that one, please tell me because I honestly don't know. I mean, I meet interesting people all the time, but I just never connect with them.

"Are you sending off that I don't want to be bothered signal? Or are your expectations not being met?

"Mmm, are you trying to profile my dating methods or something?" Chase smiles, "No, I'm not, beautiful. I just want an understanding of what I need to do to get a date with you."

"Oh, okay, well, the easiest way for *you* to get a date is to simply ask."

"Mmm, somehow, I didn't get the impression that it was that easy."

"Well, it's not difficult at all. I guess the reason I'm still single is because men are afraid to ask me out. The ones that do are not my cup of tea, and I'm not one to play dating games. I value my time. When I commit to dating, then I'm all in. I want to be stimulated. Not necessarily sexually, but intellectually. I was never a party girl. I'm more of a long walk in the park, summer picnic, and long drive to the countryside type of girl. It's just hard to find a man that enjoys doing those things, you know what I mean?"

"Mmm, well, most guys will fake it like they want those things to be with you. I'm sure because I don't know if you know this, but you are one of the most beautiful women I've yet to lay my eyes on. I am only saying this because it's true.

"I just so happen to like long walks, picnics, or a drive up to one of those cabins around Wisconsin, and hopefully, I will get snowed in with you. That's a dream date for me. I like fishing and hunting. With a few of my buddies, we always go to Lake Tahoe and get up close with nature. It's beautiful there."

"Mmm, I like frying a fresh catch. That sounds like fun."

"Yeah, it is. So, what do you think about us going out regularly?"

"Well, that sounds good, but I'm leaving for Louisiana next week to be with my daughter. She's two, and she has a birthday coming up next month. I don't know how much James has told you, but I'm sorta back and forth from Louisiana to Chicago.'

"Yes, I know about your little girl. I think that it's wonderful that you are raising your best friend's daughter. I happen to love little people, so that's not an issue. I guess what I'm hoping to do is get to know you in any way I can. I can see you here, or I can come down to Louisiana and take you out. It's not a problem for me at all," Chase replies.

"Okay."

"Okay meaning yes, you'll be happy to date me?" Chase tries to clarify.

"Yes, I will be happy to date you."

Chase reaches over and takes her hand, "Whew, yes! Now that we got that out of the way thank you for allowing me to come into your space. I hope I can stimulate you intellectually." He kisses her hand and continues holding it.

"You are welcome. Thank you for being the perfect gentleman tonight. It's really nice to meet you, Chase. I really mean that, ok?"

"Ok, so when I drop you off, are you going to feel safe in your place alone tonight?"

"Oh, James told me about you sleeping on the sofa, but I'll be okay. Just answer your phone if I call."

"Always, for you. I'll be no more than 15, maybe 10 minutes away, okay?"

"Okay. Thank you, so I guess we should go on back, huh?"

"Yes, I guess I've taken up enough of your time. Oh, do you have a portable phone?"

"No, not yet."

"Ok, I'll get you one on Monday. What about your car? Are you one of those people who only fills their tank halfway?"

Gia laughs, "I think it's at half a tank. I don't know, why?"

"You need a full tank because if you're out running errands, I wouldn't want you to be pulling up to a random gas station with some stalker after you. So, I'll swing by in the morning and fill up your tank, ok?"

Gia smiles.

"What?" Chase asks.

"Now I remember what it feels like to have a real man in my life; thank you."

"You're welcome, beautiful."

CHAPTER 33

Marteen and Karen are just leaving the doctor's office. Marteen is eight weeks pregnant, and all is well with the baby. Marteen says, "I can't wait to call James. He's waiting to hear back from me."

"Ok, do you think you can eat something?"

"Yes, I'm hungry."

Karen says, "Ok, let's go to Germaine Street and eat lunch at that Bistro.

After lunch, they head back home, and Marteen immediately calls James. James picks up, "Hello?"

"Hello, handsome," Marteen answers.

"Hey you, how did everything go today?"

"Oh, nothing but good news. I'm good, and our baby is good."

"Yes! Thank goodness! What took so long? I was starting to worry."

"Oh, we stopped and had lunch. I was starving."

"Ok good. What did you eat?"

"Steak and potatoes."

They both laughed.

"Damn, you really were hungry, huh?"

Marteen says, "Yes, I was. So how did the event go last night? I was trying to stay up to hear from you, but I guess I missed your call, sorry."

"That's ok, we did great. We got a lot of donations, and everyone was calling and thanking me, so it was solid."

"Oh, that's awesome. I'm glad you did well, and I'm sorry I wasn't with you."

"Yeah, me too. What else have you two been doing in DC?"

"Mmm, well, the same day you guys left, we went to this restaurant and got hit on by so many men we lost count. It was so much fun to get out with my little sister."

"Oh, okay, well, I know they were hitting on y'all, the two dynamic duos. As long as you told them to move along, right?"

"Oh absolutely. It was just fun to watch until it got annoying, and we had to change over to a private booth."

"Mmm. Ok, when is Karen leaving?"

"Tomorrow morning."

"Oh, ok, so you're going to work tomorrow?"

"Yes," Marteen answers.

"Ok, good. Are you going to ask for the, uh, transfer?"

"Well, I was thinking about that. I have a really good doctor here in Washington, so I was kinda hoping to wait till after I have the baby."

"What? When did you get that idea?"

"Well, the move wouldn't happen for a while anyway, so I thought we could just continue commuting until after the baby. I'll work on the transition. I have a shot at a big promotion, and once I'm promoted, my schedule will ease up, and I can do a lot of work from home," Marteen explained.

"Mmm, so what about us? Don't you wanna be in the same city with me? I thought we agreed."

"We did. I'm just putting it off until after I deliver the baby."

"Marteen, now, what if the baby comes early or late? I could miss the birth if you got your butt in DC. Why are you making these decisions without discussing it with me? Don't I get a vote? It's my baby, too."

"Baby. I'm talking about my career. I can't just up and move and lose everything I worked so hard to obtain. When I'm closer to my due date, I'll take my maternity leave and move back temporarily. I'll find a different doctor, okay, so we'll be together, and I'll take ample time off so we can both bond with our baby, ok?"

"Well, it sounds like you have your mind all made up. I guess you're pulling all the strings again."

"Don't talk like that. I'm not pulling any strings. I don't like living apart either. Things are just complicated. This all happened so fast, so let's just take a moment to adjust, okay? Don't be upset with me."

"Okay, I'm not upset, just surprised, that's all. I thought everything was good and settled. But I see you got people all in your ear, and now you are second-guessing yourself. I know your sister is in our business because you know we talked about you moving to Chicago. I told you I got a lot of businesses to run, and moving isn't an option. You were going to move your ass here. Now, how are we going to live apart? Baby please, just, mmm, look, let me stop before I say something I'll regret. Let's just talk more about this in person. I'll be out there this weekend."

"Okay."

"Alright, goodbye baby."

"Bye, sweetie, love you."

"Love you too. Oh, and before I hang up, I want you to think about this more thoroughly. I'm not just your baby's daddy; I'm your man also. We are going to be a family, and families are supposed to be together, okay? So whatever sacrifices you make are for your family, it's for us. Think about that, okay? I love you, and I'll talk to you later. He hangs up.

* * *

Chase was just leaving the hospital where Mama Jo was admitted. He interviewed her nurses and doctors and found that Mama Jo had a male visitor almost every day. He seemed very fond of her. Her daughter Mona was apparently away at the University of Illinois.

Chase had a good description of her visitor, and he headed to Gia's place to see if she recognized him. He knew this person of interest could possibly be Gia's stalker. He was getting close to solving the case. He just needed to talk to a few more people and put a name to the mystery visitor.

So far they had been on a few dates, and things were going very slow. She was keeping him at arm's length, and it was making him even more anxious to get to know her more intimately. Maybe tonight would be his chance to hold her and maybe get a real kiss.

* * *

Chase was on his way up, and they were going on another date. He was taking her to a blues club in Indiana. He made sure she was unfamiliar with the club, and so far she had never heard of the place. He made her so nervous, and she didn't trust herself with him, so she made sure he didn't get too close. He gave her butterflies, and she was afraid of what was underneath his neatly pressed clothes. She could only imagine. Lord have mercy on him because when the time came, she wasn't holding anything back!

Gia buzzed Chase up, and she quickly checked her image in the mirror. She opened her door to Chase, and boy, did he look delicious, thought Gia as she smiled and kissed him on the cheek. "Hey beautiful, wow, you look amazing as always," Chase says. "Thank you, babe."

"You are welcome. So, are you ready to spend some quality time with me?"

"Yes, always."

Suddenly, Chase makes a bold move. He pulls Gia into his arms and kisses her on the lips. He couldn't help it. She was so sexy. Gia wrapped her arms around him and kissed him right back. When they break apart, Chase lifts her chin and says, "No more pecks on the cheek. I think we are passed that, okay?"

"Okay," as she kisses him again. This time Chase takes a step back and says, "Okay, let's get out of here before I forget my manners."

"Okay, I'm only following your moves."

"Mmm, is that right? So, if we don't come back here tonight, you're okay with that?"

"Yes, because I know you wouldn't take advantage of the fact that I am allowing you to lead me."

"Awww, see...I knew it was too good to be true. You too smart for ya own good."

"Mmm hmmm, that's right. So, you know nothing happens unless I want it to, right?"

"Ok, beautiful, whatever you say," and he grabs her by the waist and kisses her on the lips again, and he whispers, "You're killing me."

* * *

Marteen walks into her boss's office wearing her power suit. She's dressed in a Brooks Brothers gray pinstripe skirt suit with a white high collar shirt and her black Chanel pumps. Mr. Arnel walks around his desk to welcome Marteen back to work.

"So, you look great, but are you sure you are ready to come back?"

"Well, I wanted to talk to you about that."

A half-hour later, Marteen walks out of her boss's office on a paid leave of absence. She was cleaning up her work area and then going home to pack. Her mind was made up, and she was going back to Chicago to be with her man. Life was short.

She found her guy, and although he was cocky and opinionated, he challenged her, and he loved her so hard. She felt the love. She never had to guess or wonder. He showed her in more ways than one. Marteen didn't know if they would get married, but she knew for sure that they would be happier and stronger together living in the same city, under the same roof.

She was stepping out on faith and a pinch of unconditional love! After all, she knew she could hold her own. Her finances were solid. She had an aggressive savings account, stocks, bonds, and an upscale condo. So, God forbid if things ever went left, she could easily take care of herself.

* * *

James was having a hard time accepting Marteen's decision to stay in DC. Later that evening, he was sitting in his living room watching a Bulls basketball game with Carl and Chase.

Carl says, "Man what's up with you? Why the somber face?"

James replied, "What? Somber, man, get out of here. Trying to sound like you read books."

They all start laughing. Carl says, "Hey Chase, am I right or wrong? Doesn't he look like somebody just stole all of his weed?"

"Yep, you do look a lil green. What's going on? You miss Marteen, don't you?"

James replied, "Man, I just got shit on my mind, that's all. And yes, your sister got me all messed up."

Chase said, "Mmm, well, I think y'all will be okay. Just give whatever it is some time and try not to overthink anything."

Carl said, "Yeah, whatever it is, y'all will be okay. So, sit your green ass down and watch Jordan do his thang!"

James smiles, "Yeah, ok, pass me my joint, and get yo feet off my table!"

They continue watching the game, and James pretends that all is good. But he's dying inside because he wants his woman with him. He doesn't like the idea of her being pregnant and alone in DC. He had to figure something out, and she wasn't answering her phone.

Back in DC, Marteen was leaving the post office. She shipped some of her stuff to Chicago. She locked up her condo and arranged to have her mail forwarded. Her car was all packed up, and she got on the road. She was driving her white two-seater Corvette all the way to Chicago.

Marteen purposely didn't call anyone, because she had a lot on her mind, and she knew the 10-12-hour drive would bring some clarity to her soul. Besides, she couldn't wait to lay her head on her man's chest and listen to the beat of his heart. With him, is exactly where she's supposed to be.

* * *

James tosses and turns all night. He hasn't heard from Marteen, and he's on edge. He gets up and tries calling her cell phone, but it goes straight to voicemail. He takes a quick shower, brushes his teeth and packs a bag. Where the hell was she? Suddenly he heard some noise in his living room. He walks out of his bedroom, and Marteen is standing in the entry hall, staring at him.

He rushes over to her and lifts her off her feet, and hugs her so freakin tight she can hardly breathe. "I was on my way to DC. Baby, why didn't you call me? I was losing my mind. Are you okay?" James says.

"Yes, I just wanted to get here. I drove all the way, I'm sorry, I just wanted to get here. I'm starving."

James laughs, "Okay, I'll fix you something. Are you sure you're okay? Damn, you feel so good and smell so good, baby, so damn good!! I love you so much, man. You had me imagining all types of shit!"

"I'm so sorry. Can you let me go just long enough so I can soak in the tub? I'm tired from driving all night."

"Oh, yes, yes. I'll run your bath and make you something to eat, okay?"

Marteen walks into the bedroom and notices his duffel bag on the bed. "Oh, you really were on your way to see me, huh?"

James comes up to her kisses her again, and says "Yes, damn right I was. I didn't know if you were somewhere hurt. I told you; I was scared as hell. I still can't believe you drove all the way here! I guess you really love my black ass, huh?"

"Yes, I do," and she kisses him with so much love. He picks her up and the only thing she's hungry for is her man. They make love over and over until the sun pours into the window. James looks into her eyes and says, "You're in trouble, you know that, right?"

"For what?"

"For driving all night and not calling me back. You lucky you pregnant because I would spank you."

"You spanked me before, and I think I was pregnant."

"Oh, so you like it when I spank you, huh? Damn, I forgot you were a freak." They both laugh.

"Yes, and that's why you love me so much."

James replied, "Yep! You put it on me the first time, coming over here in that dress and no draws on. You know, you raped me that night. I was like, damn, she a straight gangster. Because afterward you were like don't say shit to nobody!"

Marteen laughed so hard.

James continues, "You made me make you some coffee, and then you grabbed my butt on your way out. You told me to wait 10 minutes and then follow your ass over to your sister's house. You remember that?"

Marteen is laughing so hard she can't breathe. James was actually telling the whole truth and nothing but the truth.

CHAPTER 34

Carl receives the test results, and he is the father. Carly is 99.5% his daughter. The news knocked him to his knees. He can't believe Dana took those precious years away from him. He calls James, but James can't talk because he is out with Marteen. Carl sits in the dark, trying to figure out how to tell Karen.

His heart is beating so fast because he wants to hold his daughter. He needs to see her, kiss her, and tell her he loves her. He goes into the bedroom, grabs a duffel bag, and starts to pack.

Suddenly, he hears Karen coming back from her hair appointment. He snaps back into reality and shoves the bag back into the closet just as Karen walks into the bedroom. Not paying any attention, Karen says, "Hey baby, I'm sorry it took me all day. But you know I can never get out of that shop at a reasonable time. Karen finally looked over at Carl and immediately knew something was wrong.

Karen asks, "What's wrong?"

"Baby, uh, why don't you sit? We need to talk."

"What is it? Is my sister ok?"

"Yes, she's fine. It's about us."

"What about us, baby? Just tell me because you are scaring me."

"Ok, but let's sit down first okay?"

He pulls Karen over and sits her on his lap, and she hugs him.

Carl kisses her so hard and whispers that he loves her so much.

This is starting to worry Karen because now she's scared. She says, "Please, baby what's wrong? Tell me!!!!"

Carl tells Karen everything, and when he finally stops talking, Karen stands up with her hands over her mouth. She paces back and forth for a few minutes. Carl is silently watching her and praying she understands. Karen looks over at Carl, with fresh tears in her eyes, shakes her head, and says, "I can't do this. I just don't know, I don't know if I can. She grabs her purse and keys and walks out.

Carl jumps up and follows her. He beats her to the front door, blocking her from leaving, and says, "Baby let's just talk about this, please. I didn't know about this, I'm just as shocked as you are. Please, please talk to me. Just tell me what you want me to do. Just don't leave me, okay?"

Karen screams, "Just let me go, I can't breathe, just let me go!!!

Carl holds her, and she slides down. He picks her up and carries her back to the sofa, and he holds her while she cries. He sits and rocks her for the longest time. Between crying, she mumbles that she wants a baby too. Carl says, "Ok, we can have like a hundred!"

Karen laughs and says, "A hundred?"

"Hell yeah! I'm gonna put you in the Guinness Book of Records."

"Boy, you are so crazy. You better be glad I love you."

"I am, baby. I'm so sorry. When you are ready, we can, uh, go visit her, okay?"

"Oh lord, give me strength. But no, uh, damn! Uhm, I think you should go alone and spend some quality time with your baby. I'll be here when you come back, and I'll fix the guest bedroom for her, okay?"

Carl lifts Karen's chin, and he's fighting back the tears, and he says, "I love you so much. I wish I could take away your disappointment and pain and whatever else you endured because of me. I know I don't deserve you, but I promise before God that I will spend the rest of my life making you happy and giving you everything you thought you wanted. You hear me, baby?"

Karen replies, "I hear you. I know you love me. This is just another freaking test, you know? Just when things couldn't be better, a damn rock is thrown at our house. Well, I guess that's why we have broomsticks so we can just sweep this mess up and get back to life now. I am not saying I'm okay, but I will be because I cannot change anything. She's yours, so she's automatically welcome. I know I'll fall in love with her too because she's a part of you, you know?"

Carl said, "Yeah, I know."

"But, I want my baby, I mean, our baby, but maybe not now. I was just in my feelings earlier. I can't give you your first, and that hurts me. It really hurts. But we have time, so let's just get to know Carly, okay? she says as she wipes her eyes.

"You sure?"

"I think so. I could change my mind tomorrow because I'm just living on autopilot right now. You know, I never saw this one coming. So, anyway I'm sorry you didn't get to see your baby come into the world. I know you are dealing with a lot. Are you okay?"

Smiling, Carl kisses the tears on her face and says, "I'm good. You are so freaking amazing. I think I need another heart because you got this one full." He kisses her again, picks her up, and carries her to the bedroom.

That night they made love, and it was so magical. The strength of their love, the bond that they have, can withstand the test of time because of the power invested into it. The glue that holds it all together makes it truly, truly unbreakable. Man, oh man, the power of love. It's a beautiful thing.

* * *

Chase had a lead on the mystery man. He was seen out with Mama Jo on many occasions. From years of experience, he knew he had to back pedal. So, he talked Gia into driving with him to Champaign, Illinois, to see Mona. They took Mona out to dinner, and she told them about Bobby, a.k.a. Bugger.

They left Mona and drove to a hotel and checked in for the night. Chase was still acting like a gentleman, so he slept on the sofa, giving Gia the king-size bed. Gia woke up before Chase, and she was staring at him. He was sleeping so peacefully. He had one arm over his face, and the other one was on his stomach. He was so muscular and fit. She wanted to jump on top of him and take full advantage of all that masculinity. But she didn't want to make the first move.

He was taking his gentlemanly behavior business to another level of pain and torture. God, he was so handsome. She was wondering what he looked like when he was angry. Does he shout or hit the wall? Does he even have a temper? Oh, and when he smiles, his eyes light up. She loves how he claps his hands when he laughs. Dammit, she had to think of something else.

Gia takes her shower, a cold one. Chase opens up his eyes and looks at the ceiling. He's thinking damn, she's in the shower, shit. He grabs his manhood and curses out loud. He sits up just as the bathroom door opens. He waits a few minutes, grabs his overnight bag, and goes into the bathroom. The smell of coconut and sweet strawberries fills the air. He is tempted to go back into the bedroom, but he doesn't want to mess up his chances. He wanted her to want him as much as he wanted her.

After his ice-cold shower, he puts on a pair of shorts. His chest is bare because he plans on going to the pool to cool off. Gia walks in and says good morning. She's wearing a sarong with a two-piece bikini. He's thinking she's doing this shit on purpose, what the hell.

She walks up to him. He's still sitting because he's afraid to stand. She leans down and kisses him on the lips. He pulls her closer, kisses her belly button, and licks her stomach. She moans, and Chase looks up and into her eyes. She's so beautiful. He says, "You feel it, baby?" Gia says, "Yes."

Boy, did she feel the heat from his kiss. Her stomach was on fire, and what happened next will forever be a mystery. Gia would never figure out how Chase got her undressed so fast and under him. One minute she was standing in front of him. She blinks, and she's completely naked and he is deep inside of her. He was worth the wait.

Chase is by far the greatest lover and, apparently, a very talented magician.

CHAPTER 35

Chase and Gia are on the road driving back to Chicago. They are behaving much differently than two days ago. Chase is rubbing Gia's thigh, and Gia has her hand over his. They are exclusive, and Chase is making plans to take her camping with him and another couple.

He is so happy to have such a beautiful woman as his girlfriend. He is floating on a cloud, and he has a sneaky feeling that she is floating on the same cloud. They made love all day yesterday and stayed an extra night. Chase was now familiar with every inch of her body, and she took her time getting acquainted with his.

Gia jokingly said, she could pick just his body out of a lineup She didn't need to see his face because she gave him a full body examination. And she wasn't lying. Lord have mercy, she was incredible, Chase thought. Last night was unforgettable. He was almost certain that he had experienced a glimpse of heaven.

When he thought he was drained and dead to the world, Gia bought him back to life. She rose the dead. She kissed him from head to toe. She turned him over on his stomach and kissed the rest of him. She slid her tongue down his back, and before she went further she whispered, "You can't say I never kissed your ass!" And she plants a kiss on each of his ass cheeks. Then she kisses the back of his thighs and calves. She turns him over and she sees she has awoken the dead. She sits on his manhood and rolls her hips slow and steady.

Just when the world starts spinning around, she picks up speed. Chase sees a glimpse of heaven. He explodes and shakes uncontrollably because this woman, his woman, is the baddest woman alive! He would kill Bugger with his bare hands for even thinking about hurting her because she was his to protect. Yep, Gia Soja Dubai was his Queen.

* * *

Gia is packing to go back to Louisiana. It's so bittersweet, she's excited to see Carly but sad that she is leaving Chase... He is a Godsend because he has been so attentive to her every want and need. She was cooking dinner for them, because tonight was her last night in Chicago for a while...He was coming for a visit in a few weeks to meet her family. She was so excited to have him in her life. They promise to talk everyday. She felt like a teenager again because she had butterflies just thinking about him... she just couldn't get enough of him... they were always kissing and holding hands...he brought out her inner freak.. she couldn't believe she kissed him all over his body, if she could pour herself inside of him, God knows she would do it. He was so good in bed, he made her toes curl, it was all unreal.

* * *

Chase was in traffic, waiting for a freight train to pass. His mind drifts off to Gia. She was everything he ever dreamed of and a little extra. From the way she moaned when he barely touched her. Lord have mercy. The things she did to him, the way she moved, and the way she kissed had him floating on air. Damn, he couldn't get enough. The stares she got when they were together, made him crazy with jealousy. He wanted to lock her away just so he could have her all to himself. The other day, he was meeting her for lunch. He watched her walk into the restaurant, and every man had to do a double-take at her. He was all smiles because she was coming to his table. Her sexy ass walked right into his arms and kissed him on the lips. He was beaming with joy! He didn't want her to leave, but he knew she had to be with her family. But as soon as he got that damn Bugger, he was coming to Louisiana to claim his woman! The train had finally passed, and he drove on to Gia's condo.

Chase arrived just in time. Gia gave him a big kiss and hug. He sat down to eat with her, and they barely touched their plates because they were so eager to hold each other. Chase holds Gia at arm's length and says, "Let me just look at you, mmm, ahh, I see."

"What?" Gia asks.

"Mmm, I see. You are more beautiful than you were yesterday."

"Boy, I thought something was wrong with me!"

"Baby, nothing is wrong with you." He takes her hand and places her hand on his heart. "Feel how fast it's beating? Because whenever I'm this close to you, it feels like my heart is going to explode!" He pulls her into his arms.

"I know! Just come with me. We can get a small place together. You can be an agent in Baton Rouge, right?"

"Well, it's not that simple, baby. But trust me, I'm going to think of something. I know I cannot make it too long without you in my arms. Damn, you feel so good to me. This is tripped out because I've never felt this way before. I think you put something on me!"

"I know and you put the same thing on me. I don't wanna leave you, I swear I don't." Gia and Chase kiss and take their time, hoping that their few hours together will last a long, long time.

* * *

Chase wakes up and Gia is up singing and making breakfast. He smiles because he loves the sound of her voice. She's singing that silly song of hers, 'Never trust a man.'
Gia sings:

> Never trust a man with a badge in his hand...
>
> Say never trust a man, never trust a man
>
> With fingers and a hand...he ain't the one...
>
> Learn from me, ya hear me?
>
> Never trust a man.
>
> Never trust a man if he's driving a mus-tanggg
>
> He'll tear you apart, he'll break your heart,
>
> Learn from me, please hear me...
>
> I'm all for having fun; ain't trying to block no one...
>
> But if...

"Oh, hey babe, good morning," Gia says to Chase.

"Don't let me stop you from singing your male-bashing song."

Gia laughs, "Baby I'm just singing the gospel truth, you know. Now, if I cannot trust myself with you, then why should I trust you, with me...think about it."

"Awww, sweetie, it's too early for that philosophical debate, ok? Fix me whatever you're cooking. I'll be back in a minute."

Gia remembers she is out of bread, so she knocks on the bathroom door and tells him she's running to the market on the corner. Chase screams back, "Ok, sweetie." Gia grabs her wallet and keys and walks to her elevator.

Chase stops in the middle of lathering up and dries off as quickly as he can. He throws on his jeans, t-shirt and grabs his gun and badge. He runs after Gia. He has a feeling that Bugger is probably waiting for an opportunity to catch her alone. His heart is beating fast. He takes the stairs two at a time.

As soon as he makes it to the street, he looks down toward the market and a man is dragging Gia into an alley. Chase takes off, with lightning speed. Gia is struggling with Bugger, and he has his arm around her neck. With his left hand, he pulls out a box cutter. Chase enters the alley just as Bugger has his left hand in mid-air and Chase screams, "FBI!!! Don't move you son of a bitch!"

Bugger throws Gia to the side and takes off down an adjacent backyard. Chase runs to Gia, checks her out, and asks if she's ok. He then tells her to call 911 and he runs after Bugger.

Sirens are blasting as Chase is almost on Bugger's ass. He has Bugger cornered and tells him to drop his weapon and get on his knees. Bugger drops his box cutter and slowly turns around and Chase says "Move. Please move so I can send your punk ass straight to hell." Bugger says, "I surrender. Please don't kill me, I wasn't doing anything."

"Nigga save that shit. So, you wanna terrorize women, huh? Well, let's see if you can go toe to toe with a man."

Chase pats down Bugger, steps back, and then puts his gun in the back of his pants. Chase says, "Come on, if you make it past me, I'll let you go free."

"Uh no, uh, I don't want no trouble. Man, I didn't do anything."

Chase walks over to Bugger, shakes his head, and slams Bugger into the garbage can a couple of times. He throws him hard on the ground and pins his hands behind his back. Bugger is bleeding and screaming Chase tells him to stop crying like a bitch! And just then two patrol officers run over. Chase identifies himself and they cuff Bugger and take him away.

Chase runs back to Gia, and she is sitting in the back of an ambulance, arguing with the paramedics. She refused treatment until she knew her man was okay. Chase says "Hey, I'm here baby, are you okay?"

Gia hugs him so tight and asks if he's hurt. She's rubbing all over his face and arms and she's crying now because she knows another minute and she would've been gone. Chase saved her life!

* * *

James was trying to leave the house, but he was having a hard time leaving his woman. He was watching her as she slept. She looked so beautiful laying there all wrapped up in his sheets. He couldn't thank God enough for sending her to him. He kisses her one more time.

He leaves out the door, gets in his car, and drives to work with the biggest smile on his face. He turns the radio on, and the voice of

Herb Kent, the cool gent, fills his car. He's wondering when would be the best time to propose to Marteen.

Back at home, Marteen spent the day unpacking and cleaning up the house. She also washed his clothes and linens. After everything was neat and clean, just the way she liked it, she started dinner. She had never cooked for James because he always wanted to cook, and she loved his cooking.

James walked into his house, and something smelled so delicious. He also noticed that the house was cleaner and smelled fresh. Marteen walks into the living room, kisses him, and asks him how his day was.

James looks at her and says, "So you can cook?" They laugh.

"Of course I can cook. What type of question is that?"

"Well, you never cooked anything before, so I just assumed you didn't know how."

"Boy, stop playing. You know I can cook. Dinner will be on the table in 15 minutes, ok?"

"Yes, ma'am," and he goes into the bedroom to change out of his work clothes.

James starts adding things up in his head. He's thinking so, let's see...uh...she can cook, she keeps a clean house, she's a freak, she's smart and successful, she's beautiful, she's having my baby, and she loves me? Wow, oh yeah, I'm proposing tonight. James sits down to eat, and everything is delicious.

Damn, if his baby can cook just as good as Gia, if not better, God knew exactly what he was doing when he sent Marteen to Chicago. He will forever thank the lord for sending him his queen. After dinner, James puts one of his jazz tapes in, and he pulls Marteen up from the sofa.

He slowly dances with her and when the song ends, he looks into her eyes and says, "So you drove for over 10 hours to get to me," and he points to her heart "Because your heart told you to do it. And the other day in DC, you washed my clothes and packed them all neatly in my suitcase because, again, your heart told you to. I'm so happy that I have a woman who listens to her heart and not other people who don't know anything about us."

Well, a few weeks ago, I walked into a jewelry store because my heart told me to and I bought this ring. Marteen covers her mouth with her hands, and tears are forming in her eyes. He gets down on one knee and says, "I wasn't planning on shopping that day, but just like you, I listened to my heart. And right now, my heart is beating a mile a minute because I'm hoping and praying that you will make me so happy. So baby, I want to spend the rest of my life following my heart and making you smile. Will you marry me?"
Marteen shakes her head and says "Yes, yes James, I will marry you!!!"

He slides the ring on her finger. They kiss and hug and James looks into her eyes and says, "No long engagement, let's do this as soon as possible, ok?" Marteen agrees. "Ok." That night they sit on the sofa, watching the news, talking about the future, and laughing at something James said. She can't stop smiling and she can't stop looking at her ring!

* * *

James wakes up and tiptoes into the bathroom to take his shower. He doesn't want to wake up Marteen. He kept her up late last night, and he wanted her to get her rest. James comes out of the bathroom, and Marteen is up making coffee for him. He smiles and Say, "Good morning baby, I'm sorry, did I wake you?"

"No, I set the alarm so I can get up and make you something to eat. You want a big breakfast or just toast?"

"Baby I can fix it. Why don't you get some rest?"

"I will when you leave. I just wanna make sure you eat something. I know you left out of here yesterday with nothing in your stomach."

"Yeah, but I'm a big boy. I stopped and got something."

"Mmm hmmm, well, I can cook you something. I'm not doing anything, okay?"

"Ok, just toast and scrambled eggs are good, no meat, ok? So, do you like your ring?"

"Yes! Of course, I love my ring. You did really good. Didn't I thank you enough last night?" Marteen says.

"Mmm hmmm, yes you did, that's why I didn't want to wake you. I thought I would let you sleep."

"I'll go back to sleep when you leave. I just want to fix my fiancé's breakfast. Is that okay?"

"Oh yeah, you better be careful not to spoil me because I might want this every day."

"Okay, I can do this every day," Marteen says as she walks over and kisses him. Then she says, "Baby, we need a house, because you know I need a walk-in closet."

James laughs, "I know, trust me. I know. I was thinking about that, so I have a realtor that has some sweet ass houses for us to look at."

"Ooh ok, when?"

"Uh, how about Saturday?"

"Ok, and I can put my condo up for sale, so we'll have more than enough money to get whatever we want."

"No, don't sell your place. I love your condo. We should keep that; you know for weekend getaways or something."

"I know, I don't wanna sell it either, but the type of house I want, baby we are going to need a lot of cash, so..."

James jumps in, "Baby, it's ok. I can buy us a house, just keep your place, for now, ok?"

"But," Marteen says.

He kisses her and says, "What did I tell you, about trying to get ahead of what I'm trying to do? Trust me. I can buy you a big house and anything else you want, okay?" He kisses her again. He pulls away from her with that look in his eyes. That look that Marteen is very familiar with. He says, "So how do you feel?" As he unbuttons her pajama top. "You think you can uh.."

Marteen answered him by untying his robe and said, "Absolutely, never too tired to please you, baby...never!" They make love in the kitchen. Breakfast was sooo delicious.

* * *

Not long after the proposal, James and Marteen exchange their wedding vows during a quick courthouse ceremony with family and friends. They were thrilled to be true partners in the name of real love.

* * *

The week after Gia's attack, Karen is washing the breakfast dishes, and Carl is packing to go to Louisiana to see his daughter. Then he's off to L.A. Carl walks into the kitchen with his bags all packed, hugs Karen, and says "So, I guess I'll see you in a few days. Are you sure you don't want to come with me?"

"Yes, I'm sure. I'm still trying to wrap my brain around everything. But I'm thinking I might take a quick trip to Mexico or the Bahamas just to relax until it's time to meet you in L.A., okay?"

"Mmm...uh, see now I don't want to leave you. Baby, why don't you come with me? It's nice and hot in Louisiana and you can chill by yourself when I'm hanging out with Carly. I don't want you going off, somewhere alone."

"No, I don't wanna go to Louisiana, baby, I just don't. I'll take Randy or Marteen with me. I'm not going alone."

Carl takes a seat at the island and puts his head down on the table. Karen walks around and stands next to him and says, "Now what? So you're upset because I'm going on a little getaway? Baby, I need to breathe or just scream at the top of my lungs. I'm just overwhelmed." Carl looks up, pulls Karen over to him, and says, "Okay, as long as you come back and marry me because I don't want this to take you away from me."

"Baby, I'll probably be planning our wedding while I'm on the beach. You know I love you."

"Now, see, you're going to be on a damn beach somewhere and some friggin, Ricky Ricardo, ass muther f'r is going to be hitting on you. Baby, I don't want you to go, just come with me. We can stop somewhere or something, damn!!!" He slams his fists down and stands up and starts pacing.

Karen, familiar with his temper, walks away and gives him his space. Carl runs his fingers through his hair. He goes over to Karen and holds her. "I'm sorry, okay, I'll see you in L.A., okay? Just send me your itinerary."

"Okay, I just wish you wouldn't get so angry, like that. I don't give you any reason to be jealous, so..."

"Man, I don't know why. You probably put something on me 'cause I was never this crazy."

Karen laughs, "Well you need to calm down and stop all that. You know I'm not going anywhere. I mean, look at you!"

Karen steps back whistling. She walks over and rubs his chest and arms and says "Baby you are fine as hell. I'm the one that's crazy, so trust me, I'm not going anywhere, seriously. I would have to catch you like in the act before I leave you, so stop! Please, I'm not leaving all this. She caresses him and kisses him until the kitchen becomes the bedroom. Once again, Carl is running through the airport trying to make his flight!

* * *

Karen is finally alone with her thoughts. She could never reveal to Carl how hurt she was because he would carry the same burden. She knew he had to be in a good frame of mind for his daughter. That damn Coco took those first years away from him, and she knew he was hurt. She saw it in his eyes. It's funny how love will make you selfless and thoughtful. It will turn you into a healer and a psychic. It will have you doing and saying anything to cover up your pain. Karen's heart was so heavy. It felt like she had bricks on her chest.

She wanted to give him his first child, but that moment was gone. So, she didn't feel the need to rush and have his baby. Maybe she wouldn't have any, at all! She felt so much pain and she just needed to laugh and feel special. Not that Carl didn't give her enough attention, but she just needed a carefree moment. She picked up the phone and dialed Randy's number.

Randy answered, "Hello?"

"Hey Stranger"

"Hey lady, what's going on with you?"

"Well, I was wondering if you wanna go on a lil trip to Jamaica with me just for a few days this weekend. It's my treat."

"What? Girl, you better stop playing with me! Are you for real?"

"Yes! Do you think you can get the time off? I know it's short notice."

"Gurl, I don't have any vacation time left until November, but (he starts coughing) I think I'm catching a cold or coming down with a 3–4-day flu!" More coughing.

Karen laughs, "Boy, don't lose your job over this."

"Oh no, I'm gonna work this cold so good, they gonna be like, just feel better and take your time coming back. Girl just tell me the dates and I'm there!"

"Okay, I'll call you back. I'm gonna book them right now!"

"Okay, love you friend."

"Mmm hmmm, boy, bye."

Jamaica, here they come!

* * *

The resort in Ocho Rios was exactly what the doctor ordered. Karen and Randy took advantage of all the activities. They went horseback riding, climbing waterfalls, snorkeling, sailing, and club hopping. On their last night, they were sitting by the pool enjoying a lazy afternoon, and Randy was counting how many men were checking out Karen in her new bikini. She was wearing the one Randy talked her into buying in the gift shop, and it was hot and sexy. Randy says, "Girl please don't tell Carl I picked out this suit you're wearing. Because I just counted 14 men, low checking your ass out!"

"Fourteen? When?"

"Since you walked out and sat your ass down. They low checking, but they checking. So, be prepared because you are accepting every drink, this time because this is our last night, ok?"

"I'm not drinking until tonight. I think I'm still high from yesterday's shenanigans!"

"I know, that's right! And I'm blackmailing yo ass because you were dancing all night!"

"So, I can dance! It was a club. I got tired of dancing with yo no-rhythm butt. And what was all that hand circulating around mess?"

"Girl, bye! That weed had me doing my tribal white dance."

"Yes! I swear you gave me a headache; I was laughing so hard."

"Yeah ok! I'm calling Carl tonight. When I finish tricking on ya ass, he's going to fly his ass out here and beat the shit out of every man on this island."

"Boy, stop, I can't with you."

"Girl, you know how he is. Because I'm going to say, uh, hello, can I speak to Carl? He's going say, this is Carl. Imma be like, uh yeah, these guys are looking at Karen down here. He's going to say point their ass out. I'm going to be like, shit, all of them!"

They burst out laughing.

"Yep! He is going to shut this whole mother fucking island down! You hear me! Everyone will be out of a job!!"

Karen laughs, "Boy, you are so silly, you got me crying over here. But please, please don't play with him because he will bring his ass to Jamaica."

"Yep, I know. Anyway, so back to the wedding. Are you having bridesmaids and stuff?"

"Mmm, no. Just you and Marteen."

"What about Constance?"

"Oh, well, I didn't think she'd want to be in a wedding."

"Girl, that's all she is talking about at work. You better put her in it or something."

"Oh, are you serious? She wants to be in the wedding?"

"Yes, she is waiting for you to ask her."

"Omg! I didn't know."

"Girl, if you don't have her participate, she will put a hex on your firstborn."

"Boy, stop playing."

"I'm as serious as Carl beating these guys up for looking at you!"

"What, really?"

"Listen to me, if you do not ask her to be in your wedding, she will be so hurt and disappointed. She thinks she's your BFF."

"Oh, damn! Well, I'm going to call her and ask her to walk down the aisle with you, ok?"

"Thank you. Because she will kill herself, and you don't want that on your conscience."

"Boy, she is not that crazy."

"Mmm, okay. Oh look, here he comes, that Brazilian man.

"Ooh shit, he is fine as hell!"

"I'm calling Carl."

"Stop playing. I can talk to him. There is nothing wrong with being polite."

"Well, you know I can't fight. So, if Carl whoops yo ass, I can't do shit for ya!" He laughs.

"Ooh, he's smiling at me, damn."

The Brazilian says, "Well, hello, beautiful."

Karen replies, "Hello."

And so it begins, Karen is having the best time, and she hasn't even thought about lil Carly or that damn Coco. She is getting in all the sun and having all types of fun.

* * *

The first time Lucas laid his eyes on Karen was the day she checked into the resort. She walked in wearing some cut-off shorts, a white halter top, high heel sandals, and Gucci sunglasses. Her long black hair was bouncing with every step. She was laughing at something her companion was saying.

Suddenly she took off her sunglasses, and her eyes lit up the entire lobby. She was beautiful and he had to meet her. He wasn't worried about her companion because it was clear that he was gay. Lucas was in Jamaica for his best friend's bachelor party. He and six other men were having a good time.

Lucas wasn't interested in all the shenanigans that his friend was planning so that morning, he wandered off to the pool. There he saw the most beautiful creature. Suddenly, he was thrilled to be in Ocho Rios. The American dollar was like pure gold to the Jamaicans. So, he bribed the desk clerk into giving him Karen's itinerary for the duration of her stay, as well as her full name, and the hunt was on.

When Karen and Randy went sailing the next day, he rented a boat and talked the guys into sailing with him. He told the fellas that Karen was off-limits because she was his. Reluctantly they stuck their tails between their legs because Lucas was not the one to be played with. Every man on the island was looking at her. But Lucas wasn't looking for just a vacation fling, he was looking for his queen. Lucas was on a mission, and he wanted Karen's undivided attention!

* * *

Karen was treating Lucas to breakfast. He saved Randy from a big fistfight last night at a Samba dance-off. He was very attentive to her, and yesterday evening, Karen received three designer handbags with matching wallets. Chanel, Fendi, and Bottega Veneta bags were all sent to her room. The same bags she was drooling over yesterday.

From the moment he sat down next to her by the pool, they immediately connected. He was charming and funny, and he hung on to her every word. It was as if she had known him forever. Last night, they danced the Samba. It was so hot and sexy that they won the contest.

The night was going well until Randy got into an altercation with another gay man. Lucas stepped in, wrestled the guy to the floor, and took the knife from him. He was so smooth with his moves that no one knew what happened until it was over.

"Thank you for breakfast. Last night was magnificent. You are a wonderful dancer. We won because of our chemistry; you agree?" Lucas asks Karen.

"If you say so. Thank you again for helping my friend. He's upstairs sleeping off everything. They laugh.

Lucas says, "No problem. For you, I'd rearrange the world!"

Karen, blushing, replies, "Well, I told you I'm engaged. I don't want to mislead you, ok? I'm getting married to a wonderful man, who I love very much."

"I know you keep saying that. Is it to remind yourself because you are feeling something for me?"

Karen lowers her eyes and again says, "I am getting married Lucas, and I cannot accept the gifts. I'm so sorry."

Lucas reaches across the table, holds her hand, and says, "It is just a gift. To not accept would be considered very rude in my country. So, you see, you are too polite, so you must accept, and I insist. There are no strings attached. You are engaged, as you have said a hundred times. I will not pursue you, only if you are uncertain." He waits for an answer, but Karen doesn't say anything. He says, "So are you uncertain...please tell me...do you want to see me again?"

"I uh, I don't know, if by accident. I guess but I'm getting married Lucas, please."

Lucas smiles, "Mmm I see, you are loyal to your fiancée. He is very blessed. Very, very blessed. You are exquisite, and my heart is broken. So, my sweetness, I will see you to your room, yes?"

"Okay, thanks again for everything."

"There is no need. I will snatch the moon from the sky if you ask for it. I'm sorry. I am making you uncomfortable, yes...?"

"Uh yes, a little bit."

"Well, I cannot remove what is already in my heart, but I will respect your commitment to this lucky fella. I hope he knows what a gem you are. I will leave my personal number with you. If you find yourself uncertain, I will come to you or fly you to me."

Karen is silent as they approach her room. They are standing outside of her room, and Lucas touches her hair and her cheek and says, "Have a safe flight back home. He stares at her, leans in, kisses her softly on the lips, and whispers, "Forgive me." He kisses her on the cheek, puts a gold business card in her hand, and quickly walks away.

Karen is in a daze, surprised by the kiss. She touches her lips, and her lips are on fire. She rushes inside of her room and leans against the door. She looks up at the ceiling and says to an empty room, "Lord have mercy on me. Who is this man? My goodness." Suddenly, she feels sick and runs to the bathroom to wipe away the kiss. She stares into the mirror and thinks, 'I love my man, and this is just a test. I will remain faithful and strong. Don't tempt me satan, because you will lose...'

Karen quickly takes all of the gifts and arranges to have them sent back to Lucas Santos' room. She could not accept them; she knew she couldn't. She checked on Randy to make sure he was awake and all packed. They were leaving in a few hours. She couldn't wait to see her man! She missed him so much.

CHAPTER 36

Karen and Randy were boarding the aircraft. The minute they were seated on TWA, Randy started talking about Jamaica.

"Girl, thank you so much. Jamaica was beautiful, and I had a lot of fun!" Karen was unusually quiet, but she agreed with Randy. Jamaica was truly incredible.

She looks out of the window and pulls the gold business card out of her wallet and stares at it. She knows she will never call him because Carl will always be the only man for her. She puts the card back inside her wallet and she closes her eyes. She can still feel his lips on hers. She will remember that feeling for the rest of her life.

"Hey, why are you so quiet?" Randy asks her.

"Oh, just wondering how Carl's trip went with his daughter."

"Mmm hmmm, well, you know it's okay to miss him."

"Miss who?"

"The Brazilian, what was his name, uh Lucas?"

"You think so? You know, he kissed me. Well not a real kiss, he just touched my lips with his lips. It felt so good, and I hate that I liked it. Was that cheating?"

"Nope. You didn't kiss him. He kissed you. Nothing wrong with that.

"But I don't know how Carl will see it."

"So, promise me you will never tell him because I know how you think. What happened in Jamaica, needs to stay in Jamaica, ok? That man saved my life, so he will always be okay in my book. And memorize that number just in case Carl fucks up! But knowing Carl, he won't. He loves you. And what are you going to do about those handbags?"

"I don't know. I just couldn't leave them because, you know, I tried to send them back to his room, but he had already checked out!"

"I know, just put them in your closet. Carl doesn't pay any attention to your handbag collection, does he?

"Uh no, he doesn't, but Marteen does. If she sees me carrying one, she'll be like, 'When did you buy that, right in front of Carl!'"

"Oh, you are just overthinking things. Carl can afford to buy you those handbags. Just continue living your best life, okay? Because when I grow up, I want to be just like you. You are a bad bitch, and I'm riding with you, no matter what, you hear me?"

"Yep, thanks for being my BFF. You always have my back."

"You know it. Now, let's rehearse what we can and cannot say about Jamaica."

"Well, we can mention everything, just not my winning that contest and not Lucas. Because that dance with him almost had my eyes rolling in the back of my head." They laugh.

"Girl, stop. Are you serious?"

"As a heart attack, and I think he knew it because he had that smirk on his face, like, yeah I can do that shit! I had to run to the ladies' room and take off my underwear!"

"Damn, that mother fucker would have rocked your world. Did he say anything?"

"He kept smiling at me. And when we made it back to the hotel, he whispered in my ear, "Glad you enjoyed the Samba" and then he rubbed my ass. So, he knew I took my panties off."

"Man, oh man, Carl don't know how much you love his ass because it couldn't have been me. I would've climbed all over that fine-ass millionaire because y'all had chemistry. I even felt that shit! But I guess you followed your heart. And that's what love is, you know, showing restraint and knowing when to say no! I'm so proud of you! You are my shero, girl! My super friend."

They laugh, and Karen says, "Oh yeah, so what's my superpower?"

"Yes! The ability to break a millionaire's heart and walk away. You know how to love someone." More laughter.

"Mmm, thanks and I guess I did the right thing. But now, I gotta come back to reality because I have to be a stepmom. I am not looking forward to it. I know it's not his fault but sometimes I wanna slap the shit out of Carl for even fucking with her. I am tired of living in a dead woman's shadow! She's still hurting me from her grave."

"No, I don't believe that! You just need more time to get used to everything. Nobody's hurting you, well, except you! You are a good person. Just try being good to yourself and stop hiding your feelings. Tell Carl how you are feeling because maybe he needs to give you some space. Now, not to change the subject, but I want you to teach me how to do the Samba!"

"Boy, I never did the Samba until last night. That man led me on that dance floor, and I just moved with him. He was right. We had chemistry."

"Damn! Omg! Girl, y'all were looking like professional dancers on that floor. Like I said, you got superpowers."

"If you say I do. Now, tell me why you were fighting that guy in the club?"

"Oh, he was just jealous because I was flirting. But I told him I'm on vacation, and I am flirting with everyone, and that fool tried to kill me!"

"What? Well damn, you got your own superpowers. We definitely need to make this a yearly thing, okay? Let's take a vacation every other year, okay, just the two of us."

"Bet. And swear to it because you know Carl ain't going for it, so you better persuade him, okay?"

"Ok, maybe we'll go to Rio de Janeiro next."

"Ooh, isn't that in Brazil?"

"Mmm hmmm," she smiles, puts her sunglasses on, and leans back in her seat.

"Go head superwoman! But you too chicken anyway, let's just go to Las Vegas."

"Nothing wrong with dreaming. Now be quiet so I can dream about my baby."

"Which one?"

Karen gives him the finger, and Randy laughs out loud.

* * *

As soon as Karen and Randy collect their luggage, Carl is outside waiting for her. Carl says, "Damn baby, I missed you," He hugs her and picks her up. Karen wraps her arms around him and says, "I know, I missed you so much!"

Randy interrupts, "Well, my ride is here, too. I guess I'll talk to you later. Hey Carl, thanks for the trip! We had fun." He kisses Karen, hugs her, and waves goodbye as he gets in the car with some handsome man.

Carl looks down at Karen and says, "You know I didn't like the thought of you on a beach without me, right?"

"I know. But sometimes it's needed. You have your trip soon with James, right?"

"Yeah, but we are fishing, and ain't no sand around or women, so it's not like that."

They make it to the car, load up, and drive off.

"Well, we can discuss it later. I just got off the plane baby. I don't want to argue about this because I'm home now, ok?"

"Yeah, ok, but we need to talk about it. So, tell me, how many dudes were hitting on you because I know they were."

Karen replied, "Well, it doesn't matter because I'm back home with you, and I wasn't thinking about them. I was relaxing and chilling with Randy, okay?"

"Yeah right, well, I hope you got it out of your system because don't even think about leaving me like that again, ok?"

"Okay, sweetie."

"I'm serious, baby. Let's get married this weekend. I have a few days free, and we can just elope. What do you think?"

"Uhm, I thought we agreed to a destination wedding. I don't wanna elope, I want a ceremony with friends and family around us."

"Well, I'm on tour next year, so we need to take advantage of my downtime."

"Well, let's pick a spot where you are touring and get married there."

"Baby, let's just elope, please. Don't you wanna marry me?"

"Yes, I do. Well okay, let's do it your way." Karen gets quiet and stares out the window.

"Baby, what is it? You want the big wedding, don't you?"

"Yes, but you're right, it's okay. It doesn't matter as long as we get married, right?"

"Are you sure because I don't want you holding stuff in, and later you tell me you need a damn vacation without me because you didn't have your dream wedding?"

"So, I guess we're going to do this, huh? You wanna yell at me for going on vacation without you? Are you still mad at me?"

"Yep!"

"Why? Just speak your mind. Why are you so mad?"

"Yeah, I'm mad because you take your butt on a vacation without me, on a got damn beach and you don't wanna be around my daughter. You still tripping on me and Dana. So, this is where my head is. Let's just clear the air, ok?"

Karen shakes her head and says, "Baby, I don't know what you want from me. I love you, and I want to marry you. I've always dreamed of a big wedding with my prince, you know, but if you want to elope, then let's elope. It's not the end of the world. As far as your daughter, yes, I do need to adjust. But this isn't about me not wanting her in our life. I know she's going to be forever a part of our family. So don't say things to hurt me because I went on vacation without you."

Carl is silent as he drives. He doesn't say anything until they pull up to Karen's place. He looks at her and says, "I didn't like you going, I just didn't. I was hurt that you chose to go on a trip with Randy instead of going with me and getting to know my daughter. It just bothered me. I'm sorry I snapped like that, so you're right. Let's put off getting married. Maybe wait till you get used to Carly, okay? Because I'm going to court for custody, I got a lawyer."

"Ok, that's awesome. I think you are doing the right thing. So, are we still engaged?"

"Yes, of course, we are still engaged. I'm just giving you your space because once you are my wife, your space is going to be limited. I don't wanna hear about you flying off to an island trying to find yourself. Take as long as you want, and when you are good with being a stepmom and wife, then we can get married, okay?"

Karen is silent as she walks into her place.

"Tell me what you think," Carl asks.

"Well, I don't want to wait to get married. I'm good with being a wife and stepmom, ok? But if you wanna wait, then we will wait, ok?"

She walks into the bathroom and locks the door. As soon as she's inside, she slides to the floor and screams, "Uhhhhhh!!!"

Carl walks back into the living room and sits on the sofa, and curses out loud, "Dammit!!"

He sits there until Karen opens the door, and he walks back into the bedroom and says, "Are you okay?"

"Yes, I'm ok?"

"What do you wanna do? Are you okay with me filling for custody?"

"Yes, of course, baby, I'm in this. So, if we are going to court, then let's get married now so we can show the court that we can provide a family-style environment for her."

"Are you sure? Because please don't do this for me. I need you to do it because you want to."

"I am. I'm okay because I'm not going anywhere except right here, with you, and I'm sorry for everything, okay?"

"I'm sorry too. I was raw with you, but I don't want you on a beach as fine as you are because I know you had them going crazy over you. Because I'm crazy over you, so can you understand that?"

"Yes, and you were right. They were hitting on me, but I'm home, and we are stronger than ever, right?"

"Yes, we are. Now, how many guys were hitting on you?"

"Well, Randy counted 14 at the pool we were at."

"Damn, so you really gonna tell me that shit? Baby don't say anything else about that. Save it for your girlfriends, okay? Now you can't leave the house, ever! Damn, 14?"

"Well, you asked me."

"Well, just keep that to yourself. Come here, you know you got a jealous man. So please stop doing stuff to mess with me, okay?"

Karen replies, "Okay, but all I did was put on a string bikini and sit by the pool. I didn't even get in the water."

"Oh, so you don't wanna shut up about that, huh?"

"Nope, because you are going to keep asking, so I'm clearing the air.

Carl walks away, goes into the kitchen, and grabs a beer out of the refrigerator.

Karen says, "Ok, I was just joking. I thought we were still playing around."

"Nah, you had that shit on. But it's cool, I'm not tripping." He stares at her, puts the beer down, and bites his bottom lip. He runs his hand through his hair, and he's staring at her as if he wants to choke her.

Karen, not sure of what she had just started, walks over to Carl. She smiles up at him, grabs his hand, and leads him to the bedroom. She says,

"So, I uh, wanted to show you how much I missed you..."

When they are in the bedroom, Carl finally speaks. "You must wanna be single, huh?"

"No, why would you say that?"

"Because you are on the beach alone, in a string bikini, uh, that screams single." He takes his hand back and sits down on the bench at the foot of the bed.

"Ok, well, I know I'm not single, baby. I was just joking around."

"You don't know by now that you cannot joke with me about this? So don't lie to me because I know you were out there wearing that shit."

He reaches for Karen and puts her directly in front of him. He looks into her eyes and says, "If you continue to do this shit and dress like you're single, then you are going to be single for real. Okay? Because before I put my hands on you, I'll leave you. I'm not joking.

This is real talk. I don't know what to do with you because you just open up your mouth and get in all types of trouble, don't you?"

"Mmm, well you asked me and..." Karen replies, feeling nervous and worried.

"Alright, I just want you to know how serious I am about my fiancée being out there showing all her goodies to the world. I don't care what other women are wearing; I only care about you. You are going to be my wife, so when I'm not around, you are representing us, okay? So, dress like you got a damn man! Can you please do this for me? And I know you were flirting! It is all in your face! Because you are too innocent. Yeah, I know you were flirting in that damn string bikini! I can see you now. Smiling and being all polite and shit. I know you baby, that's why I didn't want you to go alone."

He shakes his head and continues, "A damn string bikini, huh? You went to Jamaica and lost your mother fuckin mind! Don't wait up! I'm going to take a long drive and try to calm down, okay? I'll be back later."

"Oh, ok, but don't leave. She tries to kiss him, but he stands up and walks out the door."

Karen is looking lost and confused, wondering why she opened her big mouth.

* * *

Karen is pacing from room to room. It's been hours since Carl left the house angry. She unpacked and washed her dirty clothes, soaked in the tub, and rearranged her bookshelf. She picked up the phone and dialed his cell phone number, and he picked up.

"Hey, are you ok? I'm worried," Karen says.

"Yeah, I'm sorry, I just came home and fell asleep. I'll just stop by tomorrow, ok?"

"Uh, why are you sleeping at your house? I want you to come back, ok?"

Carl replies, "Baby, I'm too tired to talk right now, and I'm still pissed, so I'll see you tomorrow, ok?"

"Uh, no that's not okay! Bring your ass home right now. I'm serious Carl, now. I'm not playing with you; come home!!"

"Ok, I'll be there in 20 minutes," Carl answered.

Twenty minutes later, Carl walks in, and Karen is sitting on the sofa.

"So, you still pulling my strings, got me all fucked up," Carl tells Karen.

"Why are you trying to sleep somewhere else? And why are you so fucked up?"

"Because I'm not gonna put up with you trying to maintain your single life, ok? I'm not dealing with that shit. So, either act like you're my fiancée, or we can stop acting, period. You understand what I'm saying?"

Karen looks into Carl's eyes and says, "I understand that you think because you are pissed, I'm supposed to be ok with us sleeping apart, and I'm not. I know, I should have never put that sting bikini on, and maybe I should have gone to Louisiana with you instead of Jamaica, but I didn't. I cannot change what happened. But going forward, I will be cautious of your feelings, and I will continue to behave like I always have. Because with the exception of going to

Jamaica and wearing that damn bikini, I am always in my girlfriend mode. I always behave like a lady, and you know it! But if you want to punish me by staying out all night, then so be it. I'm done defending myself."

Carl is up and on her so fast! He looks at her with that crazy love in his eyes because he can't imagine life without her. He says, "Baby, I have four days before I'm needed in LA, so let's elope. I really want to marry you. We can have your big celebration later, as big as you want, ok?" He pulls out two first-class tickets to Las Vegas. "I wanted to surprise you with these at the airport, but I was angry, and my pride was hurt. I'm so sorry, baby, please marry me now. I can't wait another day. The flight leaves in a few hours," Carl pleads. "Okay, let's get married before one of us has a stroke!" Karen laughs. Karen and Carl fly to Vegas and are married the next day. They honeymoon for three days, and when they land in L.A., Karen is Mrs. Carl St. John.

CHAPTER 37

Watching the waves reach the sand, the taste of salt in the air, wondering if he'll ever see her again. The most beautiful creature, and that's no lie. He had to try. He couldn't forget the sway of her hips, her long silky hair, and her sweet lips. He wanted her, and he was going to Chicago to L.A. he was going to find her, and she was worth the try! Meet Lucas Santos, a wealthy businessman with Karen in his mind and his heart. What the hell happened in Jamaica?

* * *

Karen is looking at herself in a floor-length mirror inside the Wiltshire Hotel in L.A. So far, she's been married for two months, and she still looks the same; she just feels differently. Carl walks up to her, wraps his arms around her waist, kisses her on the neck, and nibbles on her ear.

Karen says, "Ooh, you better stop! Now look at me. Do I look any different?"

"Mmm, like how? Did you do something different to your hair?"

"No, I mean since we've been married, have I changed in some way?"

"No, you're still beautiful baby. Why? Are you feeling like you could be pregnant or something?"

"Mmm...maybe. I just feel different. Maybe I'll take a home pregnancy test."

"I thought you didn't care for those tests."

"I don't, but my doctor is in Chicago, so I'll buy a few of them later today, ok?"

"Okay, just call me later. I'm going to the studio. Don't forget that they are playing another one of my singles on the radio this afternoon."

"I won't! You know, I'm not missing that. I'm so proud of you." She turns around to give her husband a big kiss. She is so in love with him. It's like she's living in a fairytale. They are still honeymooners because they cannot get enough of each other.

Karen kisses him with so much passion that he picks her up, and they make love again and again. She is so happy, and nothing can take her happiness away; well nothing that she would have ever imagined.

She doesn't know this yet, but happiness doesn't last long when you're married to a handsome rock star. When past discretions resurrect, when friends become ill, and when death takes a loved one away, you learn to hold on to happiness for as long as you can. Because when tragedy strikes and you kneel down to pray, you long for those happy days.

* * *

It was an ordinary morning at the house. James and Marteen were going about their morning routine when James saw an extraordinary transformation in Marteen. She was brushing her teeth when he walked past the bathroom and noticed the glow on her. It stopped him right in his tracks.

She looked up and smiled at him, and his heart skipped a beat. At that moment, she was more beautiful than ever. He walked over, hugged her, and said, "Damn baby, you are so beautiful. I think you are glowing today. Look in the mirror. Do you see what I see?" Marteen replied, "Mmmm uh, no, just that toothpaste on my chin. What are you talking about?"

"Never mind," he said as he kissed her and wiped away the toothpaste. He looks into her eyes and says, "What are your plans for today?"

"Mmm... I was going to wash the linens and go to the grocery store, which is stuff I usually do. Why?"

James, still holding her in his arms responds, "I think I'm going to rearrange some things so I can stay home today. I wanna spend time with you. Is that okay?"

"Okay, if that's what you want to do. But I thought..."

James interrupts, "I can't explain why baby, but you are glowing right now. I don't wanna be anywhere else, okay? So, get dressed. I'm taking you to breakfast."

"Oh, I was going to prepare breakfast for us..."

"I know, but I wanna take you out. Let's make today all about you, okay? Whatever you want to do." He bends down and kisses her belly, and he stands up. He kisses her, and he says with that familiar look in his eyes that he was so blessed to have her in his life, and he thanks her again for having his baby.

Marteen puts her arms around him, and she whispers, "You always know just what to say to me." She smiles up at him, and there are tears in her eyes. She continues to say, "I feel so fat today because I can't fit most of my clothes, and I'm worried that you'll be turned off or something."

James turns her around, and he points at her image in the mirror and says, "Baby, look at you. You are more beautiful to me right now than the day I first saw you. Feel that?" He pulls her closer to him. "I'm turned on right now. I don't wanna work today because you're so sexy to me. Baby, you are gorgeous." He takes her back to bed and shows her how in love he is with her.

They spend the afternoon shopping. Later they go to a movie and last they have dinner at Barbara Jeans. Marteen is wearing one of her new dresses. She is still glowing and beautiful. James can't take his eyes off of her, and suddenly he asks her, "Babe, why do you love me? You can be with any man. Why me?"

Marteen thinks for a minute and says, "You're not any man. You are everything I need in a man. I love the way you take control and challenge me. You have this magnetic field around you that draws me to you. That force that made me leave my job and drive here to be with you. Now that I cannot explain. But I'll tell you the moment I knew I was in trouble. You remember when we had lunch at that red restaurant on the day of Karen's doctor's appointment?

"Yeah, I remember that it was all four of us."

"Well, we were leaving the restaurant, and you opened the door for me. You placed your hand on my back to guide me out the door. Well, when you touched me, my back felt like it was on fire. Your touch sent chills down my spine, and I was like, oh my goodness, I'm feeling this man!"

"Oh, for real? Damn, I thought you hated my ass! I wish I'd have known that. But I guess it all worked out because you married me."

"Yes, I did," Marteen replied.

"So, do you feel cheated out of your dream wedding?"

"Mmm, no, not really. I'm happy you asked me, and one day, we'll renew our vows with our children watching. So, knowing that makes up for not walking down the aisle."

"Okay, and did you realize you just said our children? So, more than one, right?"

"Yes, baby, more than one..."

"Yes! Thank you, sweetie. Now tell me something sweet."

Marteen laughs, "What, are you fishing for more compliments?"

"Yep, starting to feel all insecure and stuff because you are so fine, and I still don't understand why you wanna be with a fool like me.

Marteen laughs. "Boy, you know you got that swag and those moves you be putting on me. I'm wondering why you are with me! You are so sexy with those light brown eyes and that six-pack. I'm like, damn, I hit the jackpot with you! And you know you're smart too, and successful and caring. So don't sell yourself short. And if you flirt one more time with these sales ladies, I'm going to beat your ass, okay? Because you are always talking shit to them. Like 'You have a beautiful smile' and 'Have a nice day beautiful!' What is up with that? It didn't bother me before, but now that I'm pregnant, I wanna slap you!"

James laughs, "Oh, okay, you know I'm calling the police if you start hitting on me. But baby, I'm sorry, I'll try not to be so charming, alright?"

"Mmm hmm, you can't help it; that's your trademark, but my hormones are on ten. So just be cool until this baby comes because I'm warning you, I might slap you next time I hear that mess, ok?"

"Okay, I got it. I'm sorry sweetie. Anything else you want me to stop doing?"

"Mmm, yes, and stop smiling so damn much. You smiled at our waitress and asked her about her damn life. Just stop it. It bothers me, okay?"

"Okay, anything else baby?"

"Mmmm, not that I can think of."

"You are still glowing, baby, and you are so cute when you are jealous. Do you know that?"

"Well, just don't make me jealous because..."

"Okay, okay, I'm sorry. Baby, I think I need to relax your mind. So, when we get home, I'm going to take care of my diamond, ok?"

Marteen smiles and says, "Okay, I wanna go home now."

"I thought you wanted the strawberry shortcake?"

"Uh, well, we can get it to go..." Marteen replies.

They are all smiles as they exit the restaurant because they have what is called that real love!

CHAPTER 38

Gia found out that Carl was suing for custody of Carly, and she was heartbroken, so she decided to call James. If anyone could talk Carl into sharing custody, it would be his best friend. Gia dials James's house. James answers, "Hello?"

"Hello James, how are you?"

"Hey, you, how are you doing? Are you still in Louisiana?"

"No, we're back for a court hearing. Did you know Carl is suing me for full custody of Carly?"

"No, I haven't talked to him since a few days before he got married."

"Well, he is, and I was hoping you could talk to him. Carly is like my own flesh and blood. I have loved her since the day Dana told me she was pregnant with her."

"I'm sorry, but I don't know what I can do because she's his flesh and blood, so I don't wanna get involved."

"Mmm, well, I understand. But did I ever tell you how I became Carly's guardian?"

"No, I don't think so."

"Well, I'm all she knows." Gia is crying as she tells her story. "Since the day Carly was born, I took care of her. Dana wanted to give Carly up for adoption, but it was me who talked her off that ledge. I fell in love with Carly the minute I saw her come into the world. I'm the one who held Dana's hand, wiped her forehead, and wiped her tears.

There wasn't much I wouldn't do for my friend. So, when she started talking crazy about giving Carly away, I stepped in with no hesitation. I knew Dana was just angry because Charles was holding her hand instead of Carl! Dana knew she wasn't mother material, and Charles wasn't fatherly. Besides, she always felt that her days were numbered. She knew Carly deserved the best upbringing, and Dana's world didn't include a baby, so she gave Carly to me. By God's grace and my relentlessness is the only reason Carl even has a daughter," she sniffs and says.

"I saved Carly's life twice before she was born. In the beginning, Dana tried to abort Carly. I once dragged Dana from an abortion clinic, and another time, I risked my own life by interrupting a crazy lady from performing an illegal abortion on Dana. I had to beat that lady off of my friend because she was screaming that she needed that money! *I* pleaded with Dana to keep her baby!! If I could have switched bodies with her, then I would have carried Carly. I loved her from the womb. "So, when I say I saved her, it's an understatement because I went through hell to keep her alive. So, she is as much like my baby as she is his. I love her with all my heart. So please talk to him, please!"

James replied, "Ok, I'll talk to him. I'm sorry, Gia I didn't know. I'm so sorry. I'll call you back, ok? I'll try my best. Uh, take care of yourself and tell Chase I said what's up, alright?"

"Okay, thanks James. Tell Marteen hello for me and thank you again." James calls Carl in L.A.

* * *

Marteen was up early one morning singing and making breakfast for her husband. All of a sudden, a sharp pain ripped through her body. She screams and bends over. James is in the shower, and he can't hear her screams. Marteen is dizzy and afraid something is wrong with the baby. She somehow makes it to the phone in the living room and collapses before she can dial 911.

Minutes later, James is out of the shower, but he goes into the bedroom to dress and doesn't notice Marteen lying unconscious on the floor. Five minutes later, James walks into the living room and sees his wife on the floor. He runs to her, and he's freaking out. James screams, "Oh God, what happened? Please, baby wake up! Open your eyes, please! Oh no! Oh no, come on, please!" He dialed 911.

Marteen opens her eyes, but she closes them again, so he picks her up and carries her to his car. He can't wait any longer. As soon as he makes it outside, the ambulance arrives, and they take over. James jumps in and rides to the hospital with Marteen. Marteen is admitted and is experiencing pre-labor pains. She is only 7 1/2 months pregnant, and the doctors are preparing for the possibility of an early delivery.

James is a wreck. His mother is with him. They are in the middle of praying when the doctors tell him that they have to perform an emergency C-section because the baby is in distress. James is taken to another waiting room, where he is given some scrubs and a mask to put on. The family is en route to the hospital.

James is so nervous, and he is praying for God's mercy because he can't imagine life without his wife. Back in the other waiting area, the family gathered together: Karen, Carl, Chase, and Gia waited with James's mom. Everyone is in their own space and silently praying for Marteen and the baby.

Karen breaks the silence and says to Carl, "Hey, I'm going to see if I can find a doctor who can tell us something because I'm going nuts, ok?"

"Okay, I'll come with you," Carl responds.

"Okay, thanks."

Karen tells everyone that they are leaving to check on Marteen when suddenly James comes in smiling. He tells them that Marteen is doing well in recovery and his newborn baby girl is doing fine. She's healthy, and she weighs 5lbs 8oz which is pretty big for less than 8 months old. The doctors are calling her a super-baby!! Her lungs are super strong, and she is just healthy and beautiful!

James is joking that his baby girl came into the world, breaking through glass ceilings. He is beaming with pride and joy because less than an hour ago, his entire world was turning upside down! He hugged his momma so tight that she smacked him playfully upside the head and told him, "Boy, you going to squeeze my brittle bones to pieces." Everyone laughed as they all took turns congratulating him on his new baby girl. The already spoiled little Jazmine Simone Knight has arrived.

CHAPTER 39

Randy was training a new associate on product knowledge when a familiar face walked into the department. Randy is shocked as he walks around his workstation and says, "Uh, is this a dream, or am I looking at the brave man who saved me? Lucas Santos smiles and says, "In the flesh, my friend. How are you doing?" They hug and shake hands.

"I'm great. What brings you to Chicago?" Randy asks Lucas.

"Oh, I have many businesses my friend, and I remember you were working at this establishment with my little heartbreaker. So, you know if she is here today?"

"Uh, no, Karen is still on vacation. Not sure how long she'll be out. I'm sure she's sorry she missed your visit."

"Mmm... that's unfortunate. Well, you must join me for lunch or dinner. I have a meeting across the street and will be free after 1:00. Let's have a bite to catch up!"

Randy replies, "Ok, I would love to. I'm actually going to lunch at 2:00."

"Oh, perfect. Where would you recommend? My treat, of course..."

"Oh no, my city, my treat. After all, I owe you my life! Uh, let's go to Houston's, which is a nice American restaurant. The food is delicious, and it's close enough. I'll write down the address."

"Ok, thank you. I'll see you soon, my friend."

Lucas takes the info and leaves. Randy panicked and ran to the back office to call Karen. Randy dialed Karen's cell phone.

Karen answers, "Hello?"

"Hey, are you alone?"

"Uh yes, what's wrong?"

"Girl, you will never believe who is in town and looking for your ass!"

"Looking for me? Who?"

"Girl, Lucas. And he is even finer than he was in Jamaica. Girl, he had on an Armani suit and Ferragamo shoes. His hair is a little shorter, but he was looking for you, and I told him you were on vacation!"

"OMG! Lucas is here? What is he doing here, and how did he know where I work?"

"I told him we worked together. Do you remember when we were talking to him at the pool? Who knew he was taking notes? Girl, he is here to see you. He said he had business here, but I bet he is here for you! So don't come anywhere near Michigan Avenue, ok?"

"Oh hell, I'm down the street at Northwestern Hospital. Marteen had her baby here...damn!"

"Oh, rats ass! That's right, I forgot. Well, I'm meeting him for lunch at 2:00 at Houston's."

"What? Why?"

"He asked me!"

"Oh, Randy, you should have said you were busy or something, dammit!"

"Well, he was so nice to us, and I like Lucas. He saved my life. I couldn't brush him off. I just couldn't, but don't worry, I'll tell him you are happily married."

"Don't tell him that!

"Why not? I'm confused!"

"Uh, oh, okay. Yeah, that's right, tell him. Then maybe he'll stop looking for me. Yeah, that makes sense."

"Yeah, it does. Now, is Carl with you?"

"No, he is meeting Gia about His daughter. I think he's going to agree with joint custody of Carly."

"Oh ok, well, I know you are happy with that."

"Yes! I didn't wanna act too happy about it, but I was celebrating in my head. I didn't want to be a full-time stepmom. I'm just not ready for all that, but you know, I would have been."

Randy says, "I know. Well, I need to get back to work. Tell Marteen I'll stop by on my way home, ok?"

"Ok, and call me. I wanna know everything y'all talked about, ok?"

"Ok, friend, bye-bye."

"Goodbye."

Marteen asks Karen, "Now, who the hell is Lucas, and what have you gotten yourself into?"

"Oh, I thought you were sleeping."

"Mmm... girl, what's going on with you? And help me with these pillows; my back is hurting me."

Karen helps her sister and then tells her everything.

"Wow! You should have taken me with you. Well, that was your bachelorette party. You better hope like hell that Carl doesn't find out! And I want one of those handbags."

Just then, James walks in and says, "What handbag? What are you ladies up to?" He kisses Marteen and hugs Karen.

"Nothing you need to know sweetheart. Did you see Jazzmine?"

"Yep, she's doing good. They're going to take you down to see her in a few minutes."

"Okay, finally! I guess I dozed off. These meds got me all groggy today."

"You want me to get them to lower the dosages or something?"

"No, it's okay. And baby, you can go home and rest. I'm okay, plus Karen's here. You need to shave and stuff."

"Oh, I was growing a beard. You don't like it?"

"Uh, I don't know why you are trying to grow a beard!"

"I'm just messing with you. I'll shave it tomorrow. I'll go home after you fall asleep tonight, okay?"

"Okay, sweetheart."

Karen stands up and says, "Well, I'll be back y'all. I'm going to the food court to grab a salad. Can I bring you something?"

"No, I'm good." Karen kisses Marteen on the forehead and leaves the room.

James says, "So what's up? I heard some of that conversation?"

"Nothing's up. Just girl stuff, okay?"

"Okay, because I'm glad you didn't take your butt to Jamaica. Because you know, you, in a string bikini, would've set me off, just like Carl! That wasn't cool, you feel me?"

"I know. Well, I was pregnant, so that wasn't happening."

"Ok, but what if you weren't? Would you have?"

"I don't know. I've never worn a string one, but I would've definitely had on a bikini. That's the beach, baby! It's what people do."

"Ok, that's true. Just do me a favor and don't wear a string bikini without me, okay? I would appreciate it, baby."

"Yes, sir! Now, how much of our conversation did you hear?"

"Mmm... apparently, not enough."

The nurse walks in with a wheelchair for Marteen.

* * *

James was sitting with Marteen in her hospital room.

Marteen says, "Sweetheart, I really want you to go home and have a good night's rest, okay?"

"I will, as soon as you go to sleep."

"Why are you so stubborn?"

"Because I love you baby, and seeing you on the floor like that with my baby still inside you got me feeling overprotective, you know?"

"Mmmm ok, I see. But we're okay. Isn't she beautiful?"

"Yes, just like her mom." He takes her hand, kisses her palm, and then places his head down on the side of her bed.

Marteen rubs his hair and says, "Baby, how much of the conversation did you hear today?"

James looks up and says, "Mmm, enough to know that Karen is playing with fire, and she needs to sit Carl down and talk to him. Because if he finds out she's keeping shit like that, he's going to think it's more than what it is. I know she wouldn't cheat on him, but that man flew

here from just meeting her in Jamaica. Shit, he wants her badly, and I'm telling you, Carl will beat the dog shit out of that dude, so she needs to talk to him. I know what he's capable of. We from the hood, baby..."

"Boy, you heard everything!"

"Yep, and I heard you talking shit about how you wish you were there."

"Yes, because I could have talked her out of stuff, that's all."

"Yeah, I know because I'm not like Carl. I trust you completely, and I know you can handle yourself around aggressive men. But Carl will see her dancing with that dude as a form of cheating. He was fucked up every day she was in Jamaica. I talked him out of flying out there. Now I'm glad I did because he would be in jail right now! Talk to your sister because she acts like she doesn't know her man. She should know how he is."

Marteen replied, "Mmm, okay. I think she should tell him also, but she shouldn't mention that he's here in Chicago asking for her because then he'll be looking for that man."

"Yeah, I agree. Normally, I would tell you to stay out of it, but I think you need to talk to your sister because this is serious stuff, okay? That dude could be dangerous. But for now, you need to take your butt to sleep."

Marteen laughs. "I will, sweetheart. But first, go check on our baby girl, please."

"Alright, I'll be back."

* * *

Randy stopped by and told Karen about his lunch date with Lucas. After he left, Karen prepared dinner for Carl and was making a salad when Carl came home and walked into the kitchen. He kisses her and asks what's for dinner. Karen tells him, and he is grinning like a little boy.

"Wow! Now that's exactly why I married you! Thank you baby. How long before we eat?"

"Give me 10 minutes, and I'll set the table, ok?"

"Alright, I'll take a quick shower then."

"Ok, baby."

While Carl is in the shower, Karen is feeling nervous because she has to talk to him about Lucas because he may hear about him from someone else. Lucas could come into the store again looking for her and talk to one of Carl's buddies. She had to say something. After dinner, they were sitting in the living room. Karen grabbed Carl a beer from the fridge, and she decided to tell him about Lucas.

Karen sits on the sofa next to Carl and says, "Uh baby, I wanna talk to you about something, and I just want you to listen before you say anything, okay?"

Carl looks confused and says, "What's wrong?"

"Oh, I'm fine. It's just something that happened while I was in Jamaica.

Carl sits up and says, "Wait a minute, don't tell me you were cheating on me because I..."

Karen interrupts, "Oh goodness no!! I didn't cheat on you. Now, why would you even think that? Just listen, ok?"

"Oh well, if it's not that, then just don't tell me, okay? You know you don't have to tell me every damn thing, okay?"

"I know, but we're married now, and I don't wanna keep anything from you."

"Mmm, did somebody try and do something to you?"

"Baby, please just listen to me. So anyway, Randy and I met this man from Brazil named Lucas. I think he developed a crush on me, which I didn't know until our last day because he was always showing up everywhere we went. On our last night, we went to a dance club, and Randy got into a fight with some guy and Lucas came from nowhere and stopped this guy from stabbing Randy. So, I thanked him, and I told him to meet us for breakfast the next morning. But Randy was hungover, so I met him. He made me a little uncomfortable because he told me I was pretty and stuff, and he knew I was engaged from the start. But anyway, I told him he was making me uncomfortable, so he stopped. He told me about this business, a nonprofit organization for men. He gave me his card because I told him that I knew someone who sort of did the same. Anyway, he walked me to my room and left. Today, he popped up at Bajem's asking for Randy and me. Because when we met, Randy told him where we both worked. I don't have his card anymore because I could show it to you. I only took it to give it to James. I had no idea that he was so infatuated with me. So, as a thank you, Randy went to lunch with him today, and now he wants to talk to me. So, I thought you should know, okay?"

Carl, still silent, reaches into his pocket, pulls out Lucas's business card, and says, "Yeah, I know about this dude. He was sniffing around the store yesterday, asking about you. Joseph called me yesterday. And I found this in your purse when I was putting the new American Express card in your wallet. I put two and two together, called his ass, and left him a message. But thanks for explaining everything. I kinda figured it was something like you said. But I need you to tell me if you did anything like flirting with him to make him think he had a chance. Because why did he bring his ass all the way to Chicago, since you wanna clear your conscience and shit!"

Karen says, "Mmm, so you knew and weren't going to talk to me?"

"Yep, and I figured if nothing was going on, you would tell me."

Karen shakes her head and says, "Anyway, I danced with him. We entered a dance contest and won. We did the Samba, so he had his arms around me and stuff. He was sniffing my hair a lot and telling me how blessed you were to have me. The dance was the only contact we had. I was just dancing, but maybe he felt something from it, I don't know. I told him I was taken, and he knew this, so I didn't mislead him. I promise you, I didn't."

"Mmm, so you dance with him, huh, like with moving your hips and stuff like that? Why didn't you mention this in the beginning?"

"Because it wasn't anything to mention."

Carl shakes his head, stands up, and is pacing back and forth. Karen gets up, walks over, stands in his path, and says, "What are you thinking? You know I would never cheat on you. What's going on in your mind baby? Just tell me so we can get past this, okay?"

Carl looks down at her, "I told you something like this would happen. I know you can't help that men are attracted to you, but you should have shut it down! You know you shouldn't have been dancing with someone who was obviously attracted to you. That dance gave him some hope. Have you ever looked in the damn mirror? You are a beautiful woman. Men are going to shoot their game on you! That's why I didn't want you in a string bikini. I'm not trying to tell you how to dress. I'm a man, so I know how we think! And you need to sit your ass down and stop dancing with mother fuckers, ok?"

"Okay, I didn't know he liked me like that..." Karen replies.

"Don't do that. Don't play with my intellect, because you know when a man is feeling you, you know!!! Because maybe you were feeling him, too!!"

"No, and don't tell me how I felt; that's not true."

"Yeah, well, it better not be true. Because now, I don't trust you. How can I when you were rolling your hips up against some fucking stranger!!"

He runs his fingers through his hair and sits back down on the sofa, holding his head in his hands. He is visibly upset, and Karen says, "I love you, baby, you know I do! It was just a dance."

"I know, but you are really testing me. I'm not playing with you because this man could be psycho, and now I gotta beat his ass. Because you wanna go on vacation, wearing a string bikini and shake your ass."

"Carl, I don't want you fighting anyone. You can just talk to him because we are not teenagers, so please don't fight him, okay?"

"Baby, if he says one word out of pocket, I'm going to beat his ass. He cannot be stalking you and shit! So, pack some stuff because you are going to LA with me tomorrow. You know I have a recording to do."

"Uh, I was gonna stay with Marteen and my new niece,"

"Not anymore. Just pack your stuff, okay, and I'm not asking you, baby!"

Karen frowns but decides not to push her luck, "Okay, well, can we stop by the hospital before we leave?"

"Yes, we can do that."

"Okay, I'll pack in the morning. Let's go to bed."

"Nah, you go ahead. I'm going to sit here and relax my mind because you know I'm angry about this, right?"

"I know you are." She walks over and kisses him on the lips, and he doesn't respond. She reluctantly goes to bed without him.

Karen is so sorry about the mess she has caused, and she prays and hopes Carl forgives her because she loves him so much. Later that night, Karen wakes up, and Carl is asleep next to her. He has his arm around her waist, and she cuddles with him. Smiling, she falls back to sleep.

* * *

Karen wakes up, and Carl is already up and dressed. She goes into the bathroom and takes her shower. While she's brushing her teeth, he comes into the bathroom and asks her if she wants to go out for breakfast. Karen responds, "Do we have time because I can cook something real quick?"

"Yes, we have time. I'll be back in 45 minutes; will you be ready?"

"Yes."

"Mmm, alright by the time you finish packing, I'll be back, and we can grab something, ok?"

"Okay, baby."

Carl stares at her for a few minutes and turns around. Karen calls out, "Carl, wait, and she walks over and gives him a hug. He hugs her, but not the embrace she is used to. She kisses his lips, and he kisses her back, but it's not the same. Then he walks out.

Karen is left looking crazy because they always have morning sex, and today was the first time they didn't. Now she knows he is really angry.

She calls Marteen's hospital room and James picks up.

Karen says, "Hey, good morning. Is Marteen up?"

"Good morning, hold on."

Marteen picks up, "Hello?"

"Hey, how is Jazz doing?"

"She is good. She gained an ounce, so she may be coming with us in a few days."

"Oh, that's awesome! Well, I told Carl everything. He's making me go to LA, so I cannot stay at the house with you. I'm so sorry. Maybe..." She starts to cry.

"It's okay, I understand. He's right, y'all should be together."

"I know. I think he's so mad with me."

"No, you didn't do anything bad. Just give him time, stop crying because I don't wanna cry, okay?"

"Okay. Well, I'll stop by before we leave town and see you and my little niece, okay?"

"Okay, now stop crying and get it together. It's not as bad as it seems, and don't let this break you, okay?"

Karen takes a deep breath, "Okay, I'm okay. I'm sorry. I'll see you later, ok?"

"Okay, call me back if you wanna talk. I'm here if you need me, okay?"

"Ok, sis, bye."

"Did she talk to him?" James asks Marteen.

"Yep, and he is angry at her. So anyway, she can't stay with us. He's taking her with him to LA."

"Okay, we'll be fine. I'll get my mom to help you, ok?" James replies.

"Okay, I just wanted my sister though, you know?"

"Yeah, I know. But he's just trying to protect her. She's not his girlfriend anymore. She's his wife! And just so you know, he doesn't have a mean bone in his body, ok?"

"Okay," Marteen replies.

* * *

Across town, Carl and Karen stop at Maxine's for breakfast and they order their usual. Karen is a little sad about leaving her sister. Carl is in his own head because he feels betrayed by Karen. He thinks something else happened, and it is killing him inside.

"So, how is your mom doing?" Karen asks Carl.

"She's good! She said hello. She's keeping Carly for a few days, so I was able to see her and stuff."

"Oh, I didn't know she had Carly over. I would've gone with you this morning."

"Oh, well, I knew you had to pack and stuff. We'll do something with her when we get back, okay?"

Karen reaches across the table for Carl's hand and says, "I wish you would forgive me so we can make up. I don't know how long I can take you being so indifferent to me."

"I know. I'm just trying to erase the image of you and this guy hanging out together. I can't get it out of my head, but we'll be okay. Just give me a minute, alright?"

"Okay, well, we have the rest of our lives because I'm not going anywhere. But don't take that long, ok?"

Carl smiles and says. "Yep, I hear ya..."

They finish eating and head to the hospital.

* * *

Carl and Karen made it to L.A. late that evening and Carl is checking out the house they are renting, temporarily. Karen is putting the groceries away and then making up the bed when Carl walks in, with their luggage.

Karen asks, "Hey, are you hungry?"

"Nah, I'm good. Do you mind unpacking my stuff for me? I'm going downstairs to work on some music, okay?"

"Okay, don't be long. You know you have to be out of here at 7 am."

Carl replies, "I know. Don't wait up, okay?"

Karen sighs, "Baby please stop this. I cannot take this treatment anymore. Just come to bed early tonight, okay?"

"I need to work, okay? Maybe next time you'll think before you shake your ass with another man, okay? Now I got work to do and I don't know how long I'm going to be. My brain is messed up because my wife has some psycho stalker on her ass! You think a few kisses is supposed to make me forget that! No! So, leave me alone, okay? Just stop, I need to work!!" He goes down below and slams the door.

Karen sits down on the bed and stares into space. Tears are forming in her eyes, and she lets them fall. She can't move...not for a while. She finally goes to bed and as soon as she closes her eyes, Carl is moving around. He finally gets in bed and eventually, he sleeps. Karen turns over, hugs him, and falls asleep with tears in her eyes.

Carl is up and dressed the next morning. Karen is still asleep when he leaves for the studio. Karen finally wakes up and is sick to her stomach. Carl is really upset, and he needs time, and he made it crystal clear. Karen finishes fixing up the house and starts dinner. Carl was late coming home. He had been drinking and said he had eaten dinner with his band. So, she packed away the food and sat in the family room reading a book she picked up at the airport.

She finally goes to bed, and Carl is asleep and snoring. So, she goes into the guest bedroom and falls asleep. In the middle of the night, Carl wakes up and crawls into bed with Karen, and he falls back to sleep. The next morning, Karen wakes up and Carl is in bed with her, with his arm across her waist. She smiles because she knows he is slowly coming back to her.

* * *

Karen is up fixing breakfast, and Carl comes into the kitchen, sits at the counter, pours a cup of coffee, and says, "Good morning baby. Please fix me a big plate of everything."

"Good morning," she walks over and kisses him on the lips. He kisses her back and apologizes for coming home late.

She's surprised that he kissed her back.

"Hey, I'm sorry I was late last night. It was Bob's birthday, and I had too many shots. Man, I'm hungover, so I need something," Carl says, sounding like his old self. Karen gives him some Tylenol and laughs, "Yeah, I know. That's why I slept in the guest room; you were snoring so loud."

"Oh ok, I was wondering why you were in the other room. I'm sorry baby."

Karen and Carl enjoy breakfast. Karen is making up the bed when Carl comes up behind her, picks her up, and lays her on top of the bed. He pulls her pajama bottoms off and stares at her. Then he puts her legs up and kisses her until, like a volcano, she erupts and is paralyzed. Minutes later, she experiences an aftermath. Carl leaves her in a fetal position as he walks away and goes to work.

When she is finally able to move, she is so blown away because she had just experienced the longest organism of her life, and her husband just left out the damn door! She is tempted to go to his studio and bring his ass back home to finish what he started. So, she calls him.

Carl answers, "Hello?"

"Baby, what the hell was that?"

"Mmm, what was what?"

"Don't play with me! Come back and finish what you started."

"I can't. I'm in a meeting. I'm sending a car for you tonight." Remember I have that duet with Basha, so put on that dress I bought you in Las Vegas."

"Oh, I forgot about that. Why didn't you remind me?"

"I'm sorry. How are you feeling?"

"How do you think? I'm frustrated with you. I want you to come back. Oh, my goodness, that was amazing baby."

"Good. I'm glad you enjoyed it. I'll see you later, ok?"

"Awwww, I could choke you! But ok, I need to get my hair and nails done. I guess I'll see you later."

"Alright. Mmm, you know, I can still taste you...?"

"Oh shit, baby, you better stop. Why are you messing with me?"

"Because I'm frustrated too. I still can't get the image of you dancing with that dude. Can you understand that?"

"Mmm...yes, I think so."

"Alright, I'll see you tonight."

They hung up. Karen was sorry for hurting her husband. Carl had not touched her sexually in days. He was still in his feelings about Lucas and they were living together like roommates until this morning. She didn't know what to expect from him, but she was going to get her husband back, come hook or crook, because enough was enough!

* * *

Karen is running late for Carl's video event. She finally gets into the limousine, and she's thinking about Carl and his duet with this chick named Basha. Basha was another new artist with a beautiful voice that meshed well with Carl. They were singing their new hit called 'Can You Feel It.' Karen hated the way she looked at Carl when she sang with him. Basha was always trying to hook up with him. Karen was sick and tired of talking to her. Tonight, she was going to beat her ass if she even looked cross-eyed at her husband!

The L.A. women were notorious for taking each other's man, but they didn't know Karen. Tonight, she was going to reintroduce herself. Karen walks into the party, wearing a black silk mini with her black and tan stilettos by Fendi. She looked gorgeous and her hair was beautiful as it bounced off her shoulders.

As she walks over to Carl, Carl spots Karen walking his way, and he is mesmerized by her beauty. He's thinking, damn, my wife is gorgeous. He meets her halfway, gives her a long kiss, and whispers in her ear, "Tonight, I'm going to finish what I started." Karen smiles, looks into his eyes, and says, "Promise?"
Carl responds, "I promise."

Carl reintroduces her to everyone and he takes her to her seat because he is performing with Basha in five minutes. They are in an old theater in Hollywood and it's staged to look like a grand ballroom. Carl takes the stage. He is in a black tuxedo, sitting behind a grand piano. He's so handsome, and he quietly sings as Basha appears in a long flowing gown. She is fanning herself as Carl is singing to her. Towards the end of the duet, Basha goes off script and runs her fingers through Carl's hair and passionately kisses him. He is trying to avoid her lips, but she lands one on him. Karen is livid and thinks this bitch has gone way too far!

Some of the band members are looking at Karen and wondering how she feels about Basha's behavior. But Karen is cool as a cucumber. When the song ends, they wrap up, and people are dancing and drinking. Later on in the evening, Karen follows Basha into the ladies' room.

Carl walks over to Karen, and she tells him she's going into the ladies' room to talk to his little costar. He tries to stop her, but she pulls away and goes into the powder room. Basha is laughing with one of the guests, and she looks over at Karen and says, "Oh, hello, how are you?"

Karen, ignoring Basha, turns to the other lady and says, "Would you mind leaving us alone? I need to speak to Basha."

The lady runs out and bumps into Bob, Carl's friend, and tells him what's happening. Bob repeats what she said to Carl, and he laughs, takes a bill out of his wallet, and says he got $50 on Karen.

Carl is not amused. Karen locks the door, and Basha stands up straight with one hand on her hip and says, "I know you ain't mad over that little kiss; that's how you sell songs, okay?"

Karen replies, "How many times have I told you to stay away from my husband? You try to push your fuckin tongue down his throat? I'm tired of talking to yo ass. Karen puts her purse on a table and grabs Basha by her fake ass hair. She turns her around and pushes her face up against the mirror. She puts her knee in her back and bangs her head against the mirror.

Karen tries to pull her arm out of the socket. She swings her into a nearby garbage can, and while she is trying to stand, Karen pops her upside her head with her fist and says," Now try that shit again, and I'll break every bone in your body!"

Karen straightens out her dress and grabs her purse. She checks her hair and leaves Basha on the floor. She unlocks the bathroom door and walks out.

A few ladies run into the bathroom and try to help Basha. Carl looks down at Karen, and then he hears someone screaming that Basha got her ass beat! Karen looks up to Carl, takes his drink out of his hand, and takes a sip. She says, "Take me home before I kill that bitch."

Carl is looking at his wife, who is calm and untouched. He's wondering what happened, and Bob comes over and says, "Man, I should have put a million dollars on Karen. She tapped that ass!"

Carl replies, "Yeah ok, we're out of here. Is Basha going to be okay?"

Bob replies, "I guess so. She said her arm was broken, and she has a goose egg growing upside her head."

Carl looks at Karen, shakes his head, and says, "You better hope she doesn't press charges. Karen replies, "What? She threw the first punch. I was defending myself. It's not my fault, and she walked towards the exit! While the chauffeur drives them home, Karen is fusing at Carl, "Why did you let her put her damn mouth on you, you should have pushed her ass off?"

Carl replies, "Baby, she was so quick, and the camera was rolling. What was I supposed to do?"

"Awww, I'm so sick of these bitches all over you! I'm so sick of this Hollywood drama!"

"You know you can't be fighting everybody."

"Baby, I had to tap that ass. If she pulled that mess in front of me, just imagine what she would do when I'm not around. I had to show her because she was too bold."

They pull up to the house and as soon as Karen walks in the door, Carl is all over her. They finally makeup, and Carl keeps his promise. Karen is floating above the earth because she has her man's back. Carl is happy because his woman just beat the shit out of his costar. The realization of it turned him on, but of course, he will never admit it. And he cannot keep his hands off of her. Although happiness doesn't last long, true love will last a lifetime. Their bond is truly unbreakable.

CHAPTER 40

'Can you feel it' is a hit! Billboards are all up and much to Karen's surprise, the kiss is what everyone is talking about! Maybe Basha was right, but she still shouldn't have gone off-script, like that. Guess it was worth that ass-whooping!

Carl says, "Baby, you know we gotta do that kiss at the music awards?"

"She ain't gonna do it, trust me."

"Baby, stop bullying her."

"I'm not thinking about Basha, but if she puts her tongue in your mouth, her career and your career are over!

They laugh and Carl says, "So you going to give up this house and those shopping sprees at Neiman Marcus?"

"Yep! We are going to get regular jobs and live in a regular neighborhood with regular people. I wouldn't miss this Hollywood drama because as long as I am with you, I'm already rich baby. You feel me?"

"Yeah, I feel you." He kisses her, taps her on her butt, and says, "Let's go to that party tonight."

"Oh, I don't feel like being around a bunch of phony people."

"Yeah, I know, but I need to be seen there."

"Well, okay but let's not stay too long."

"We'll leave whenever you want to."

"Okay, we can go. Oh, I cannot wait to see my lil niece! I'm so glad they're coming to L.A. Randy is coming too!"

"Yes, me too. Carly is coming the week after, with Gia and Chase. You are going to have a house full!"

"Yes, I know. I was thinking we should do Thanksgiving here and Christmas in Louisiana."

Carl agrees, "Ok, whatever you want is cool with me."

"Why are you so agreeable?"

"Because no matter what I say, we always end up doing it your way. I'm just learning to agree with you."

"Well, I want you to have some input also. We are a team baby."

"Alright, I'll remember that. Well, anyway, Basha wanted me to ask you if it's okay for her to kiss me at the music awards show..."

"Uh, no! She cannot kiss you. Tell her NO!!"

Carl laughs. "Baby, come on, this song and video is a hit, and that kiss sold it!"

"Boy, why are you so eager for her to kiss you?"

"This is business."

Karen agrees, "Okay, tell her she can kiss you. But no tongue, and that's non-negotiable. If I see a tongue, I'm going to beat her ass into the floor, tell her!!!"

Carl laughing, "Baby, I'm not telling her that. Stop messing with her like that!"

"I'm just so over these people in LA. It's too much! And every woman in the business is sniffing around you; they are so desperate! Baby, I'm going to kill one of these helfa's over you!"

"When did you become so violent? You used to be so quiet and non-confrontational."

"When Basha put her tongue in your mouth! I can beat her ass again and again, just thinking about it!"

"Alright, let's change the subject."

Karen agrees, "Please do."

* * *

Randy was the first to arrive in LA, and Marteen was set to arrive in a few days. Karen gives Randy a tour of the house, and then they get ready for the awards ceremony. Randy is on 10! The music awards show was off the chain! Celebrities were all over the place. Carl and Basha were up next and Basha was feeling nervous.

Backstage, Basha knocks on Carl's dressing room door and opens the door as soon as he says 'enter'. Basha says, "Hey, so you ready?"

"Yeah, I'm good, are you ok?"

"I don't know. I just don't want any problems with your wife because she is crazy!"

"Nah, she's just territorial. And you know you were flirting with me in front of her. But she's good on the kiss. Just don't put your tongue in my mouth, and you'll live to sing another day, alright.?" Carl laughs, "Now cheer up, we got this. We can win tonight, okay? Let's get that nomination."

Basha takes a deep breath, "Ok. Well, pucker up because we are on in 3 minutes."

As the curtain opens, Carl is sitting at the piano and he starts to sing as his fingers play the piano.

Can you feel it

Can you feel it

Baby, do you hear my heart...

It skipped a beat when your lips touched me...

The earth moved beneath our feet...

Oh girl, can you feel it...or is it just me...

Basha walks out.... singing

Oh, baby I can't take this heat... (she's fanning herself)

When you are near me... I can hardly breathe...

I must admit...way across the ocean in the sea...

Yes! I can feel it...

The way you kiss me... got me so weak...

Your lips like candy...ooh so sweet

Ooh baby I must admit ...I can feel it...

Carl sings:

Girl, if you feel it too...

Here's what we gotta do...

Take off your dress and your high-heeled shoes...

Ooh baby, let's make the Earth move

Basha:

Ooh baby, I feel it!

Yes, I feel it...

She rubs her fingers through his hair and kisses him...

Carl sings:

"Mmm, I feel it...

And they sing together:

"Let's make the earth move.

The crowd explodes! They are nominated in three categories. Can you feel it, it is a hit!!!!

Back in the audience, Karen is sitting next to Randy, and she whispers to him, "Why do I feel like he just cheated on me?" Randy replies, "Girl, I know because I can feel it too!" They both laugh.

Karen says, "Boy, I can't with you!"

They stand up and clap.

* * *

After breakfast the next day Karen and Randy were relaxing by the pool. Randy was nursing a Bloody Mary for his hangover and Karen was sipping on a mimosa. Randy says, "Girl, I never had so much fun. Last night was incredible! I was smoking that Hollywood weed with Snoop and I swear Janet Jackson winked at me, with her weird ass."

"Uh uh, you know I love her. She's just real and not phony like the rest of them. Now, what did you think about Basha?"

Randy replies, "Oh, she alright. Now is that the one you beat the shit out of?"

"Yeah, that's her. I can't stand her! I know, she enjoyed that kiss! Aww, I'm so mad at Carl! I wish he had a regular job because this show business mess is too much for my heart! Didn't it look like that kiss lasted a little too long?"

"Mmm hmmm. I told you I was feeling it. They were all into it. Oh, but not Carl, but that Tasha or whatever the heck her name is, now she was rubbing all in his hair and stuff!"

"Ok, stop! I'm going in here to talk to his ass. I'll be right back!"

Randy says, "Girl, stop! I'm just playing with you! It was just a show; you know Carl wasn't feeling that."

"Yeah right, I'll be right back!"

"Oh hell!!" Randy replies,

Carl is down in his studio working on a new hit when Karen calls him upstairs. Carl walks into their bedroom, "Hey, what's up baby?"

"Uh, I'm sorry to interrupt your studio time, but I'm feeling like that kiss last night was too much. I just can't."

"Aww come on now! Baby that didn't mean anything to me. You know I don't want Basha or anyone else!" He hugs her, "Stop this, okay! I love you and you know I do!"

"Awwww, I know. I'm just so jealous of her kissing you and touching you. It just makes me crazy. It's all on the television, every network is showing it over and over! I don't mean to be like this. But I'm feeling hurt, or something..."

"Okay, well think of it as a job, you know, baby? That's all it is. And trust me, you don't have anything to be jealous about. Basha could be naked, and it wouldn't phase me. You got me locked up, tight!" Carl replies as he taps his chest. "I'm all yours baby."

"Mmm okay. You know I'll kill you if you ever cheat on me! And I don't want her rubbing in your hair. I don't even do all that!

They both laugh and Carl replies, "Alright baby. So... uh, you good?"

"I guess so."

Carl smiles, "Okay because you know, she's going on tour with me. We are going on the Morning Show, and I'm being featured in Ebony. Rex, my agent, just told me that I'm being considered for a spread in GQ. So, I'm going to need you to put on your big girl drawls. Because if I get that spread in GQ, they are coming by the boatload! I don't want you fighting anybody, because I love you. And I'm not throwing what we have away for a piece of ass, okay!"

"Okay, you're right baby, I'll get it together. I'm sorry, I'm just going through some stuff. I hope I'm not pregnant because that would explain the way I've been feeling lately on everything."

"What do you mean you hope not? I thought we were trying to get pregnant?"

"Uh, no. You remember we agreed that we would focus on Carly and try next year? I got the IUD put in."

"Nah, take that mess out. I don't want to wait. Let's extend the family a couple of babies. At least two more, and that'll keep your mind off this stupid stuff. You feel me?"

"Okay, I'll make an appointment for early next week."

"Cool. I'm going to try and finish up, so I can hang out with y'all ok?"

"Ok, baby."

He stops at the door, smiles, and says, "Hey, what are you doing for the rest of your life?" He winks.

Karen replies, "Mmm, beating the shit out of these hoes that's coming for you."

They laugh and Carl says, "I see I got my hands full with you. You something else girl."

Karen replies: "Mmm hmmm."

CHAPTER 41

Imagine sitting at a dinner table with James, Randy, Marteen, Carl, and Karen. It was an evening of laughter, shit-talking, and some great entertainment. James says, "So, where is the damn butler and maid of this big ass mansion?"

Karen answers, "Uh, that would be me!"

Carl says, "Hey that's because you don't trust anyone. Y'all don't know, her...."

L.A. has turned my wife into 'Get Christie Love' around here!"

Laughter fills the table.

Karen says, "Uh, no, these trifling women got me like that!"

James asks, "What are they doing to you sis?"

Marteen jumps in, "She handling her business, right sis?"

They bump fists across the table.

Randy chimes in, "Yep! She sure is, and I ain't mad at her!"

James says, "What's up? Am I missing something?"

"Oh yeah, I didn't tell you that my wife beat up my costar in the ladies' room for kissing me on stage, Carl says as he winks at Karen.

James replies, "Oh, Wow! When?"

Carl says, "Last month at the premiere of the video, man she didn't have a scratch on her, and you know my buddy Bob?"

"Yeah, I remember him!"

"Man, we were betting money on Karen. He told me Basha got an old-fashioned ass whooping!"

James laughed, "Get the fuck out of here!!!" Looking at Karen, "Damn sis, yo lil self, did that! Man, I'm scared of you! But I don't blame you, that's how we get down in Chicago!"

Laughter fills the table.

Jazz is crying in the next room. Marteen tells James, "Baby, you woke up Jazz, with yo loud mouth."

"Oops, sorry, I'll go."

"No, it's ok, I got her."

Marteen goes in and soothes her back to sleep. Karen and Carl tip-toe in the room behind Marteen. They look at baby Jazz with so much love and admiration.

Carl whispers, "Wow, she's beautiful, isn't she baby?"

"Yes, I can't wait to have our baby. Now I really want one."

"Yeah, me too. I never saw Carly at this age." He hugs Karen as they look at their niece while she sleeps.

Later that evening, James and Carl were hanging out in his studio and laughing about Karen fighting on Basha. Carl laughs, "Man, my baby went crazy on that girl, I was like, damn! She doesn't know what she did though. I had to talk Basha out of pressing charges, and I had to pay her doctor's bills. But she shut down the peep show though. Because all the girls are staying out of my way, they are so bashful and respectful now! It's comical."

James says, "Wow! But I told you that girl is crazy about you. Don't fuck around on her, please don't!"

"Oh no! Man, there isn't a woman dead or alive that even comes close to my sweetheart. She is everything I want and everything I need! I love her to death, you feel me?"

"I feel you. But what about that Rochelle? You almost killed a dude over that girl!"

"Nope, not even her. I'm good. I love Karen man. And I'm not gonna lie, the way she took care of Basha, man oh man, that shit, had me hard as a brick! Watching her get all angry and trying to cuss, I was like, yeah, I'm tearing yo ass up, as soon we get in the house!"

James laughs, "Alright then! So you and lil Tyson doing alright out here, huh?"

"Man, Mike Tyson ain't got nothing on my baby. Shit'd, when I tell you she beat the shit out of Basha's ass, please believe it! I saw Basha the next day. She had a black eye, some big ass knots upside her head, and her wrist was all bandaged up! I was like, damn, my wife did all that? And Basha got at least 20 pounds on Karen! It is a mystery because I cannot bring myself to ask her, so I'm just mystified!"

James says, "Wow! She ain't playing with them. That's funny as hell, though! Lil Karen out here beating the shit out of people!!"

They laughed, throughout the evening. Two old school partners, shit-talking and reminiscing. Back upstairs, the girls and Randy were doing the same.

Everyone is gathered around the grand piano as Carl sings one of his songs called:

I'll Dry Your Eyes

I see the hurt...

Hidden deep in your eyes...

I'll erase your pain...

Just let me inside

I'll dry your eyes, ooh

I'll dry your eyes

The world is changing...

No more rules in this game...

They'll break your heart...

And say you're the blame..

Don't ya worry

Don't ya cry...

You're not to blame

I'll tell ya why...

I'll dry your eyes...

Ooh I'll dry our eyes

Ooh ooh

Societies Low ...

Low on brains

And the Excuses...

The excuses are lame..

The world is changing...

No more rules in this game...

I see you hurt ...

It's in ya eyes

Time is wasting...girl

Just let me inside

I'll dry your eyes...

Ooh ooh

I'll dry your eyes

Just Open up,

Let me in

Too soon for love

We'll just be friends

I'll dry your eyes

I'll dry your eyes

Can't lose if you don't try...

I'll erase your pain...

Just let me inside

I'll dry your eyes

Ooh Ooh

I'll dry your eyes

Ooh ooh

Girl, if you wanna

Wanna rebound

I'll be your pillow

You can lay it on down

I'll dry your eyes

Mmm mmm

I'll dry your eyes

Mmmm mmm

I'll dry your eyes

He finishes singing, and everyone is clapping.

Karen says, "Yes, I love it baby, it's sexy!"

James asks, "Alright, so you singing about, uh trying to get with this chick on a rebound?"

Marteen jumps in, "Uh, well, I think you wanna like ease in while she's at her lowest and take advantage of a recent breakup, right?"

James laughs, "Uh, isn't that what I just said?"

Randy says, "Uh yeah, what y'all just said! I love it. That's beautiful man."

"Thanks. It's just a draft. I gotta clean it up," Carl replies.

Karen walks over and sits next to Carl behind the piano and says, "Baby, can you teach me how to play?"

Marteen sighs, "Oh lord, on that note, I'm going to bed. But that was beautiful brother-in-law. I'm so proud of you."

James says, "Yeah, man that's smooth and catchy!"

Randy agrees, "Yep, what y'all just said."

They all laugh, and Karen says "Boy, you a mess. I guess we'll see y'all in the morning. And uh, Randy is on breakfast tomorrow!"

Randy agrees, "Yep, what she just said. Goodnight everyone."

More laughter fills the room.

Carl tells everyone, "Ok, thanks, and see y'all in the morning."

Karen and Carl stay up playing around on the piano before going to bed. It was a good day hanging out with friends and family.

CHAPTER 42

Karen and Marteen have planned a surprise girls' trip for
Randy. His birthday is the next day and out of desperation, she and
Marteen decided to take him to Las Vegas for one night. Karen
was hoping they could fool Randy into thinking they were going
shopping. Las Vegas was on his bucket list, and Karen wanted to
make his birthday an epic night! Now, if she could just talk Carl into
letting her go.

After breakfast, she cornered him in the bedroom. "Hey, uh,
can I get your approval on something?"

"What? I already know y'all are going shopping for Randy's birthday.
It's cool, baby. Buy whatever you want." Carl replies.

"Ok, but uh, I wanted to talk to you about this last night, but it slipped
my mind. Marteen and I planned a uh, one-night trip to Vegas as a
surprise birthday for Randy. He will lose his mind because he has
never been to Vegas. So, uh is it okay because James is cool with
keeping Jazz. We'll be back right around the time Chase and them get
in..."

Carl is quiet and looks annoyed. Karen keeps talking, "I know it's
short notice, but we just thought of it last night. Is it cool baby?"

"No, it's not. You got more company coming tomorrow and Carly!
Why would you plan something like this? Y'all can take him
somewhere in LA."

"I know, but he's never been to Las Vegas and it's his birthday baby."

"Nah that's not going to happen. You know Carly, Chase and Gia are coming in the morning. That's a lot of people, and you wanna hang out in Vegas! Now you know that's some irresponsible stuff! So uh, I don't think you should do that. Just take the credit card and take him out to eat or shopping but bring your ass back here tonight. And I'm not playing with you, so don't be looking at me all sad and shit! You need to be here, okay?"

Karen walks over, unpacks her overnight bag, and says, "Ok, we'll just go out for lunch, and I'll be back in a few hours, ok?"

Carl grabs her arm, "Alright. You know I'm right. Don't be mad at me. Can I get a kiss before you go?"

Karen gives him a kiss and walks out. She looks at Marteen and shakes her head. Marteen rolls her eyes, shakes her head, and walks back into the guest bedroom. James is sitting on the bed putting on his shoes and Jazz is sleeping.

Marteen unloads the clothes out of her bag and says, "I can't stand his jealous ass!"

"What?" James asks.

"I guess Carl told Karen she couldn't go to Vegas for one night. One freaking night! He acting like he's her damn daddy!"

"Well, it is last minute. And baby, stay out of it please, okay?"

"I'm not gonna say anything to him. But if you were okay with me leaving Jazz for a night, why is he tripping? I'm telling you, he's trying to control her, and that ain't cool. I know that's your boy, but right is right."

"Yeah, well that's their stuff. We ain't got nothing to do with it, okay? Hey, did you hear me? Don't interfere okay?"

"I heard you the first time." She walks over, kisses Jazz, and then kisses her husband. She walks into the living room and the three of them go out to lunch.

Karen is trying to seem happy but inside she's a little embarrassed and sad. Her sister is looking at her with that look. She can't deal with her, so she's going to make today a good day for Randy. Later that evening, the boys are shooting hoops and Karen and Marteen are sitting out by the pool, talking to Randy.

"So have you decided what you want to do tomorrow, because we can chill here or go out. I know I can get Carl to get us into any one of those clubs, so you can see some more celebrities," Karen asks Randy.

"Uh, you know what, I just want a nice home-cooked meal, with my BFF! Just being in L.A. hanging with you is going to make my day epic. You inviting me here, with your family, means so much. I couldn't have prayed for a better friend. I love you so much."

With tears in her eyes, Karen replies, "Awww, thanks." They hug each other.

Marteen says, "Awww, you guys are making me cry. Now make some room and share the love."

James and Carl walk over and look at them hugging wondering what they missed.

James says, "Hey, what's up?"

Carl jumps in, "Yeah, what did we miss?"

Randy wiping his eyes says, "Just showing my appreciation to your lovely wife. She is my best friend, and I love her to the moon. So don't be jealous because you ain't the only man that loves her, ok?"

Carl replies, "Mmm, yeah I know, she's something. I'll be right back."

Carl goes into the house to make a few calls and an hour later, he calls Karen into the bedroom.

Karen asks, "Hey, what's up?"

"Well, I called in a favor. If y'all leave right now, my buddy can fly y'all to Vegas on his private airplane." He gives her a business card. "You just call him when y'all are ready to come back, ok? I'm sorry for being a prick but I know Randy is your boy. So go on, have an epic night! I love you sweetie."

Karen was speechless, and suddenly she screamed and jumped into his arms, "Oh thank you, thank you, so so much! Oh my goodness, did you tell Marteen and Randy?"

"Yep, they're probably waiting for you. I got a limo waiting to take y'all to the private plane."

Karen looks into his eyes and says, "Baby, as soon as I get back, it's going down, like your birthday. You hear me?"

"Ooh, like my birthday?"

"Yes!"

"Really? You gonna do that thing you do? Shit, but we got company and shit."

Karen laughs, "I don't care. We'll wait until everyone is asleep or we can do it in your studio, it's soundproof. Because I'm going to rock your damn world, you hear me?!"

"Damn! Ok, ok, well go, so you can get yo ass back, ok?"

Karen kisses him with so much passion and then whispers in his ear, "I think we need some more whipped cream."

"Oh, got damn! I'll run to the store. Now get out of here before I change my mind!"

"Ok, see you tomorrow." She playfully sticks her tongue out as she walks out.

Carl falls back on the bed and says, "Awww shit!!! Hurry back baby!!!

Karen, Marteen, and Randy climb into the limo. They pop open the champagne that's already on ice and they toast to an epic night! Randy is laughing and crying at the same time. He knows that anytime he and his girl are alone, and out of town, baby, it is going down!!!

* * *

Lil Jazz has James and Carl running around in circles. She is grabbing everything in reach and trying to put it all in her mouth. They have a new respect for mothers, and they can't wait for their wives to come home. Carl says, "Now you see why, I didn't want Karen to go?"

"Yep, because Jazz doesn't even act like this with Marteen. I think she's playing me," James replies and laughs.

"Probably. Just wait until she's walking and talking, because Carly won't let me out of her sight. And her favorite word is "why." She uses that word in every sentence. I asked her if she missed me over the phone, and she said, "Why daddy?" But I cannot wait to have another one. I love kids, they keep you humbled, you know?"

"Yeah, I feel you. I asked Marteen if she was ready for another one, and she looked at me like I had three heads! So, I took that as an infinitive NO."

Carl laughs, "Well, I told you to give her some time. Maybe a couple of years at least.

* * *

Early the next morning, Marteen, Randy, and Karen drag themselves into the house wearing sunglasses. The girls are still dressed up in party clothes and all three of them have a long blond streak in their hair, even Randy. Karen takes her heels off and walks into the bedroom. Carl is asleep. She takes her clothes off and takes a shower.

Carl is up when she comes back into the room. He says, "Hey you! Oh damn, what is that in your hair?"

"Oh, it's just a blonde streak. I'll get it out later. I'm so sleepy. I haven't slept since yesterday morning."

"Mmm, ok. What did y'all do?"

"We were club hopping and just having a good time. But I'll tell ya all about it tomorrow."

"You mean later today? It's 8 am baby."

"Oh, well, let me just close my eyes for a few hours, ok?"

"Yeah, ok. You remember what you promised me, right?"

"Yep, I got you. Just let me rest some."

As soon as her head hits the pillow, she's asleep. Carl is left staring at her, because doggonit she promised him his birthday treats!

He wanted to shake her ass awake but he decided to let her rest for an hour because she friggin promised him.

James was watching Marteen undress, and then she took a long shower. When he went to check on her, she was asleep on the shower floor.

"Oh shit, Marteen!! Baby wake up, what's wrong with you?"

"What, what? I'm ok; I just fell asleep."

"You better get it together. What the hell were you drinking?"

"I don't know baby. How is my baby girl?"

"She's sleeping, so please don't wake her up."

"Ok." She grabs one of his T-shirts to put on, crawls into bed, and falls instantly asleep.

James is looking at her and wondering what the heck happened because he has never seen her drunk. As soon as he climbs in bed, she sits up and says, "Oh my god, where is Jazz?"

James shakes his head and says, "Baby just go to sleep. Jazz is sleeping over there, ok? Now lay your ass down and sleep that shit off!"

"Oh okay." And she falls back asleep.

Randy is sleeping like an angel in all of his clothes because he couldn't make it to the shower. He barely made it to the bed and passed out! Well, I can't write about their epic night, because y'all know, what happens in Vegas, stays in Vegas.

* * *

The afternoon after the three amigos returned from Las Vegas was full of tension. Karen slept most of the morning and didn't get out of bed until 2 pm. Carl was fuming. Marteen slept until 3 pm and

James was pissed off!!! Randy's ass was still sleeping when Karen went to check on him. She pulled his shoes off and slapped him until he responded because he scared her for a minute. She cut the shower on, undressed him and half dragged him until he finally got into the shower. She straightened up the room and found him some cutoffs and a T-shirt to put on. When he was dressed, she told him, "Randy, now remember what we said, ok?" He shook his head and they both repeat their oath, "To the mother fucking grave!"

She goes to talk to Marteen. When James is out of earshot and they repeat the same oath, "To the mother fucking grave!" Randy's birthday celebration was beyond any experience any of them had ever had!! Last night they took the word EPIC to another level!! The good news was that Carly, Gia, and Chase weren't coming until the next day. They had missed their flight, and Karen was thanking God for small favors! She was not ready to entertain a three-year-old!

James made dinner for everyone, and they all finally sat down at the table. For them, history was made. Because for the first time, no one said a word, well except Jazz. She was sitting in Marteen's lap doing her baby talking! Everyone ate in silence. Karen was the first to speak.

"Mmm mmm, this is so good, James. Thanks for cooking tonight."

"Yep, because we had to eat, and y'all still walking around here like zombies and shit."

Marteen covers the baby's ears and says, "I wish you wouldn't curse around her."

"Oh shit, I mean shuts."

Marteen rolls her eyes and says, "Ok, so when her first real word is 'shit,' don't look at me."

They all laugh as James lowers his head.

Marteen says, "Awww, but you still win father and husband of the year!" She rubs his leg.

"Yeah, ok. But I hope you got whatever it was out of your system because I'm about to start putting my foot down, alright?"

"Alright, I hear you, baby. Love you."

"Yeah, ok, just so you know. Love you too."

Carl jumps in, "Yeah, what he just said."

More laughter fills the table and Karen says, "Well we are going to bed early tonight." She looks at Carl and says, "And why don't we sleep in your studio baby so you can finish teaching me my piano lesson?"

Carl smiles when he realizes the significance of her suggestion.

"Oh, okay, well, let's get ready then."

"Boy, not this early; it's only 6:00 o'clock!

"Ok baby, let me know when you're ready, ok?"

"Ok, sweetie, and thank you again for flying us to Las Vegas. I cannot wait to show you my appreciation."

"Yeah baby, I'm glad you guys had fun. And on that note, he brings out a cake for Randy. They sing happy birthday to him, and he is overwhelmed.

Randy says, "Thanks, everyone. There are no words, no words." He makes a wish and blows out the candles.

Later that evening, everyone is inside their rooms. Karen is making good on her promise to her husband. They are downstairs in his studio on the sofa bed, and Carl is singing a new song called 'Oh Karen, Karen, Karen, Karennnn!! And oh, Sweet Jesuuuussss!!!' Normally, he is a silent lover, maybe a grunt or two. But tonight, Karen is giving him his birthday treats, and he loses his mind every damn time!!! He continues to scream out her name. OhKarenkarenkarenkarenkaren, all night long!!! I think he has another hit song!!

Upstairs, James and Marteen are making love as quietly as they can. But Marteen can't take it, and she screams out as James takes her back to the motherland!! He tries to muffle her screams with a kiss but it's useless because she is having an out-of-body experience! Jazz opens her eyes, but she doesn't cry. She's just looking into the darkness like babies do. She puts her pacifier back into her mouth, closes her eyes, and falls asleep. She's being a good baby for her mama!

And Randy, well Randy is smiling in his sleep because he is reliving the best night of his entire life!!! And the sad part was, he knew he could never ever tell a soul.

CHAPTER 43

Carl is up bright and early, and he is in a great mood. He serves Karen coffee and biscuits with honey, (her favorite) in bed. He wakes her up with kisses. When she opens up her eyes she smells the scent of dark roast coffee. Karen sits up and says, "Mmmm, thank you baby. You're in a good mood!" Karen sips her coffee.

"Yep! This is a beautiful morning baby, and I love you so much. You know, I think I wanna marry you again!"

"Again, what are you talking about?"

"I want us to have a wedding, in our house, with this long staircase we have. Baby you can put on a wedding gown and walk down those stairs. I can watch my bride walk down those stairs. I was thinking about that all night. I know you missed your special day, so let's do it while we have everyone here. I can get my mom here, and baby we can have a wedding, what do you think?"

Karen replies, "Baby, I'm not trying to be funny, but did last night's birthday treats do something to your mind because I don't know about that. I mean, you are on tour in a few days. I can't throw a wedding in a few days!"

"Yes, you can baby. All you need is a dress, and we can cater the rest. We can have some flowers sent in. We can do this, it will only be a few of us. Maybe 15 to 20 people. Please? I'll help and you have your sister and your best friend right here in the house."

She is shaking her head in amazement.

Carl continues, "Alright, now listen, did you know I get teased a lot about you? Not just by James, but by my band members too. Because I'm always eager to come home to you, I don't hang out with them after work. I'm always the first to leave an event or party. My behavior is unheard of in this industry. I'm around beautiful women every day, and although I can admire their beauty, baby they don't hold a candle to you! You hold my heart. It's crazy because the old me was something else. But you, baby, you tamed this old dog." He points to his chest. "I just wanna marry you again. Sometimes, I feel like my heart is going to burst because it's filled with so much love for you. Sweetie, you just don't get it, and I can't explain it. I'm not trying to force this on you, so if you don't wanna do it, that's cool. Just think about it." He kisses her and then removes his T-shirt. He is looking at her with that look in his eyes and whispers, "I wanna see you in a wedding dress, okay? Please think about it."

Karen looks at his muscles, and she rubs his chest. She noticed a small scratch mark on his biceps, and she traced it along his arm and asked, "When did you get this?"

"Oh, yesterday, when I was shooting some hoops with James. He grabbed my arm and scratched me. It's nothing."

"Mmm...well, James is gonna get his butt whooped for scratching on your arm. You tell him to be careful, okay?"

Carl smiles, "Oh, is that right?"

She kisses him on his chest and arms, and she says, "Yes, that's right. Tell him to be careful because I don't want any marks on you unless I put them there."

"Ok, sweetie, I'll tell him."

"Good. Now let's say our vows in front of the people who love us. And I'll find a dress, ok? Because you are so happy about doing this and all I want is to make you happy."

"Yes! Ok, thank you so much. I already wrote my vows this morning."

"Boy, that's not fair because you know you write better than I do."

"Not if you write it from your heart. You can do it, look at all those poems you wrote when you were a teenager. You got this. Now give me a big hug." She hugs him tight.

"Yeah, that feels good. I love the way your hair smells. It's so fruity mmm... you feel so good, baby!" And he holds her so tight because he really, really loves her. The wedding is on!

* * *

Chase and Gia arrive with Carly, and they are immediately given a list of things to do for the wedding. Carl's mom made it in from Chicago and Carly is running around following her dad. Carl is on ten because he has his three favorite girls together under one roof! He is smiling so hard and of course, James is teasing him, "So you know you now have two anniversaries to remember, right?"

"Oh, yeah, I guess you're right, and why do you find that amusing?"

"I'm just saying, because as your best-man, I need to keep you informed about everything. Just doing my job player."

"Well, did you organize my bachelor party yet...player?"

"Oh, you didn't hear your wife threaten me? So, we ain't having one. Sorry, but you know, your lil Mike Tyson, don't play! She is not beating my ass. But we can get drunk and watch a movie."

They both laugh and Carl says, "Man, she did not say that."

"Man, on my mama and your mama, she said all that shit!"

"Oh damn."

"I don't know why you're mad because yo whipped ass wasn't going to do anything, anyway!"

"Whatever, just plan what we talked about...damn!"

Karen, Marteen, and Randy are out shopping for the perfect wedding dress and then they are picking up Constance from the airport. They enter an upscale boutique and are immediately given VIP treatment. Karen tries on a few dresses and narrows it down to two because the alterations aren't necessary.

They all vote on the same dress and while they are wrapping everything up, Randy brings up an incident that happened in Vegas.

Marteen says, "Uh, sis, check his pulse because he better be dead, bringing up Las Vegas."

Karen says, "I know, right? Boy, what's wrong with you?"

"I'm just saying y'all going to hell for setting that shit up. And I'm breaking out with some type of rash!"

Karen says, "Boy, ain't nothing wrong with you. You're just allergic to pussy, that's all." They burst out laughing.

"Fuck both of y'all and hell is ya destiny. I'm telling you the truth."

Karen replies, "Uh uh...I already asked for forgiveness, and Marteen did, too. Right sis?"

Marteen says, "Yep, we good and saved!" They give each other a high five.

"Mmm hmmm, y'all ain't right in the head because I'm getting phone calls and shit."

Marteen laughs, "Because you put it on em!! That's why! Now stop whining, we heard y'all screaming for Jesus."

Karen says, "Yep, at first I was like calling security, and then I recognized that sound, so we left y'all alone.

Randy asks, "How long was I in there? Because that shit was off the chain!!"

Marteen answers, "Most of the night, right Karen?"

Karen says, "Yep, and later, we all went to that club where all hell broke loose. You were doing that nerdy white dance, and you were like, I'm hot! So, we threw..."

And the salesperson walks up, and they shut up.

Later that day, special equipment is delivered, and the house is transformed before their eyes! Flowers are arriving, and Gia and Carl's Mom are directing everyone. Karen and her wedding party are still out doing their personal shopping. Everything is coming together! Carl is thrilled because tomorrow he is going to see his bride in a wedding dress.

Just as a limousine is pulling out of the entryway, Karen and the guys pull up. Carl and James step out of one of the limousines. Marteen asks James, "Hey babe are y'all leaving?"

"Yep, Jazz is sleeping, and Gia is keeping an eye on her, ok?"

"Okay, well have fun!"

They kiss, and James walks back and climbs into the limo. Carl kisses Karen and says, "So you good on everything?"

"Yes, and I know y'all better not be going to a strip club." She walks around and taps on the window.

James rolls down the window, and she says hi to Bob and Chase. She looks directly at James and says, "He better not be in any strip clubs, and don't get him too drunk because I don't want him all hung over. Y'all hear me?"

They all say okay, and she walks back to Carl and gives him the longest kiss. She whispers in his ear, "You better behave yourself."

"I will, baby, see you later."

As soon as Carl gets back into the limo, James shakes his head and says, "Man, you better not ever tell her where we're going. I swear I'll choke yo ass."

Chase says, "Yep, don't say anything because it's going down with the ship tonight my brother. You hanging with the big dogs now!! Ruff ruff!!"

They start barking while Bob cracks open a bottle of Vodka and James lights up a joint. Carl reaches for the joint, leans back and takes a long pull, and says, "Fuck y'all, it's my party, motherfuckers!! Las Vegas, here we come!!"

James says, "Oh yeah, it's about to be like the old days, my brotha!"

They bump fists.

Chase says, "Hey, don't forget y'all are married to my sisters, so watch yourselves!"

Bob says, "Oh snap, I thought they looked alike! Damn, y'all got some good-looking women. Shit'd I know y'all ain't messing up nothing."

"Nope!" Carl says as he winks at James.

James smiles, "What he just said..."

* * *

The day is finally winding down, and the kids and Karen's mother-in-law are in bed. So, Karen, Marteen, Gia, Constance, and Randy are all sitting in the living room, drinking champagne and listening to some music. Karen says, "I wonder what our husbands are up to because I know some funny stuff is going on."

Marteen agrees, "Mmm hmm, I bet they are in a strip club, with some hoochie giving them a lap dance."

Gia says, "Yep, probably, and he better get his butt in the shower before he crawls in bed with me."

Karen replies, "I know that's right, and I bet they took their ass out of town. Because Carl has the hook up with his friends' private airplane. I just hope he doesn't cheat on me."

Randy says, "Nah, he ain't gonna do that."

Constance agrees, "Yeah, I'm with Randy. He might get a lap dance, but he's not going any further."

Marteen replies, "Well, I'm checking his clothes and everything when he brings his butt in here. Because if anything is suspect, I'm going off because I don't play that mess!"

Karen interrupts, "Well, not to change the subject, but I just wanna thank everyone for being here and helping us pull off this last-minute wedding, just in case I forget to say thanks. Okay? I appreciate y'all so much!!"

They stay up talking and playing cards until the wee hours of the night. Randy shows them his nerdy dance moves, and everyone is on the floor laughing. Good times for all!

And at 7 am, the boys are back in town. James, Carl, Bob, and Chase exited the limo, looking tore down! Bob is sleeping downstairs in the studio on the sofa bed. Chase is in the guest house with Gia and Carly. James looks at Carl and says, "Hey, you good man?"

"Yeah, I'm ok, thanks. That was the shit!!"

James says, "Ssh ssh, ok, ok, keep it down. Now get some rest because you are getting married again in a few hours."

Carl agrees, "Yeah. I love you man!"

"Alright negro, go to sleep. See you in a few."

James walks into the bedroom, and Marteen is up waiting for him. He says, "Oh, hey baby, what are you doing up?"

"It's 7 am, and you know the wedding is at 2 pm. Where have you been all night?"

"Baby, it was a bachelor party, so we stayed out, ok? Now I'm going to take a shower and go to bed, okay?"

"Okay, but if I find out you cheated on me, I'm divorcing yo ass. You hear me? Because I can smell that shit all the way over here."

"I'm not arguing with you. I haven't done anything except smoke weed and have a few drinks, that's all. Stop accusing me of shit."

Marteen lays back down and pulls the sheets over her head. James undresses and gets into the shower. Marteen gets up and checks his clothes and wallet. She finds nothing, and his clothes smell like weed and cigarettes.

She goes into the bathroom and opens the shower. James looks at her and says, "Baby, I didn't do anything, okay? What you wanna do? Get in here with me?"

"No, but I'm serious. Because if you did anything, I mean anything, I'm kicking your ass. Because I know yo ass did something." She closes the door, climbs back into bed, and goes to sleep.

Karen is awake when Carl gets in, and she doesn't say anything Carl says, "Oh, you up? Were you waiting for me baby?"

In silence, Karen stares at him. She lays down, covers up, and tries to go to sleep.

Carl says, "Ok, you don't wanna talk to me, well, I'm gonna take a shower."

Karen replies, "I swear on everything, if you cheated in any way, I'm going to cut it off, you hear me!"

"Baby I didn't do anything."

"I know yo ass did something. Coming home in the morning, yeah, just pray it never gets back to me!"

Carl shakes his head, takes his clothes off, and gets into the shower. Karen gets out of bed, checks his clothes, and finds receipts from a hotel in Las Vegas. She puts them back in his pocket, walks into the bathroom, and opens the shower door.

Carl says, "What?"

"Where did you go, and don't lie to me."

"Las Vegas."

"Mmm, ok."

She closed the shower door and got back into bed.

Carl gets into bed and kisses her. As soon as his head hits the pillow, he starts snoring. Karen puts a pillow over her head and goes back to sleep.

Chase walks into the guest house and never makes it to the bedroom. He falls asleep on the sofa. Gia walks over to him and takes his shoes off. She covers him up and stares down at him. He mumbles, "Hey, baby." Gia lightly pops him upside his head and says, "Boy, if you did anything, I'm beating ya ass, you hear me!"

"Yes, baby," and he falls asleep snoring.

Gia goes back into the bedroom, and she falls back to sleep. A few hours later, Gia is in the kitchen with Marteen, and they are making breakfast for everyone. James and Chase are still sleeping, and the wedding is in a few hours.

CHAPTER 44

The house is beautifully filled with fresh flowers. Carly is so cute in her white dress with tiny roses in her hair. She's following her daddy around, and he picks her up because she's stepping on his heels. Gia is making sure everyone is seated, and Constance and Randy are waiting down by the staircase. Constance is so thrilled to finally be in her best friend's wedding. Well, in her mind, she really is Karen's BFF.

James is following Carl around because he is the best man, and he can't think straight because he's hungover. Gia takes Carly from Carl and places her in front of the staircase with a basket full of rose petals. She instructs her to walk slowly up to her dad as soon as the music starts. Of course, Carly asks her 'Why.' So, Gia tells her again that her dad is waiting for her because that's the only way it makes sense in Carly's little mind.

Karen is upstairs with Marteen, getting ready to walk down the staircase. She is nervous because she doesn't want to fall and break anything. Marteen is trying to calm her down, and she tells her that if she falls, then she'll fall with her. Karen laughs at the thought of them tumbling down the stairs because that would make today memorable.

The guests are seated. Basha and the band are attendees, and she has her eye on James. Carl invited everyone, so Basha assumed that she was included. Karen doesn't know she's a guest and James is low checking her out. Chase is officiating the ceremony, and he's hungover.

Suddenly, the music starts playing, and they get ready to walk out. Carly takes off walking fast, and Gia tries to slow her down. But she's determined to get to her dad. James and Constance walk down the aisle. James goes left, and Constance goes right. Marteen walks down the stairs wearing a long platinum straight off-the-shoulder silk dress, and she is beautiful. James is beaming at his wife and he's feeling ashamed for even thinking of Basha because Marteen is stunning!

Bob is mesmerized by Marteen and has developed a crush on her. Gia sings 'At Last' by Etta James as Karen takes the stairs. Everyone gasped because she looked incredible. She is wearing an ivory beaded gown. It's fitted with a long flowing train and the back is cut low. She has a small Tiara on her head full of hair. In honor of her mom, she is wearing pearl earrings as her something 'old.'

Carl is smiling from ear to ear as his bride walks down the stairs towards him. Carl takes her hand as she passes her bouquet to Marteen. Chase begins to speak, and when he's done, Carl slides a bigger diamond onto Karen's finger. He looks into her eyes and says his vows.

"The first time I saw you, my heart knew. My heart was beating fast. You smiled at me, and that did it. First, I wanted you for selfish reasons. Then we dated for those four seasons. I wanted your

commitment and your heart. Because I craved you, I had to have you!
I'm so thankful God blessed me with the Queen I prayed for you.
I promise to love you unconditionally, to care for you, to
inspire you, to fight for you, and to cherish you till my last
dying breath. You are the absolute love of my whole life.
Thank you for saying yes!"

Karen smiles, slides a platinum band on Carl's finger and says,
"When I wake up by your side, my heart is so full. I'm afraid it could
burst from the inside. I pray every time you walk out the door and ask
for your protection and safety. I loved you the moment I laid eyes on
you. I had rules in place to shield my heart, but you broke through
those barricades. No words could ever describe how much I love you.
And a hundred times over, I'll marry you. You are the reason I
breathe and sleep so peacefully. I am yours, baby. You complete me.
Don't ever doubt what's in here (she touches her heart) because I'll
love you a million times a million. And if that isn't long enough, then
multiply it by two. Because there aren't enough numbers in the
world, to ever explain how much I love you."

He wipes her tears away, and she wipes away his.

Chase announces, "By the power invested in me, I now
pronounce you husband and wife. Again, you may kiss your bride."
Carl kisses his bride for the longest time and then pulls away and
whispers, "Damn girl, you are wearing that dress." He grabs her hand,
and they turn and jump the broom. On cue, the music starts playing,
and everyone is hugging and congratulating the lovely couple. Their

love isn't picture book perfect, but it's the real thing! And their bond remains unbelievably unbreakable!

* * *

The wedding reception is coming along smoothly. Marteen is holding Jazz, and James has been missing for a while. Karen changes into a black and white mini jumpsuit by Chanel, which is gorgeous. She's wearing her hair down, just the way Carl likes it. Marteen is wearing the black version of Karen's outfit.

Karen notices her sister staring off from across the room, so she walks over and says, "Hey, why are you looking so strange?" Marteen replies, "I was trying to find James because I need to use the ladies' room. He hasn't held Jazz all day and he is acting really weird. "Mmmm, well, I'm looking for Basha. She was not invited, and I wanna talk to her about putting her damn hands in Carl's hair, but she's avoiding me."

Marteen laughed, "Oh, leave that girl alone; she got the message. Oh, I see him and James is talking to Basha." He's laughing so freely with her, and all of a sudden, Marteen is instantly jealous. She begins to walk towards him, and before she makes it halfway, James brushes his hand slowly across Basha's butt, and he whispers something in her ear. They share a laugh.

Basha is still laughing as she walks away. James looks over and makes eye contact with Marteen. He quickly walks towards her. Marteen is so confused and is holding Jazz so tightly. Jazz starts to cry, and before James makes it over to her, she turns and gives Jazz to

Karen because she suddenly can't breathe. Maybe she's seeing things because why on earth would her husband touch another woman's ass, who in their right mind would do that in front of everyone!

She's taking deep breaths because she just got the wind knocked out of her. James is standing in front of her, and he says, "Hey baby, what's wrong?"

Marteen looks at him, and she shakes her head and whispers, "You asshole. You know I saw it."

"Baby, I didn't do anything. I don't know what you think you saw, but.."

"I know what I saw."

Karen says, "Yeah, I saw it too." Randy runs up and asks Marteen if she's okay because, apparently, he saw it too.

Karen gives Jazz to Randy and tells him to hold her while she searches for Basha. "I'm kicking that heffa out of my house because she wasn't even invited."

Karen walks away, and Marteen looks at James with so much hurt in her eyes, and she says, "Who is she?"

James looks around and says, "Let's go in the room, ok?"

He reaches out for her hand, and she snatches it from him.

As they walk into the bedroom, Bob is watching from across the room. He is shaking his head and thinking James had to be stone crazy to cheat on his beautiful wife. He was baffled because people would pick the leaf instead of the flower.

Marteen slaps him as soon as they are inside, and she pokes him in his chest and says, "Who is she?????"

And she doesn't wait for a response as she grabs her suitcase and starts packing whatever is in sight.

James says, "Baby, stop, listen. I didn't, uh baby, just don't do anything crazy, ok? I love you. I don't really know her, ok?"

"Okay, just stop. Now you are really making me angry because you know damn well you know her! You probably fucked her because why would you feel comfortable enough to grab her ass! Where were you after the wedding? Were you with her? And why in God's name would you touch her in my sister's house in plain view...why?? Just tell me why?"

"I don't know. I don't know why. I was joking around with her, that's all. It was just stupid baby. Let me explain, please don't leave. Just don't leave me because I promise you I didn't cheat on you, please."

"What the fuck is wrong with you? Who grabs another woman's ass in front of their wife!! Really?? I try to be the best wife to you," Her voice is cracking. "I cook, I clean, I give you sex whenever, wherever, I don't have anything else to give." She's shaking her head. "And I even left my six-figure paying job, I left my home...and for what? You don't like my ass? Because my ass is the only ass you should be rubbing! James, I swear I could kill you! What is wrong with you? Are you still high, or what!!"

"I'm sorry, I'm probably still high, though. I'll tell you everything; just stop packing and sit down. Okay, please. You know I love you; you know it. I swear on everything that I didn't cheat. I was just joking around with her. She said her feet were sore, and I told her that her ass was probably too big for her feet to carry, and she laughed out loud. That's why I touched her butt. Ok, listen, I uh...I met her when I worked with Carl on that rap video, and we just talked shit and laughed at stuff. We ain't on that shit. She knows I'm happily married. You can talk to her and ask her anything."

"Why would I talk to her? I'm not married to her; she didn't take any vows with me. I'm talking to yo ass! Because you are crossing a thin mother fucking line!"

She sits on the bed and puts her head in her hands. She is silent for a minute, and when she looks up, there are fresh tears in her eyes. She wipes them away and says, "I'm going to get my baby, and I think you should figure out if you want a wife or your plaything because you can't have both...ok?"

"I want you, my wife. There's nothing to figure out."

"Uh, yeah, there is because you were looking at her like you wanted her, and I cannot unsee that. So, find out what you want, and don't come back until you know for sure. I'm not competing with anyone. I'm not fighting anyone over a man that's unworthy of me! It's one thing if she was flirting with you, then yes! I'll kick her ass to the moon. But you were flirting with her, and I am not fighting over that! Get your priorities straight, and then we'll see, okay?"

James replies, "What do you mean? Are you leaving me? I didn't do anything! Please, I'm sorry, I was wrong for touching her butt. I know that now. But I don't want her. I don't want her,

I want you, and only you. I'll do anything you want. Just tell me what you want, please, please. I'm begging because I don't care about my pride. I'm begging for your forgiveness and understanding. I'll spend the rest of my life making it up to you. Please, baby please, just give me a chance! I messed up, ok? I grabbed her ass, and I was just joking about something. It was nothing, and I'll never touch anyone again, ever. Okay, please baby. I'm sorry sweetie. You know you love me, and I love you."

He's wiping tears from his eyes because he's scared. Marteen starts crying, and she shakes her head and says, "I'm so embarrassed. Everyone saw you. My friends and family. How can I trust you again, how?"

"You will in time. I will earn your trust, baby. I'll earn it back because you are my priority, you and Jazz! I know that now, and I won't put you through this anymore because I know what it feels like to almost lose you. I just can't live without you; I can't."

He holds her and kisses her, but she's not responding. James looks at her and says, "I'm so sorry I hurt you, okay? Let's go for a walk with Jazz and get some fresh air, okay? I'll take some time off when we get back home, and we can go away. Just us and Jazz and we can renew our vows in Paris if you want. Or on a beach, you said you wanted to go, and we can do that. Okay, just tell me and I'll make it happen. I'll do anything for you."

"No, I don't want to renew the vows you are breaking. You don't give a damn about our vows. Not if you are rubbing up against another woman and smiling like you can't wait to fuck her. So don't talk about that, because you don't want me. You can't want me the way you're behaving in plain sight. You know what? I'm tired; just go get our baby so I can get her ready for bedtime, ok? And James, before you go, uh, I don't know if I can sleep in the same bed with you, ok...not right now."

"Okay, I understand. I'll be back."

Karen walks into the room and asks Marteen if she's okay.

"Yes, I'm good. I'm going to get Jazz ready for bed, and then I'm going to bed, okay?"

Karen says, "Ok. Well, Carl found Basha and sent her ass on home. Everyone else left too, okay? So, I'll talk to you tomorrow. Let me know if you need me, ok?"

"Ok, and you looked beautiful today. Sorry for this mess; I don't know what to do."

"Thanks, and take a moment and think before you do anything, ok? He was just being a dog, but it probably was harmless. Are you sure you are okay, because we can stay up and talk, you know? There are a lot of rooms in this big ass house...and you are welcome to any one of them as long as you need it because I got you! Ok?"

"No, I know, thanks. But I'm going to bed. Let's talk tomorrow."

"Ok."

James walks in with Jazz, and she's already asleep in his arms. Karen rolls her eyes at him and walks out. Marteen takes Jaz, undresses her, and she curls up and falls back asleep. James takes his tux off and sits in a chair next to the bed. Marteen undresses and takes her shower. As soon as she is inside the shower, she starts to cry.

She can't remove the image from her mind. James opens the shower door and joins her.

Marteen says, "Don't touch me, don't you dare..."

He ignores her, takes the soap, and washes her up. He holds her, and again he begs for her forgiveness. She hits and punches him. He takes her hands and holds them. He holds her until she stops fighting him and tells her he's not going anywhere no matter what.

He dries her off as she looks off into space. He slips one of his T-shirts over her head and puts his wife to bed. He sits in the chair and watches over the two people he loves the most. He vows to never hurt his wife again. Of all the dumbest shit he's done, today was the stupidest and most fucked up of all time, and he's not losing his wife.

CHAPTER 45

Karen and Carl are up early and feeling like newlyweds again. Karen makes Carl breakfast in bed, and they share a long walk around the grounds. Life was good!

Gia and Chase spend the morning inside the guest house. Chase is swimming in the pool while Gia is catching up on her beauty sleep. Carly is hanging out with her grandma. They are taking full advantage of their alone time.

Randy and Constance are getting ready to hit Rodeo Drive for lunch and some sightseeing. Bob is hanging out at the pool, taking in some sun, and reading a Stephen King novel.

James is up early, and he lets Marteen sleep in. He gives Jazz her bath, gets her dressed, and takes her out for some fresh air. They sit by the pool, and he makes small talk with Bob. Then he grabs some orange juice, a bagel, and cream cheese and takes them into the room for Marteen.

James and Jazz enter the bedroom. Marteen is almost dressed, and she says, "Oh hey, thanks for letting me sleep in. Is she fussy today?"

"No, she's in a talkative mood this morning." He starts talking to Jazz in baby language.

Marteen smiles, "Mmm, that's good. She was a little fussy yesterday. I think the noise and the crowd were bothering her."

James replies, "Yeah, she's good. How are you feeling? I got you a bagel and some orange juice."

"Thank you," Marteen says.

James walks over, kisses his wife, and says, "Hey, is there anything I can do for you today? I'm so sorry for yesterday. You want to go somewhere since it's our last night?"

Marteen replies, "I'm just no longer in the mood. I'll just hang out here until it's time to leave tomorrow. I just don't wanna talk to anyone, ok?"

"Why, because of me?"

"I'm just ready to go home. So uh, I'll take Jazz off your hands, and you do whatever you wanna do okay?"

"Baby, I can keep her. I mean, I wanna be with you today. Let's go out for dinner tonight. We can talk about whatever is bothering you. How long are you going to punish me?"

"Maybe forever, why? Am I keeping you from your girlfriend?"

"Of course not. You know I don't want anyone else. Baby, I'm in love with you and only you. So, if you don't wanna do anything then we won't, okay?"

Someone is knocking on the door. Karen walks in and asks Marteen if she wants to go swimming. Marteen says no, she was going to relax in her room. Karen says, "No, you are not going to be cramped up in this bedroom. Come on, let's hang out. You'll feel better. And Randy is gonna do his dance for us when he gets back."

Marteen laughs, "Ok, I'll be out there in a minute. I'm going to put Jazz's bathing suit on so she can look like mommy, ok?"

Karen says, "Yeah, nope, my mother-in-law is on childcare duty tonight, so you can chill, ok?"

"Mmm, well, I don't know. I'll keep Jazz with me, but we'll be over there in a minute, ok?"

James speaks up, "Babe, I'll keep my baby girl with me. Go on and hang out, okay?" He takes Jazz and her bag with him. And before he leaves, he kisses Marteen again and says, "I'll see you, ok?"

Marteen looks at him as he walks out the door.

Karen tells Marteen, "Ok, so I'll see you in a minute, ok?"

Marteen changes into her two-piece bathing suit. She wraps a towel around her waist and grabs her straw hat and sunglasses. A few minutes later, she walks out towards the pool. James and the guys are starting a game of spades as she walks past. She drops her sunglasses , and Bob breaks his neck to pick them up for her.

Marteen tells him, "Oh, thank you. And I'm sorry I forgot your name, you are...?"

"Oh, I'm Bob. I manage the band for Carl."

"Oh, that's right. Well, thanks again, Bob. It's nice to meet you."

She walks around and leans over to give Jazz a little kiss. She tells James she's going for a swim and will be back to take Jazz.

James says, "Okay, sweetie. You look beautiful baby."

Marteen doesn't say anything. James grabs her and says, "I'll keep Jazz with me. Go on and enjoy the pool; I got her."

"Ok," Marteen says as she walks off. She removes her towel from around her waist and throws it over her shoulders. Bob is staring.

James says, "Man, why are you always eyeballing my wife? I'm starting to think you crushing on her."

"Man, I'm just noticing how beautiful she is, that's all. I don't mean no harm, alright?"

"Yeah, ok, just as long as that's all you do."

"What's that's supposed to mean?" Bob says to James.

"Man, you know what that means."

Carl interrupts them as he walks over, "Hey, hey we ain't on that shit now! Come on, let's just play cards. I got James and Bob. You and Chase are partners okay?"

James says, "Yeah, I'm cool." He gives Jazz her bottle to hold.

Chase just shakes his head and starts dealing. Jazz falls asleep on the second hand. James lays her down in the bed and puts pillows around her. He brings the monitor back out with him.

Bob brings up Basha. Carl says, "Yeah, I know she's pissed. But she knew she wasn't invited. If she pulled out on us, well we can just edit her part out."

Bob replies, "Man, her part was too long. Just talk to her because we kinda need her to sign off."

James asks, "Needs who to sign off?"

Bob replies, "Basha. She's trying to back out because Carl asked her to leave yesterday and she's in her feelings."

"Oh, well, I don't think my wife is going to let me do anything with her involvement."

Carl says, "I know because you copping feels on her ass, in front of her!"

"Man, whatever. Karen didn't like her anyway."

"No, but she was cool with it until you did that shit yesterday."

"Look who's talking, you ain't no saint. You cheated on her with Dana!"

"I did not have sexual relations with her."

"Stop lying. You know you hit that."

"I did not have sexual relations with her..."

"What the hell is sexual relations? Stop saying that. You know you tapped that ass, period."

Carl says, "Man, I did not have sexual relations with her."

"Ok, say that shit one more time, and I'm going to smack your ass."

Carl laughs, "Man, I wish you would. I'll kick ya ass!"

James says, "Say that stupid shit again, and I'll jump over this table."

Carl says, "Jump fool because I did not have sexual..."

James jumps up, and Chase grabs him. Bob helps him because James is overpowering Chase. Carl flips the table over and screams for them to let James go. Chairs are flipped over, and cards are everywhere.

Marteen, Gia, and Karen are playing splash ball in the pool when they hear the guys fighting. Marteen is the first one out of the pool because she can hear James's mouth. Karen and Gia are on her heels.

Marteen asks, "What is going on?!"

James says, "Man, let me go."

Carl is saying yeah let his ass go, and Marteen says, "Okay, James, calm down. Baby, y'all too old for this."

Karen runs over to Carl and begs him to walk away with her. Carl pushes her away until his mom comes out of the room and screams for them to stop! Carl calms down, and Chase and Bob let go of James. Marteen pulls James to her and begs him to let it go, "Please stop. Come on, let's go, baby. Come on."

James walks backward with Marteen. Carl is breathing hard, and Karen is begging him to calm down. James walks into the room with Marteen. She grabs a robe because she's wet and shivering from playing in the pool. James sits down and puts his head in his hands.

Marteen checks on Jazz and then walks back over to him, "Are you okay?"

"Yeah."

"Why are you trying to fight your best friend?"

"I don't know, baby. I'm just mad at the world because you're mad at me. And I'm taking it all out on Carl. I'm sorry."

"Well, I've never seen you so angry. You almost picked Chase up! Baby, that's a lot of anger. So, I hope you apologize to everyone, okay?"

"Yeah, well, pack our stuff. Let's go to a hotel close to the airport so we can get out of here in the morning, okay?"

"Let's just stay and leave..."

James interrupts and raises his voice, "Baby, I need you to pack up, Okay? Please."

"Okay." Marteen starts packing, and James goes out to apologize.

* * *

James walks out and everyone is putting everything back in place. James walks over to Carl's mom and apologizes to her. He hugs her and hugs everyone else, too. He saves Carl for last.

James tells Carl, "I'm sorry, man. I'm just taking my anger out on you. I hope you know I didn't mean any of that stuff. I love you, you're my brother, ok?"

"It's cool, man. I'm sorry too."

"Cool. Well alright, we are going to get out of here and get a hotel for the night. I just want to talk to Marteen in privacy before we get to Chicago, ok?"

"Oh, okay, I understand. Well, I'll see you in a few weeks."

James goes back to help Marteen pack, "Hey, I apologized to everyone and told them we were going, okay?"

"Okay, I miss my bed."

"Yeah, me too and I miss you. How long am I on punishment because I'm dying a slow death. I'm picking fights with people. Baby, you gotta give me some."

"No, you're not getting off that easy. Just take a cold shower, and you'll be just fine."

"Damn, why are you so mean?" He walks over and puts his arms around her. "Can I have a real kiss?"

"No, because you..."

James kisses her, and she kisses him back. She wraps her arms around him. James begs her for more, but she breaks away and stares at him. "Why are you so mean?" James asks her.

"Just keep your hands off of Basha's ass. And buddy, you know you can forget about doing a video with her. And I mean it, are we clear?"

"Crystal, baby. I'm not doing shit!"

Marteen laughs, "Mmmm, you better not. Okay, we're packed. Now, let's get out of here."

CHAPTER 46

James and Marteen finally make it back home. Marteen was doing laundry and fixing dinner. James was feeding Jazz and reading to her. Looking at them now, one would have never known how close they came to breaking up.

Marteen was still in her feelings about Basha, but she was on the road to forgiveness. And James was determined never to hurt her again. James finally gets Jazz to sleep. He puts her in her baby bed, tiptoes out, and joins Marteen in the kitchen.

"Hey, she's knocked out. Can I help you with dinner?"

"Nope. Just give me five minutes, and we can eat, ok?"

"Ok, you want me to open up some wine?"

"Mmm uh, yeah, I can use a glass, thanks."

James walks over to her, hugs her, and says, "Thank you for making dinner tonight. I'm sorry about everything, okay?"

"You're welcome, but we still have to eat. So, I'm just doing what I have always done. So, open the wine and let's eat, okay? I know you are sorry, and I'm working on forgiveness, ok?"

"Okay, that's more than enough." He kisses her, and she kisses him back. He's thrilled about that.

He grabs a bottle of wine, and they eat dinner. They laugh about the good memories of L.A., and they don't mention the bad ones. Later that evening, James wonders if he can sleep with his wife again. He was hoping he could because it was killing him inside.

He really wanted to make love to her, but he didn't want to set her off. He was going along with whatever signs she sent to him.

James asks, "Uh, so I was wondering if I was sleeping in here tonight?"

Marteen looks at him from across the room, climbs into bed and just pulls the covers over her and doesn't speak a word. James, taking her silence as a yes, climbed into bed. After a few minutes, he turns over, hugs her, and kisses the back of her neck. Feeling more confident, he turns her over, climbs on top, and they make love.

When it's over, Marteen asks him to sleep in the guest room because apparently, he's still in the doghouse. "What? I thought we were good. Why I gotta sleep in there? Come on, now..."

Marteen says, "Because you don't rub your hands on another woman and think you can just ease back in bed with me. You're still in the doghouse; I just needed to get off! Goodnight."

"Awww, come on."

"No, and leave the door open when you leave. Now I'll see you in the morning. Goodnight, baby."

James curses and reluctantly leaves and goes into the guest room to sleep. He's thinking she is on some bullshit until sleep catches up to him. Marteen is smiling, and she is sleeping like Jazz, just like a baby, because she knows he has to learn to respect her and appreciate her in every way. She has something else planned for his ass tomorrow.

* * *

Marteen was still having nightmares about James grabbing on Basha's ass. It was destroying her confidence, and she was still angry and confused. She didn't want him to know, but she needed some outside attention. So, she got James's mom to babysit and went out with Randy for some harmless flirting. The hottest club in town was called Jay Bar, and to get on the VIP list you had to know someone. So, Marteen called Karen, and Carl made it happen.

Back in L.A. Carl tells Karen, "Alright, I got them on the list; Marteen, James, and Randy."

"Ok, I told her. But James is on a retreat with the boys club, so it's just Randy and Marteen."

"What? I didn't know she was going without him."

"And? What difference does it make? She can go without him, with his ugly cheating ass!"

"Uh, nah, this ain't cool. That's a pick-up place, and I'm not taking the blame for this. So, call her back and tell her to go somewhere else."

"Boy, they're probably already there."

"You should have told me James wasn't with them."

"I didn't know all that was necessary."

Carl shakes his head and walks into the other room, where he dials James's cell phone. James answers, "Hello?"

"Hey, what's up?"

"Oh, not a lot, just making sure these knuckleheads are sleeping and not playing and shit, what's up with you?"

Carl tells James, "Uh, Karen told me you were up at the lake house, and Marteen was going out with Randy."

"Yeah, she's taking him to, uh dinner for a belated birthday gift."

"Oh, well, she's on her way to Jay Bar with him because I just put them on the VIP list."

"What? Man, stop playing. I know she ain't going in there."

"She's going, man. So, I just thought I'd tell you because I thought you were with them, so I put your name down also."

"Ah shit, man, I'm squeezing her ass around her neck...she fucking with me... alright, I'll talk to ya later."

James hangs up and calls Marteen's cell phone, but she doesn't answer, so he leaves a message and calls her again! Still no answer. James tells one of the leaders that he has an emergency and has to leave. James drives to Jay Bar with fire in his blood because Marteen is walking into a player's den, and he was going to get his damn wife.

* * *

Marteen and Randy are sitting in the VIP room amongst all types of rappers and artists. They order a bottle of champagne, and Marteen is in rare form because she is getting all the attention. Someone sends a bottle of Dom over, and Randy is like, "Oh shit, it's going down again. Every time I'm out with one of y'all, we don't pay for shit!"

"Uh, no, we cannot accept that. I'm buying our drinks because I don't want them over here sweating me."

"Oh damn, now why not?"

"Because I just wanted to feel sexy because James is making me feel jealous with his latest shenanigans."

"Well, I could have told you, you are beautiful and sexy.

Shit'd you bring the drinks and the men everywhere we go! We could be in McDonald's, and someone will buy us Big Macs!"

They burst out laughing. "Basha can't touch you or Karen, so don't be feeling like that, girl. Don't you know, you got it going on?" And oh shit, here they ass come."

Two basketball players walk over and start talking to Marteen.

James was breaking every speed limit, and he was pissed because he knew Jay Bar wasn't a place for his wife to be at. He could not wait to see her ass; she was in deep trouble. Guys were known to drug pretty girls, especially the business ones like Marteen, because she wasn't up on that shit! And he was gonna kill someone tonight, damn it! James' thoughts were all over the place. He was less than 10 minutes away.

Marteen was dancing with a businessman from Detroit. He was the owner of a few car dealerships, and he was sniffing around her like new money. But she was just glad to get away from the basketball players. They were too aggressive. So, when he asked her to dance, she gladly accepted!

James walks into the VIP area. It's decked out in white leather seats and a medium-sized dance floor with big crystal chandeliers hanging from the ceiling. He sees Marteen dancing with a big country dude. She's shaking her ass in a mini skirt and a silk halter top. Her breasts are up and out, she has on high heels, and she's moving her hips to the music.

James is steaming hot as he walks towards the dance floor. James grabs Marteen by her waist, and she turns around. Before she can speak, he says, "Hey, time to go baby."

The businessman says, "Whoa, I'm dancing with her fine ass!"

"Not anymore. Just walk away because, trust me, you don't want this ass whooping."

The businessman says, "Fuck you and swings at James."

James ducks. He hits him one time and knocks him on his back, and he's out cold. Everyone is backing away, and people are staring. One of his friends runs over, and James quickly grabs him, and body slams him to the floor, and tells him to stay his ass down.

The bouncers come over, and one of them recognizes James and says, "Oh, okay, he's cool. Let's get these fools out of here."

Marteen is in shock because everything's happening so fast.

Security picks up the dude James knocked out. James shakes hands with one of the bouncers and says, "Hey, what's up player? Sorry, but he was hitting on my wife, and you know how it is..."

The bouncer replies, "Oh, for real?"

"Yeah, and when his ass wakes up, tell him if I see him, imma finish that ass whooping."

"Hey, don't worry, he ain't coming back. But tell Carl I said what's up because he is blowing up! I love that new hit 'Can You Feel It.' Man, that's the shit. And tell him to hook a nigga up!"

"Will do, and yeah, he's doing that shit. I'll tell him. Well, just send me the bill, okay? I'm out."

"Oh, it's cool. His ass is paying before he wakes up. Take care of yourself and your pretty lady."

Marteen is as quiet as a mouse because she knows she's in trouble.

James guides Marteen out, and Randy is right behind them.

James makes sure Randy drives off safely, and he and Marteen walk over to his car. He helps her into the passenger seat and then gets into the car and says, "Why are you testing me baby? What happened to going out to dinner and then going home? Why are you in that pick-up market of a club?"

"I didn't know it was like that, and we just decided at the last minute." James slams his hands on the steering wheel. He takes a deep breath, starts the car, and they drive home in silence.

Marteen's heart is beating so fast because she's never seen him so angry, so she doesn't say anything. When they are in the house, Marteen takes off her shoes and walks straight to the bedroom. James pours a glass of bourbon and drinks it down. Then he pours himself another one and sits down on the sofa. He's too angry to talk to her because raw anger is inside of him, and he doesn't want to say or do anything to hurt her. If she opens up her mouth and says some goofy stuff, he's going to choke her, as God is his witness.

He's rubbing his hand when Marteen comes over to him with a wet cloth and rubbing alcohol. She's still wet from her shower, and he looks up at her. She sits next to him. She takes his hand, and she silently takes care of it. She walks away, and she comes back.

She grabs his hand and leads him into the bedroom. He sits on the bed, and she looks at him and says, "I'm so sorry baby. I wasn't thinking, I wasn't thinking."

James pulls her down onto the bed, kisses her, and holds her. He tells her he loves her. "I love you, don't you know?" She nods. "I know you are a grown woman, and you have been taking care of yourself before I came along. But now you're my wife, okay? You are my WIFE. So please don't set me off again, please. Okay?"

"Okay, I'm sorry. How is your hand?"

"It's been better."

He stands up and undresses. Marteen pulls the covers back, and she climbs into bed. James climbs in and hugs her so tightly. He looks at her, smiles, and says, "I see I have to take you out more often because you look so good swinging those hips, you know that?"

"Oh, did I? Well, you scared me, fighting like that."

She rubs his hand and kisses him all over. All of a sudden, she couldn't wait to feel him. Watching him fight two big guys over her has her on fire. She goes insane as she is kissing him and rubbing him. She takes him as deep as she can take him, and she makes passionate love to her baby daddy, her husband, her boo thang, and most importantly, her strong, capable superman.

She has her confidence back and her man. And yes, she forgives him, and she'll never bring it up. She doesn't need to, because she has his undivided attention! Throughout every room of the house, you can hear her screams. Because this time, he's not smothering her cries. He wants to hear her scream out his name. Because she's his wife and he loves her to the very core of her being. He would tear someone to pieces over her, and she knew. Yep, she knew.

CHAPTER 47

James was up early, looking out of his bedroom window. Marteen was taking a shower, and he was thinking about last night. He knew he had his hands full with Marteen. She was strong-willed, and he liked that. But seeing her dancing in a club like Jay Bar made his blood boil, but what could he do? He couldn't choke her because he'd be under the jailhouse. So, he had to talk to her and give her more attention, hoping she wouldn't get curious about that type of life.

Marteen comes over and hugs him from behind. He quickly responds with, "Good morning baby," and kisses her.

"Good morning. Where were you just now? You had that serious look on your face."

"Mmm, just wondering what made you put on your party clothes and go to that club last night."

"Oh, well, uh, you said we didn't have to talk about it anymore."

"Yeah, I said it because I was angry inside, and I couldn't handle your excuses then. But I'm in control of that anger now. So, I wanna know why my wife was out shaking her ass last night when she told me she was going to a restaurant?"

Marteen takes her arms off of James. She senses his negative body language, so she gives him some distance. She walks over and sits on the edge of the bed and says, "Well, honestly, I was still in my feelings about you and Basha. I just wanted someone to tell me I was beautiful. Someone other than you, because..."

James interrupts, "But I tell you that every day, baby. Don't I show you love? Why do you need a stranger to tell you what I tell you every day?"

"Ok, just let me finish baby. I needed to feel better about myself because seeing your attraction to another woman made me feel unattractive to you. I just wanted to feel beautiful. Saying it out loud doesn't make sense now. I was so hurt and embarrassed that I needed to feel like I wasn't losing my sexy side. Can you understand that?"

"I guess. So did you want to make out with another man, or something like that?"

"No, of course not. I even refused all of the drinks that were sent to me. I just wanted the attention and nothing else. I love you so much, and I was scared you were bored with me or something. Because why else would you wanna grab another woman's body part?

"Mmm, baby, I told you in L.A. that I didn't want anyone else and that I was in love with you. I don't know what else to do. But I know I don't want you back in that club. Because whatever you were looking for wasn't in there, okay? So, I need you to understand something: I love you to death. No doubts, ok? You need to believe that shit! Because if I ever see you with another man, I cannot be responsible for what will happen. Do you understand that?"

"Yes, I understand that, and you won't. Because I know now I'm secure with you and your feelings for me. I'm sorry I put you in that position; I'll never do anything like that again, okay?"

James walks over and kisses her. He looks down at her and says, "Please don't do that again. I'm going to pick up Jazz, and I'll be right back, ok?"

"Okay."

She thinks for a second and says his name out loud, "James! I'm sorry baby. Are we okay?"

He stops and turns around, "Yeah, we're good." He walks back, lifts her up, looks into her eyes, and says, "I love only you. You don't have to look for love anymore, okay? Believe me, because I'll die for you without hesitation. I don't understand why you can't feel it." And he kisses her with so much love and the deepest passion until she is dizzy.

When he finally lets go, he walks out the door. Marteen stares after him. She touches her lips and then her stomach because she has the same butterflies swarming around in her stomach as their first kiss. She should have never doubted his love. She felt it in her bones, all the way down in her toes. God knows she felt it.

CHAPTER 48

Gia was stepping out of her comfort zone, and she introduced her first rap song to Carl, and she called it,

'Happy Doesn't Last Long'

So, you ain't feeling those sad songs...

You think I'm hating n' I want some...

Well Ms. Lady, you got it all wrong...

Cause I left his cheating ass alone...

Cause happy doesn't last long...

Why u hating on them sad songs...

He'll be chasing bitches in ya home...

Happy doesn't last long...

Wait til ya pick up his phone...

Those bitches calling...all night long...

He got Susie cause she real thick

And Betty because she does them tricks...

So, trust me, I'm long gone..

Ain't trying to mess up a home...

Who u protecting yourself from...

Yeah, happy doesn't last long

Why you hating... he getting his freak on...

Why you hating on them sad songs..

That's why I left his cheating ass alone...

As soon as I let him drop I ran and I didn't stop..,

Doing better, and I love myself...

Happy, because I know where I've been...

Won't ever worry me again.

Now I'm blessed in my new home.. trust me...

Happiness doesn't last long...

All smiles and living life

Soon...you'll be his ex-wife

He's already in his next home.

While u hating ...your man is long gone

Trust me...happy doesn't last long

Now he left you and you're all alone...

Bet u wanna play a sad song...

Told ya happy doesn't last long...

Yeah...bet u wanna play a sad song

Balled up...crying ...cause you're all alone

Yeah....Sorry you had it all wrong.

Wipe your tears and play your sad song...

Yeah ...play ya sad song

Happy doesn't last long...

Happy doesn't last long...

Of course, Gia wasn't a rapper, but Carl was smiling because he knew someone who could rap the heck out of Gia's new song, a chick called Missy. With a little tweaking, it could be a hit! Carl turns to Gia and says, "Yeah, I like it. Let me see what I can do, and I'll holla at you. Now, is there something else you wanna play?

Karen told me about this man-bashing song you wrote with Dana."

Gia laughing, says, "Oh, yes. 'Never Trust a Man.' I'm still working on it, but you are going to crack up whenever you hear it."

"Oh, is that right?"

"Yep, because we were inspired by you and Dana's on-and-off relationship. It sorta goes like this...

She sings in her soulful voice:

I say never trust a man

Never trust man

If he drives a Mustang.,

Ya, hear me...

Learn from me...

Carl falls over laughing, "Oh, hell nah. That's messed up. Y'all wrong for that. Man, I love my Mustang!"

They both begin laughing.

* * *

James was on a conference call with Carl and Bob. They were trying to resolve the problem with Basha and their rap video. Carl finally talked Basha into signing on, but now they had to talk their wives into letting them release the video.

James says, "Uh, man, I don't know. My wife will kill me if she ever views that video. So, I need to tiptoe around this and butter her up. Shit'd because I'm telling you, if she says no, then I cannot do it."

Carl agrees, "Yeah, I know, same here. But I know if Marteen is cool with it then Karen will be. I'm not really singing with Basha in this one. But yo ass is rapping with Basha so I don't know if Marteen will feel comfortable enough, you know?"

James says, "Yeah, I know. Well, when she comes back from the park, I'll talk to her, alright?"

Bob says, "Ok cool. Just hit us back up, and we'll take it from there."

Carl says, "Sounds good. So, I won't mention anything to Karen until I hear back from you, ok?"

James says, "Okay, I'll holler at ya later, bye."

They end the call just when Marteen is coming in. Marteen and Jazz are just getting back from their stroll in the park and Jazz is asleep. James says, "Hey baby, how was y'all play date?"

"Oh, she tired herself out, playing with her little friends. She's starting to take stuff from people. I don't know where she gets that from, but she was acting bad today."

"Mmm, well, that's why we need to make another baby, sweetie. She needs a sibling."

He walks over, pulls Marteen into his arms, and kisses her. Marteen pulls away and says, "Mmm, there you go with that mess. I swear if I'm pregnant again, I'm going to stop speaking to you. You are praying way too hard for us to have another one, and my body just got back to its original form. Dang!!"

"So, you not going to give me another baby? Don't you want our kids to grow up together like you and Karen did?"

Marteen puts Jazz to bed, walks back into the living room and says, "Yes I do, but baby can we just give it another year, please!" She flops down on the sofa and asks James how his conference call went with Carl.

James says, "Well, I'm glad you asked because I wanna run something by you, ok?"

"Mmm, well if it's about that rap video with Basha the answer is hell no!! I'm serious about that, ok?"

"Baby, why can't I do this rap? Everyone is counting on me because without me, there's no song, period. And Basha is just in it for a few minutes with me, and I'm not touching her at all. I'm just rapping baby, ok, that's all!"

"Baby I just don't want you in this Hollywood drama. Because you know if this is a hit, women are going to be all over you. And I swear if you touch anyone or..." She gets up, walks over, and gently grabs his stuff, "Give my stuff away, I will kill you, and that's the gospel!"

She then kisses him with so much love. He grabs her butt, pulls her closer to him, picks her up, and carries her back to the sofa. He says "Baby, I'm not giving anything away. I'm all yours, you know that. Please let me."

They are wrapped up inside each other, and neither one is listening.

Later that evening, James asked Marteen again if it was okay for him to release the video, "So, is it okay for me to do the video?" Marteen is carrying Jazz on her hip and replies, "I don't care. You know you want to be in that Hollywood drama. So go on and do it, but I'm telling you, if any drama with another woman develops, I'm gone. I'm not forgiving you, and I don't wanna hear, baby please, and all that. I will walk away and never look back. Just so we are clear.

And I'm not sweating you because I have a daughter to raise, and I don't have time to be no damn detective, so just do the damn video, okay?"

She walks into the bedroom with Jazz in her arms and shuts the door behind her. James is standing in the kitchen looking off into space. He takes a deep breath and calls Carl. He tells him he can't do it because his wife is not on board, and he loves her more than a rap video.

Carl says, "Yeah, I figured as much. So, I'll call Bob and listen to him whine about it."

"Alright, I'll talk to you later."

James goes into the bedroom and Marteen is lying down with Jazz. He gets in the bed and Jazz is sitting in the middle. She's playing with her blocks and doing her baby talking. James picks her up and plays with her for a few minutes. He sits her back down and puts her bottle within her reach. He looks over at his wife and says, "I just called Carl, and I told him I couldn't do the video, okay sweetie?"

"Mmm, why did you do that? I thought you wanted to do it."

"Yeah, but it's not worth upsetting you. I don't want my wife mad at me."

"Well, I wasn't mad; I was just worried about the drama. You saw how it changed my sister, and I just don't want that to happen to me. I'm a mother now, and I have to keep my priorities straight."

"Yeah, I know. That's why I love you so much, and you're right. We don't need any distractions because I think you're pregnant again."

Marteen immediately sits up and says, "Omg, why would you say that?"

"Mmm, because I know your body inside and out, baby and I can see a change in you. You were sick this morning and you went to the grocery store and bought two gallons of orange juice. You didn't start your cycle last month because we've been having sex every day and every night. So yeah, you're probably 6-8 weeks pregnant."

"Awwww schutz, I think you're right. Awwww, I know you did this on purpose because remember when you couldn't wait, and I changed my birth control pills? You remember when I told you to use a rubber, and you were like those days are over, and we made love all night? I know that's the night. OMG!"

James smiles, leans over, kisses her, and says, "I'm sorry baby, but you better make an appointment just to be sure, okay?"

"Mmm, well you can just wipe that smirk off of your face." She picks up Jazz and rocks her to sleep. "Because I'm not talking to your butt. I can't believe this. I'm getting my tubes tied in triple knots, after this birth, trust me."

"No, you're not. I wish you would do that. Baby you know we agreed to a big family, so no tubes tying, okay?"

"Well, you need to use rubbers when I'm in between birth control methods because you are always poking me and acting like you are allergic to condoms. I am not having all these babies, back-to-back." Jazz is closing her eyes.

"Okay sweetie. I'm sorry but I cannot wait for you to find out, for certain."

He reaches over and gently lifts up Jazz and takes her to her baby bed because she has fallen asleep in Marteen's arms. He comes back and Marteen is brushing her hair in the mirror. He walks over, takes the brush, brushes her hair and says, "Baby, I'm the luckiest man alive to have you. I'm sorry you got pregnant before you were ready but I know you will be glad when he is born because I think it's a boy this time."

Marteen rubs her stomach and says, "Mmm I hope so, because if it's another girl, you are going to drive me crazy until we have a boy." She turns around, hugs him, and says, "Thanks for not doing the video. I don't wanna share you with the world."

"Yep, anything to make you happy baby. And I think we better take a trip somewhere, just us before you start showing. Because I wanna see you in a string bikini, okay?"

"Ooh yes, and before my taste buds go away. We need to plan something ASAP!"

James starts to undress her. Marteen wiggles away and says, "Really James, we just made love a few hours ago. You are a maniac."

"Hey, I can't help it. I'm married to a goddess, and you know, I gotta have it, so bring your ass over here."

She starts backing away, "No, and don't wake up Jazz."

"Uh, that's you, screaming like I'm killing you. I won't make a sound. Now come on, because if I have to chase you, I'm hitting it all night long. So, you better get over here. I just want a quickie baby."

Marteen sighs and says, "What is wrong with you? You are never satisfied." She shakes her head and removes her clothes. James watches her as he removes his sweats, and he says, "It's your fault, with all that good stuff. Come here and tell me you love me. You know I need to hear that shit."

Marteen walks over to him and says, "I love you, baby."

"Oh yeah, tell me again baby."

"I love you so much."

He makes love to her over and over until she screams out and wakes up Jazz again because she just can't hold it in. James is smiling as he gives his daughter her pacifier and soothes her back to sleep so Marteen can enjoy the aftermath.

James was the happiest man alive. He had it all: a beautiful daughter and a classy, beautiful freak of a wife. He had to thank God again tonight for sending him exactly what he prayed for. He smiled as he watched his daughter slowly fall back asleep with her pacifier and his wife curled up in a fetal position. Yeah, he was truly blessed with two beautiful babies.

CHAPTER 49

Carl was working at his record studio doing paperwork when Bob busted into his office out of breath. Bob had run down the hallway. He had just listened to Gia's sample tapes, and he was beyond thrilled. Bob says, "Man, who is this Gia? I just listened to her tape, and she sounds unbelievable!"

"Oh, she's family man. She's the one that's engaged to my wife's brother."

"Oh yeah, she sang at the wedding, and she can rap a little bit. I like her sound."

"Yeah, I know. She has another song about men. It's corny, but I love it."

"Well, you know what, I think we should replace Basha with Gia, and then James can do it because his wife was only tripping because of Basha!"

"Mmm, well, you know James used to date Gia, so I don't know."

"Oh damn! Who hasn't he fucked with? Man, he is a trip. I'm telling you, I thought I was on to something, God dammit!!" And he sits down in the chair across from Carl's desk.

"Hold up, now!! Uh, well, you might be. Let me run it by Gia and James and see, okay? Because they dated a long time ago, and Marteen is cool with Gia."

"Mmm, okay, because we are sitting on a hit because that slick ass James can rap his ass off! He could be the next Snoop Dog!"

"Yeah, I know. And we need to give him a name. Now go rest your nerves and stop running and shit. You know you could've just picked up the phone and called me."

"Man, I know. I was just excited and shit, because man, you got papers! I'm trying to get some papers, you feel me?"

"Yeah, I feel you, but don't kill ya self."

They both laugh, and Bob says, "Man, bye."

* * *

James was feeling hopeful because he knew he could rap with Gia because they had good vibes. So, it was up to his buddy Carl to convince Marteen because he wasn't doing anything to set her off. James was working at the Boys Club today and he was meeting Marteen later for an early dinner. He wanted to take her out and show her off, because she was starting to get cabin fever, and she needed a break from Jazz.

Carl and Karen were in town for a few days, so they were babysitting Jazz for the day. He was hoping Carl could later persuade his wife to let him do the rap video because he really wanted to do it. It was eating at him, but he needed to keep peace inside his house, so he wasn't bringing it back up.

Across town Karen was down on her living room floor in her old apartment playing with Jazz. She was helping her build a castle with her blocks, but Jazz wanted to eat them all. Carl walks into the living room and cracks up laughing. Man, she puts everything in her mouth! Look at her."

Carl gets down on the floor with them, and he pretends to eat one of her blocks. Jazz snatches her block from him, throws it across the room, and starts screaming at him with that baby talk. They laugh at her.

Karen says, "You better leave her stuff alone. She ain't sharing with you.

"I'm sorry, Jazz, I know now you're a bad baby, like your Auntie Karen."

"Boy, don't tell her that. I'm her favorite Auntie, right Jazz?" She picks up Jazz, and they rub noses together. Jazz is so tickled.

Carl smiles, "She's so cute, isn't she?"

"Yes, she is, right? Tell him, yes, yes, tell him Jazz. I'm cute and smart just like my mommy and my auntie."

Karen takes her into the bedroom and checks her diaper because they are going on a little shopping spree. Carl is standing in the doorway, and he says, "Baby do I have to go with you?"

"Nope, I'm meeting Randy and Constance, so you are off the hook, okay?"

"Alright, cool. I'm going to the Boys Club to hang out with James, so just call me when you're ready, and I'll pick you up. So uh, where am I dropping y'all off?"

"Oh, uh, Neiman Marcus because they have cute girl stuff."

"Okay, I'll put the car seat in. You want me to carry something down?"

"Yes, grab her bag and stroller for me."

"Okay."

Carl picks Karen and Jazz up from Neiman Marcus, and they drive to James' house. Marteen opens the door and takes Jazz from Carl, kisses her, and tells her how much she missed her. James comes over, hugs Karen, and thanks her for babysitting.

Karen says, "Oh, anytime. She is a delight and such a good baby. She didn't cry or anything. Oh, and we went shopping and got her some stuff." Karen has two large shopping bags.

Marteen says, "Omg girl what did you buy, the entire store? Ooh, let's go in the room and look at them!" They go into the bedroom and James shakes his head and offers Carl a drink.

Carl says, "Uh, I'll take a beer. So, I brought the tape with me, and I have it on film so let me know which one we should show them."

"Mmmm, well, I'm thinking the cassette tape so she doesn't have a visual of Basha, and then you can tell her that we're replacing Basha with Gia, ok?"

Carl agrees, "Yeah, ok."

James goes into the bedroom and asks the girls to come out and listen to one of Carl's new songs. James takes Jazz from Marteen's arms, and they sit down on the sofa. Carl puts the tape in. When Marteen recognizes James' voice she puts her hands over her mouth and looks over at her husband.

The song is called *'Hey Sexy'*

James raps:

> *Hey sexy in those daisy dukes,*
> *Damn girl, can I talk to you..*
> *Call me daddy because I'm so strict*

You can't stop me...til I'm finished

Love you hard just like a Queen

Girl, I'll give you all the finer things

Satisfaction guaranteed

I'll give you what you want and what ya need...

Come on Sexy, just talk to me

Basha sings:

I don't know, you talk a good game...and you so smooth,

But I'm not into material things... I'm sorry,

I'm with another...dude

James raps:

Oh, yeah .... I'm sorry too...

But you ain't listening

You blind and don't see...

I'm that dude to take ya from these streets ...

Come here baby, I wanna wine you

And ooh Girl can I dine with you...

I'll have you whinny like a baby...

You'll be smiling in ya damn sleep...

Yeah come on n talk to me

Carl sings:

Don't explain bro...

She aint on this brick...

She busy chasing these knuckleheads

She ain't down like them other chicks...

You feeling her cause she is so thick!

James's rap:

Yeah and that's the damn truth!

Like em thick and super cute

Yeah She got that phat ass too

Come on sexy, can I talk to you

Basha Sings:

I don't know, you sound a little slick...

Not easily impressed like those thirsty chicks

You want my digits; I'll have to ponder it...

But I don't think you can handle this

Carl Sing:

Ooh shit! She just challenged you

James:

Damn baby what you tryna do?

I know talk is cheap, but I got something that'll make ya weep...

Baby I don't brag cause it's childish...

The truth is you ain't ready for me

I'll have you speaking in your native tongue...

Trust me girl, I'll get ya sprung...

Don't challenge me...

When I get you in these sheets...

Girl you'll be crowning me...your new king!

I'll take your ass around the globe ...cause I'm nasty!

Truth be told...

You can't handle me!

I'll have you screaming and calling me daddy...

Cause I'm so strict... trust me,

Baby you ain't ready

Yeah check my references,

Talk is cheap...

Let's get a room and you can sample me...

Basha swings her hips and walks away.

James raps:

Hold up Sexy, where you running to...

Don't leave me hanging...can I talk to you...

Got my heart in the danger zone...

Give me yo digits or let me take you home...

Get with me and I'll put you on a throne...

Picket fence all around our home...

Carl sings:

She ain't on no real dude

She like fuckin with them old fools

Move along n go fishing in the sea

She likes those sharks with the gold teeth...

She blind and can't see...

You the one to take her from the streets

Keep it moving where she wants to be...

Yeah snatch another from the blue sea...

James Raps:

Hey sexy! Will ya talk to me...

Basha:

Here's my number

I think I've heard enough.

James Raps:

Thank you, baby., I'll hit you up!

Yeah, sexy... I'll hit ya up...

Hey sexy you'll be crowned a Queen..

Tell ya man to pack up all his things!

Carl and James sing:

His time is up! Yeah his time is up

James:

Yeah...tell ya man, his time is up!!

Carl stops the tape. Marteen stands up, shakes her head, looks at her husband, and says, "Okay, so you doing this, huh?"

"No, I just wanted y'all to hear it, and Carl was thinking of putting Gia in and removing Basha. But uh if you still don't want me to do it then I won't, okay?" James says looking at his wife.

Karen says, "Y'all sound good as hell and I didn't know James could sing or rap like that, man that's a hit! I love it, and baby you know you sounded good!" She walks over and hugs Carl.

Carl says, "Thank you, sweetie. So, uh, what do you think? I'm waiting to hear what you have to say." He looks right at Marteen.

Marteen agrees, "Yeah, it sounds good. Y'all know y'all don't need my approval because it sounds like it's already done. She stares at James, rolls her eyes at him, and sits down.

James says, "Okay man, uh, well I guess I'll think about it because it's not up to me. So, uh tell Bob to put it aside for now, okay? So uh, y'all wanna play some spades or something?"

Sensing the tension, Carl declines and says they'll take a rain check. He and Karen say goodbye and leave.

CHAPTER 50

Marteen is furious with James. As soon as Karen and Carl leave, she goes completely off. "Really James? I thought this matter was put to rest." She puts her hands on her hips and mimics James's voice, "What the hell happened to, uh, oh, I love you more than rap, and I don't want to upset you and all that garbage that came out of your mouth! You sound just like that slick-ass mess on the tape. I swear to Jehovah if you release that, you are going to be in a world of trouble. Do you understand me?"

"Yeah, I hear you."

He hands her Jazz, grabs his keys, and walks to the door.

"Where the hell are you going?" as she switches Jazz to her left shoulder and soothes her.

"For a drive because I'm not trying to argue with you, okay?"

Marteen switches Jazz to her right shoulder and responds in a whisper, "Well, we need to talk about this because I'm really confused. You tell me one thing, and then you do another, and now you wanna walk out."

"Yeah, because if you continue talking to me like that, I'm going to say something I know I'll regret. So why don't you try to cool off and when I return we can talk, okay? Because trust me you need to calm down. And I know exactly what I said, but this matter isn't as easy as I thought to just walk away from."

"Well, I don't want my husband singing rap songs. And where are you going?"

James stares at her for a brief moment and says, "Just out, ok?" And he opens the door and shuts it behind him.

Marteen sighs and walks back into the bedroom with Jazz. She sits down in the rocking chair and rocks her baby until she falls asleep too. James rides over to the Boys Club, goes into the gym, and shoots free throws until his arms are numb.

Back at home, Marteen is pacing back and forth because now she is worried. This is the first time he has left without telling her where he was going. She calls the Boys Club, hoping he is in his office. James picks up on the third ring and says, "Hello?"

"Hey, it's me," Marteen says.

"What's up, baby."

"Please come home."

"Okay, have you calmed down?"

"Yes, so please come home."

"Alright, I was just shooting some free throws. Let me lock up and I'll head back."

"Okay, are you hungry?"

"Yeah, I can eat something. Do you want me to pick up something?"

"No, I just need you to come home, ok? I'll order a pizza and make a salad. Is that cool?"

"Yeah, that's cool, I'm on my way."

Marteen is at the kitchen island preparing a salad when James walks in and says, "Hey you, is Jazz asleep?"

"Hey. Yes, she's asleep. Do you want to eat in the kitchen or the dining room?"

"Whatever, it doesn't matter."

"Hey, can you come here please?"

James walks over to his wife. Marteen walks around the island, stands in front of James, and says, "I'm sorry for yelling and although I felt blindsided, I understand why you wanted me to hear the tape. It sounded good and I'm proud of you, baby. You are a man of many talents." She hugs him and he hugs her back.

* * *

James and Marteen are flying to LA for some alone time and to record his new rap song with Gia. James's mom was babysitting Jazz for a week. They are happily in love and ready to enjoy the sun. James and Marteen were spending three days with Carl to record and then they were off to Maui for four days of relaxation.

The first day of recording was not a good day for James. He was joking around with Bob and a few of the other guys from the studio. Gia was flying in later that night and Carl was doing some last-minute sound checks. Marteen and Karen were on their way over after enjoying a little retail therapy.

It was a record-breaking hot day in L.A. so, Marteen and Karen decided to buy some matching daisy dukes and dress like twins in honor of the new rap video, called 'Hey sexy'. Marteen had practiced Gia's lines, and she was playing on singing it for James. It was supposed to be all in good fun. But James and Carl didn't find it the least bit entertaining.

James was in the middle of recording when Marteen and Karen walked in, switching in their daisy dukes on cue while James was rapping. Marteen raises her arms over her head and starts singing Gia's lines and swinging her hips. Karen is dancing with her, and everyone is staring at them, like, what the heck?

Bob is choking on his iced tea as he watches Marteen dance, and James looks over at her. He and Carl exchange looks...what the hell! James stops singing and leaves the booth, and Carl is right behind him. One of the guys is like, hold up, that was great and another one of the guys says, damn they're fine as hell!!

James says, "Hey, what are you doing baby? I'm in the middle of recording?"

"I know; I just wanted to cheer you on and have a little fun. Did I do something wrong?"

"Absolutely! This ain't no damn club. Why are you walking in here with all these nigga's in here half naked and shaking your ass?"

Marteen, feeling hurt, "Omg are you serious baby? I was just trying to play a joke on you, just to show my support. Awww... I can't believe you."

Marteen turns to walk away. James grabs her arm, pulls her to the side and whispers, "Hey don't embarrass me, okay? Just let me work and I'll talk to you about this later, okay?"

"Why are you making me feel like I did something wrong?"

"Because you did! Now take that shit offyou ! And please cover your ass up!" He is looking crazy, and he's grabbing her arm really hard because her breasts are out, and her ass is busting out of her shorts, and he is furious at her!

"You're hurting me!"

Realizing what he was doing, James let go and walked back inside. Carl is whispering to Karen and when he walks away she is staring at him with a confused look on her face. Back inside James walks back into the booth and Carl walks in behind him. He apologizes for the interruptions and tells everyone to take a 15-minute break.

James leaves the booth and shakes his head at Carl. James says to Carl, "Man, what the fuck were they doing?"

"I don't know! Karen knows I don't care for those damn shorts on her and she doing all that damn shaking and shit! Man, sometimes I wish I could slap her ass and not be judged."

"Hell yeah, I could squeeze Marteen's neck until her ass just passed out! She was testing me ever since she took her ass to that got damn club and was shaking her ass with some country-looking dude! Man, I swear I wanted to grab her by her throat, but you can't do that shit. We'll be in jail!

"Yep! Let me go check and see what she's doing because I know her feelings are hurt and shit."

"Alright, well I can't even look at Marteen right now because I don't wanna go to jail today.

They both laugh and part ways.

* * *

Marteen was beyond confused. She knew her husband was angry with her, but she couldn't care less about it because he was acting juvenile. Marteen and James were staying at Carl's guesthouse. The view from the master bedroom terrace overlooks the gigantic pool area. Marteen is inside the master suite and changes into a two-piece bathing suit, slips her daisy dukes back on over her swimsuit bottoms, and walks a few steps to the pool.

Karen is sitting out alone, and she has on a one-piece orange swimsuit with a sarong as her cover-up. Karen says, "Hey sis," as she lifts up her sunglasses. "Ooh I thought you were taking those shorts off?"

"Girl, I am not thinking about James. He is not my damn daddy!"

"Well, I like having peace in my house. I took them off because my husband is crazy as hell, and I'm not trying to mess with him over those shorts."

"I know because Carl has you wrapped around his finger. But James is not telling me how to dress. It is 104 degrees outside. I'm wearing these shorts, so he better get over it."

She takes her shorts off and jumps into the pool. Karen shakes her head when Carl suddenly walks over and kisses her.

He says, "Hey, you feel okay?"

"Mmm hmmm, I'm good, just relaxing. I'm sorry we interrupted your recording."

"It's cool. I'm sorry I snapped at you. But you know these guys are easily distracted, and I don't want them eyeballing you like a piece of meat. That's all sweetie."

"Yep, I'm good! How long y'all going to be because Gia isn't coming until later tonight."

"Uh yeah, we should be done in an hour or so. I was just checking on you."

"Mmm, well I'm good baby. Are we entertaining your band tonight because I can set up the grill?"

"Nah, I'm sending them jokers home. I'm spending some quality time with my gorgeous wife." He kisses her with so much passion before he walks back to his studio.

Marteen steps out of the pool, wraps a towel around herself, and sits down.

Marteen says, "Damn, your husband is checking on your ass, huh?"

"Mmm hmmm, he was just trying to make sure he didn't piss me off. That's all that was about. Because as quiet as it's kept, his butt is wrapped around my finger!"

They both laugh.

Marteen replies, "I heard that, but my husband is on a trip! He is one complicated man. But I love his ass, so I guess I'll stop wearing these daisy dukes."

"Thank you, because James was looking at you like he wanted to beat yo ass!"

Marteen laughs, "I know he was thinking about it because he grabbed my arm so hard and then turned his back on me."

Karen says, "Well, I'm going in this water." She takes off her sarong and jumps into the pool. Marteen jumps back in, and they swim and play poolside games until they tire themselves out.

After hanging out with Karen all day, Marteen decides to call it a day. She exits the pool, dries off, slips back into her shorts, and says goodbye to her sister. She walks back towards her room just as James is walking with Carl and Bob. The guys are on a break and are walking towards the pool. James is laughing at something when he looks over and sees his wife walking to their room, still in her daisy dukes.

James is furious and asks Carl if he has his bail money. Carl replies, "Yep, I got you, and I got Cochran on speed dial."

Bob says, "Man, y'all are some serious dudes!"

"I'll see y'all later." He jogs over to catch up with his wife.

Marteen opens up the door. James is right behind her, and they walk inside together.

As soon as they are inside, James taps Marteen on her butt and says, "Why are you so fuckin hardheaded and don't listen to half the stuff I tell you?"

"Baby, it's 104 degrees outside, and I was at the pool, in case you haven't noticed."

"Yeah, but your sister listens to her man, but you don't give a damn about anything I say!"

"I am not my sister, and I do listen to you when you make sense."

James takes a step toward her, stops, and stares at her. Marteen takes a step back and unconsciously rubs the arm he squeezed.

Marteen breaks the stare, takes off her shorts, and grabs a robe to put on. James asks, "Would it have hurt you to just take the shorts off baby like I asked you to? Sometimes things don't have to make sense. But because it was important to me, you should have done what I asked. I know you are not Karen, but you could learn something from her because she knows how to be a wife!"

"Oh, so I'm not a good wife because I kept my shorts on."

"Baby, those things are not shorts. They're attention grabbers! Men are attracted to those types of shorts. I don't want them staring at your ass cheeks!! So next time I ask your ass not to do something, listen to me!!"

James is raising his voice, "I listen to everything you tell me. When you told me to stop flirting with waitresses, even though it was harmless to me and didn't make sense, I stopped because it bothered you. Because that's some shit you do when you love someone! But you so fucking hardheaded, and your stubbornness is going to get yo ass choked up." His phone rings.

* * *

James is staring into Marteen's eyes as he answers his call. "Hello? Yeah, ok, I'll be there in a minute." James ends his call, looks at his wife, and rubs his fingers through his hair. He shakes his head and says, "Why is it so hard for you to do what I asked?"

He walks over to her, and Marteen takes a step back. She extends her hands out and says, "I'm not my sister, but I'm a damn good wife. I do listen to you, but I don't like it when you talk to me like I'm a child!"

"Baby, I just asked you to change your shorts, that's all. How is that treating you like a child?"

"It's how you say things. I am working on my attitude, but you need to work on your temper. I'm sorry baby, I was going to change, but I went to the pool, so I didn't..."

James cuts her off, "It's cool, you already told me. It didn't make sense. Well, I'm going back to the studio. That was Carl on the phone. Gia just got here, so we are going to start recording. I'll talk to you later."

He opens the door and walks out. Marteen sits on the bed and screams, "Ahhhhh!" She flops down on the bed and sighs. James gets to the studio, and Gia hugs him and says, "Hey, I was just explaining to Carl that I can't wear any daisy dukes for the video because Chase is dead set against it, so we need to..."

James interrupts, "Yeah, that's cool, I understand."

"Oh, wow. Okay, I thought you were going to argue with me, but alright then, let's get it started."

They get into the booth, and on Bob's cue, James starts rapping:

"Hey sexy in those daisy dukes damn girl, can I talk to you..

Call me daddy because I'm so strict

You can't stop me...til I'm finished

Love you hard just like a Queen..,

Girl, I'll Give you all the finer things...

They practice most of the night. When James gets back to the guest house, Marteen is asleep. James undresses, and he stares at his wife while she's sleeping. He notices how she's all curled up, like Jazz when she's sleeping. Marteen is wearing one of his T-shirts. She's always in his T-shirts. He walks over and covers her up, and kisses her cheek. He strokes her hair. He's thinking the love of his life is so damn stubborn and so incredibly beautiful.

Marteen wakes up and immediately reaches for James, but he's not in bed with her. She sits up yawning, looks around, and calls out his name. Silence. She gets up and sees the note on the bedside table, and she reads aloud."

Didn't want to wake you, I'm going into town with Carl to talk business, and I'll see you later this evening.
Love, James

Marteen crumbles the paper and throws it across the room. She calls him on his cell. James answers, "Hello?"

"Hi, why did you let me sleep? I thought we were supposed to talk?"

"We will baby. I just didn't want to wake you up, ok?"

"Well next time, wake me so I can at least kiss you goodbye. How long are you going to be gone?"

"Uh, probably all day. We are meeting some producers for dinner, so it'll be later tonight. I'm sorry baby."

"Are you serious? You should've woken me up! We got to talk because I don't like you being mad at me, okay?"

"I'm not mad, just a little irritated. But can we talk later tonight because I'm going into a meeting, okay?"

"Mmm, okay. I love you."

"Love you too baby, bye."

"Bye, sweetheart."

Marteen gets dressed and walks over to the main house. She greets Karen and Gia, "Good morning ladies."

Gia says, "Hello!"

Karen replies, "Hey lady, guess you had a nice night. Walking in here, and it's almost noontime."

"No, I didn't, and James left without saying anything. He left me a damn note. I'm so mad at him!"

Karen asks, "Oh, he didn't tell you about the meeting today?"

"No, not till I called his cell phone."

"Well, he knew about it yesterday because Basha is threatening to sue them if they pull her off the record."

"Mmmm really, well, you can't blame her because she was all in and set, so..."

"Yeah, I know," Karen replies

Gia says, "Well, I didn't know anything about her because I was not trying to take money out of her pocket. So, I told them I was going back home tomorrow. This isn't my type of thing anyway. Y'all know I prefer soulful music."

Marteen says, "Mmm hmm well, I think they wanted you because of me. But I told James I was okay with Basha singing it because I trusted him. But if she even looks sideways at him, you think you fucked her up, trust me, I will kill that bitch! And that's on my baby, Jazzmine!" They all laugh.

Karen says, "I know that's right. But I don't want her in it. But Carl told me either they use Basha, or they drop it and write another song because his lawyers are saying that Basha was in her right to sue." Marteen says, "Oh well, let's go out and put a hurting on our husband's credit card because Mama needs a new dress!

They hit Rodeo Drive!

CHAPTER 51

James and Carl were enjoying an early dinner with a few producers discussing their up-and-coming rap song, and so far, all was good. They were at the Wilshire Hotel, dining in their upscale restaurant. Marteen and the girls were all dolled up and wearing their new dresses, so they decided to have an early dinner on rodeo drive. After getting their hair and nails done, they are looking like three stunning queens!

James was listening to one of the producers when three beautiful women walked into the dining area and captured the eye of all the male patrons. James looks over and sees his beautiful wife walk in looking as gorgeous as the day he met her. He turned to Carl and said, "Man, I'm out of here. Are you good without me? Because my wife is looking too damn good! Check out who just walked in here."

Carl looks over and spots Karen, "Oh shit, is that my baby too? Lawd, have mercy. Oh yeah, let's close out."

While Carl is closing out their bill, James walks over to his wife's table and says, "What's up beautiful?"

Marteen says, "Omg! Hey baby, and they kiss."

James says hi to Karen and Gia, complimenting them, and then he steals Marteen away.

Marteen and James request a private booth, and Marteen is blushing like a teenager because her husband is blowing up her head with so many compliments.

"Damn baby, can I get your phone number or something? Shit'd because the only meal I'm hungry for tonight is you."

"Boy, stop that before I come over there and give these people something to talk about."

"Well, bring your sexy ass over here. I swear we need to get this food to go because I'm going to be all over you in 10, 9, 8, 7, 6...."

Marteen grabs the nearest waiter and asks him to make their order to go. James goes to the front desk and pays for a honeymoon suite for the night because he can't wait a minute longer! He wants his wife, as sure as the world is round and a dollar bill is green.

* * *

James was in bed holding Marteen in his arms. They are lying in a heart-shaped bed in a beautifully designed honeymoon suite at the Wilshire Hotel. Marteen was still a bit light-headed from making love with her husband. James had mastered the art of making her scream out loud. He was incredible, and Marteen loved every inch of him! She couldn't imagine living without him because he and Jazz were her whole life.

James nibbles on her earlobe and whispers, "Tell me you love me." With no hesitation, Marteen says, "I love your whole ass, baby. I'm talking about the top of your head to the soles of your feet! And everything in between! You hear me baby?" She turns around and kisses him with so much passion and pure love that he feels a tug on his heart. He looks down into her beautiful eyes and says

"Damn baby, what has gotten into you? You are swelling my head up, shit'd, both of them!"

Marteen giggles, "Mmm...I just want you to know that I do listen to you, and I'm sorry I didn't take the shorts off. I was being prideful because I thought you were trying to control me."

"I wasn't trying to do that baby. I couldn't control you if I tried. You are much too strong and level-headed. That's what I love about you. I don't worry about you because I know I have a strong, independent woman. I just need you to allow me to be your king. Okay? Because if I tell you to fall back, then you can fall back, and I'll catch you, baby!" He lifts her chin and kisses her. Hey, I'll always catch you...every time! You just need to believe it!"

"Okay, I know! I'm working on it. I hope you can be patient with me and control your temper because I still have a bruise on my arm. You were squeezing my arm so tight, and you weren't even aware that you were doing it."

"I'm so sorry. I didn't mean to hurt you. You know I would never lay a hand on you. I might think about it, but I'll never hit you. Never! Especially now that I know you bruise so easily..."

They laugh. Marteen says, "Boy, you are a fool!"

"Yeah, I am! I'm a fool for you. So, what do you think about Basha performing with me? We may have to go back to her, baby..."

"I told you I was okay with that. To be honest, I don't think Gia really wanted to do a rap song."

"Mmm, did she say that?"

"Not in so many words, but it was implied."

"Yeah, but she was good at it because of our chemistry. But I think Basha will bring the song to life because she has that rawness about her. I just need you to be cool with it."

"I told you I was. Why are you so concerned about it?"

"Because I know you will be jealous once I start spending time away from you, and your mind will be playing tricks on you."

"As long as you stay true to our vows, I will be just fine. And absolutely no touching or anything like that. She better not try that mess she tried on Carl because on everything I believe in, I will kill that bitch! Trust me."

"See, that's what I'm afraid of. Baby, you don't have to kill anyone. Just calm down, damn! I don't know if I should even do this; maybe I can..."

Marteen interrupts him, "Baby it's okay. Just do your song, and I promise you, I won't be that crazy jealous wife. I'll support you. Just don't give me any reason to be concerned. I will be your biggest fan. I promise. Just do your thing, okay?"

"Alright baby, I'll get it out of my system, and then I'll walk away and never look back."

"Okay, now call your mom and check on our baby."

"We just talked to her a few hours ago!"

Marteen says, "Mmmm...baby, it was more than a few hours ago. Can you just call please?"

"Alright, but you should have just bought her with us because you cannot be checking on her 10 times a day, baby. You're probably getting on my Mama's last nerve!"

"So, I can check on my baby..."

"Baby you so damn hard-headed! Give me your arm, so I can squeeze it again...."

They both laugh.

* * *

Basha was in her studio waiting on a call from her agent when her best friend Carla walked in, making noise from the click of her shoes. Carla says, "Hey girl, why are they checking IDs like you the damn president, or something."

"Girl, ever since Carl's wife attacked me, security is back on point. But we can't leave yet because I'm still waiting to see if we got the spot for that rap song."

"Oooh yes, that fine brother I met in Vegas, they call Chase, was checking me out. But he's not in the song, right?"

"Nope, but my future baby daddy is. You remember him? He's the rapper named James. I'm in love with him, and I know he wants me. But he's married to this real pretty lady. But I don't care because I want his ass!"

"Mmm girl, you need to leave these married men alone because l know you don't want another beat down."

"Girl, for James, I'll take that ass whooping. I gotta have him. And as soon as we get the thumbs up, I'm putting on my daisy dukes, and I'm going to perform my ass off, trust me!

"Well, don't say I never warned ya."

"Girl, I'm not gonna be in his face like that. I'm going to flirt when we're alone and make him chase me. He is so sexy and smooth, lord have mercy!!!" The phone rings.

* * *

James and Marteen are back in the guesthouse. James is on his way into town with Carl to meet up with Basha. Marteen says, "So Basha is back in for good."

James replies, "Yep! We are going to review the original tape we did with her and record another one. I made a few changes, so we'll see."

"Okay, well, I'll start packing so we can leave tomorrow for our belated honeymoon." She wraps her arms around him and gives him a big kiss.

Mmmm, oh yeah, can't wait, baby. So, I'll see you later tonight. And don't be calling my mama, because Jazz is good, okay? We'll call her in the morning, alright?"

"Why are you limiting my calls to check on our baby?"

"I'm not; I just know how my mom is. So just cool it a little bit, okay? Please baby, if anything happens, she'll call us immediately, okay? You know Jazz is in good hands."

"Okay, well good luck and behave yourself. And don't be checking out Basha's ass because I know she's going to be showing off her assets."

"Yep, see here we go, with you being jealous, and I haven't even hit the stage!"

"Baby, you are fine as hell, so she's going to come for you. I'm just saying don't fall in her trap because you know I carry a loaded gun."

"Oh boy, just calm your ass down, nobody's trapping me."

Across town, James and Carl go over the lyrics with Basha, and Bob does sound checks. James says, "So it's basically the same. Just throw a little sass into this line, okay?"

"Mmm, you mean like this... "But I don't think you can handle this." She nails it!!

"Yeah, just like that, and in the video, you will walk away with Carla and give her a high five! But we'll practice that later. Let's just record the song okay?"

"Okay, I know it like the back of my hand, I'm ready," Basha says. James replies, "Okay, cool."

Carl says, "Ok, let's start fresh and see where we stand with the background sounds. I think we need a catchy beat, but let's just go with what we have for now."

James and Basha go into the sound room and James starts to rap. Later, when Carl and James are in the car driving back to the house, James brings up Basha, saying, "Man, Basha got it down on the first run. She is perfect for this!"

"Yep, I told you. She killed it. That girl got a lot of skills, but she's just thirsty for a man in the business. So watch her, because I think she likes you."

"Yep, I know she does. She grabbed my ass when you weren't looking."

"What? Oh shit, that girl is too much, I'll talk to her agent."

"Yeah, because I don't want any problems. You know my Achilles heel."

"Yeah, so be strong and don't get caught up because Marteen is my wife's sister."

"Man, I'm not messing up my marriage for Basha! I love my baby, but Basha... Basha...Basha got a pretty ass on her, damn!!"

"I know. It sits up perfectly and wait until she puts on them daisy dukes. Shit'd we gotta have a closed set, absolutely no wives."

"Oh yeah, shit'd, I am going to have fun with this rap video. I wish I could spank that big ass!"

"I know, but be strong, nigga! Because it's going to blow up, player!! I'm about to reinvent yo ass! Real talk."

They laugh and bump fists.

* * *

The ladies are back at the main house inside the game room Gia says, "Well, I guess it's final. I'm going home tomorrow, and Basha is back in."

Karen says, "I know, and I don't like it."

Marteen says, "I know, me either. But she's going to do well with that big ass she has. Hey, let's play a game of pool."

She walks over to the big pool table in the middle of the room.

They set up and rack the balls and pick their pool sticks. Marteen and Gia play the first game while Karen watches from the circular bar area that's built into the wall.

Marteen says, "I must be crazy to allow James to work with her after what happened. But I wanna trust him, you know?"

Gia says, "I know, but these women are so thirsty for attention, and James is a smooth operator, so I hope you know what you are doing."

Marteen says, "I'm nervous about it but he better keep it in his pants. Because I don't know what I'll do if he cheats on me."

Karen says, "Girl, you can't trust them around women like Basha 'cause they throw it in their face. So, by instincts, they gonna look and wonder...my husband included."

Gia says, "Yep! That's why I'm working on this song called 'Never Trust a Man.' It sums it all up."

Marteen says, "What? Girl, how does it sound?"

Karen says, "Yeah, sing it Gia; I'm curious."

Gia puts down her pool stick and sings:

"Never trust a man...never trust a man...

I say never trust a man with a prize in his draws...

Learn from me...ya hear me....

If he ever calls...if he ever calls...

Turn your phone off...turn your phone off...

Learn from me, ya hear me

Never trust a man, never trust man,

With a tongue in his mouth...

Y'all hear me...ya hear me...

Cause when he takes it out...when he takes it out..

Girl you'll be climbing up the walls.

Learn from me...ya hear me...

The girls laugh in the background.

I say never trust a man... never trust a man....

Listen little one...I'm all for having fun

Ain't trying to block no one...

If the prize is in his draws, a long tongue in his mouth

He ain't the one...

Girl, you better run...you better run...

Learn from me ...ya hear me

Marteen and Karen are laughing and giving each other a high five. Karen says, "Omg! I love it, let's produce it and get it on the charts!"

Marteen says, "Yes! Girl, did you let Carl hear that?"

Gia says, "Yep, but I'm still writing it. But y'all like it, huh?"

They both say, "Love it!!"

Marteen says, "Girl hurry up and finish it, and we'll help you get it out there. Because I got some cash, and we can do it by ourselves!"

Karen says, "Yep, and Bob, who works with Carl, will help us, especially if Marteen asks him. Because that man worships her!"

"Who the hell is Bob?" Marteen asks.

Karen says, "Girl, never mind. But trust me, we can do this without our husbands because I wanna do something, and I got a little stash too!

Gia says, "Okay, well, let's stay in touch and I'll work on finishing up."

Marteen says, "Cool, but seriously, who the hell is Bob?"

They all laugh.

* * *

James and Carl return and find the ladies playing pool and giggling. James walks into the game room first, says hello, kisses Marteen, and steps to the bar to pour himself a glass of bourbon.

He says, "What's so funny?"

Marteen replies, "Oh, just girly stuff. So how was Basha's debut?"

"She was alright, not as strong vocally as Gia."

Gia says, "Thank you, but her butt is bigger, so I know she will put a hurting in the video."

James replies, "Yep! She got some junk in her trunk."

Carl walks in and says, "Who got junk in their trunk?"

Karen says, "Basha baby, who else? Are you guys hungry?"

Carl replies, "Nope," and hugs his wife.

James says, "Nah, I'm good." He grabs Marteen and places her in his lap.

Marteen whispers, "Did you behave yourself?"

"Yes, of course. Did you miss me?"

"Yes!" and she gives him a long, passionate kiss.

Karen says, "Damn, y'all need a room or what? Because we have a house full."

James replies, "Yep, let's go, baby. I'm tired. It's been a long day. We'll see y'all tomorrow morning."

Marteen replies, "Okay, well, goodnight family. See y'all at breakfast. Gia's cooking!"

Everyone, in unison, shouts, "Yes!!!"

Gia says, "Well damn, thanks Marteen for volunteering me!"

Marteen laughs, "You're welcome, sista!!"

As soon as they make it into the guesthouse, James says, "So what was y'all laughing so hard about? I thought I heard Bob's name."

Marteen replies, "Oh, I don't know anyone named Bob baby... we were just having fun, that's all." She takes her sandals off.

"Yeah, ok. You not cheating on me, are you?"

"Of course not. Why would you think that?" She stops what she's doing and looks at him with confusion.

"Okay, because I know a Bob, and I will beat his ass. Because I know he be checking you out...so..."

"James, I don't know a Bob. Are you being serious?" She's standing with one sandal on and one sandal off.

"Just saying baby, that's all. You had that shit on the other day, and that joker's eyeballs almost fell out. That's why I didn't want you in that shit!!!

"I swear I don't know a Bob, and we were just laughing at this song Gia wrote about men. Why are you tripping out?"

"Because I'm jealous baby. I'm telling you; I'll kill yo ass and that creepy mother fucker!"

"OMG! James, please stop it. I'm not doing anything, and I swear I don't know anyone named Bob... what is going on with you?"

James is silent. He sits down in a chair across from the bed and calms down. She finally takes her other sandal off.

James speaks, "I don't know, baby, I'm sorry. I know you're not doing anything; it's just me in my head, that's all." He stares at her, "Tell me you love me."

"I love you, so stop thinking crazy. You are scaring me."

James walks over, kisses her, picks her up, and carries her to the bed, "I'm sorry. I'm tripping. I love you baby. I love you so much, I'm going crazy!"

"I understand baby because I'm crazy too."

They tear each other's clothes off and make mad, passionate love. The type of love that brings your animalistic behavior to the surface.

Gia hears Marteen's screams out by the poolside just as she is about to take a late-night swim. She smiles to herself because she knows that scream all too well. James is an animal in the bedroom. Sweet Jesus, she shakes her head as she jumps into the pool to cool off! Side note: when a man who isn't the jealous type suddenly becomes jealous for no reason, it's usually because he's feeling guilty about what he's thinking of doing or what he has done.

* * *

James wakes up holding his wife in his arms, and he feels guilty for lusting over Basha. He needed to talk to Carl again about checking her ass because she needs to keep her hands to herself. Marteen was stirring in her sleep, and he pulled her closer because he couldn't get enough of her.

He loved her so much, and he knew she loved him just as much. He loved the way she screamed out his name last night. Damn, she had some vocals on her. But he had to talk to her about all that screaming because she was forever waking Jazz up out of her sleep. And with the new baby on the way, something had to give.

He smiled as he slowly began to make love to her again, and like clockwork, she moaned in her sleep. Lord have mercy on any man who ever tried to take her from him. She was his for life. He picks up speed because she feels so good. He's screaming omg in his head as he climaxes, and she joins him as she shakes and screams out, "Oh, James!!! Music to his ears.

When it's over, he whispers good morning beautiful, love me some you, baby.

Back at the main house Gia is up cooking breakfast and humming her song when Carl and Karen enter the kitchen and say good morning. Carl grabs a cup of coffee, sits at the island and reads the newspaper he has in his hand. Karen helps Gia with breakfast, and they hear James and Marteen sharing a laugh as they walk into the kitchen.

Minutes later, everyone is sitting at the island enjoying a wonderful breakfast. Karen gets up and pours everyone a glass of mimosa. James gets another glass, fills it with orange juice and hands it to his wife. Marteen says, "Guys we have an announcement to make." She looks at James.

"It's been confirmed that Marteen is eight weeks pregnant. So y'all got another niece or nephew coming in a few months."

Karen says, "Omg! You guys are so blessed! Congratulations!" She hugs them.

Carl says, "Damn man, you weren't playing, huh! Congratulations." He embraces his friend.

Gia replies, "Oh wow! Congratulations!" She walks over and joins everyone with hugs and more congratulations!!!

Marteen says, "Thanks so much. We are so happy, and we are hoping James gets his son this time."

After breakfast, James pulls Carl aside and reminds him to report Basha for touching him because he doesn't want her actions to escalate. Karen overheard the conversation and wondered if she should say something to Marteen. She decided not to because she didn't want to wipe the smile from her sister's eyes.

CHAPTER 52

Gia leaves for the airport right after breakfast. Chase and Carly are picking her up at the airport in Chicago, and she can't wait to see them. Karen and Carl are having lunch with Marteen and James before they leave for Maui. Karen is riding into town with Carl, and she has her new Bottega Handbag sitting on a chair. Marteen's jaw drops when she sees it, "Girl, when did you get your bag?"

"Oh, I got it in Jamaica."

Marteen picks it up, nudges James, and says, "Baby, I want this in brown. They have this same one but larger."

"Ok, well, buy it."

"Really? It's expensive."

"Sweetie buy it if you want it. Shit buy two, I don't care."

Marteen squeezes James' neck and shouts, "Thank you! I love that bag. It's the best style this year!"

"This year? So, you want another one next year?"

"Mmm hmmm"

"Damn, I better hurry up and record this song, so I can keep my wife happy!" He pecks her on the lips, and says, "Are you ready to leave?"

Marteen stands up and walks over to her sister and says, "Well, I guess we will see you guys in a few weeks."

They hug and kiss Karen and Carl goodbye and take a limo to the Airport.

* * *

James and Marteen receive a warm welcome from the natives as they check into their 5-star hotel suite. The hotel is hidden in the heart of Maui, and they have the entire upper floor all to themselves with a personal maid and butler. James went above and beyond to please his beautiful wife.

Marteen jumps into his arms as soon as they are alone and she gives him a big kiss, "Omg baby, this is unbelievable. I love it!" She runs into the master bedroom and squeals. She runs back, grabs James's hand, and drags him into the bedroom.

Marteen says, "Baby, did you arrange this?"

"Yes, do you like it?"

Marteen, with tears in her eyes, nods. She can't believe it. The bed is almost identical to the one she has in D.C., and it is full of rose petals. In the center is the Bottega Veneta Handbag she wanted in brown and black, and a dress is draped over the black handbag.

Marteen is crying for real because it looks like the latest Versace dress that she showed him in the magazine a few weeks ago!

Marteen says, "Oh my goodness, I love it!"

"You see, I'm always listening to you, baby. I'm going to give you the world because your wishes will always be granted! I love you so much."

He gets down on one knee and presents her with another ring.

"I think you deserved a bigger diamond, so I hope you like it. So, uh, will you accept this ring in addition to the one you have? And will you promise to try and stop screaming so loud when I'm making love to you? And will you stop being afraid to fall back and allow me to catch you because I will always catch you. I love you more than the air I breathe, baby. You are my everything!"

Marteen gets down on her knees beside him and with tears in her eyes, she says, "I promise to listen to you, and I will allow you to catch me. But I can't promise that I won't scream when you make love to me, because you make me feel so amazing. It's a feeling that invades my body and I lose control. I scream because it feels so incredible. But I'll try my best. Thank you so much. You are the best husband and father; I will give you a house full of babies!"

James slides her old ring off, replaces it with a bigger ring, and says, "Thank you for choosing me. Now tell me you love me."

Marteen smiles and screams "I LOVE YOU JAMES KNIGHT!!!

The next three nights in Maui were like a dream because Marteen had fallen in love all over again! Because happy doesn't last long.

CHAPTER 53

Carl and Basha are nominated for best collaboration. Carl was nominated for Best New Artist and "Can You Feel It" is nominated for Best R&B Song. Carl is nervous because he and Basha are presenting the Album of the Year award, and they are performing the new rap song with James called "Hey Sexy."

He is riding high, and thankfully, his wife is with him to bring him back down to earth. They are in their suite, and Karen is giving him a birthday treat to calm his nerves. He is in another world as she drains the tension from his whole body.

James and Marteen are across the hall getting dressed for the red carpet, and they are laughing as Marteen is trying her best to tie his bow tie. James is rapping in her ear because she can't get the damn thing tied! He's rapping,

Come on sexy, I'm getting hot.

You can't tie a damn knot...

Baby, haven't you heard...

I'm singing at the awards...

Marteen is laughing so hard at her silly husband and James is trying to take his mind off of what's really happening. Basha is nervously practicing her introductory lines while her hair and makeup is being applied by her stylist. Bob is as nervous as a mouse in a house of cats. He wants the new rap song to be a hit so he can finally make a name and get paid!! This is the moment everyone has been waiting for, limousines are pulling up and the red carpet is laid. Imagine two young boys growing up in the projects of Chicago. Now imagine those same young men about to perform together live on stage in front of the world!! Ready or not Hollywood, here they come!!!

* * *

James's mom is anxious to see her son on television. She and Jazz are watching the performances from their hotel suite. Carl's mom is beaming with pride and joy. She is in the audience sitting between Karen and Marteen, waiting to see her one and only son perform at the Music Awards Ceremony!

James and the crew are up next. The song is called "Hey Sexy." Curtains open to the beat of the song. Carl is singing in the background

...Oh, she so sexy
...Oh, so sexy

Basha has her back to the audience singing. James walks out bobbing his head and singing, waving his hand in the air. Basha turns around and sings and dances to the beat. The crowd goes wild for Basha and James' rap.

Hey, sexy in those daisy dukes, damn girl, can I talk to you..
Call me daddy because I'm so strict
You can't stop me...til I'm finished
Love you hard just like a Queen
Girl, I'll Give you all the finer things
Satisfaction guaranteed

I got what you want and what ya need...

Come on sexy...just talk to me

Basha sings:

"I don't know you talk a good game...mmmm..and you so smooth,

Mmmm...but I'm not into material things,

Sorry, I'm with another...dude"

James raps:

"Oh, yeah...I'm sorry too...

But you ain't listening

You either blind and don't see...

I'm the nigga that'll take you from these streets ...

Come here baby, I wanna wine you

...and ooh Girl can I dine with you...

(Basha is up close to James)

I'll have you whinny like a baby...

You'll be smiling in ya damn sleep... yeah

Come on sexy n talk to me

Have you living your best life...

Just be loyal and you can be my wife...

Carl takes a cordless mic and comes to the front stage rapping and the crowd goes wild.

Carl sings:

"Don't explain bro...

She ain't on this brick...uh,

She busy chasing these knuckleheads

She ain't down like them other chicks...

You feeling her cause she is so thick!

James raps:

"Yeah, and that's the damn truth!

Like em thick and super cute

Yeah and that phat ass too

Come on sexy, can I talk to you

Carl is singing in the background. Basha raps:

I don't know, you sound a little slick

...Not easily impressed like those thirsty chicks

If you want my digits,

I'll have to ponder it...

But I don't think you can handle this

Basha dances while Carl raps:

Ooh shit! Did she just challenge you?

James raps:

Damn baby what you tryna do...

I know talk is cheap

Uh, but I got something that'll make ya weep...

Baby I don't brag cause it's childish...

The truth is you can't handle me, uh.,

I'll have you speaking in your native tongue...

Trust me girl, I'll get ya sprung...

Uh...challenge me... 'n I get ya in these sheets

...Girl you'll be crowning me your new king!

I'll spin your ass around the globe ...cause I'm nasty!

Truth be told...you can't handle me!

The crowd explodes. Carl is singing in the background:

Hey, hey, hey, sexy.. hey hey sexy ...

James raps:

I'll have you screaming and calling me daddy

...Cause I'm so strict...trust me,

Baby, you can't handle this

Yeah, check my references,

I'll have ya screaming cause I'm nasty

Hold up sexy,

Where you running to

...Don't leave me hanging

...Can I talk to you...

Got my heart in the danger zone...

Get with me, and I'll put you on a throne...

picket fence all around our home...

Carl sings:

"She ain't on no real niggs

She like fuckin with them knuckleheads

Move along n go fishing in the blue sea

She like those sharks with the gold teeth

...She either blind and can't see

... You the one to take her from the street

Keep it moving she where she wanna be

...yeah snatch another from the blue sea...

Carl and James sing*:*

      Hey hey hey sexy... hey hey hey sexy

James raps:

      Hey sexy! Will ya talk to me...

Basha:

      Here's my number...

      You can call me...

      I think I've heard enough.

James raps:

      Thank you, baby,

      I'll hit you up!

      Yeah, sexy .. I'll hit ya up...

James licks his lips and raps:

      Hey sexy, you'll be crowned a Queen

      ...Tell ya man to pack up all his things!

Carl and James sing;

      His time is up! Yeah, yeah his time is up...

James raps:

      Yeah...

James and Carl slap hands, turn their backs, and walk off right behind Basha!! The audience is on their feet clapping, "Hey Sexy" is a hit!

Carl wins all nominations! He walks to the mic to accept his last award, Best New Artist. The audience is clapping for him. His family and friends are cheering for him. He is living his dream. Carl speaks into the microphone, "Thank you, thank you. Wow, you know something my mom often says, God is good! Yes he is." The crowd explodes.

He takes a moment before saying, "I would like to thank the Music Awards for this honor, my loyal band members, my relentless agent, Josh, and Mr. Teddy Riley for seeing my gift. My hometown of Chicago and all my friends back home, Joe, Joseph, Randy, Constance, and Big Mike! My assistant Bob Jones, Ms. Basha for that kiss (laughter), all the fans who supported me and bought my records, my sister-in-law, Marteen, who's married to my best friend, my ride-or-die. Trust me, y'all will remember him. My boy James Knight, love you brother, uh, shoutout to my beautiful daughter Carly, who I hope is asleep in bed. I wanna thank my incredibly strong and beautiful mother. She sacrificed her dreams so that I could live mine. Love you beyond the moon, Mama! And finally, the love of my whole life. This woman has been my rock, my inspiration, my everything... my gorgeous wife, Karen. Stand up baby, stand for me, please! Oh yeah, isn't she beautiful?" Karen stands. Thank you for putting up with this crazy life, love you so much and I can't wait to hold you baby!"

He lifts up his trophy and looks to the heavens and continues on.

"Thank you, God for blessing me with a beautiful wife and a beautiful life. Thank you everyone!! And may God bless us all!!!"

He leaves the stage to step into the real Hollywood! Lots of interviews, parties, and more parties. This is only a tip of what is going to transpire for the talented Mr. Carl St. John!!!

CHAPTER 54

The American Music Awards was a mind-blowing experience! The 'Hey Sexy' rap song is on fire, and the video will be released in a few days. James is on his way to LA to finalize everything and to perform with Basha and Carl at the release party.

James is checking his suitcase, and Marteen is watching him with Jazz on her hip. Jazz is pulling on her mother's hair, so Marteen puts her down and she crawls over to her dad. James picks her up and gives her a big kiss. He puts her back down and she is holding on to his leg as he continues to pack his carry-on bag. Marteen says, "Are you missing something?"

"Yeah, where is the picture of you and Jazz?"

"Oh, it's on the side. I took it out of the glass frame, and it's in a plastic sleeve."

"Oh, I want to keep it framed so I can put it out in the hotel."

He looks over and all of a sudden, Jazz is walking!

Marteen says," Omg, she's walking!"

"Wow! I told you she would do it before I leave for L.A. Look at her; her legs are strong baby!"

Marteen walks further away and Jazz walks faster to catch up with her. James runs to grab a camera. After he takes a few pictures, He goes over and picks her up. He holds her and tells her she's a big girl and Jazz is smiling and baby talking to him. Marteen walks into a three-way hug.

James kisses his wife and says, "I don't wanna leave right now. This is the best feeling to see my baby girl walk! Thank goodness I was here to witness it."

"I know. She's growing up, isn't she?"

"Yep, we gotta watch her like a hawk."

"I know, she's quick and sneaky, aren't you!" And she kisses Jazz.

"Well, I'll be back in four days, okay?"

"Wait, I thought you said three days?" Marteen says looking puzzled.

"Oh, I meant three nights and four days sweetie, okay?"

"Mmmm, that sounds like forever. We're going to miss you, right Jazz?"

Jazz says, "Da Da!"

James replies, "Did she just call me da da?"

"Yep, she sure did!" They both laugh.

Jazz says again, "Da Da Da," and reaches for him.

"Hey baby, you want your da da!" He holds his baby girl. "Awww you're breaking my heart sweetie. Yes, I love you munchkin. Man, I cannot leave today!"

He looks over at Marteen and tells her to call and change his flight for the following day. He can't leave his little girl right now, she's growing up too fast. Later that night James is holding his wife, and he tells her, "Baby, why don't you come with me to California? We can take Jazz and be together because I don't want to leave her. She's becoming a daddy's girl!"

"I know, but you'll be back in a few days. We'll go next time because she has a doctor's appointment tomorrow."

"Mmm, okay. It sounds like you want to get rid of me."

Marteen turns around and hugs him, "Baby I don't want you to go but I know you have to. I don't ever want to get rid of you. I love you so much and you know I do."

"Yeah, I know. Mmm...wow, I don't wanna leave you, baby. I swear I don't. I'm done with this rap shit after the hype is over. Then, uh, we are going to get back to our original lives! I promise you, and after this baby, (he rubs her belly) we'll be careful, so you don't get pregnant again for at least a few years, Okay?"

"Okay sounds good baby."

The next day, James leaves for California to film the rap video, and Basha is once again, up to no good!

* * *

Maybe Marteen should have gone with her husband to LA. Or maybe she should have never agreed to Basha being in the video. The crew is staying in Hollywood in a hotel next to the venue where they are performing the debut of the video. James was taking a shower in his hotel suite, when Basha sneaks into his room after telling the maid that she was locked out of her room.

Basha, dressed only in a hotel robe, placed the ice bucket on a nearby table and walked into the bathroom. She unwraps her robe and opens the shower door. James, completely taken aback, blinks at Basha's naked body and says, "Hey, what the fuck are you doing?"

"What does it look like I'm doing? You know you want me!"

She drops her robe to the floor, steps into the shower, and tries to kiss James.

"No, no, come on now, you gotta leave baby. I mean it, get some clothes on, now, damn! Come on...!"

James steps away, but he's trapped. So, he pushes past her and stumbles out of the stall. Basha is on him as she follows him out. She pushes him onto the bed and climbs on top. James pushes her off and tells her to leave before he calls security. She giggles.

Basha walks closer and drops to her knees and tries to kiss his manhood and says, "Ooh baby, damn, you got exactly what I need. Let me taste you. I promise I'll leave afterward!" James hesitates and Basha takes advantage of the opportunity. She wraps her tongue around his manhood and James moans. Then he quickly grabs her by the hair and pushes her away. He grabs a pair of boxers and quickly pulls them on his wet body. He picks up the phone.

Basha laughs and walks back into the bathroom, puts her robe back on, and, licking her lips says, "Mmm...okay, sexy, I'm leaving. But if you change your mind, I'm only a few steps away. I will run back and rock your whole damn world because I want yo fine ass!" She walks up to him and kisses his lips, "Baby, we can do this on the low. I won't tell a soul, okay?" She rubs up against him, smiles, and leaves the room. James puts the phone into its cradle, falls back onto the bed, grabs his manhood, and says out loud, "Oh, shit!!!"

Karen sees Basha leaving James's suite, and she runs back into her room and screams for Carl. Carl runs out of the bathroom. "What! What is it!!"

"Go talk to James because I just saw Basha leave his room with nothing but a robe on. You better find out what the hell is going on!" Carl says, "Oh shit, are you for real?"

"Yes! My sister is pregnant with his second baby, and that mother fucker is cheating on her!"

"Hey, we don't know that." He gestures with his hands and says, "I'll be back." Carl grabs his wallet and walks to the door.

"You better talk to him because I'll kill his ass if he hurts my sister. I promise you!!!

"Calm down baby, and don't tell your sister anything. Let's see what's going on, okay?"

Karen stays silent. Carl says, "Hey, you hear me?"

"Yeah, I heard you. But blood is thicker than water so, we'll see. Now go and find out." Carl leaves out.

* * *

James is pacing back and forth in his hotel room when Carl knocks on his door. He is nervous about Basha returning so he looks through the peephole. James quickly opened the door for Carl and he immediately tells him about Basha. Carl says, "Ok, ok, hold up! Are you telling me she walked into your bathroom?"

"Yes! Man, I don't know how she got in. But she was all over me, and I told her to leave me alone, shit!! Man, that girl is troubled and I'm telling you, I cannot work under these conditions. She almost made me forget I was married!"

"Oh man. Well, Karen saw Basha leaving out of here, and you know she thinking crazy."

"Oh, hell nah, man please don't let her tell my wife this shit! I don't know how that girl got in here. And I swear I didn't do anything. I told her to get out and that was hard as hell! She was buck naked in here and she was touching me and shit. But I put her out and that's the truth."

"Yeah I know. But uh, maybe you should call Marteen and get ahead of any drama because my wife has a mind of her own. So, she might be talking to Marteen right now!"

James sits in a nearby chair and puts his head in his hands, and he sighs before saying, "If I lose my family over this bullshit, I'm going to choke that crazy girl! I can't believe this mess, man. I swear I don't know how she got her ass inside my locked room. I gotta tell Marteen before your big-mouth wife does."

"Man, she probably bribed someone. I told you she was thirsty for you. But just be cool and call Marteen. I'm going to talk to Basha's agent, and I'll call you later, ok?"

"Okay, I'm going to call my wife and pray she believes me."

"Alright, but whatever happens, we have to perform tomorrow night, okay? We got money riding on this."

"Man, I guess. But my head is somewhere else."

"I feel you. But I need you to square up with your wife and then get your mind right so we can get this shit over with! You know we gotta perform tomorrow night. I'll rap with ya later!" Carl walks over to the door.

"Tell Karen what happened ok? I'm going to call Marteen right now!" Carl leaves, and James calls home.

Marteen answers, "Hello?"

"Hey baby, uh, how are you doing?"

"Ok, just put Jazz to sleep. How are you doing? You sound a little nervous."

"Uh baby, I uh, had an uh, run-in with Basha today, about a half an hour ago."

Marteen's heart is beating fast, "What happened?"

"Basha bribed her ass into my room while I was in the shower and kinda threw herself on me..."

"What?!! Are you kidding me, what the fuck is wrong with her, OMG! I am going to hurt her. Are you okay?"

"Yes, she left after I threatened to call security. I already complained to her agent about her because she's been hitting on me. But I thought it was harmless and I didn't want to upset you. But now, she's going too far."

"Wait a minute! So, she's been hitting on you from the beginning?"

"Yep, don't be mad, baby. I was handling it. And I told Carl immediately and we called her agent. But she apparently didn't listen because she's way out of hand!"

"Mmm... you better be telling me the truth because I can't deal with you cheating on me. I just can't!!"

"I'm not. I swear I did everything to stop her, except hit her. You know I don't want anyone except you."

"Well, I'm coming out as soon as I get a flight okay? Because that bitch is fucking with the wrong husband! I'll call you later."

"Baby, I can handle this. I was only calling because I'm thinking of taking legal action. I don't want you getting upset with the baby and stuff, ok?"

"I'm ok. You know I'm coming so, don't even try to stop me. And of course I'm upset, you just told me that bitch is throwing her stuff at you. Oh, hell yeah, I'm on my way to you! I'll call you later."

"Okay, just don't let this upset the baby, okay? And thank you for believing me. I'm so sorry about this."

"Of course I believe you, I know that bitch wants you!! This is why I didn't want you doing it because if it's not her, it would be another one of them thirsty ass bitches! She's just lucky I'm pregnant because I could kill her, with my bare hands.

"Alright baby, please calm down. This is why I didn't want to call you. But Carl told me to because you might find out and think I was cheating on you. But I know you don't blame me because I'm innocent, baby! I love you so much and I really want you to calm down because I'm going to take care of it! I promise I will."

"Did she put her mouth on you?"

"Come on now, baby why are you asking me that?"

"Mmmm...did she see you naked?"

"Yep."

"Dammit!" A crashing noise occurs.

James says, "What happened?"

Marteen sighs, "Nothing. I, uh just broke a glass."

"Did you cut yourself?"

"No, I'm good."

"Okay. I know I can't stop you from coming! Call me back baby, and love you so much, I swear on everything."

"I love you too and we will talk about this again, in person, ok? And lock up and keep your damn clothes on, ok?"

"Ok sweetie. See you soon."

"Bye."

* * *

Carl walks back into his hotel suite, and Karen is just hanging up the phone. Karen asks, "Did you talk to his slick ass?"

"Baby, please don't tell me you already called Marteen..."

"Hell yeah, but her phone was busy, and she didn't pick up her cell phone."

Carl shakes his head, "Well, it's good you didn't talk to her, damn! You need to relax."

"Oh really, your friend ain't no damn good. My loyalty is with my sister, and I'm telling her what I saw."

"Well, I talked to him, and Basha bribed her way into his room while he was in the shower. He put her out as soon as he saw what she was trying to do. Hold up before you start accusing him, alright?"

"Oh, come on, I don't believe that mess. And no way will he refuse Basha after he rubbed her ass in front of everybody! Yeah, I'll believe that shit, when pigs fly!"

Karen picks up the phone, and Carl quickly grabs it out of her hand and says, "Hey, stay out of it, and let your sister decide what she believes."

"Uh, excuse me, I'm telling her what I saw, and you can't stop me. So, hand me the damn phone because my sister needs to know what I saw leaving her husband's room! And I don't care how you feel, because that's your homey! My sister ranks your homey. And I better not ever see a bitch coming out of your hotel room with a damn robe on. Because trust me, when I tell you, everybody is dying, except me!"

Carl laughs, "Come on now, sweetie... calm down. We are solid and you know it! But that Basha is on some bullshit. I need to call her weak-ass agent and set some boundaries because I am going to fire her and rip up her contract!"

"Mmm, well, you should have never hired her. I'm sure there's another singer out there with better morals!"

Carl puts the phone down, grabs his wife and hugs her. Baby just let them work it out. You can call her later, okay? Please, baby."

"Mmm... I just need to talk to her. I know James is probably smooth-talking his way out of trouble so, by the time I talk to her, it won't matter, anyway."

"Well, they can work this out on their own. And you know, that lil hood talk of yours is starting to turn me on baby."

Carl holds her closer and kisses her until they are breathing hard and taking each other's clothes off.

* * *

Marteen arrived in L.A. hours before anyone knew she was there. She flew in on her best friend's private jet. Marteen had a small circle of friends and her college roommate, Monica, was her sister from another mother. She was a well-known Entertainment Lawyer, and she had a private practice right in the heart of L.A. Although they didn't talk every day, whenever they did, they picked up right where they left off. It was as if time had stood still, for them.

Monica's mom was from Kenya which is where she has been for the past year, tending to her sick mother. Monica's business partner, Victor Lance, arranged Marteen's travel arrangements. They shared a brief lunch as he prepared documents for her. Marteen hired the firm to investigate Basha. She needed some leverage because Basha had stumbled upon the wrong husband! She wanted to hit her where it hurt the most, her pockets!!

Victor was very intrigued by Marteen, and although he had seen several photographs of her, to see her walk into his office with so much beauty and grace, totally blew him away! Victor was spellbound by her presence and he was trying desperately not to stare at her legs! After lunch, Victor shook hands with Marteen and arranged her transportation to her hotel. Marteen walked into the quaint little Hollywood hotel, rolling her luggage behind her and looking as beautiful as ever. She used her cell phone to call her husband.

James picks up, "Hello?"

"Hey, I'm downstairs."

"Huh? Are you in LA?"

"Yes, and I forgot your room number."

"Wow. How? Well, just stay right there. I'm on my way to you, ok baby?"

"Ok."

Marteen's cell rings as soon as she hangs up with James.

Monica says, "Hello, have you arrived yet?"

"Oh, hey Monny, I'm here, and thanks so much! Victor did a great job. My husband is meeting me now, so, I'll call you back as soon as I talk to him and stuff, ok?"

"Okay, girl! Your husband, huh? Damn, I still can't get used to that. Anyway, glad you made it. If you need anything just ask Victor, he will make it happen. He is a godsend!

"Ok girl, thanks so much. Kiss ma for me! I'll call you later, ok?"

"Ok bye. And remember you are pregnant so don't be trying to fight and stuff!"

"Oh, don't worry, I can beat her ass with one hand tied behind my back. You already know that."

"Yeah, but don't do anything until I have Victor check things out. I'll be back in the States sooner than later, ok?"

"Okay, bye. Thanks again!"

"No worries, you know I got you! Goodbye friend."

James steps off the elevator and smiles as he walks towards his gorgeous wife!

James steps out of the elevator and scans the room for his wife. She is standing by the desk looking like a model in her mini dress and high heels! She's showing off her long sexy bowlegs and he can't believe she's his mother fucking wife! James immediately walks over, hugs and kisses her! James says, "I missed you baby. Look at you, you look so good! And where is my baby?"

"Thanks, sweetie. I told you over the phone that your mom is watching Jazz."

James touches her stomach, "No, I'm talking about my unborn baby. You don't even look pregnant in this dress. So where are you carrying our baby, sweetie? He grabs her luggage and leads her to the elevator. Marteen rubs her stomach, "Well, I feel every bit of this baby, and I am showing. Just wait until I take this dress off; you'll see."

"Oh, it's coming off as soon as we make it to the room. Damn, you look amazing, baby!" He grabs her hand and kisses it.

As they wait for the elevator, James asks, "How did you get here so fast?"

"I miss you too, baby! I left you a message that I was taking my friend, Monica's company jet! She's our new attorney and investigator. We need to talk about Basha. I want you to talk to our new attorney because we should press charges against her butt! She entered your room, unlawfully."

They step into the elevator and ride to the 18th floor. James replies, "I know but Carl already has his attorney looking into it and I thought your friend was in Africa somewhere."

"Mmm, well that's nice of him, but I want our own attorney to take care of this. Carl has enough on his plate right now and Monica's business partner is handling our case. I met with him earlier."

"Oh ok, well, whatever you want to do, baby! I'm just happy you're here! Oh wait, you met with a dude in that dress, today?"

"Yes, in this dress. Why, is something wrong?"

"No, but uh, what's this dude's name, and why did you meet him without me?"

"Baby, it was just a brief hello. He arranged my flight for me, that's all. His name is Victor Lance, and he is strictly about business so stop being jealous."

"Mmmm...well don't meet with him again without me, ok? Now come on in here and show me what's under that dress! With your sexy ass! I'm going to have to lock your fine ass up! You can't leave this room, without me, ok?"

They both laugh and Marteen says, "Boy stop. I am the one that should be locking your butt up!"

As they enter the suite, Marteen kicks her heels off, pulls her husband closer, and kisses him. James picks her up, with that crazy look in his eyes and he carries her to the bed. He slowly makes love to his wife, and he is so grateful to have her and his family still intact! Because truth be told, if he was a weaker man, he would've cheated on her as soon as Basha put his manhood into her mouth! Real talk!

* * *

Marteen and James were meeting Carl and Karen for lunch. Tonight is the unveiling of the video, and so far, Basha is still in the group. Carl supposedly has some news of Basha and their performance to share later that evening. Marteen was anxious to hear the updates, and James was worried about performing with Basha, in front of his wife.

Karen was in her feelings because her sister was clearly avoiding her ever since she expressed her thoughts about James. She hasn't seen Marteen since she arrived in LA. Back inside James's suite, he and Marteen were getting dressed, when Marteen's cell phone rang.

Marteen answers, "Hello?"

Victor is on the other end and says, "Hello Mrs. Knight, this is Victor Lance. I hope I'm not disturbing you."

"Oh, hello Victor. No, my husband and I were just talking about you. Have you found anything on Basha?"

"Well, as a matter of fact, we have. I was wondering if you could stop by my office later, or I could come to you."

"Oh, ok, uh, can I place you on a brief hold?"

"Sure."

Marteen walks into the bedroom and tells James the news. They decide to stop by Victor's office after lunch! As soon as Marteen hangs up with Victor, there is a knock at the door. Marteen opens the door to Karen and Carl. Karen and Carl come inside with hugs and kisses. Karen says, "Hey girl, you look good! Why haven't I heard from your butt, did James lock you down or something?"

James walks over and says, "Yes, she was on lockdown as soon as I saw her fine ass. How y'all doing?"

Carl says, "We good. So y'all ready? Because Basha and her agent are uh meeting us at the restaurant."

Marteen and James say in unison, "What?"

"Uh yeah, we are discussing her contract and I'm pulling her ass out! So, we'll see what's up. And my lawyer is also stopping by."

"Uh, this ain't cool at all because I don't know if I can look at her without snapping off," Marteen replies.

James says, "Ok, ok, uh, calm down baby. Let's just think about this for a minute, alright?"

Karen says, "Well, you should have thought about it before you rubbed up on her, and maybe she wouldn't have walked her bold ass in your room, shit! Think about what?"

Marteen says, "Ok wait sis, that's over with. And please stop blaming my husband for some shit that bitch did on her own."

James sensing the tension says, "Well, I'll tell y'all what, just go on and talk with Basha and her agent. We'll sit this one out because I don't want to upset my wife."

Karen says, "Upset! Shit you the damn reason."

Carl says, "Hey, hey come on baby, let it go, alright let's go. We'll see y'all later ok?"

Marteen shakes her head and stares at her sister as Carl pulls her out with him. James says, "Ok, just call us with the details and we can meet up in the hotel bar area or something alright?"

Marteen walks out behind them to talk to her sister, but James pulls her back inside, closes the door, and begs her to calm down.

Marteen says, "I'm ok. I just don't want her to continue blaming you all the time."

"I can take it baby. She's just looking after you. And she's right, I started this shit."

"Well, she could be a little more sensitive because you are my husband, and I forgave you. So, she should tame her anger! I'm sick of this shit being thrown in my face!! Damn!!"

James holds her and rubs her back. He lifts up her chin, looks into her eyes, and says, "You are my whole world. And as long as we are together, fuck what they say and fuck what they think, ok? I love you, and you love me. So, roll it off because you got our baby to think about. If you're upset, the baby is upset. You feel me? Now relax, baby, please."

"Mmmm, ok let's just head on over to my lawyer's office and hear what he has to say."

"Ok sweetie. I'm so sorry about all this. I'm so blessed to have your understanding, and you know I'm crazy about you, right?"

"Yes, I know. I love you too, baby! Let's just go okay?"

"Alright."

* * *

Carl and Karen made it to the meeting spot early and decided to sit at the bar and order a cocktail. They are having lunch at The Blue-Moon Room, a well-known spot for celebrities to come and enjoy a peaceful meal! Karen sips her wine and says, "Baby I know you think I'm being mean to James, but he is newly married, and he has a baby. When you factor all of that in, no way should he be putting himself in these situations. So, I don't trust him, and I'm sorry I can't hide my frustrations."

"I get that you love your sister, but she is a grown woman and whatever happens in her marriage is her business, not yours. I know you wouldn't want her in our business and talking shit about me! You know you would be upset! So don't say stuff without thinking because when you hurt James, you hurt her!"

"Mmm... I know, I have to just bite my tongue and mind my business. But I'm telling you, he is going to hurt my sister because he is not ready for her. It's like they got together too soon. He needs to be cultivated. He still has that itch, and one day he is going to scratch it! That's if he hasn't already. Don't ask me how I know, but I know!"

"Well, you still have to bite your tongue, baby and respect their marriage, ok?" He checks his watch. "So, uh let's close out and see if our reservations are ready."

"Okay," she says as she leans in and kisses Carl.

"Mmm, what was that for?"

"Just thankful that I have a good man, and I'm not stressing over any drama. You make me so happy baby; I love you so much!"

"I love you more baby, especially when you give me my treats!"

"Mmm... well maybe, if you stop throwing hints about it, maybe I'll surprise you one day, ok?"

"Alright...fair enough."

Just as they are being seated, Basha, her agent, and her bodyguard walk over. Karen unconsciously rolled her eyes at Basha and pondered to herself, 'Ooh I could beat her ass to the floor. Lord help me. Here we go.' Karen's thoughts are interrupted as she is introduced to Basha's agent.

* * *

Marteen and James arrive at 'The Law Office of Tunda and Lance and are immediately led to a conference room. They are offered coffee and fancy pastries. James is impressed by the layout, and he is wondering why his wife hired an attorney without his knowledge. Marteen is so ready to get this over with because she is more anxious to know what's going on inside the meeting with Basha, across town.

Mr. Victor Lance walks into the conference room wearing the hell out of a Navy Armani suit and Hermès silk tie with Ferragamo monk strap shoes. James is getting a strange vibe from this dude, and once the introductions are made, they get down to business. Victor's investigators have discovered how Basha entered James's suite, and with the hotel's cooperation, they can file a motion against Basha. Once the incident is leaked to the press, it could damage Basha's career and release James from his contract.

James says, "Hold up wait, so what exactly are we talking about? Correct me if I'm wrong but did my wife hire this firm to destroy Basha's career?"

Marteen answers, "Well basically yes. And to free you from your contract. I thought that's what you wanted to do."

James looks over the paperwork, glances over at Victor and says, "Uh, I'm sorry we wasted your time, but I'm not agreeing to any of this, and my wife didn't explain this to me. So uh, just send me the bill." James stands up, opens his wallet, and gives Victor his business card.

Marteen looks shocked, stands up, and says, "Okay, wait a minute, uh, I'm sorry, Victor. Could you please give us a minute alone?"

"Sure. Just stick your head outside the door when you're ready for me."

As soon as Victor leaves Marteen puts her hands on her hips and snaps off, "What did you think this was about? I told you I wanted her to pay for what she did and now you're acting like you don't know shit!"

"Baby, I had no idea you were trying to strip her of her livelihood, and I'm not down with that. So, let's get out of here because I think your hormones are clouding your judgment."

"No, my love for your ass is what's clouding my judgment! Awww! I can't do this. If you want out of this lawsuit, then fine. But I'm still looking into it."

"Baby, we need to talk about this, so let's go back to the hotel and put this matter on hold, okay?"

Marteen sighs, "Yeah ok. We definitely need to talk because I'm starting to feel like you don't want to hurt Basha for personal reasons."

"Oh, come on, that's not true! I'm all for revoking her contract with the group but I don't want to take away her career! Now let's go because we can discuss this in private, alright?"

Marteen shakes her head, grabs her purse, and walks out. She informs Mr. Lance that she will be in touch. James shakes his hand, and they exit the building in silence. For the second time in their marriage, they rode back to the hotel in complete silence.

As soon as they are back at the hotel, James hears from Carl that they have a rehearsal for the video in 20 minutes. Basha is joining them on stage but, as a result of her behavior, she is not joining them on the road. Basha's contract has been revised. She cannot have any form of communication with James, or she is fired on the spot, losing all residuals, and all monetary benefits!

Marteen is not happy, and she forbids James to perform on stage with Basha. James pleads, "Baby, please, I am under contract. Carl and I both have money riding on this. It's just for a few minutes of singing, and she isn't going on the road with us, next month, okay?" So please just calm down."

"I don't want you anywhere near her, and if you would've had my lawyer handle this, we wouldn't be having this conversation."

"Baby, I'm going on stage tonight. So, you need to stop yelling at me and calm down. I'm sorry about everything but I'm not losing all this money over Basha so please just chill, okay?"

"Chill, you want me to chill, while you are on stage with this crazy ass bitch, that tried to fuck you! No! I'm not chilling, and I don't want you to perform!!!"

James tries to hold Marteen, but she snatches away and stares at him.

"I mean it, James. I don't want you doing this, because I don't know if I can watch you do this!" Her voice cracks.

James stares at the ceiling and then picks up his phone and calls Carl.

"Hey, I'm going to miss rehearsals okay? I'm good, I know what to do. Marteen is upset and I need some time to calm her down."

"Damn! We need to rehearse though, the layout is different. Awww hell, man. Just come down as soon as you can, because this shit is live and we gotta be on point!"

"Man, look, I'm talking to my wife. So, I don't give a damn about this rehearsal shit, okay? My woman is upset, so I'll call you back."

"Aw damn!!! Uh...ok."

James pulls Marteen into his arms and kisses the top of her head. He then walks with her over to the table and they sit down and look at each other. Marteen is the first to speak. "Mmmm...I know my hormones are at an all-time high, but I'm still angry with Basha. I feel like she should be held accountable for what she did. Pulling her from the tour just isn't punishment enough. Can you understand that?"

"Yes, I understand your frustration, but you are being extremely vindictive and I'm hoping you will find it in your heart to forgive her so that you can have some peace in all of this. You have a baby to think about sweetie. I don't want you holding on to anger because it will consume you. I know you are not a vengeful person, so please don't let Basha turn you into someone, you are not! I am going to perform tonight and although Basha is singing with us, she's not going to distract me from doing what I have worked so hard to accomplish. I love you and when I get off that platform, I'm coming back to you, and we are going home to be with our daughter! So, if you can't sit through the performance then I understand and I promise to come back here as soon as I can, okay?

"Well, I guess I don't have a choice. I'll uh, just pack up and go back home. I know you need to stick around for the after party and take some photos so why don't you go before Carl has a stroke. I'm going to take a bath and lie down, because I know I can't watch you and her together. I just can't. I need to rest my nerves, alright?"

Marteen stands up and walks back to the bedroom and James is left staring after her. James gets up and walks out. He has said all he can say. Marteen hears the door close, and she lets the tears fall. James is waiting for the elevator staring down at the gold and brown carpet as Basha comes out of her room. Basha sees James standing at the elevator and immediately goes back inside and does not come out until he has left the floor. She feels awful about what she has done, and she prays that he and his wife will one day forgive her.

James walks into the auditorium and sees Carl on stage talking to Karen and Bob. Karen climbs down the stage and walks over to James, "Hey, is uh Marteen coming to rehearsal?"
"Uh no. She's taking a bath and then leaving for Chicago. She said she doesn't want to watch the show. Excuse me..."

James steps on stage and talks to Carl and Bob. Karen takes out her cell phone and calls her sister. Marteen lets the call go to voicemail. She is rolling her suitcase out of the room, and she's going home to be with her daughter because she cannot stomach looking at her husband singing to Basha!

* * *

Marteen made it to the airport early. She sat inside her gate area in deep thought as she rubbed her stomach. She suddenly realized she needed to eat something. Marteen walked over to a Mexican restaurant.

Back at the venue, rehearsal was solid, even though Basha's presence made everyone uncomfortable. James and Carl were backstage getting ready when Bob ran into their dressing quarters breathing hard and says, "Man, guess who is in the audience?"

James says, "Who?"

Carl says, "Man, calm down and breathe, shit!!"

Bob replies, "Oh I'm sorry. But uh, Sean John and Eddie Murphy are sitting in the audience! And I heard Sean was here to ask y'all to collaborate on his next song, real talk."

Carl says, "Oh, for real?"

James answers, "Man, I'm done with this rap shit! Forget Sean John, my wife might leave my ass. Shit'd...And that's real talk!!"

They all laugh.

Carl says, "Well let's just do this show and worry about that shit when and if it happens!"

Bob says, "Alright, well, did y'all talk to Basha about the switch-up?"

Carl answers, "Uh, yeah, I told her, and she's cool with it."

James says, "Well don't look at me. You know I'm not supposed to talk to her or look at her, which is going to be tough, seeing that I have to sing with her ass!!

They all laugh some more.

Carl says, "Alright man, I heard you, damn!! And you got a point, but it is what it is. So, let's just do everything as planned and we will be ok. Did you hear from your wife?"

Bob steps out and James replies, "No and I'm starting to worry because she's still upset with me. I don't know if she left yet or what!

But I'm going to sit her ass down and talk to her about not answering her cell phone when I call her."

"Yeah, I feel you. Karen hasn't heard anything either."

"Nope! But my mom told me she heard from her. But uh, you know, I'm out of here as soon as this show is over because I need to be with my family, alright?"

"Ok, well, let's hit it then." They bump fists and walk out towards the stage.

The band is already on stage with Basha and Carla. The MC introduces them and Carl and James walk on stage singing 'Hey Sexy.' The crowd goes wild as Basha and Carla are singing and dancing in the background. James is rapping to the audience, (hence the switch) when his heart suddenly skips a beat. Sitting up front with a spark in her eyes is his beautiful wife! Man, oh man, the night just got better as James sets the stage on fire. 'Hey Sexy' is undoubtedly a hit!!!

CHAPTER 55

Marteen and Karen were having lunch in the hotel dining room. Marteen was full of life and her eyes sparkled as she laughed at her sister's imitation of her husband. Karen says, "I was like have you seen Marteen? And he looked at me and said...all proper like... "Uh no, I have not, and uh can you excuse me!" I was like excuse you, for what? Girl, you had him all messed up. He didn't know if he was coming or going! Please don't do that to him, again...because he can't take it..." They burst out laughing.

Marteen replies, "I'm sorry. I was just in my feelings. But we talked it out, and he is back to his silly-acting self. And he is seriously considering leaving the music industry and I'm like thank you! I'm so sick of this business and I don't like him on the road and stuff. You know what I mean?"

"Yes, I do. And Carl is trying to ease out. As soon as he has satisfied all of his obligations, he is going to focus on writing and that's it! I can't wait to have my husband to myself, again."

"Oh yes, I feel you on that one! This music industry is for the birds!"

* * *

James is having a meeting with Carl and Bob about the hype from last night's performance. Carl says, "Do, uh, you think we should meet up with Sean John tomorrow, or are you serious about leaving for Chicago?"

James replies, "Yes, I'm serious about going back home. I'm done man! I have a family to enjoy.

This business is making my wife nervous, and she's my whole world. So, I'm out, for sure! Sorry, man."

Bob says, "Well, I understand that. Because if she was my wife, I would be at her beck and call."

James says, "See, there you go with that shit. Man, stop saying that! She ain't your wife. And I better not catch you dreaming about her!!" They all laugh.

Bob says, "Man, whatever. I was just saying I understand, that's all! Damn!"

Carl says, "Yeah me too. But I was hoping we could at least get another song out of you before you call it quits! Everyone was asking about you and saying how good we were out there. We rocked last night, and you know it!!"

James tells him, "Man stop tempting me. You know I can't do anything. I already promised Marteen and she'll kill me, for real! I am done! It's a wrap, so..."

Carl replies, "Ok, ok, I feel you! Well, I'm going to hang out with Bob and the fellas, you coming out?"

"Nah, I'm spending the rest of this day with my baby, so y'all have fun. I'll rap with y'all later! Alright?"

Carl says, "Alright, player, see ya later."

Bob chimes in, "Later, man..."

James walks out and nods to a couple who recognize his face. He takes a taxi back to the hotel to be with his wife. He can't shake the feeling of last night's performance. He was trying so hard to hide his excitement from everyone because in his head he was flying, and he had another song floating around inside his brain. Man, oh man, he was thrilled. But sadly, he couldn't show it! Damn, thought James as he exited the taxi and headed up to his room to spend time with his beautiful wife.

* * *

The girls were on their way back to their rooms when they bumped into Basha in the hallway. Marteen was laughing out loud when the elevator doors opened, and suddenly Basha was standing right in front of her. Surprisingly, the two had not seen each other since the stage performance, and thankfully, Karen was the first to break the ice.

Karen says, "Oh, so you're still here, huh?"

Basha replies, "Uh, excuse me please," as she tries to step past and get on the elevator.

Marteen jumps in, "Uh, I was hoping I could have a word with you." Karen and Marteen block the elevator door, and Basha is forced to wait for the next one. Feeling uncomfortable, Basha backs away and decides to go back to her room. Marteen says, "Oh, so now you can't talk to me? I just want to talk to you, woman to woman, that's all. My sister is not going to mess with you, okay?"

Basha picks up speed as she walks back down the hallway towards her room. Marteen quickly catches up with her and grabs her arm. Basha snatches her arm away and says, "Look, I already said I was sorry, and I wasn't going to talk to him anymore, so..."

Marteen cuts her off and says, as Karen looks on, "Listen, I know you are sorry, but you crossed the line, and I can't let that go. I don't know what possessed you to even think you could throw yourself at my husband and not get your ass tossed!"

Marteen pokes Basha in her chest and pushes her, "Hmmm.., I mean, what the hell were you doing in my husband's room, naked? Huh? Do you think saying you're sorry is supposed to patch up everything?

Marteen's voice is high, and her fists are balled up. Basha is crying and shaking her head as she slowly walks backward.

Suddenly, James steps off the elevator, and hearing the commotion, he runs past Karen and grabs his wife before she attacks Basha!

"Hey, now! Come on baby, what are you doing out here? You need to calm down!"

Marteen snatches away as Basha runs and locks herself inside her room. Karen is for once, on James's side, "Yeah, come on sis. You don't need the stress right now, ok? Listen to James, please! Just let it go for now."

Marteen is quiet as she walks back down the hall to her room.

Karen goes into her hotel room, and James leads Marteen into their room. Once they're inside, James says, "Baby, are you okay? You know you shouldn't be getting upset while you are pregnant. What happened out there?"

Marteen takes a deep breath and says, "Nothing, I just lost it. But I'm okay. It's just that I cannot stop thinking about what she tried to do to you! It's making me crazy; you know what I mean?"

"Yeah, I know. But you know you were weak with Jazz's birth, so you can't let her complicate this pregnancy, okay? I know you want to choke her up, but you can't be physical like that, not in your condition. You need to relax, ok? I'm so sorry baby, but we are leaving tomorrow morning, okay?" He hugs her, and she hugs him back.

CHAPTER 56

Marteen and James finally made it back to Chicago. James was in the living room getting ready to drive to his mom's house to retrieve Jazz when he heard Marteen's scream! James rushes to his wife and finds her on the bedroom floor, holding her stomach and in what seemed to be the most horrific pain!

He immediately calls 911, praying that his wife and unborn child are okay. He was in the same nightmare he was in before Jazz was born. This time, he couldn't move his wife because she was screaming, and his heart was beating so loudly and fast. It was clouding his brain cells. The noise was deafening.

As soon as the paramedics arrived, Marteen went into shock, putting her and the baby's life in extreme danger. James called Karen and Carl with the news. It sent Karen into hysterics as they rushed to get back to Chicago. Marteen was fighting for her life after losing too much blood and unfortunately, the baby as well!

The infant was too weak to survive, and the little boy died on the delivery table! James's world had literally turned upside down!! Carl and Karen made it to Northwestern Hospital at record speed. Carl's business partner got them on a private jet as soon as he heard the news about James's wife! The story had leaked, and Marteen's condition was all over the news! Reporters were trying to talk to James. Carl said, "No comment" to a rude reporter.

Karen was on her cell phone, speaking to Chase, when James suddenly appeared with tears in his eyes.

Cameras were flashing. Thankfully, security rushes over to clear the waiting area! Karen takes one look into James's eyes and faints!!

* * *

Heartbreaking news travels fast. Monica, Marteen's best friend, was on the other side of the globe packing her bags and preparing for her long trip back to LA when she heard the news about her friend! Monica froze in front of her computer and grabbed her chest before she frantically started to search for her cell phone, to call someone, dammit, anyone, because no one had called her, and she needed updates!! 'Please, God, hear my prayers,' says Monica as she continues to pray for her sorority sister and search for her personal Blackberry.

Chase was still holding the phone, shouting into the receiver for Karen to talk to him, not knowing that she had just dropped the phone and fainted! Chase finally hangs up and turns to Gia, with tears in his eyes, and says, "It's Marteen. She's in critical condition at Northwestern Memorial. I, uh, need to get there, ok?"

Gia says, "OMG!! Of course, baby. I'll call the airlines."

Chase walks into the bedroom to pack a bag, praying his sister makes it!

Randy is eating a late lunch with his friend Tom when he gets the call from Carl about Marteen! Randy gasps, jumps up, and apologizes to his friend as he runs out of the restaurant and flags a taxi to take him to the hospital.

Bob is in his hotel suite when he sees the news flash, and he's wondering why he didn't know sooner. Bob's heart is heavy as he makes a call to Carl while he packs a bag to go to Chicago. James and Marteen are like family to him, and he needed to be close in case he was needed!

Everyone is trying to get to Northwestern Memorial Hospital. People from all over the world are praying for James and Marteen. But no one is praying harder than Basha! Basha is in her hotel suite when she hears the breaking news about a rap artist flashes on the screen: ****"James Knight, who just launched the biggest hit song of the summer, called 'Hey Sexy' Mr. Knight was seen entering Northwestern Memorial Hospital with his pregnant wife who is reportedly in critical condition. New R&B artist of the year, Carl St. John, was said to have flown in on a private jet to be with his best friend and sister-in-law...details pending.... ***reports from ABC****
To be Continued...

Hello readers,

As far as I can remember, I've always had a pen in my hand and stories in my head. I wrote my first poem when I was eight years old. I lost my mom early on, and my emotions and survival were fueled by my writing energy as I traveled down the highway of my life - trying to trust the journey! With no roadmap, I leaned on my faith and ancestors. I wrote about every heartfelt encounter I experienced along the way. I invite you to take this journey with me.

Enjoy!